THE CRIT

"With every new b

more, for his feisty

passion for the und... and his willingness to strike out in new directions." —*Entertainment Weekly*

"John Grisham is exceptionally good at what he does. . . . Grisham's books are also smart, imaginative, and funny, populated by complex, interesting people, written by a man who is driven not merely by the desire to entertain but also by genuine (if understated) outrages at human cupidity and venality." —*The Washington Post*

"John Grisham is about as good a storyteller as we've got in the United States these days."

—*The New York Times Book Review*

"John Grisham owns the legal thriller." —*The Denver Post*

"John Grisham is not just popular, he is one of the most popular novelists of our time. He is a craftsman and he writes good stories, engaging characters, and clever plots." —*The Seattle Times*

"A mighty narrative talent and an unerring eye for hot-button issues." —*Chicago Sun-Times*

"A legal literary legend." —*USA Today*

BY JOHN GRISHAM

A Time to Kill
The Firm
The Pelican Brief
The Client
The Chamber
The Rainmaker
The Runaway Jury
The Partner
The Street Lawyer
The Testament
The Brethren
A Painted House
Skipping Christmas
The Summons
The King of Torts
Bleachers
The Last Juror
The Broker
The Innocent Man
Playing for Pizza
The Appeal
The Associate
Ford County
The Confession
The Litigators
Calico Joe
The Racketeer
Sycamore Row
Gray Mountain
Rogue Lawyer
The Whistler
Camino Island
The Rooster Bar

THE THEODORE BOONE BOOKS

Kid Lawyer
The Abduction
The Accused
The Activist
The Fugitive
The Scandal

THE ROOSTER BAR

A NOVEL

||||

JOHN GRISHAM

DELL BOOKS • NEW YORK

The Rooster Bar is a work of fiction. Names, characters, businesses, organizations, places, events, and incidents are the product of the author's imagination or are used fictitiously. Any resemblance to actual persons, living or dead, or locales is entirely coincidental.

2018 Dell Mass Market Edition

Published in the United States by Dell, an imprint of Random House, a division of Penguin Random House LLC, New York.

DELL and the HOUSE colophon are registered trademarks of Penguin Random House LLC.

Originally published in hardcover in the United States by Doubleday, a division of Penguin Random House LLC, in 2017.

ISBN: 978-1-101-96770-6
Export edition ISBN: 978-1-5247-9884-0
ebook ISBN: 978-0-385-54120-6

Cover design: John Fontana
Cover photograph: © Georgii Shipin/Shutterstock

Printed in the United States of America

randomhousebooks.com

2 4 6 8 9 7 5 3 1

Dell mass market edition: June 2018

THE ROOSTER BAR

||||

1

The end of the year brought the usual holiday festivities, though around the Frazier house there was little to cheer. Mrs. Frazier went through the motions of decorating a small tree and wrapping a few cheap gifts and baking cookies no one really wanted, and, as always, she kept *The Nutcracker* running nonstop on the stereo as she gamely hummed along in the kitchen as though the season *was* merry.

Things were anything but merry. Mr. Frazier had moved out three years earlier, and he wasn't missed as much as he was despised. In no time, he had moved in with his young secretary, who, as things developed, was already pregnant. Mrs. Frazier, jilted, humiliated, broke, and depressed, was still struggling.

Louie, her younger son, was under house arrest, sort of free on bail, and facing a rough year ahead with the drug charges and all. He made no effort to buy his mom anything in the way of a gift. His excuse was that he couldn't leave the house because of the court-ordered monitor attached to his ankle. But even without it, no one expected Louie to go to the trouble of buying gifts. The year before and the year before that both of his ankles had been unburdened and he hadn't bothered to shop.

Mark, the older son, was home from the horrors of law school, and, though even poorer than his brother, had managed to buy his mother some perfume. He was scheduled to graduate in May, sit for the bar exam in July, and begin working with a D.C. firm in September, which, as it so happened, was the same month Louie's trial was on the docket. But Louie's case would not go to trial for two very good reasons. First, the undercover boys had caught him in the act of selling ten bags of crack—there was even a video—and, second, neither Louie nor his mother could afford a decent lawyer to handle the mess. Throughout the holidays, both Louie and Mrs. Frazier dropped hints that Mark should rush in and volunteer to defend his brother. Wouldn't it be easy to stall matters until later in the year when Mark was properly admitted to the bar—he was practically there anyway—and once he had his license wouldn't it be a simple matter of finding one of those technicalities you read about to get the charges dismissed?

This little fantasy of theirs had some rather large holes in it, but Mark refused to discuss it. When it became apparent that Louie planned to hog the sofa for at least ten hours on New Year's Day and watch seven straight bowl games, Mark made a quiet exit and went to a friend's house. Returning home that night, while driving under the influence, he made the decision to flee. He would return to D.C. and kill some time puttering around the law firm where he would soon be employed. Classes didn't start for almost two weeks, but after ten days of listening to Louie bitch and moan about his problems, not to mention the nonstop *Nutcracker,* Mark was fed up and looking forward to his last semester of law school.

He set his alarm for eight the following morning, and over coffee with his mom explained that he was needed back in D.C. Sorry to leave a bit earlier than expected, Mom, and sorry to leave you here all alone with your bad boy, Mom, but I'm outta here. He's not mine to raise. I got my own problems.

The first problem was his vehicle, a Ford Bronco he'd been driving since high school. The odometer had frozen at 187,000 miles, and that had happened midway through college. It desperately needed a new fuel pump, one of many replacement parts on the Urgent List. Using tape and paper clips, Mark had been able to wire and jerry-rig the engine, transmission, and brakes for the past two years, but he'd had no luck with the fuel pump. It worked but at a lower capacity than normal, so that the Bronco's max speed was forty-nine on level ground. To avoid being clobbered by 18-wheelers on the expressways, Mark stuck to the back roads of rural Delaware and the Eastern Shore. The two-hour drive from Dover to central D.C. took twice as long.

This gave him even more time to consider his other problems. Number two was his suffocating student debt. He'd finished college with $60,000 in loans, and no job. His father, who seemed happily married at the time but was also in debt, had warned him against further studies. He'd said, "Hell, boy, four years of education and you're sixty grand in the hole. Quit before it gets any worse." But Mark thought taking any financial advice from his father was foolish, so he worked a couple of years here and there, bartending and delivering pizza, while he haggled with his lenders. Now, looking back, he wasn't sure where the idea of law school had originated, but he did remember overhearing a conversation between two frat brothers who were pondering weighty matters while drinking heavily. Mark was the bartender, the lounge was not crowded, and after the fourth round of vodka and cranberry juice they talked loud enough for all to hear. Among many interesting things they had said, Mark had always remembered two: "The big D.C. law firms are hiring like crazy." And, "Starting salaries are one-fifty a year."

Not long after that, he bumped into a college friend who was a first-year student at the Foggy Bottom Law School in D.C., and the guy gushed on about his plans to blitz through his studies, finish in two and a half years, and sign on with a big firm for a fat salary. The Feds were throwing loans at students, anybody could qualify, and, well sure, he would graduate with a mountain of debt but nothing he couldn't wipe out in five years. To his friend, at least, it made perfect sense to "invest in himself" with the debt because it would guarantee all that future earning power.

Mark took the bait and began studying for the Law School Admission Test. His score was an unimpressive 146, but this did not bother the admissions folks at the Foggy Bottom Law School. Nor did his rather thin undergraduate résumé with an anemic grade point average of 2.8. FBLS accepted him with open arms. His loan applications were quickly approved. Sixty-five thousand bucks were simply transferred from the Department of Education each year to Foggy Bottom. And now, with one semester to go, Mark was staring miserably at the reality of graduating with a combined total, undergrad and law school, principal and interest, of $266,000 in debt.

Another problem was his job. As it happened, the market wasn't quite as strong as rumored. Nor was it as vibrant as FBLS had advertised in its slick brochures and near-fraudulent website. Graduates from top-tier law schools were still finding work at enviable salaries. FBLS, though, was not quite in the top tier. Mark had managed to worm his way into a midsized law firm that specialized in "governmental relations," which meant nothing more than lobbying. His starting salary had not been established, because the firm's management committee would meet in early January to review profits from the previous year and supposedly jiggle the pay structure. In a few months, Mark would be expected to have an important talk with his "loan counselor" about restructuring his student debt and somehow repaying the entire mess. This counselor had already expressed concern that Mark did not know how much he would be earning. This concerned Mark too, especially when added to the fact that he didn't trust a single person he'd met at the law firm. As much as he tried to fool himself, he knew deep in his gut that his position was not secure.

Another problem was the bar exam. Because of demand, the D.C. version of the test was one of the more challenging in the nation, and FBLS grads had been bombing it at an alarming rate. Again, the top schools in town did well. The year before, Georgetown had a 91 percent pass rate. For George Washington it was 89 percent. For FBLS, the pass rate was a pathetic 56 percent. To succeed, Mark needed to start studying now, in early January, and hit the books nonstop for six months.

But the energy simply wasn't there, especially in the cold, dreary, depressing days of winter. At times the debt felt like cinder blocks strapped to his back. Walking was a chore. Smiling was difficult. He was living in poverty and his future, even with the job, was bleak. And he was one of the fortunate ones. Most of his classmates had the loans but not the jobs. Looking back, he'd heard the grumbling even in his first year, and with each semester the mood at school grew darker, the suspicions heavier. The job market worsened. The bar exam results embarrassed everyone at FBLS. The loans piled up. Now, in his third and last year, it was not unusual to hear students verbally spar with professors in class. The dean wouldn't come out of his office. Bloggers blistered the school and screamed harsh questions: "Is this a hoax?" "Have we been had?" "Where did all the money go?"

To varying degrees, almost everyone Mark knew believed that (1) FBLS was a subpar law school that (2) made too many promises, and (3) charged too much money, and (4) encouraged too much debt while (5) admitting a lot of mediocre students who really had no business in law school, and (6) were either not properly prepared for the bar exam or (7) too dumb to pass it.

There were rumors that applications to FBLS had fallen by 50 percent. With no state support, and no endowment, such a decline would lead to all manner of painful cost cutting, and a bad law school would only get worse. This was fine with Mark Frazier and his friends. They would endure the next four months and happily leave the place, never to return.

MARK LIVED IN a five-story apartment building that was eighty years old and visibly deteriorating, but the rent was low and this attracted students from George Washington and FBLS. In its earlier days it had been known as the Cooper House, but after three decades of frat-like wear and tear it had earned its nickname as the Coop. Because its elevators seldom worked, Mark took the stairs to the third floor and entered his cramped and sparsely furnished flat, for which he paid $800 a month for five hundred square feet. For some reason he'd cleaned the place after his last exam before the holidays, and as he flipped on lights he was pleased to see that everything was in order. And why shouldn't it be? The slumlord who owned the place never came around. He unloaded his bags and was struck by the silence. Normally, with a bunch of students, and with thin walls, there was always a racket. Stereos, televisions, arguments, pranks, poker games, fights, guitar playing, even a trombone played by a nerd on the fourth floor that could rattle the entire building. But not today. Everyone was still at home, enjoying the break, and the halls were eerily quiet.

After half an hour, Mark was bored and left the building. Walking along New Hampshire Avenue, with the wind cutting through his thin fleece and old khakis, he decided, for some reason, to turn onto Twenty-First and stop by the law school to see if it was open. In a city with no shortage of hideous modern buildings, FBLS managed to stand out in its unsightliness. It was a postwar edifice covered with bland yellow bricks on eight levels slung together in asymmetrical wings, some failed architect's effort at making a statement. Supposedly, it once was an office building, but walls had been knocked out with abandon to create cramped lecture halls on the four lower floors. On the fifth was the library, a rabbits' warren of large, retrofitted rooms packed with seldom-touched books and some replicated portraits of unknown judges and legal scholars. The faculty had offices on the sixth and seventh floors, and on the eighth, and as far away from the students as possible, the administration carried on, with the dean solidly hidden in a corner office from which he seldom ventured.

The front door was unlocked and Mark entered the empty lobby. While he appreciated its warmth, he found the area, as always, utterly depressing. A huge bulletin board covered one wall with all manner of notices and announcements and enticements. There were a few slick posters advertising opportunities to study abroad, and the usual assortment of handmade ads offering stuff for sale—books, bikes, tickets, course outlines, tutors by the hour—and apartments for rent. The bar exam loomed over the entire school like a dark cloud and there were posters extolling the excellence of some review courses. If he searched hard enough he could possibly find a few employment opportunities, but at FBLS those had become scarcer by the year. In one corner he saw the same old brochures hawking even more student loans. At the far end of the lobby there were vending machines and a small coffee bar, but nothing was being brewed during the break.

He fell into a battered leather chair and soaked in the gloominess of his school. Was it really a school or was it just another diploma mill? The answer was becoming clear. For the thousandth time he wished he had never walked through the front doors as an unsuspecting first-year student. Now, almost three years later, he was burdened by loans he couldn't imagine paying off. If there was a light at the end of the tunnel, he couldn't see it.

And why would anyone name a school Foggy Bottom? As if the law school experience itself wasn't dreary enough, some bright soul had, some twenty years earlier, tagged it with a name that conveyed even more cheerlessness. That guy, now dead, had sold the school to some Wall Street investors who owned a string of law schools that were reportedly producing handsome profits while cranking out little in the way of legal talent.

How do you buy and sell law schools? It was still a mystery.

Mark heard voices and hurriedly left the building. He hiked down New Hampshire to Dupont Circle, where he ducked into Kramer Books for a coffee and a quick thaw. He walked everywhere. His Bronco lurched and stalled too much in city traffic, and he kept it tucked away in a lot behind the Coop, always with the key in the ignition. Unfortunately, so far no one had been tempted to steal it.

Warm again, he hustled six blocks north along Connecticut Avenue. The law firm of Ness Skelton occupied a few floors in a modern building near the Hinckley Hilton. The previous summer Mark had managed to weasel his way inside when he accepted an internship that paid less than minimum wage. At major law firms, the summer programs were used to entice top students to the big life. Little work was expected. The interns were given ridiculously easy schedules, along with tickets to ball games and invitations to fine parties in the splendid backyards of the wealthy partners. Once seduced, they signed on, and upon graduation were soon thrown into the meat grinder of hundred-hour weeks.

Not so at Ness Skelton. With only fifty lawyers, it was far from a top-ten firm. Its clients were trade associations—Soybean Forum, Retired Postal Workers, Beef and Lamb Council, National Asphalt Contractors, Disabled Railroad

Engineers—and several defense contractors desperate for their share of the pork. The firm's expertise, if it had any, was maintaining relationships with Congress. Its summer intern program was designed more to exploit cheap labor than to attract top students. Mark had worked hard and suffered through the stultifying work. At the end of the summer, when he had received an offer that somewhat resembled a position upon passing the bar exam, he couldn't decide if he should celebrate or cry. Nonetheless, he jumped at what was being offered—there was nothing else on the table—and proudly became one of the few FBLS students with a future. Throughout the fall, he had gently pressed his supervisor about the terms of his upcoming employment but got nowhere. There might be a merger in the works. There might be a split. There might be a lot of things, but an employment contract was not one of them.

So he hung around. Afternoons, Saturdays, holidays, anytime he was bored he would stop by the firm, always with a big fake smile and an eagerness to pitch in and help with the grunt work. It was not clear if this was beneficial, but he figured it couldn't hurt.

His supervisor was named Randall, a ten-year guy on the verge of making partner, and thus under a lot of pressure. A Ness Skelton associate who didn't make partner after ten years was quietly shown the door. Randall was a George Washington law grad, which, in the city's pecking order, was a step down from Georgetown but several notches above Foggy Bottom. The hierarchy was clear and rigid, and its worst perpetrators were the GW lawyers. They detested being looked down upon by the Georgetown gang; thus they were eager to look down with even more disdain on anyone from FBLS. The entire firm reeked of cliques and snobbery, and Mark often wondered how in hell he wound up there. Two associates were from FBLS, but they were so busy trying to distance themselves from their school they had no time to lend Mark a hand. Indeed, they seemed to ignore him more than anyone else. Mark had often mumbled, "What a way to run a law firm." But then he figured that every profession had its levels of status. He was far too worried about his own skin to fret over where the other cutthroats had studied law. He had his own problems.

He had e-mailed Randall and said he would be dropping by to do whatever grunt work was available. Randall greeted him with a curt "Back so soon?"

Sure, Randall, and how were your holidays? Great to see you. "Yeah, got bored with all the holiday crap. What's up?"

"Two of the secretaries are out with the flu," Randall said. He pointed to a stack of documents a foot thick. "I need that copied fourteen times, all collated and stapled."

Okay, back to the copy room, Mark thought. "Sure," he said as if he couldn't wait to jump in. He hauled the documents down to the basement, to a dungeon filled with copiers. He spent the next three hours doing mindless work for which he would be paid nothing.

He almost missed Louie and his ankle monitor.

2

Like Mark, Todd Lucero was inspired to become a lawyer by booze-tinted conversations he'd overheard in a bar. For the past three years, he had been mixing drinks at the Old Red Cat, a pub-style watering hole favored by students from GW and Foggy Bottom. After college at Frostburg State, he'd left Baltimore and drifted into D.C. in search of a career. Finding none, he hired on at the Old Red Cat as a part-timer and soon realized he had a fondness for pulling pints and mixing strong drinks. He'd come to love the pub life and had a gift for schmoozing with the serious drinkers while placating the rowdies. Todd was everybody's favorite bartender and was on a first-name basis with hundreds of his regulars.

Many times over the past two and a half years he had thought of quitting law school to pursue his dream of owning his own bar. His father, though, had strong opinions to the contrary. Mr. Lucero was a cop in Baltimore and had always pushed his son to obtain a professional degree. Pushing was one thing, but paying for it was something else. And so Todd had fallen into the same trap of borrowing easy money and handing it over to the greedy folks at FBLS.

He and Mark Frazier had met the first day, during orientation, back when they were both starry-eyed and envisioning big law careers with fat salaries, back when they, along with 350 others, were horribly naive. He vowed to quit after his first year, but his father yelled at him. Because of his commitment to the bar, he had never found the time to knock on doors around D.C. and hustle for summer internships. He vowed to quit after his second year and cut off the flow of debt, but his loan counselor strongly advised against it. As long as he was in school he did not have to confront some brutal repayment schedule, so it made perfect sense to keep borrowing in order to graduate and find one of those lucrative jobs that, in theory, would eventually take care of the debts. Now, though, with only one semester to go, he knew only too well such jobs did not exist.

If only he'd borrowed $195,000 from a bank and opened his bar. He could be printing money and enjoying life.

MARK ENTERED THE Old Red Cat just after dark and took his favorite place at the end of the bar. He fist-bumped Todd and said, "Good to see you, man."

"You too," Todd said as he slid over a frosty mug of light beer. With his seniority, Todd could comp anyone he damn well pleased, and Mark had not paid in years.

With the students away, the place was quiet. Todd leaned on his elbows and asked, "So what are you up to?"

"Well, I've spent the afternoon at dear old Ness Skelton, in the copy room sorting papers that no one will ever read. More stupid work. Even the paralegals look down their noses at me. I hate the place and I haven't even been hired yet."

"Still no contract?"

"None, and the picture gets fuzzier every day."

Todd took a quick sip from his mug stashed under the counter. Even with his seniority, he wasn't supposed to drink on the job, but his boss wasn't in. He asked, "So how was Christmas around the Frazier house?"

"Ho, ho, ho. I lasted ten miserable days and got the hell out. You?"

"Three days, then duty called and I came back to work. How's Louie?"

"Still seriously indicted, still looking at real jail time. I should feel sorry for him but compassion runs thin for a guy who sleeps half the day and spends the other half on the sofa watching *Judge Judy* and bitching about his ankle monitor. My poor mom."

"You're pretty hard on him."

"Not hard enough. That's his problem. No one's ever been hard on Louie. He got caught with pot when he was thirteen, blamed it on a friend, and of course my parents rushed to his defense. He's never been held accountable. Until now."

"Bummer, man. I can't imagine having a brother in prison."

"Yeah, it sucks. I just wish I could help him but there's no way."

"I won't even ask about your dad."

"Didn't see him and didn't hear from him. Not even a card. He's fifty years old and the proud papa of a three-year-old, so I guess he played Santa Claus. Laid out a bunch of toys under the tree, smiled like an idiot when the kid came down the stairs squealing. What a rat."

Two coeds walked to the bar and Todd left to serve them. Mark pulled out his phone and checked his messages.

When Todd returned, he asked, "Have you seen any grades yet?"

"No. Who cares? We're all top students." Grades at Foggy Bottom were a joke. It was imperative that the school's graduates finish with sparkling résumés, and to that end the professors passed out As and Bs like cheap candy. No one flunked out of FBLS. So, of course, this had created a culture of rather listless studying, which, of course, killed any chance of competitive learning. A bunch of mediocre students became even more mediocre. No wonder the bar exam was such a challenge. Mark added, "And you really can't expect a bunch of overpaid professors to grade exams during the holidays, can you?"

Todd took another sip, leaned even closer, and said, "We have a bigger problem."

"Gordy?"

"Gordy."

"I was afraid of that. I've texted and tried to call but his phone's turned off. What's going on?"

"It's bad," Todd said. "Evidently, he went home for Christmas and spent his time fighting with Brenda. She wants a big church wedding with a thousand people. Gordy doesn't want to get married. Her mother has a lot to say. His mother is not speaking to her mother and the whole thing is blowing up."

"They're getting married May 15, Todd. As I recall, you and I signed on as groomsmen."

"Well, don't bet on it. He's already back in town and off his meds. Zola stopped by this afternoon and gave me the heads-up."

"What meds?"

"It's a long story."

"What meds?"

"He's bipolar, Mark. Diagnosed a few years back."

"You're kidding, right?"

"Why would I kid about this? He's bipolar and Zola says he's off his medication."

"Why wouldn't he tell us?"

"I can't answer that."

Mark took a long drink of beer and shook his head. He asked, "Zola's back already?"

"Yes, evidently she and Gordy hurried back for a few days of fun and games, though I'm not sure they're having much fun. She thinks he quit his meds about a month ago when we were studying for finals. One day he's manic and bouncing off the walls; then he's in a stupor after sipping tequila and smoking weed. He's talking crazy, says he wants to quit school and run off to Jamaica, with Zola of course. She thinks he might do something stupid and hurt himself."

"Gordy is stupid. He's engaged to his high school sweetheart, a real cutie who happens to have money, and now he's shacking up with an African girl whose parents and brothers are in this country without the benefit of those immigration papers everyone is talking about. Yes, the boy is stupid."

"Gordy's in trouble, Mark. He's been sliding for several weeks and he needs our help."

Mark pushed his beer away, but only a few inches, and clasped his hands behind his head. "As if we don't have enough to worry about. How, exactly, are we supposed to help?"

"You tell me. She's trying to keep an eye on him and she wants us to come over tonight."

Mark started laughing and took another sip.

"What's so funny?" Todd asked.

"Nothing, but can you imagine the scandal in Martinsburg, West Virginia, if word got out that Gordon Tanner, whose father is a church deacon and whose fiancée is the daughter of a prominent doctor, lost his mind and quit law school to run off to Jamaica with an African Muslim?"

"I can almost see the humor."

"Well, try harder. It's a scream." But the laughter had stopped. "Look, Todd, we can't make him take his meds. If we tried to he'd kick both our asses."

"He needs our help, Mark. I get off at nine tonight and we're going over."

A man in a nice suit sat at the bar and Todd walked over to take his order. Mark sipped his beer and sank into an even deeper funk.

3

Three years before Zola Maal was born, her parents fled Senegal. They resettled in a Johannesburg slum with their two young sons and found menial jobs scrubbing floors and digging ditches. After two years, they had saved enough for a boat ride. Using the services of a broker/trafficker, they paid for a miserable trip to Miami aboard a Liberian freighter, along with a dozen other Senegalese. When they were safely smuggled ashore, an uncle met them and drove them to his home in Newark, New Jersey, where they lived in a two-room apartment in a building filled with other folks from Senegal, not a single one of whom held a green card.

A year after they arrived in the U.S., Zola was born at Newark's University Hospital and instantly became an American citizen. While her parents worked two and three jobs, all for cash at less than minimum wage, Zola and her brothers attended school and assimilated into the community. As devout Muslims, they practiced their religion, though at an early age Zola found herself attracted to

Western ways. Her father was a strict man who insisted that their native tongues of Wolof and French be replaced with English. The boys absorbed the new language and helped their parents with it at home.

The family moved often around Newark, always to cramped apartments, each one slightly larger than the last, and always with other Senegalese close by. All of them lived in fear of being deported, but there was safety in numbers, or so they believed. Every knock on the door brought a brief shudder of fear. Staying out of trouble was imperative, and Zola and her brothers were taught to avoid anything that might attract the wrong kind of attention. Even though she had the right papers, she knew that her family was in jeopardy. She lived with the horror of her parents and brothers being arrested and sent back to Senegal.

When she was fifteen, she found her first job washing dishes in a diner, for cash of course, and not much of it. Her brothers worked too, and the entire family scrimped and saved as much as possible.

When Zola wasn't working she was studying. She breezed through high school with good grades and enrolled in a community college as a part-time student. A small scholarship allowed her to become full-time and also landed her a job in the college library. But she still washed dishes, and cleaned houses with her mother, and babysat children for family friends with better jobs. Her oldest brother married an American girl who was not a Muslim, and though that meant an easier route to citizenship, it caused serious friction with her parents. The brother and his new wife moved to California to start another life.

At the age of twenty, Zola left home and enrolled as a

junior at Montclair State. She lived in a dorm with two American girls, both of whom were also on tight budgets. She chose accounting as a major because she enjoyed working with numbers and had a knack for finance. She studied hard when time allowed, but the juggling of two and sometimes three jobs often interfered with the books. Her roommates introduced her to the partying scene and she discovered she had a knack for that too. While she clung to the strict Muslim prohibition against alcohol, and she really didn't like the taste of any of it anyway, she was more receptive to other temptations, primarily fashion and sex. She was almost six feet tall and was often told how great she looked in tight jeans. Her first boyfriend happily taught her all about sex. Her second introduced her to recreational drugs. By the end of her junior year she silently and defiantly considered herself a nonpracticing Muslim, though her parents had no clue.

Her parents would soon have more serious problems. During the fall semester of her senior year, her father was arrested and jailed for two weeks before bail was arranged. At the time, he was working for a painting contractor, another Senegalese with proper documents. Evidently, his boss had underbid a union contractor for a job painting the interior of a large office complex in Newark. The union contractor notified Immigration and Customs Enforcement (ICE) and reported that illegals were being used. That was serious enough, but some office supplies were allegedly missing and fingers were being pointed. Zola's father and four other undocumented workers were charged with grand larceny. He was served with a Notice to Appear in immigration court, along with a criminal indictment.

Zola hired a lawyer who claimed to specialize in such matters and the family forked over a retainer of $9,000, virtually all its savings. The lawyer was extremely busy and seldom returned their phone calls. With her parents and brother hiding in and around Newark, Zola was left to haggle with the lawyer. She grew to despise the man, a fast talker who liked to stretch the truth, and would have fired him had it not been for the retainer. There was no money to hire another. When he failed to appear in court, the judge kicked him off the case. Zola eventually convinced a legal aid lawyer to step in and the indictment was dismissed. The deportation, however, was not going away. The case dragged on and became so distracting that her grades suffered. After several court appearances and hearings, she became convinced that all lawyers were either lazy or stupid and that she could do a better job herself.

She fell for the scam that easy federal money could make law school possible for everyone, and took the first bold steps that would lead to Foggy Bottom. Now, halfway through her final year of law school, she owed more money than she could imagine. Both parents and Bo, her unmarried brother, were still facing deportation, though their cases were languishing in the backlogged immigration courts.

SHE LIVED ON Twenty-Third Street in a building not quite as dilapidated as the Coop but similar in many respects. It was packed with students crammed into small, cheaply furnished flats. Early in her third year, she had met Gordon Tanner, a handsome, athletic blond boy who lived directly across the hall. One thing quickly led to another, and they began an ill-fated affair, one that soon led to conversations about living together, to save money of course. Gordon finally nixed the idea because Brenda, his pretty fiancée from home, loved the big city and visited often.

Juggling two women proved too much for Gordy. He'd been engaged to Brenda for practically his entire life and now wanted desperately to avoid a marriage. Zola raised far different issues, and he had not convinced himself he was brave enough to run off with a black girl and never see his family and friends again. Add the strain of a soft or even nonexistent job market, suffocating debt, and the prospect of flunking the bar exam, and Gordy lost control. He had been diagnosed as bipolar five years earlier. Meds and psychotherapy worked well, and, with the exception of a frightening episode in college, his life had been pretty normal. That changed around Thanksgiving of his third year at Foggy Bottom, when he stopped taking his meds. Zola was shocked at the mood swings and finally confronted him. He admitted his condition and went back on the meds. The ups and downs leveled out for a couple of weeks.

They finished exams and went home for the holidays, though neither wanted to. Gordy was determined to provoke the final fight with Brenda and blow up the wedding. Zola did not want to spend time with her family. Even with his troubles, her father would find the need to unload lectures and tirades on her sinful Western lifestyle.

After a week they were back in D.C. with Gordy still engaged, the wedding still on for May 15. But he was off his meds and behaving erratically. For two days he never left his bedroom, sleeping for hours, then sitting with his chin on his knees, staring at the dark walls. Zola came and went, uncertain about what to do. He disappeared for three days while sending her text messages that he was on the train to New York, to "interview some people." He was on the trail of a great conspiracy and had a lot of work to do. She was asleep in her apartment when he barged in at four in the morning, ripping off clothes and wanting sex. Later in the day he disappeared again, chasing bad guys and "digging for dirt." When he returned he was still manic and spent hours with his laptop. He told her to stay away from his apartment because he had so much work to do.

Frightened and exasperated, Zola finally went to the Old Red Cat and talked to Todd.

4

She met them at the stoop in front of the building and they followed her up the stairs to her apartment on the second floor. When they were inside she closed the door and thanked them for coming. She was obviously worried, almost frantic.

"Where is he?" Mark asked.

"Over there," Zola said, nodding toward the hall. "He won't let me in and he won't come out. I don't think he's slept much in the past two days. He's up and down and right now he's bouncing off the walls."

"And no meds?" Todd asked.

"Evidently not, at least none from the pharmacy. I suspect there's some self-medicating going on."

They looked at one another, each waiting for someone to make the next move. Mark finally said, "Let's go." They stepped across the hall and Mark knocked on the door. "Gordy, it's Mark. I'm here with Todd and Zola and we want to talk."

Silence. Springsteen could barely be heard in the background.

Mark knocked again and repeated himself. The music died. A chair or a stool was kicked and fell over. More silence, then the doorknob clicked. A few seconds passed, and Mark opened the door.

Gordy was standing in the center of the cramped room, wearing nothing but an old pair of yellow Redskins gym shorts, the same pair they had seen a hundred times. He was staring at a wall and ignored them as they eased into the room. To their left, the kitchenette was a wreck with empty beer cans and liquor bottles left in the sink and strewn along the counters. The floor was littered with paper cups, used napkins, and sandwich wrappers. To their right, the small dining table was piled high with papers in random stacks around a laptop and printer. Under it, the floor was covered with papers and files and discarded magazine articles. The sofa, television, recliner, and coffee table had been shoved as tightly as possible into one corner, as if to clear everything away from the wall.

The wall was a maze of white poster boards and dozens of sheets of copy paper, all arranged in some crazed order and secured with colored pushpins and Scotch tape. With black, blue, and red markers, Gordy was in the process of piecing together a gigantic corporate puzzle, some grand conspiracy that led to the ominous faces of a few men at the top.

Gordy appeared to be staring at the faces. He was pale and emaciated and had obviously lost a lot of weight, something Mark and Todd had not noticed two weeks earlier during final exams. He was an athlete who loved the gym, but the toned muscles were gone. His thick blond hair, the source of immense vanity, was stringy and had not been washed in days. Sizing him up, and taking in the condition of his apartment, they knew instantly that their friend had gone over the edge. They were in the presence of a manic artist, secluded and deranged and hard at work on an enormous canvas.

"What's the occasion?" Gordy asked as he turned and glared at them. His eyes were sunken, his cheeks hollow, his beard a week old.

"We need to talk," Mark said.

"Yes we do," he said. "But I'm doing the talking because I have a lot to say. I've got it all figured out now. I've caught the bastards and we have to move fast."

Tentatively, Todd said, "Okay, Gordy. We're here to listen. What's up?"

Gordy pointed to the sofa and calmly said, "Please have a seat."

"I'd rather stand, Gordy, if that's okay," Mark said.

"No!" he barked. "It's not okay. Just do as I say and we'll be fine. Now sit down." He was snarling, suddenly angry, and seemed ready to throw a punch. Neither Mark nor Todd would last ten seconds in a fistfight with Gordy. They had seen two in their law school days, both quick knockouts in bars with Gordy still on his feet.

Todd and Zola sat on the sofa and Mark pulled a stool over from the snack bar. They stared at the wall in disbelief. It was a maze of flowcharts with arrows jutting in all directions and linking together dozens of companies, firms, names, and numbers. Like schoolchildren who'd just been admonished, they sat, waited, and absorbed the wall.

Gordy stepped to the dining table, where a half-empty

fifth of tequila was in the works. He poured some into his favorite coffee cup and sipped it as if having tea.

Mark said, "You've lost a lot of weight, Gordy."

"Haven't noticed. I'll get it back. We're not here to talk about my weight." Holding the coffee cup, and evidently giving no thought to offering his pals anything to drink, he stepped to the wall and pointed to the top photo. "This is the Great Satan. Name's Hinds Rackley, Wall Street lawyer turned investment crook, worth only four billion, which barely gets the poor guy on the *Forbes* list these days. A lesser billionaire, I guess, but nonetheless one with all the toys: Fifth Avenue mansion with a view of the park, big spread in the Hamptons, a yacht, couple of jets, trophy wife, the usual. Law school at Harvard, then a few years with a big firm. Couldn't fit there so he hung out his own shingle with a few buddies, merged here and there, and now he owns or controls four law firms. As billionaires go, he's rather shy and loves his privacy. Operates behind the veil of a lot of different companies. I've only tracked down a few but I've found enough."

Gordy was talking to the wall, his back to his audience. When he lifted his cup for more tequila, the indentions between his ribs were visible. His weight loss was astonishing. He spoke calmly now, as if spouting facts he alone had uncovered.

"His main vehicle is Shiloh Square Financial, a private investment operation that also plays with leveraged buyouts and distressed debt and all the usual Wall Street games. Shiloh owns a chunk of Varanda Capital, how much we don't know because their filings are bare-bones, everything about this guy is deceptive, and Varanda owns a chunk of Baytrium Group. As you might know, Baytrium owns, among many other companies, our dear Foggy Bottom Law School. Us and three others. What you don't know is that Varanda also owns an outfit called Lacker Street Trust, out of Chicago, and Lacker Street owns four other for-profit law schools. That's a total of eight."

On the right side of the wall in large squares were the names of Shiloh Square Financial, Varanda Capital, and Baytrium Group. Below them in a neat row were the names of eight law schools: Foggy Bottom, Midwest, Poseidon, Gulf Coast, Galveston, Bunker Hill, Central Arizona, and Staten Island. Below each name were numbers and words in print too small to read from across the room.

Gordy stepped to the table and poured another measured serving of tequila. He took a sip, stepped back to the wall, and faced them. "Rackley began piecing together these schools about ten years ago, always, of course, hiding behind his many fronts. It's not illegal to own a for-profit law school or college, but he wants to keep it under cover anyway. Guess he's afraid someone will catch on to his dirty little scheme. I've caught him." He took another sip and glared at them, his eyes wide and glowing. "In 2006, the bright people in Congress decided that every Tom, Dick, and Harry should be able to vastly improve their lives by getting more education, so the bright people said, basically, that anyone, including the four of us, could borrow as much as needed to pursue professional degrees. Loans for everyone, easy money. Tuition, books, even living expenses, regardless of how much, and of course all backed by the good word of the federal government."

Mark said, "This is well-known, Gordy."

"Oh, thank you, Mark. Now, if you'll just sit there and be quiet I'll do the talking."

"Yes, sir."

"What's not well-known is that once Rackley owned the law schools, all eight of them, they began expanding rapidly. In 2005, Foggy Bottom had four hundred students. By the time we arrived in 2011, enrollment was at a thousand, where it remains today. Same for his other schools, all have roughly a thousand students. The schools bought buildings, hired every half-assed professor they could find, paid big bucks to administrators with passable credentials, and, of course, marketed themselves like crazy. And why? Well, what's not well-known are the economics of for-profit law schools."

He took another sip and moved to the far right of the wall, to a poster board covered with numbers and calculations. He said, "A bit of law school math. Take Foggy Bottom. They clip us for forty-five thousand a year in tuition, and everybody pays. There are no scholarships or grants, nothing real schools have to offer. That's a gross of forty-five million. They pay the professors about a hundred grand a year, a far cry from the national average of two-twenty for good schools, but still a bonanza for some of the clowns who taught us. There is an endless supply of legal academics looking for work, so they're lined up begging for the jobs because, of course, they just love being with us students. The school likes to brag about its low student-to-teacher ratio, ten to one, as if we're all being taught by gifted pros in small, cozy classes, right? Remember first-semester torts? There were two hundred of us packed into Stuttering Steve's classroom."

Todd interrupted with "How'd you find out about their salaries?"

"I talked to one of them, tracked him down. He taught

admin law for third years and we never had him. Got fired two years ago for drinking on the job. So we got drunk together and he told me everything. I got my sources, Todd, and I know what I'm talking about."

"Okay, okay. Just curious."

"Anyway, Foggy Bottom has about 150 professors, its biggest expense, say $15 million a year." He pointed to a jumble of figures they could barely read. "Then you have the administration on the top floor. Did you know that our incompetent dean makes $800,000 a year? Of course not. The dean at Harvard Law makes half a million a year, but then he's not in charge of a diploma mill where someone is watching the bottom line. Our dean has a nice résumé, looks good on paper, speaks well whenever he speaks, and has proven rather adept at fronting this racket. Rackley pays all his deans well and expects them to sell the dream. Throw in another, say, $3 million for the other bloated salaries up there and it's safe to say the administration costs $4 million a year. Let's be generous and make it $5, so we're at $20 in costs. Last year it cost $4 million to operate the place—the building, the staff, and, of course, the marketing. Almost $2 million of it was for propaganda to entice even more misguided souls to sign up, start borrowing, and pursue glorious careers in law. I know this because I have a friend who's a pretty good hacker. He found some stuff, didn't find some other stuff, and was impressed with the school's security. He says they work hard at protecting their files."

"That's $24 million," Mark said.

"You're quick. Round it off to $25, and the Great Satan nets $20 million a year off dear old Foggy Bottom. Multiply that times eight and the math will make you sick."

Gordy cleared his throat and spat at the wall. He took another sip, swallowed slowly, and paced a few steps.

"So how does Rackley do it?" he asked. "He sells the dream and we took the bait. When his eight schools expanded overnight, they opened their doors to everyone, regardless of qualifications or LSAT scores. The average LSAT for entering first years at Georgetown, which we know for sure is a top-tier school, is 165. For the Ivies it's even higher. We don't know the average LSAT at Foggy Bottom, because it's a military secret. My hacker couldn't penetrate the file. But it's safe to say it's well below 150, probably closer to 140. A major flaw in this defective system is that no LSAT score is too low to be admitted. These dipshit law schools will take anybody who can borrow the federal money, and, as stated, *anybody* can borrow the federal money. The ABA will accredit a kindergarten if it calls itself a law school. No one cares how dumb an applicant might be, nor does the federal loan program. Don't want to offend anyone in this room but we all know our scores. We've all been drunk enough to talk about them, with the exception of Zola of course, who happens to have the highest of the four. So to be diplomatic I'll say that the average of our little group is 145. Based on percentages, the chances of passing the bar exam with a 145 is about 50 percent. No one told us this when we applied because they care nothing about us; they just wanted our money. We were screwed the day we walked in."

"You're preaching to the choir," Mark said.

"And the sermon is not over," Gordy shot back, then ignored them for a moment as he studied his wall. Again, they exchanged looks that conveyed apprehension and fear. The sermon was interesting, and depressing, but they were far more worried about their friend.

He continued, "We're in this mess because we saw the opportunity to pursue a dream, one that we could not afford. None of us should be in law school and now we're in over our heads. We don't belong here, but we were scammed into believing we were cut out for lucrative careers. It's all about marketing and the promise of jobs. Jobs, jobs, jobs, big jobs with nice salaries. The reality, though, is that they don't exist. Last year the big firms on Wall Street were offering $175,000 to the top grads. About $160,000 here in D.C. We've heard about these jobs for years and somehow convinced ourselves that we might get one. Now we know the truth, and the truth is that there are some jobs in the $50,000 range, something like you, Mark, managed to get, though you still don't know the salary. These are at smaller firms where the work is brutal and the future is bleak. The big firms are paying one-sixty plus. And there is nothing in between. Nothing. We've suffered through the interviews, knocked on doors, scoured the Internet, so we know how bad the market is."

They nodded along, primarily to placate him. Gordy took another sip, moved to the left side of the wall, and pointed. "Here's the really nasty stuff, the part you know nothing about. Rackley owns a New York law firm called Quinn & Vyrdoliac; you might have heard of it. I had not. In the trade it's referred to simply as Quinn. Offices in six cities, about four hundred lawyers, not a top one hundred firm. A small branch here in D.C. with thirty lawyers." He pointed to a sheet of paper with the firm's name in bold lettering. "Quinn works primarily in financial services, the gutter end. It handles a lot of foreclosures, repossessions, collections, defaults, bankruptcies, almost everything related to debts gone bad. Including student loans. Quinn pays well, at least initially." He pointed to a colorful brochure, a trifold opened and pinned to the wall. "I saw this four years ago when I was considering Foggy Bottom. You probably saw it too. It features the smiling face of one Jared Molson, a grad who was supposedly happily employed at Quinn with a starting salary of $125,000. I remember thinking that, hey, if Foggy Bottom is turning out guys who get jobs like that, then sign me up. Well, I found Mr. Molson, had a long chat with him over drinks. He was offered a job at Quinn but didn't sign a contract until after he passed the bar exam. He worked there for six years and quit, and he quit because his salary kept going *down*. He said that each year the management would study the bottom line and decide that cuts were necessary. His last year he earned just over a hundred and said screw it. He said he lived like a bum, whittled down his debt, and now he's selling real estate and driving part-time for Uber. The firm's a sweatshop and he says he got used by Foggy Bottom's propaganda machine."

"And he's not the only one, right?" Todd said.

"Oh no. Molson was just one of many. Quinn has a fancy website and I read the bios of all four hundred lawyers. Thirty percent are from Rackley's law schools. Thirty percent! So, my friends, Rackley hires them at enviable salaries, then uses their smiling faces and great success stories for his propaganda."

He paused, took a sip, gave them a smug smile as if waiting for applause. He walked closer to the wall and pointed to another face, a black-and-white photo on copy paper, one of three just under the Great Satan. "This crook is Alan Grind, a Seattle-based lawyer and a limited partner in Varanda. Grind owns a law firm called King & Roswell, another low-tier operation with two hundred lawyers in five cities, primarily out west." He pointed to the left, where King & Roswell held a spot next to Quinn & Vyrdoliac. "Of Grind's two hundred lawyers, forty-five came from the eight law schools."

He took another sip and walked to the table for a refill.

"Are you going to drink that whole bottle?" Mark asked.

"Only if I want to."

"Maybe you should slow down."

"And maybe you should worry about yourself. I'm not drunk, just sufficiently buzzed. And who are you to monitor my drinking?"

Mark took a deep breath and let it go. Gordy's speech was clear enough. His mind was certainly clicking right along. In spite of his disheveled appearance, he seemed to be under control, at least for the moment. He stepped back to the wall and pointed at the photos. "The guy in the middle here is Walter Baldwin, runs a Chicago law firm called Spann & Tatta, three hundred lawyers in seven cities, coast to coast. Same type of work, same fondness for graduates of lesser law schools." He pointed to the third face under Rackley. "And rounding out the gang is Mr. Marvin Jockety, senior partner of a Brooklyn law firm called Ratliff & Cosgrove. Same setup, same business model."

Gordy took another sip and admired his work. He turned and looked at the three. "Not to belabor what should be obvious, but Rackley has under his thumb four law firms with eleven hundred lawyers in twenty-seven offices. Between them, they hire enough of his graduates to give his law schools plenty to crow about, so that suckers like us rush in with piles of cash provided by Congress." His voice was suddenly loud and shaky. "It's perfect! It's beautiful! It's one great big fat law school scam that's risk-free. If we default the taxpayers pick up the tab. Rackley gets to privatize the profits and socialize the losses."

He suddenly threw his coffee cup at the wall. It bounced off the thin Sheetrock unbroken and rolled across the floor. He sat hard against the wall, facing them, and stretched out his legs. The soles of his feet were black with dirt and grime.

The crash echoed for a few seconds as they watched him. Nothing was said for a long time. Mark gazed at the wall and absorbed the plot. There was no reason to doubt Gordy's research. Todd gazed at the wall as if enthralled by the conspiracy. Zola stared at Gordy and wondered what they were supposed to do with him.

Finally, Gordy, almost in a whisper, said, "My number is 276,000 in loans, including this semester. What's yours, Mark?"

There were no secrets. The four knew each other well enough.

"Including this semester, 266," Mark said.

"Todd?"

"One-ninety-five."

"Zola?"

"One-ninety-one."

Gordy shook his head and laughed, not from humor, but from disbelief. "Almost a million. Who in their right mind would loan the four of us a million dollars?" At the moment, it did seem absurd, even laughable.

After another long pause, Gordy said, "There's no way

out. We've been lied to, misled, scammed, and suckered into this miserable place. There's no way out."

Todd slowly got to his feet and stepped to the wall. He pointed to the center of it and asked, "What is Sorvann Lenders?"

Gordy snorted another fake laugh and said, "The rest of the story. Rackley, through another company, and this guy has more fronts than a low-rent strip mall, owns Sorvann, which is now the fourth-largest private student lender. If you can't get enough cash from the government, then you go private, where, surprise, surprise, the interest rates are higher and the debt collectors make the Mafia look like Cub Scouts. Sorvann lends to undergrads as well and has about ninety million in its portfolio. It's a growing company. Evidently, Rackley smells blood on the private side as well."

Todd asked, "And what is Passant?"

Another pained laugh. Gordy slowly climbed to his feet and walked to the table, where he grabbed the bottle and took a long swig. He grimaced, swallowed hard, wiped his mouth with his forearm, and finally said, "Passant is Piss Ant, third-largest student loan collecting racket in the country. It's under contract to the Department of Education to 'service,' as they like to say, student debt. There's over a trillion dollars out there, owed by fools like us. Passant is a bunch of terrorists, been sued a number of times for abusive debt collection practices. Rackley owns a chunk of it. The man is pure evil."

Gordy walked to the sofa and sat next to Zola. As he passed, Mark got a strong whiff of his body odor. Todd walked to the kitchenette, stepped around the debris on the floor, opened the fridge, and pulled out two cans of beer. He handed one to Mark and both popped the tops. Zola rubbed Gordy's leg, oblivious to his odors.

Mark nodded at the wall and asked, "So how long have you been working on this?"

"That's not important. There's more to the story if you care to hear it."

"I've heard enough," Mark said. "For now anyway. How about we walk around the corner and get a pizza? Mario's is still open."

"Great idea," Todd said, but no one moved.

Gordy finally said, "My parents are on the hook for ninety thousand of my debt, private stuff I carried over from college. Can you believe that? They were hesitant, and for good reason, but I pushed them hard. What an idiot! My dad makes fifty thousand a year selling farm equipment and owed nothing but a mortgage until I started borrowing. Mom works part-time at the school. I've lied to them, told them I have a great job all lined up and I could handle the repayments. I've lied to Brenda too. She thinks we'll be living in the big city where I'll hustle off to work each day in a nice suit, eager to claw my way to the top. I'm in a bit of a jam, guys, and I see no way out."

"We'll survive, Gordy," Mark said, but without conviction.

"We'll get through it," Todd said, without specifying which "it" he was referring to. Law school? The debt? Unemployment? Or Gordy's breakdown? There were so many challenges at the moment.

Another long, dreary pause. Mark and Todd quietly sipped their beers.

Gordy said, "How can we expose Rackley? I've thought about sitting down with a reporter, someone who covers the legal beat for the *Post* or maybe the *Journal*. I've even thought about a class action lawsuit against the crook. Think of the thousands of young idiots like us who are on the same sinking ship and would love to take a shot at the guy once the truth is out."

Mark said, "I don't see a lawsuit. I mean, sure, he's put together a brilliant scheme but he hasn't done anything that's actionable. There's no law against owning diploma mills, even though he's trying his best to hide it. His law firms can hire whoever they want. Sleazy, unfair, deceitful, but not enough for a lawsuit."

"Agreed," Todd said. "But I love the idea of helping an investigative reporter hammer the guy."

Zola asked, "Wasn't there a case in California where a law student sued her law school because she couldn't find a job?"

Mark replied, "Yes, there have been several, all dismissed but for the one in California. It went to trial and the jury found in favor of the law school."

Gordy said, "I'm not giving up on the lawsuit. It's the best way to expose Rackley. Can you imagine what discovery would be like?"

"All fun and games, but he's not stupid," Mark said. "Hell, he owns four law firms. Just think of the heavy artillery he'd throw at you. The plaintiffs would spend the next five years drowning in paperwork."

"What do you know about lawsuits?" Gordy asked.

"Everything. I've been educated at Foggy Bottom."

"I rest my case."

The lame effort at humor passed and they stared at the floor. Finally, Todd said, "Come on, Gordy, let's go get a pizza."

"I'm not going anywhere but I think you guys should leave."

"Then we're not leaving either," Mark said. "We're staying here."

"Why? I don't need a babysitter. Get out."

Todd, still standing, walked to the sofa and stared down at Gordy. "Let's talk about you, Gordy, you and your condition. You're not sleeping or eating, or bathing for that matter. Are you taking your meds?"

"What meds?"

"Come on, Gordy. We're your friends and we're here to help."

"What meds?" he demanded.

"Come on, Gordy, we know what's going on," Mark said.

Gordy turned to Zola and growled, "What have you told them?"

Zola was about to respond when Todd said, "Nothing. She's told us nothing, but we're not blind, Gordy, we're your best friends and you need some help."

"I don't need meds," he snapped back, then bolted to his feet, brushed by Todd, and went to his bedroom. Seconds later he yelled, "Get out of here!" and slammed the door. They took a deep breath and stared at each other. Seconds later, the door opened and Gordy came out. He grabbed the bottle of tequila, said, "Leave! Now!" and disappeared again into his bedroom.

A minute passed without a sound. Zola stood and crossed the den. She put an ear to his door and listened. She stepped away and whispered, "I think he's crying."

"Great," Mark whispered.

Another minute passed. Softly, Todd said, "We can't leave him."

"No way," Mark said. "Let's take turns. I'll pull the first shift on the sofa."

"I'm not leaving," Zola said.

Mark looked around the den and finished his beer. Almost in a whisper he said, "Okay, you take the sofa and I'll take the chair. Todd, you sleep on Zola's sofa and we'll swap in a few hours."

Todd nodded and said, "Okay, I guess that will work." He stepped to the fridge, got another beer, and left. Mark turned off the lights and settled into the battered leather chair. A few feet away, Zola curled up on the sofa. He whispered, "This could be a long night."

"We shouldn't talk," she said. "The walls are thin and he might hear us."

"Right."

The digital clock on the microwave emitted a bluish light that seemed to grow brighter as their eyes adjusted to the darkness. It defined the shadows of the small dining table, the computer, and printer. Though they were still wide awake, the room was perfectly still. No sounds from the bedroom. Soft, distant music from down the hall. After ten minutes, Mark pulled out his phone and checked his messages and e-mails. Nothing important. The next ten minutes seemed like an hour as the chair grew more uncomfortable.

He stared at the wall. He couldn't see the picture of Hinds Rackley, but he could feel his eyes gazing smugly down at them. At the moment, though, Mark wasn't concerned with Rackley and his grand conspiracy. He was worried about Gordy. Their challenge tomorrow would be getting their friend to the doctor.

5

At 2:00 a.m., Todd slipped into Gordy's apartment without a sound and found both Mark and Zola asleep. He shook Mark's arm and whispered, "My turn." Mark stood, stretched his stiff joints and muscles, and walked across the hall, where he fell onto Zola's sofa.

Before dawn, Gordy got out of bed and put on his jeans, sweatshirt, socks, and denim jacket. Holding his hiking boots, he stood by the door and listened. He knew they were in the den, waiting for him to make a move. He gently opened the bedroom door and listened. He took a step into the den, saw their silhouettes on the sofa and in the chair, heard their heavy breathing, and silently walked to the door. At the end of the hallway, he put on his boots and left the building.

At the first hint of sunlight, Zola awoke and sat up. Seeing the bedroom door open she jumped to her feet, turned on the lights, and realized Gordy had managed to escape. "He's not here!" she yelled at Todd. "He's gone!"

Todd scrambled out of the chair and walked past her to

the bedroom, a small square space where hiding would be impossible. He poked through the closet, looked in the bathroom, and yelled, "Shit! What happened?"

"He got up and left," she said. They stared at each other in disbelief, then walked over to break the news to Mark. The three hurried down the stairs and along the first-floor hallway to the building's rear door. There were a dozen cars in the parking lot but none of them belonged to Gordy. His little Mazda was gone, as they feared it would be. Zola called Gordy's cell but of course there was no answer. They returned to the apartments, locked the doors, and walked three blocks to a diner where they huddled in a booth and tried to regroup over black coffee.

"There's no way to find him in this city," Mark said.

"He doesn't want to be found," Todd said.

"Should we call the police?" Zola asked.

"And tell them what? Our friend's missing and might hurt himself? These cops are busy with last night's murders and rapes."

Todd asked, "What about his parents? They probably have no idea what shape he's in."

Mark was shaking his head. "No, Gordy would hate us forever. Besides, what can they do? Hurry over to the big city and start searching?"

"I agree, but Gordy has a doctor somewhere, either here or back home. A doctor who knows him, who's treated him, who's prescribed the meds, someone who should know that he's in bad shape. If we tell his parents, they can at least inform the doctor. Who cares if we piss off Gordy as long as he gets some help?"

"That makes sense," Zola said. "And the doctor is here. Gordy sees him once a month."

"Do you know his name?"

"No. I've tried to find out, but no luck."

Mark said, "Okay, maybe later, but for now we gotta find Gordy."

They drank coffee and pondered the impossibility of finding him in the city. A waitress stopped by and asked about breakfast. They declined. No one had an appetite.

"Any ideas?" Mark asked Zola.

She shook her head. "Not really. In the past week he's disappeared twice. The first time he took a train to New York and was gone for three days. When he got back he didn't say much, just that he was on the trail of the Great Satan. I think he talked to some people up there. He hung around for a day or so; we were together most of the time. He was drinking and slept a lot. Then I came home from work and he was gone again. For two days, nothing. That was when he found the law professor who'd been fired from Foggy Bottom."

"Did you know what he was doing?" Todd asked.

"No. Two days ago he locked himself in his apartment and wouldn't see me. I think that was when he moved the furniture and went to work on the wall."

"How much do you know about his condition?" Mark asked.

She took a deep breath and hesitated. "This is all confidential, guys, you understand? He swore me to secrecy."

"Come on, Zola, we're all in this together," Mark said. "Of course it's confidential."

She glanced around as if others were listening. "Back in September, I found his pills, so we talked about it. He was diagnosed as bipolar when he was in college and didn't tell anyone, not even Brenda. He told her sometime later, so she knows. Through therapy and meds he's kept things together nicely."

"I never knew it," Mark said.

"Neither did I," Todd said.

Zola continued. "It's not unusual for people who are bipolar to reach a point where they believe they no longer need the meds. They feel great and convince themselves they can live just fine without them. So they stop taking them, things soon begin to spiral down, and they often turn to self-medication. That's what happened to Gordy, though he was also feeling a lot of other pressures. All this law school mess, couldn't find a job, the loans, and to make it all worse he felt as though he was getting pushed into a wedding. He was in bad shape by Thanksgiving but worked hard to conceal it."

"Why didn't you tell us?"

"Because he would hate me. He was convinced he could man up and somehow survive. And, looking back, most of the time he was okay. But the mood swings got worse, as did the drinking."

"You should have told us," Mark said.

"I didn't know what to do. I've never dealt with something like this before."

"Pointing fingers will not help right now," Todd said to Mark.

"I'm sorry."

Todd glanced at his cell phone and said, "It's almost eight. Nothing from Gordy. I'm supposed to go to the bar at noon and work a shift. What's everybody else doing today?"

Zola said, "I go in at ten for a few hours." She was working as a temp in a small accounting firm.

Mark said, "Well, I came back early to get away from home and hopefully put together a plan to start studying for the bar exam, but I really don't want to. I suppose I'll drift on over to Ness Skelton and kill the day sucking up to my future bosses, trying to appear needed and relevant. For no pay, of course. I'm sure they need some help in the copy room."

"Gotta love the law," Todd said. "I'll accomplish more in the bar."

"Thanks."

Zola said, "I suppose all we can do is wait."

Todd paid for the coffee and they left the diner. They had walked a block when Zola's phone vibrated. She pulled it from a pocket, looked at it, stopped, and said, "It's Gordy. He's at Central Jail."

AT 4:35 A.M., Gordy was stopped after an officer noticed his Mazda weaving along Connecticut Avenue. He stumbled during a field sobriety test and eventually agreed to blow. He registered 0.11 on the mobile monitor and was immediately handcuffed and placed in the rear seat of the police car. A tow truck hauled his car to the city lot. At Central, he blew again with the same result. He was fingerprinted, photographed, booked, and thrown into the drunk tank with six others. At 8:00 a.m., a bailiff led him to a small room, handed him his phone, and told him he could use it once. He called Zola, and the bailiff took his phone and led him back to the cell.

Thirty minutes later, his three friends walked through the front door at Central, got themselves scanned by a metal detector, and were directed to a large room where, evidently, families and friends came to retrieve their loved ones after a bad night. It was lined with chairs along three walls, with magazines and newspapers scattered about. Behind a large window at the far end two uniformed clerks were busy with paperwork. Cops milled around, some chatting with dazed and nervous people. There were about a dozen of them—parents, spouses, friends—all with the same spooked looks and fidgety manners. Two men in bad suits and battered briefcases seemed right at home. One was chatting up a cop who appeared to know him well. The other was huddled with a middle-aged couple. The mother was crying.

Mark, Todd, and Zola found seats in a corner and took in the surroundings. After a few minutes, Mark walked to the window and offered a sappy smile to a clerk. He said he was there to get his friend Gordon Tanner, and the clerk checked some paperwork. She nodded toward the seats and said it would take some time. Mark returned to his chair between Todd and Zola.

The lawyer chatting with the cop watched them carefully and soon came over. His three-piece suit was made of a slick bronze fabric. His shoes were shiny and black, with long pointed toes that flipped up at the tips. His shirt was baby blue and his thickly knotted tie was pale green and matched nothing else. On one wrist he wore a large gold watch with diamonds and on the other he displayed two bulky gold bracelets. His hair was greased back and bunched behind his ears. Without a smile he delivered his standard line, "Here for a DUI?"

Mark said, "Yes."

The lawyer was already passing out his business cards. Darrell Cromley, Attorney-at-Law. DUI Specialist. Each of the three got a card as Darrell asked, "Who's the lucky guy?"

"Our friend," Todd said.

"First time?" Darrell asked happily.

"Yes, first time," Mark replied.

"Sorry to hear. I can help. It's all I do, DUIs. I know all the cops, judges, clerks, bailiffs, the ins and outs of the system. I'm the best in the business."

Careful not to say anything that might show the slightest interest in hiring the guy, Mark asked, "Okay, so what's he looking at?"

Darrell deftly pulled over a folding chair and faced the three. Without missing a beat, he asked, "What's his name?"

"Gordon Tanner."

"Well, Tanner blew a 0.11, so there's not much wiggle room. First you gotta pay two hundred bucks to get him out. PRB, personal recognition bond. They'll process him in about an hour and he can go. Cost you another two hundred to spring his car. It's over at the city pound. Take half an hour or so to get it out. He'll have a court date in a week or so. That's where I come in. My fee is a thousand bucks cash."

"He keeps his license?" Todd asked.

"Sure, until he's convicted, in about a month. Then he'll lose it for a year, pay a fine of five thousand, but I can get some of that knocked off. I'm really a bargain, you know? Plus he's facing five nights in jail, but I can work some magic there too. We'll sign him up for community service and keep him out. Believe me, I know the ropes. You guys in school or something?"

Mark said, "Yes, we're law students." He was not about to give the name of their school.

"Georgetown?"

Todd quietly said, "No. Foggy Bottom."

Cromley smiled and said, "That's my school. Finished there twelve years ago."

The door opened and two more worried parents walked in. Cromley eyed them like a hungry dog. When he looked back at the three, Todd said, "So we need four hundred cash right now."

"No, you need fourteen hundred. Two hundred for the bond. Two hundred for the car. A thousand for me."

Zola said, "Okay, but our friend probably had some cash on him. How do we find out how much?"

"I can find out. Hire me now and I go to work. Your friend needs protection and that's where I come in. The DUI treadmill in this town will chew him up and spit him out."

Zola said, "Look, our friend is not doing well. He's, uh, well, he's having some problems and he's off his meds. We need to get him to the doctor."

Darrell liked it! His eyes narrowed as he moved in for the kill. "Sure. Once we get him out I can file a motion for an expedited hearing. Again, I'm tight with the judges and I can speed things along. But the fee will go up, of course. Let's not delay things."

Mark said, "All right, all right, give us some time to think about it."

Cromley bounced to his feet and said, "You have my number." He slithered away, found another cop to chat with as he surveyed the crowd for his next victim. As they watched him, Mark whispered, "That could be us in a couple of years."

"What a slimeball," Todd said, barely under his breath.

Zola said, "I have $80. Let's pass the hat."

Mark frowned and said, "I'm light. Maybe thirty."

Todd said, "Me too, but I've got enough in the bank. I'll run find an ATM while you guys wait here."

"Good plan." Todd hurried from the room as more people arrived. Mark and Zola watched Cromley and the other lawyer work the crowd. Between victims, Cromley either chatted with a cop or took important calls on his cell. Several times he left the room, always on the phone, as if attending to urgent legal matters elsewhere. But he always returned, and with a purpose.

Mark observed, "The things they haven't taught us in law school."

"He probably doesn't even have an office," Zola said.

"Are you kidding? This is his office."

TWO HOURS AFTER arriving at Central, the three left with Gordy. Since Zola didn't own a car, and since Mark's Bronco could not be trusted in traffic, they piled into Todd's Kia hatchback and made their way to the city's car lot in Anacostia near the naval yard. Gordy rode in the rear seat next to Zola with his eyes closed and said nothing. Indeed, there was little conversation, though there was much to be said. Mark wanted to get it all on the table with something like "Well, now, Gordy, are you even remotely aware of what a DUI will do to your already miserable employment opportunities?" Or, "So, Gordy, do you realize that, even assuming you pass the bar exam, you'll find it virtually impossible to get admitted to the bar because of a DUI?"

Todd wanted to drill him with something like "So,

Gordy, where, exactly, were you headed at four in the morning with two empty tequila bottles on the floorboard?"

Zola, far more compassionate, wanted to ask, "Who is your doctor and how soon can you see him?"

So much to say, but nothing was said. At the car lot, Mark handled the negotiations with the clerk. He explained that Mr. Tanner was ill and unable to function at the moment.

Probably still drunk, the clerk thought, which was not at all unusual.

Mark forked over $200, half of which came from Gordy's wallet, and signed the necessary forms. They left with Todd driving Zola to work, and Mark driving Gordy in his Mazda.

As they inched along in city traffic, Mark said, "Wake up, Gordy, and talk to me."

"What do you want?" he mumbled without opening his eyes. He reeked of alcohol and body odor.

"I want to know who your doctor is and where his office is located. That's where we're going right now."

"No, we're not. I don't have a doctor."

"Well, you damned sure need one. Come on, Gordy, stop lying. We know about the bipolar disorder and the doctor or therapist or whoever you're seeing. It's obvious to us that you're off your meds and you need help."

"Who told you this?"

"Zola."

"That bitch."

"Come on, Gordy, lay off. If you don't tell me right now who your doctor is I'm going to call your parents and Brenda."

"I'll kill you."

"Great, let's stop the car and have a knife fight."

Gordy took a deep breath and shuddered from head to toe. He opened his eyes, looked out the window, and said, "Please stop yelling at me, Mark. I've had a bad night."

"Okay, I'll stop yelling, but you've got to get some help, Gordy."

"Please take me home."

"To Martinsburg. I like that idea."

"Oh, hell no, not there. I'd blow my brains out, which is not a bad idea these days."

"Stop it, Gordy. Let's go to your apartment, where you can take a nice, long shower. Then maybe a nap. We'll get something to eat, and then I'll drive you to the doctor."

"The nap sounds good. Nothing else."

A moment later, Mark realized his friend was wiping tears from his cheeks with the back of his hand.

6

When Gordy fell onto his bed he told Mark to leave. Mark explained that was not going to happen and they argued briefly. Gordy gave up, pulled a blanket over his head, and fell asleep. Mark closed the bedroom door, sat on the sofa, and stared at his phone. Brenda had called him twice that morning and was panicked. Her rambling voice mails and text messages were increasingly urgent. She had not heard from her fiancé in two days and she was ready to drive to D.C. On the one hand, Mark almost welcomed her intervention. She needed to know what was happening. She could assume control of the situation and take the pressure off Mark and the others. She would probably get his parents involved, and at the moment they were needed.

But, on the other hand, she could make a bad situation worse. No one could predict how Gordy might react if she showed up and started barking. He would certainly yell at Mark for telling her the truth. The last thing Gordy needed at the moment was more drama.

Mark stepped into the hallway and called Brenda. He

lied and said Gordy was suffering from a nasty bout of the flu, that he was in bed, still highly contagious, and getting plenty of fluids and flu medicine. Mark and Todd were sitting with him, nursing him, and things were under control. If there was no improvement by tomorrow, Mark promised to take him to the doctor. Did she happen to know the name of his doctor? No, she did not. He would call her with updates as things progressed. When the call ended, Brenda was still concerned and said she would wait a day or so before driving over.

Mark walked up and down the hallway, feeling like a creep for lying and thoroughly confused about what to do next. Several times he almost called her back to tell the truth. If he did so, she would be there within two hours and Gordy would be hers to worry about. She knew him better than anyone. They had been a couple since the seventh grade. Mark had known Gordy for only two and a half years. Who was he to assume the role of Johnny-come-lately and get involved in their problems? Gordy needed medical attention, and perhaps his fiancée was the only person who could make that happen.

However, if Brenda arrived on the scene now, things could spiral out of control. She would hear about the DUI. She knew Mark and Todd and would resent their cover-up. She might learn the truth about Zola, a possibility that was too awful to think about. In the chaos, she might realize that Gordy was lying about a nice job after graduation. The situation would become so unpredictable that everyone would get hurt, especially Gordy. Most important, Gordy didn't want Brenda anywhere near him. He wanted to call off the wedding, but so far had not found the guts to break up.

The more Mark paced, the more confused he became. Procrastination seemed like a safe strategy, at least for the moment, and he decided to stick with the lie and see how the afternoon unfolded.

Noon came and went with Gordy still semi-comatose. Mark quietly cleaned the kitchen and hauled three bags of garbage to the dumpster. He washed the dishes, dried them, and put them away. He swept the floors and tidied up the mess around Gordy's work space on the dining table. He tried to rearrange the furniture but could not do it without making noise. He spent a lot of time staring at the wall and trying to understand the connections linking the companies, firms, and players in Hinds Rackley's empire. It was an impressive conspiracy, and Gordy had spent hours piecing it together. But was his research accurate? In his unhinged state, was he capable of thinking clearly?

With his cell phone, Mark searched the web and read everything he could find about bipolar disorder and depression. There was a lot to read. Around three, he heard noises in the bedroom and peeked in. The water was running in the bathroom; Gordy was finally in the shower. Half an hour later, he stepped into the den, freshly scrubbed and shaved with his thick blond hair as handsome as always. He was wearing jeans and a sweater. He looked at Mark and said, "I'm hungry."

"Great," Mark said with a smile. They walked a few blocks to a favorite deli and ordered sandwiches and coffee. Conversation was muted, almost nonexistent. Gordy didn't want to talk and Mark left him alone. Gordy picked at his BLT, finally removed the bread, and ate the bacon with his fingers. They drank coffee as fast as the waitress could pour it, and the caffeine seemed to revive Gordy.

With a mouth full of chips, he said, "I feel better now, Mark, thanks."

"Great. Let's finish up and go see your doctor."

"No, it's not necessary, Mark, I feel fine now."

"The doctor, Gordy, or therapist or whatever the hell he or she is. You think you're okay now, but this will pass."

"The therapist is a joke, can't stand the guy."

The waitress poured more coffee. Gordy finished his chips and shoved his plate away. He sipped from his cup and avoided eye contact. Mark finally said, "You want to talk about the DUI?"

"Not really. Let's go for a walk. I need some fresh air."

"Great idea."

Mark paid with a credit card and they left the diner. They drifted through Dupont Circle and headed west on M Street. The temperature was up and the sky was clear; not a bad day for a long walk. They crossed Rock Creek and entered Georgetown, where they walked with the crowds along Wisconsin Avenue and stopped occasionally to look at shopwindows. In a used-book store, they browsed through the sports section. Gordy had played football and lacrosse at Washington and Lee and would always be the superjock.

Whatever he was thinking he kept to himself. He seemed relaxed and smiled from time to time, but he was not the old Gordy. His cockiness and usual smart-ass banter were absent. He was troubled, and rightfully so, and Mark missed the quips and cynical observations that were so common. When the wind picked up late in the afternoon, they ducked into a coffee shop for a latte. Bunched around a small table, Mark tried again to engage him, but Gordy was in another world. When he went to the restroom, Mark sent a text to Todd and Zola with an update. He also sent one to Brenda, saying Gordy was slightly better but now he had infected both Mark and Todd. All three were now sick as dogs and taking care of one another in Gordy's apartment. The flu was highly contagious and raging through D.C.; best if she stayed away.

As they were leaving the coffee shop, Gordy said he wanted to walk along the Potomac River. They crossed M Street on Wisconsin and drifted down to the Georgetown Waterfront, a modern development of high-end shops and restaurants and cafés that, in nice weather, would be packed with students and tourists sitting outdoors enjoying the sun. But in the dead of winter there wasn't much foot traffic. Standing on the boardwalk beside the frigid Potomac, Gordy seemed to enjoy the views. To their right was the Key Bridge linking Georgetown to Rosslyn. To their left was Theodore Roosevelt Island and another bridge. Not far away was the Kennedy Center, and in the distance the Lincoln Memorial and other monuments. The air was noticeably colder near the water. Large chunks of ice inched their way down the river.

When Gordy turned around, he was smiling with an odd look of peaceful satisfaction.

"I'm freezing," Mark said.

"Let's go."

WHEN TODD AND ZOLA arrived after dark, Gordy was sleeping again while Mark read a paperback. In soft voices, the three recapped the day and tried to plan the night. They discussed calling Brenda and telling her the truth, but no one was ready for that. Especially Zola. Other than a passing thought of finding his doctor, there was little discussion about tomorrow. With hardly a sound, they moved his furniture and tidied up his den. Mark really wanted to clear off the wall. He was tired of looking at the face of Hinds Rackley and his gang. Things were bad enough being ensnared in their grand conspiracy, but it was almost cruel to have them in the room. However, Todd and Zola vetoed the idea. Gordy had slaved over his masterpiece. Destroying it might unhinge him again.

When the pizza arrived, Zola eased into the bedroom and tried to rouse her boyfriend. She returned, alone, and said he was barely responsive, and rude at that. They ate the pizza, drank nothing but water, and killed time. Mark had Gordy's keys in his pocket and that's where they would stay. They decided to tag team through the night, same as before, with Zola pulling the first shift on the sofa. Todd went across the hall to her apartment. Mark walked four blocks to his and showered for the first time that day.

After they were gone, and the den was dark and quiet, Zola began texting. To compound her miseries on this perfectly miserable day, she had received a call from her father. His latest petition had been denied by the immigration judge, and an order had been entered to remove him, her mother, and Bo, her unmarried brother. After twenty-six years in the U.S., they would be flown back to Senegal with a load of refugees. Twenty-six years of hard work in menial jobs for low pay. Twenty-six years of scraping by and saving as much as possible and obeying every law, including speed limits. Twenty-six years of considering themselves Americans and thankful to be here. Now they were being forced to return to a country they did not know and wanted no part of.

She was a strong woman who took pride in her toughness, but laden with more worries than any person could possibly bear, Zola made the mistake of closing her eyes.

AT 1:42 A.M., her phone began buzzing and vibrating. It was in the pocket of her jeans and finally woke her. Missed call. It was Gordy. It took a second or two for reality to hit, and she bolted to her feet and ran to his bedroom. She checked his bathroom, knowing perfectly well he wasn't there, and ran to wake up Todd. For the second night in a row, they raced down the stairs to the first-floor hallway and to the parking lot behind the building. Gordy's Mazda was gone. Todd called Mark and said they were racing over to get him. In Todd's car, Zola's phone pinged with a text message.

"It's him. He says: 'Zola, I can't do this anymore. There's no way out. I'm so sorry.'"

"Shit! Call him!"

"He won't answer," she said as she punched his number. Straight to voice mail. "Hello, this is Gordy. Leave a message."

"Voice mail," she said. "I'm texting him." *"Gordy, where are you? We're coming to get you."*

She stared at her phone waiting for a reply, then re-sent the same text. "Nothing," she said.

"And you heard nothing when he left?"

"Of course not. I tried to stay awake. I guess he had another key."

"Evidently. He's gonna hurt himself."

"Don't say that."

Mark was sprinting from his building, on the phone,

trying to reach Gordy. He did not. He jumped in the backseat of the car and said, "Now what?"

"You still have his keys?" Todd asked.

"In my pocket. Who keeps the other key to a car that's ten years old?"

"I guess Gordy does. He's gonna do something stupid, you know that?"

"That's very helpful right now," Zola said. "I'm sorry, guys, I didn't mean to fall asleep."

That's two nights in a row, both Mark and Todd thought, but they said nothing. Beating her up would not help matters, and she felt bad enough. If Gordy was determined to pull another stunt, they really couldn't stop him.

"Any ideas?" Todd asked, still clutching the wheel. There was no response. The three sat in an awful silence as the engine hummed away and the heater blew warm air. Zola broke the silence with "He liked to jog along Rock Creek."

Todd said, "I doubt if he's jogging tonight. It's twenty degrees."

Mark said, "Let's check out Coney's. It's always been our favorite place to sober up."

"Good idea," Todd said as he shifted into drive. "Keep calling and texting."

Coney's was an all-night waffle shop on Nineteenth Street and was favored by bums and students. Todd stopped at the corner and Mark ducked inside. He was back in seconds and said, "No sign of him. I have an idea. Let's go to the Waterfront in Georgetown. We were there this afternoon and he seemed to like the place."

"What do you mean 'He liked the place'?" Todd asked.

"I don't know. Just drive."

As they turned onto M Street, Mark's phone rang. "Oh shit! It's Brenda. Do I take it?"

"Yes," Todd snapped. "Right now you gotta take it."

Mark hit speaker and said, "Hey, Brenda."

She was frantic. "Mark, what's going on? I just got a text from Gordy. He says he's sorry, there's no way out, and he can't keep going. What the hell is happening, Mark? Talk to me."

"He's driving around D.C., Brenda. Todd and I are in the car trying to find him. He's off his meds and acting crazy."

"I thought he was in bed with the flu, same as you."

"He was in the bed sick, okay? We were with him and he sneaked out. Have you tried to call him?"

"Of course! Why didn't you tell me he's off his meds?" She was practically screaming.

"I didn't know he was on meds, Brenda, until yesterday. He never told us. You didn't either."

"It's not something we talked about. Please find him, Mark!"

"We're trying."

"I'll get there as fast as I can."

"No, not yet. Stay put and I'll call you later."

At the Waterfront, they parked at a curb and scrambled out of the car. As they sprinted toward the river a security guard stopped them. Mark said, "Sir, we're looking for a friend. He drives a little blue Mazda and he needs our help. Have you seen him?"

"Ain't nobody here this time of night," the guard said.

"Okay. We're just looking, that all right?"

"Sure."

They walked along the promenade and stopped by the

edge of the Potomac, in the same spot Gordy and Mark had been just hours earlier. To their right, a few cars crossed the Potomac on the Key Bridge. And to their left, beyond Roosevelt Island, there was an emergency on the Arlington Memorial Bridge. Red and blue lights were flashing.

7

By the time they arrived, the three westbound lanes of the bridge were blocked and traffic was backing up. Todd parked on a grassy knoll near a ramp and they hurried to the scene. Half a dozen D.C. police cars were parked haphazardly on the bridge with their doors open and blue lights flashing. Radios squawked as cops milled about. Two of them were standing on the sidewalk at the railing, peering into the dark river below. An ambulance with its siren wailing was inching through the stalled traffic trying to reach the scene. A hundred feet onto the bridge, a cop stopped them.

"Get back!" he growled. "Where do you think you're going?"

They stopped and absorbed the mayhem before them. Over his shoulder and beyond the police cars they saw Gordy's blue Mazda, sitting dead still with its lights on in the center lane. Its driver's door was open.

"What happened?" Mark asked the cop.

"None of your business. Now get away from here."

Todd said, "Sir, we know him. He's our friend. What's happened to him?"

The cop took a deep breath and relaxed. He said, "He jumped, okay? He stopped his car and jumped."

Zola screamed and buried her face in her hands. Todd grabbed her before she fell. Mark's knees buckled and he almost vomited. He managed to say, "No, there's no way."

The cop took Mark by the shoulders and nodded to his left where two officers were consoling a middle-aged woman. He said, "That woman was driving behind him when he stopped. She saw him run to the edge and jump. I'm sorry."

"There's no way," Mark said again, and Todd led Zola to the wide sidewalk a few feet away. She sat down hard with her back against the concrete railing of the bridge and wailed inconsolably.

"I'm sorry," the officer said again. "We're running his tags. He's from West Virginia, right?"

"Right. His name is Gordon Tanner. We're students."

"Come with me." Mark followed him past the police cars and the cops and they stopped behind Gordy's car. Mark stared at it in horror and shook his head. "Over here," the cop said, and he led Mark to the edge of the bridge. Two cops with handheld search beams were shining lights on the dark waters of the Potomac. A speedboat with more blue lights was racing toward them.

The cop said, "This is where he went over. There's ice down there. No one could last more than two minutes."

Mark stared at the water and watched the speedboat go under the bridge. He covered his eyes and began sobbing.

A detective in a trench coat walked over and asked, "Who's this?"

The cop said, "He's a friend, knows the guy."

Mark looked at the detective and tried to compose himself. The detective said, "I'm sorry, son. What can you tell us?"

Mark wiped his eyes and gritted his teeth. In a shaky voice, he managed to say, "He's our friend and he's been having some trouble lately. Got a DUI last night and we've been keeping an eye on him all day. We were afraid he might do something stupid."

"Does he have mental problems?"

"No, he's just off his meds." His voice cracked and he wiped his eyes again. "I can't believe this."

"I'm sorry, son. I'm Detective Swayze, DCPD. Here's my card with my cell number."

Mark took the card and managed to say, "Thanks."

"We're searching now and it'll take some time, but we'll find him. Do you know his family?"

"Yes."

"Where's he from?"

"Martinsburg, West Virginia."

"Do you mind giving them a call? They'll probably want to get over here."

That was the last phone call Mark wanted to make, but he nodded and said, "Sure. Can we help with the search, or something?"

"Sorry, son, there's nothing for you to do but wait. Text me your phone number and I'll call when we find him."

"How long will it take?"

The detective shrugged and said, "You never know with something like this. I suggest you go someplace warm and wait. I'll call you later with an update. Tell the family they can call me too. And look, we've searched the car but there's no note. Do you know where he lives?"

"I do."

"Okay. Do you mind checking his place to see if he left behind a note? They usually do. If you find something, call me at once."

"I'll do that."

Swayze put a hand on Mark's shoulder and said, "I'm sorry, son."

"Thanks." Mark began walking along the sidewalk. Another ambulance was approaching from the west and traffic was backing up in that direction as well. There seemed to be a million flashing lights. Two larger boats with search beams had joined the first and they circled under the archways of the bridge.

Mark and Todd helped Zola to her feet. They were freezing, numb, but too shocked to feel anything. They half carried her back to the car, which was blocked by traffic. Todd started the engine and the heater and they sat in stunned horror and watched the nightmare. Zola wept in the front passenger's seat. Todd slumped against his window and looked like a ghost. Mark sobbed and tried to catch his breath. Minutes passed as his phone kept vibrating. He finally took it out of his pocket and said, "Brenda's called four times. Someone has to tell her."

Todd said, "That someone is you, Mark. You have no choice."

"Why can't you call her?"

"Because you know her better. She's calling you, not me."

Mark clutched his phone and waited. A tow truck with yellow lights inched its way through the stalled traffic and weaved around the police cars. Someone with authority decided the ambulances would not be needed, so they left, along with a few of the police cars.

"You gonna call her?" Todd asked.

"I'm trying to find the courage," Mark said.

"This is my fault," Zola said, sobbing.

"It's no one's fault and you know it," Todd said, but with little conviction.

"I did this," she said. "I did this."

The yellow lights turned around, and they watched the tow truck come toward them in an eastbound lane. It passed them with Gordy's car on its rear wheels. More boats arrived and the flotilla fanned out south of the bridge, searching. The police cleared two of the westbound lanes and the stalled traffic began moving slowly.

Mark said, "What do I tell her? I can't say he's dead because we don't know for sure, right?"

Todd said, "He's dead, Mark. Tell her he jumped off a bridge into the Potomac River and they're searching for his body."

"I can't do it."

"You have no choice."

Mark took a deep breath but did not make the call. He said, "I was with him when he made his decision. We were at the Waterfront, and Gordy was staring at this bridge. When he turned around he was calm and smiling. He made up his mind and was at peace with his plans. I was too stupid to realize it."

"We are not doing the blame game, damn it," Todd said.

"Well, you can bet your ass Brenda will point fingers and I'll be the target. I lied to her all afternoon. I should've told her the truth and let her deal with him."

"We did what we could. It's not our fault he cracked up."

"It's all my fault!" Zola shrieked. "All of this."

"Stop it, Zola!" Todd snapped.

A cop with a flashlight motioned for them to move, and Todd eased off the grass and onto a westbound lane. They moved slowly over the bridge. Three patrol cars were parked bumper to bumper in the outside lane. A group of cops huddled on the sidewalk, near the spot where Gordy jumped.

"Where are we going?" Mark asked.

"I don't know."

They crossed the river, turned south onto the GW Parkway, and got off on Columbia Island. Todd parked in an empty lot at the LBJ Memorial Grove, with a marina in front of them and hundreds of boats rocking gently at the docks. They stared into the darkness as the car's heater strained and heaved. Mark's phone began vibrating in his pocket.

"Are you going to call her?"

Mark looked at his phone and said, "I don't have to. She's calling me." He opened a rear door, got out, and started walking toward the dock. He put the phone to his ear and said, "Brenda, something terrible has happened."

8

They took Zola to her apartment and laid her on the sofa. Mark covered her with a quilt and sat at the end, holding her feet. Todd made a pot of coffee and as it brewed he sat on the floor with his back to the sofa. Zola placed a hand on his shoulder. For a long time nothing was said; the only sound was that of the coffeepot rattling and hissing.

Mark's phone vibrated and he pulled it out. "It's Brenda's father again." He tapped the screen, put the call on speaker, and said, "Yes, Dr. Karvey."

"Mark, we're driving over now, should be there in about an hour. We'll check in at the Marriott in Pentagon City. Can you meet us around seven?" The voice was calm and assured.

"Sure, Dr. Karvey. I'll be there."

"Thanks. I made contact with Detective Swayze and he has my number."

"Good. See you at seven."

Mark ended the call and said, "That's exactly what I want to do. Deal with a hysterical woman."

"I'll go with you but we're not going to be abused," Todd said.

"We will definitely be abused. She's already screamed at me twice. It's all our fault because I lied to her, because we let him get away, because we didn't call the family, because we didn't take him to the doctor, because of everything."

"It's all my fault," Zola mumbled without opening her eyes.

"It's not your fault and your name has not been mentioned," Mark said. "Let's keep it that way."

Todd said, "If she starts yelling I'm walking out. I feel rotten enough without a lot of drama from Brenda and the families."

Mark said, "When we were driving away from the city pound yesterday Gordy threatened to kill me if I called her. I mean, it wasn't a serious threat, I think, but that was his frame of mind. He didn't want her to know. And he refused to talk about going to the doctor. What were we supposed to do?"

"We've hashed this out already, Mark," Todd said. He got up and poured three cups of coffee. It was almost 4:00 a.m. and they were physically and emotionally exhausted. Zola sat up on the sofa, took her cup, and tried to smile. Her eyes were red and swollen; she seemed on the verge of another breakdown at any moment. She said, "I don't think I'll go with you guys."

"No, you need to stay here and rest," Mark said.

"Good idea," Todd added. "You really shouldn't be around Brenda."

"I met her once. She thinks we're all just good friends. Gordy said she didn't have a clue about us."

"I'm sure she didn't, but she could still be jealous,"

Mark said. "She didn't like the fact that Gordy was here in the big city without her."

Another long pause as they sipped coffee. Mark broke the silence with "Oh yeah, we need to look around for a suicide note. The detective said so."

"That should be fun," Todd said. They walked across the hall, entered Gordy's apartment, and turned on the lights. Nothing had changed since they left in a panic. A note would be in the bedroom and they didn't find one.

"This place is filthy," Mark said, looking around. The sheets were in a wad with half the mattress exposed. Clothes were piled on the floor. Two empty liquor bottles were on the dresser.

"I'll clean it when you guys are gone," Zola said. "I'm sure the family will want to see his apartment." They stepped back into the den and stared at Gordy's conspiracy wall. "Any ideas?" Todd asked.

Mark said, "Let's take this mess down and save it. The family will have no use for it." Zola filled a laundry basket with dirty sheets, towels, and clothing, and took it to the laundry room in the basement while Mark and Todd carefully removed the poster boards and sheets of paper from the wall. Rackley's face and those of his confederates were placed in a neat stack to be hauled away. Next to Gordy's computer, Mark saw two thumb drives and he instinctively put them in his pocket without a word.

At six, he and Todd left the building and headed to Pentagon City. With no traffic, they arrived at the Marriott in twenty minutes and went to the café for biscuits and coffee. As they ate they tried to steel themselves for the meeting. "She'll probably say some horrible things," Todd said.

"She's already said them."

"We are not going to be trashed, Mark."

"We have to be patient, Todd, and sympathetic. Poor girl just lost a fiancé she adored."

"Well, he didn't adore her, not anymore."

"She'll never know that. Or will she?"

"Who knows? According to Zola, he and Brenda fought a lot before Christmas. Who knows what he said? He might have called off the wedding."

"He would have told us. We're his best friends, Todd, at least here in D.C. I'll bet money the wedding was still on and Brenda was dreaming of her big day. Now her childhood sweetheart is dead."

"What should we have done different?" Todd asked.

"I don't know, but I'm not sure I would've called Brenda. Gordy would've freaked out on us and the situation would have gotten worse."

"It got worse."

"It did. We'd better go."

They rode the elevator to the third floor and knocked on a door. Dr. Karvey was waiting and opened it quickly. In a soft voice he introduced himself; firm handshake, tight smile, which under the circumstances struck them as remarkable. He waved them into the room, the sitting area of a suite. He offered coffee and they declined. There was no sign of Brenda or anyone else.

Gordy had talked about his future father-in-law several times, and they knew the Karvey family was wealthy from land and a bank. Dr. Karvey was a cardiologist and highly respected in Martinsburg. He was about fifty, with lots of graying hair and a firm chin. He wore a jacket with no tie and his clothes were obviously expensive. Gordy, who habitually tossed cheap shots at everyone, had never uttered a negative word about the man.

They sat around a small table and spoke in low voices. Brenda was in the bedroom with her mother. Dr. Karvey had given her a sedative and she was resting. The police had just left after briefing the family. Gordy's parents were driving over and would be in the city within the hour.

Dr. Karvey said, "Please tell me what you know."

Mark nodded at Todd, who swallowed hard and began the recap of the past few days. A law school friend who lived in the same building became concerned about Gordy's behavior and went to the bar where Todd worked, looking for help. They found Gordy in his apartment, where he had been holed up for a couple of days. He was a mess, drinking, detached, and obviously in need of their attention. They were afraid to leave him alone, but he sneaked out. When Todd detailed the DUI twenty-four hours earlier, Dr. Karvey grimaced and shook his head, his first visible reaction. Mark picked up the narrative, and described his efforts to keep Gordy safe throughout the previous day. Gordy refused to talk about his condition and wouldn't give Mark the name of his doctor. He threatened Mark if he called Brenda or his parents. He slept a lot, stopped drinking, and seemed to be rallying. They stayed with him again last night, but he managed to sneak out. When they discovered he was gone, they panicked and tried to find him. He would not answer his phone. They raced around the city and saw the emergency lights on the bridge.

When Mark finished, he looked at Todd, who nodded. The story was almost complete and sufficient enough for the moment.

Dr. Karvey said, "Thank you. When Gordy came home on break, he and Brenda had some serious conversations about their future, as all couples do. It was definitely a rough period, but Brenda thought they had settled things. But he left without saying good-bye and returned here."

"We heard some of that," Mark said.

Todd asked, "Did Brenda know he was off his meds?"

"Well, we didn't know Gordy was bipolar until a few months ago. This was one reason for their arguments. He tried to keep it quiet, which is not unusual."

Mark and Todd shook their heads in disbelief.

Dr. Karvey said, "Look, I know Brenda said some harsh things a few hours ago, and I'm sorry for that. She is distraught and heartbroken. We're just as stunned as you are. We've known Gordy since he was a kid and he was practically a member of our family."

"It's okay," Mark said.

"We're so sorry, Dr. Karvey. We weren't sure what to do. We had no idea he was capable of something like this."

"You did your best under the circumstances," Dr. Karvey said with his calming bedside manner. As Mark and Todd relaxed for the first time since entering the suite, Dr. Karvey, in an even lower voice, hit them with "Was there another girl?"

They flinched and stared at their hands. Mark had the presence of mind to ask, "Okay, if the answer is yes, will you tell Brenda?"

"No. It would only make matters worse."

"Then why do you want to know?" Todd asked.

He thought for a moment and said, "Let's let it pass."

"Good idea."

Eager to leave before someone emerged from the bedroom, Mark and Todd wrapped things up and said goodbye. They hurried from the suite, and the hotel, and drove aimlessly past Reagan National Airport. They worried about Zola but had no desire to return to Gordy's apartment, not for a while anyway. They passed through Alexandria, drifted south, at some point turned east, crossed the river on the Woodrow Wilson Bridge, and parked at the National Harbor Marina. The Potomac stretched before them, seemingly a mile wide and flowing south as if all was well. There were no signs of a search. They had seen two Coast Guard ships and the police boats near the airport, but nothing this far below the Arlington Memorial Bridge.

Mark said, "Do you suppose they can project how far and how fast a body will travel in the river?"

"You're asking me?" Todd replied.

"I thought you knew about these things. Didn't you have a friend who drowned in high school?"

"Yep, Joey Barnes. Fifteen years old." Todd tapped his fingers on the steering wheel and thought about his old friend. "Drowning victims go under and sink to the bottom, regardless of the depth. If the water is cold it takes longer. Once on the bottom, some chemical reactions take place and these force the body to rise. Almost all of them do, usually not far from where they made a splash. There's a chance he'll get snagged on something and remain below."

They thought about this as the heater hummed away. Mark said, "He'll wash up, don't you think?"

"They'll find him. We need a funeral and a burial and a closing to this mess. I can't imagine a memorial service someday without a body."

"They'll find him. And then we'll bury him. And then

we're supposed to hustle back to law school for our last semester."

"I can't even think about that."

"Law school is the reason Gordy's dead, Todd. If he'd never gone to law school he'd be fine right now."

"Wouldn't we all?"

"I can't go back."

"Let's talk about it later. Right now we need some sleep."

EARLY IN THE afternoon, Dr. Karvey called Mark and asked if he and Todd could retrieve Gordy's car, drive it over to the hotel, and meet with Mr. and Mrs. Tanner. They couldn't think of anything worse, but at the moment the family needed them and there was no one else available. So for the second time in two days, they went to the city pound to fetch Gordy's little blue Mazda. Seconds before he jumped, he turned off the ignition and evidently stuck the extra key in his pocket. Fortunately, Mark still had his collection of keys. The city kindly waived the towing and storage fees and saved them $200.

The Karvey suite was worse than a morgue. Brenda sat on a sofa between her mother and Mrs. Tanner, two women who supposedly loathed each other and had been squabbling over the wedding plans. Now, though, that was behind them and they were suffering in unified grief.

Once more, Todd and Mark tag teamed through the painful narrative of the past few days and tried to deflect as much blame as possible. The graciousness Dr. Karvey had shown early that morning was gone, though he tried to keep things calm. Mr. Tanner asked many pointed questions about what Mark and Todd did and didn't do. Why did Mark lie about Gordy being sick with the flu? Why didn't they simply call the family for help? How did they allow Gordy to sneak out of his apartment not once but twice? What steps did they take to control his drinking? And so on. Brenda said little. She either stared at the floor and wiped her eyes or glared at them as if they themselves had tossed him off the bridge. It was a horrible, gut-wrenching meeting, and at one point everyone in the room, including Mark and Todd, was in tears. As things deteriorated, Mark finally threw up his hands, said enough was enough, and stormed out of the suite, with Todd right behind him.

They drove away in silence, sick with the knowledge that the families would always hold them responsible for Gordy's death, but also furious that they were being blamed. It was too easy now, with perfect hindsight, to carefully dissect what they did or did not do and condemn their decisions. The truth was that Gordy was sick and they did their best to help.

Zola's name had never been mentioned.

9

The waiting was excruciating. Todd killed time by working a few hours at the bar. Mark and Zola got out of the building and went to see a movie. They flinched every time their phones vibrated, but there was no news about the search. Law school friends were checking in, desperate for updates. Social media was buzzing with the news and gossip. The *Post*'s online edition was covering the story.

After work, Todd arrived at Zola's apartment with a six-pack and they ordered a pizza. As they ate, Zola told them about her parents and brother. During the afternoon, they had been taken to an immigrant detention facility in Pennsylvania. Armed ICE agents had given them an hour to pack what little clothing and personal items they could carry, then herded them, handcuffed, along with four others, into a van. Her father had called from the facility, which he described as "little more than a jail." He had no idea how long they would be kept there before the flight back to Senegal.

Mark and Todd were shocked and angry. The timing was

particularly cruel. Zola was distraught and dealing with the suicide of a boyfriend, and now this. They decided to stay together, and at midnight finally fell asleep; Zola in her bed, Mark on the sofa, Todd in a chair beside him.

EARLY IN THE morning, as the three sipped coffee and shook off the cobwebs of a hard sleep, they heard voices and movement across the hall. Mark cracked the door and they listened.

Dr. Karvey, Brenda, and the Tanners were in Gordy's apartment. They found it spotless, with every dish washed and put away, the refrigerator emptied of stale food, not a drop of alcohol anywhere. The den was tidy, its floors clean, and his work space at the dinette table was neatly arranged. His bed was made to perfection. Every stitch of clothing was clean and put away. On his dresser there was a large framed photo of Brenda, one he usually kept in a drawer. In the bathroom, his towels were folded and stacked. The floor, commode, shower, and vanity were practically shining. In his medicine cabinet there was no sign of his pills. They assumed he had gone to great lengths to spiff up the place before checking out.

Brenda broke down once. She sat on the sofa and sobbed as her father rubbed her knee. From across the hall, the three listened in a creepy silence.

The Tanners decided that a quick look around was enough for the moment. They would return later and retrieve his stuff. They locked the apartment and left with Brenda and her father. From a second-floor hall window the three watched them drive away, and felt painfully sorry for them.

IT WAS MONDAY, January 6. Classes would resume in a week, but there was no thought of law school. And while visiting an immigrant detention facility for the first time was not their idea of an exciting road trip, they needed to get out of town. Zola called in sick and Todd took a day off from the Old Red Cat. They left D.C. before noon and headed north. To avoid the Potomac River, Todd followed Connecticut Avenue into Chevy Chase and Maryland. For the first half hour, little was said. Zola, in the front passenger's seat, was subdued and stared blankly out the window. Todd sipped coffee from a tall paper cup and fiddled with the radio, finally settling on an oldies station, but at low volume.

In the backseat, Mark flipped through some paperwork, retrieved a magazine article, and began, "According to the *Post,* Immigration and Customs Enforcement maintains fifteen detention centers around the country and on any given day there are 35,000 people in custody. Last year ICE detained over 400,000 undocumented workers and deported about the same number, at a cost of over $20,000 per deportee. The entire detention system eats over $2 billion a year. It's the largest immigrant detention system in the world. In addition to the fifteen ICE facilities, the Feds contract with hundreds of county jails, juvenile detention centers, and state prisons to house their detainees, at a cost of about 150 bucks a day per person, 350 for a family. Two-thirds of all facilities are run by private companies. The more bodies they have, the more money they make. Homeland Security, which ICE answers to, has a quota, one mandated by Congress. No other law enforcement agency operates on a quota system."

"And conditions are deplorable," Zola said, as if she knew more than Mark.

"Indeed they are. Since there is no independent oversight, the detainees are often subjected to abuse, including long-term solitary confinement and inadequate medical care and bad food. They are vulnerable to assault, even rape. Last year, 150 died in custody. Detainees are often housed with violent criminals. In many cases, legal representation is nonexistent. On paper, ICE has standards for the facilities, but these are not legally enforceable. There is almost no accountability for how the federal funds are spent. The truth is, no one is looking and no one cares, except for the detainees and their families. They are forgotten people."

"That's enough," Zola said.

Todd piped in with "Yeah, enough, and why are we talking about this?"

"What do you want to talk about? Gordy? Brenda? Law school? Classes start in a week and I can't wait."

That killed the conversation for a while. Mark flipped through more articles and hummed along with the radio. Finally, he asked, "So, Zola, can we talk about your family?"

"Sure."

"Why did they leave Senegal?"

"My parents never talked much about their country. They were happy to be away from it and determined to pursue a new life here. I asked questions as I got older, but the answers were usually evasive. My father worked for some type of farmers' co-op and there was a problem with the government. He made some enemies, lost his job, and thought it best to get out. He's always been terrified of going back. Most of his family has scattered and there's nothing there for him, nothing but trouble. He's afraid he'll be persecuted if he returns."

"And your brothers?"

"Sory, the older one, married an American and now lives in California. His wife is not a Muslim and my father has little to do with him. My younger one—we call him Bo for short—was born in Senegal, so he's in trouble too. He's never married and is very devout."

Todd said, "I thought ICE had a policy of not separating families."

"It may be written down somewhere," Mark said, "but it's not always followed. I read an article last night about a family from Cameroon, parents and five kids, all living in an apartment in the Bronx. ICE kicked in the door one night, grabbed the father, and in due course shipped him back to Africa. The mother is undocumented too, and she and the kids live in fear that ICE will come snatch her too. Imagine what that's like. The kids were born here, like Zola, so they could be separated from both parents. When ICE was asked about the case, some official said something like 'The State of New York has an excellent foster care system.' Can you believe that?"

"I'd rather talk about law school," Zola said.

"Not me," Mark said. "I can't go back. Do you guys really plan to walk into class next Monday?"

"What are your options, Mark?" Zola asked. "If you drop out, you lose your job. You can't quit with one semester to go."

"I have a job only if I pass the bar exam, which, at this moment, seems impossible. Right now, I'm not mentally or emotionally stable enough to grind my way through the review courses. Are you, Todd?"

"It makes me nauseous."

"It's also seven months away," Zola said.

"Why can't we take off this semester, sort of kick the can down the road for a spell?" Todd asked.

"Because the loan sharks will eat us for lunch. If we're not in school, we have to start repayment. There might be a loophole here or there, but I doubt we could find one."

"No, we couldn't be that lucky."

"Let's talk about something else," Zola said.

"Okay, but we're running out of topics," Mark said.

Another long stretch of silence, then Mark said, "Okay, I have a confession. When we were cleaning Gordy's apartment on Saturday, I saw two thumb drives next to his computer. I took them, figured neither his parents nor Brenda would have any use for them. I had a look last night and found nothing to do with his suicide. However, he was on the trail of something."

"Rackley?"

"Yes, but there's more. Have you guys been following the scandal involving Swift Bank?"

"I saw some headlines," Zola replied.

"No, I got my own problems," Todd said.

"Swift Bank is now the ninth-largest bank in the country. A few years back, it tried like hell to get itself classified as too big to fail, but the Feds said no. Unfortunately, it didn't fail, and has done okay since then. It was up to its ears in the sub-prime mortgage scams and has a history of fraud and corruption. It's a really sleazy outfit that is involved in just about every type of low-end financing while at the same time spending a ton on marketing because it really wants to be your neighborhood bank."

"We've seen the ads," Todd said.

"Good. Well, Gordy thinks, or was thinking, that Rackley owns a chunk of Swift. How much he wasn't sure, because, as usual, Rackley operates behind a wall of shell companies, most of them domiciled offshore. These fronts have slowly and quietly purchased the stock of Swift, always keeping their acquisitions under 5 percent. More than that, as we know, and they have to register with the SEC. Gordy was on the trail of three separate and apparently unrelated shell companies that owned a total of 12 percent of Swift. Current value of about four billion, and making Rackley by far the largest shareholder, something he would like to keep quiet."

Todd said, "Ho hum. Where do we fit in?"

"Not sure we do, but it makes for fun reading, and since we can't agree on anything else to talk about, I'll just keep prattling on about Swift Bank and Hinds Rackley. Any objections? Good, now, about a month ago Swift landed on the front page with another scandal, nothing new for these crooks, but now they might have outdone themselves. So let's say you, Todd, walk into your local Swift branch and open a routine checking account. You deposit a thousand dollars, get some cute little temporary checks, all is swell and you really liked the pretty account manager, who was super friendly. Well, once you leave, she turns into a crooked little bitch and opens some more accounts for you. A savings account, or two, a money-market account, a credit card, a debit card, maybe even a brokerage account. Instead of just one Swift account, you actually have seven. She gets a bonus, a pat on the back, good girl. You know nothing about the other six accounts, but good ole Swift sticks you for a few extra bucks each month in mysterious fees to cover the accounts."

"Who squealed?" asked Zola.

"She did. Turns out that Swift account managers from coast to coast were trained in nefarious ways to push accounts on folks who didn't want them, or, if they declined, simply create the extra accounts anyway. Millions of accounts. Your girl and a few others have come forward and blown the whistle. They claim they were under enormous pressure from the top down to create the accounts. The entire bank is upside down and Congress starts hearings next week."

"I hope it's all true, for Rackley's sake anyway," Todd said.

"And litigation?" Zola asked.

"Of course. The plaintiffs' bar is in a feeding frenzy. Two class actions already, more to come. There could be a million customers affected."

"Wish I banked at Swift," Todd said. "Then I could take a shot at that asshole."

"He's got his claws into our skin deep enough."

"Let's talk about something else," Zola said.

10

The Bardtown Federal Detention Facility was in a secluded valley three miles off Interstate 99 and twenty miles south of Altoona. If there was a town nearby, it wasn't visible. The entrance was a wide asphalt drive that appeared new and ran downhill, giving them a panoramic view of the place as they arrived. Spread before them was a complex of flat-roofed, boxlike buildings, very similar to classroom trailers used at overcrowded schools. A double line of tall chain-link fencing surrounded the rows of buildings in a neat square. Thick rolls of razor wire glistened from atop the fencing and gave the entire facility a foreboding sense of being nothing more than a prison.

As Todd slowed the car, he said, "It looks like one of those old black-and-whites of Auschwitz."

"Thanks, Todd," Zola said.

It was a demoralizing sight, and Zola could not control her emotions. She was crying when Todd pulled in to the gravel lot. They sat for a few moments and stared at a two-story building at the front, obviously the place where they would check in. It, too, was flat-roofed and appeared to be made of wallboard. So far, the entire facility gave the impression of having been constructed overnight.

Zola finally said, "Let's go," and they walked to the front door. A temporary sign beside it read, "Bardtown Federal Detention Facility. Immigration and Customs Enforcement. Office of Detention and Removal Operations. Department of Homeland Security. DHS, DRO, ICE. Administration Building."

They stared at the sign and Todd mumbled, "Alphabet soup."

To which Mark replied, "Let's hope they've met the ACLU."

They walked through the doors and entered a reception area. There were no signs to guide them, so Mark stopped a thick young man in a uniform. "Excuse me, sir, but where is the visiting area?"

"What kind of visitors?"

"Well, we would like to see one of your inmates."

"They're called detainees."

"Okay, we would like to see one of your detainees."

Reluctantly, he pointed down the hall and said, "Try down there."

"Thank you so much." They drifted down the wide hallway, looking for a sign that would indicate anything to do with visitation. Because it was a federal facility, there were employees everywhere, all in uniforms that varied. Beefy young men swaggering around with guns on their belts and "ICE" in bold letters on the backs of their parkas. Clerks with white shirts and ties and gold badges over their pockets. Cops who appeared to be nothing more than county deputies.

They walked to a counter where three young ladies were camped out. One was shuffling papers while the other two were enjoying their afternoon snacks. Zola said, "Excuse me, but I'm here to see my parents."

"And who are your parents?" asked the gal with the paperwork.

"Maal. My father is Abdou, my mother is Fanta. Maal. M-A-A-L."

"Where are they from?"

"Well, they're from New Jersey, but Senegal originally. They were picked up yesterday."

"Oh, they're detainees?"

Mark bit his tongue to keep from blurting, "Of course they're detainees. Why else would we be here?" But he stared at Todd and said nothing.

"Yes, they are," Zola said politely.

"Do you have an appointment?"

"Well, no, but we've driven two hours to see them."

The officer shook her head while another put down her brownie and pecked on a keyboard. The second one, an older white lady, said, "They have not been processed yet." This, obviously, was a deal killer.

"Okay, well, then process them," Zola said.

The first one said, "We'll take care of that, okay? But I'm afraid you can't see them until they've been processed."

"You must be kidding," Zola said.

"Sorry," she said without the slightest trace of sympathy.

"How can you hold them if they haven't been processed?" Zola demanded.

Number one, a middle-aged black woman, sneered at

her as if she would enjoy putting Zola in her place. "We have our rules," she said firmly.

Mark and Todd took a step toward the counter. Todd was wearing jeans, sneakers, and an old leather jacket. At that moment, Mark was slightly better dressed in khakis, hiking shoes, and an insulated vest. Todd nodded to Mark, who leaned forward and said in a loud voice, "Look, I'm her attorney, okay? She is an American citizen and she has the right to see her family. We've driven two hours for this visit and you will not deny her. Her parents and brother were picked up yesterday and are about to be sent back to Africa. She may never see them again."

The third one stopped eating. The second one stopped pecking. The first one drew back and managed to say, "I'm afraid you'll have to see the supervisor."

"Great!" Mark yelled. "Get him out here!"

The disturbance attracted some attention and two ICE boys came over. One of them, Gibson, said, "Got a problem here?"

"Damned right we got a problem!" Mark growled at him. "My client here just drove from Washington, D.C., to see her family one last time before they are deported back to Senegal. Now we're told she can't see them because of paperwork."

The ICE boys looked at the three clerks. The first one said, "You know the rules. No visitors until they have been processed."

Gibson looked back at Mark and said, "Well, there you have it. Rules are rules."

"Can I see the supervisor?" Mark demanded.

"You can stop yelling, that's what you can do." He took

a step closer, eager for a physical confrontation. Two more agents ventured over to back up their buddies.

"Just let me talk to the supervisor," Mark said.

"I don't like your attitude," Gibson said.

"And I don't like yours. Why is attitude important here? What's wrong with allowing my client to see her family? Hell, they're being deported. She may never see them again."

"If they're being deported it's because a judge said so. You don't like it, go see the judge."

"Well, now that you've mentioned a judge, you're playing my game. I'm gonna sue you first thing in the morning in federal court. What's the first name, Gibson?" Mark took a step closer and eyed his nameplate. "M. Gibson. May I ask what the *M* stands for?"

"Morris."

"Okay, Morris Gibson. Write it down, Todd." Todd pulled out a pen and grabbed a sheet of paper off the counter. Mark looked at the next ICE agent and said, "And what's your name?"

"Why do you want to know?" he replied with a smirk.

"For the lawsuit, sir, I can't sue you if I don't know your name."

"Jerry Dunlap."

Mark whirled and zeroed in on the three clerks, all of whom looked petrified. "What's your name?" he growled at the first one.

She glanced down at the nameplate pinned above her left pocket, as if to verify things, and said, "Phyllis Brown." Todd scribbled away.

"And you?" Mark said to the second one.

"Debbie Ackenburg."

Todd asked, "Would you spell it, please?"

She did. Mark looked at the third and said, "And you?"

With great trepidation, she softly said, "Carol Mott."

Mark turned again and noticed four other ICE agents watching the dispute. "Any of you guys want some of the action? It's a lawsuit in federal court, filed first thing in the morning. You'll be forced to hire lawyers, at least one each, and I'll make it drag on for the next two years. Anybody?" The four stepped back in unison.

A man in a suit rounded the corner and asked angrily, "What the hell is going on here?"

Mark took a step toward him and said loudly, "I'm collecting names for a federal lawsuit. Are you the supervisor?"

"I am," he said proudly.

"Great, and what's your name?"

"Who the hell are you?"

"Mark Frazier, with the Washington law firm of Ness Skelton. I'm the attorney for Zola Maal, this lady right here. We've driven from D.C. so she can see her family. She's an American citizen and she has the right to see her family before they are deported. Your name please."

"George McIlwaine."

"Thank you. And you're the head guy around this place?"

"I am."

Todd was still scribbling names. Mark yanked out his cell phone, tapped it, called no one. Glaring at McIlwaine, he said to his phone, "Hello, Kelly, it's Mark. Get me Kinsey in litigation, right now. Tell him it's an emergency." Pause. "I don't care if he's in a meeting. Get him now!" A longer pause as Mark stepped closer to a third ICE agent who was standing a bit too close. Over his shoulder he barked at Todd, "Add T. Watson to the list. What does the *T* stand for?"

Watson glanced around and shifted his weight from one foot to the other.

"Come on, Mr. Watson, you don't know your first name?"

"Travis."

"Attaboy. Add Travis Watson to the lawsuit."

Todd scribbled away. Zola took a step back, a little distance between her and this wild man. Back on the phone, Mark said, "Yeah, Kinsey, look, I'm at the Bardtown Detention Facility and they are denying our client the right to see her family. I want you to prepare a quick lawsuit and file it as soon as possible. I'll text over the names of the defendants." A pause as he listened to no one. "That's right. Start with Homeland Security and ICE, then add the names of, hang on." He pointed at the three ladies, the three ICE agents, and McIlwaine. "Seven of them, individually." Mark looked at the other agents and said, "Any of you guys want a piece of this?" They backed away even farther. "Guess not. Do it quick, Kinsey." Another pause. Gibson and Watson shot fearful glances at McIlwaine. The three ladies were wide-eyed and afraid to move. Back to the phone, Mark said, "Great! File it this afternoon online. Eastern District of Pennsylvania, federal court. See if you can get Judge Baxter. He'll throw the book at them. Call me in ten minutes."

Mark tapped his phone and put it in his pocket. He glared at McIlwaine and said, "I'm suing all of you individually for monetary damages and when I get them I'll enroll the judgment, then I can garnish your paychecks and put liens on your homes." He turned around and barked at Todd, "Give me those names." Zola and Todd followed him to a row of chairs against a wall. They sat down and Mark pulled out his phone again. Holding Todd's list, he appeared to be texting the seven names.

McIlwaine finally moved. He took a deep breath and stepped toward them. With a fake smile he said, "Look, we might be able to work out something here."

TWENTY MINUTES LATER, Agent Gibson led them to a small room at the back of the administration building and told them to wait. When they were alone, Todd said, "You're crazy, you know that?"

"It worked," Mark said with a smug grin.

Zola managed to laugh and say, "I wouldn't want you to sue me."

"Who needs a law license?" Mark asked.

"Well, practicing without one can get you in trouble," Todd said.

"And you think these clowns are going to call the D.C. Bar Council and dig for information?"

Zola opened her bulky purse and pulled out a black hijab. As they watched, she draped it over her head and shoulders, tugging here and there until it was in place. "I'm supposed to wear this when in the presence of men who are not in my family," she said properly.

"What a good little Muslim," Todd said. "And you chose a long dress instead of those tight jeans we've been admiring for years."

"What jeans? It's the least I can do for my parents since I may not see them for a long time."

“I think you’re cute,” Mark said.

“I am cute, just don’t say anything, okay? My father is suspicious enough.”

“You look rather virginal,” Todd said.

“Knock it off,” she said.

The door opened. Her parents and brother Bo spilled into the room. Her mother, Fanta, grabbed her and they embraced, both in tears. She hugged her father, Abdou, and Bo, and finally looked at Todd and Mark. She introduced them, described them as friends from law school, and explained they had driven her up from D.C. Mark and Todd shook hands with Bo and Abdou, but not her mother. Her father thanked them again and again, and when the moment became awkward, Mark said, “We’ll be in the hallway.”

When he and Todd left the room, the entire family was crying.

11

Early Tuesday morning, a D.C. police boat was cruising near the inlet to the Tidal Basin on the east bank of the Potomac. An officer noticed something unusual. A closer look revealed a body, bleached white, bloated, and snagged in some undergrowth at the river's edge, a stone's throw from the Jefferson Memorial.

Mark was still asleep when Detective Swayze called. He described what they had found and said he had just talked to Mr. Tanner, who was back home in Martinsburg along with Gordy's mother and the Karveys. Neither Todd nor Mark had spoken to Brenda or her father or the Tanners since their unpleasant meeting Saturday afternoon. Apparently, at some point Monday, the families had decided they could accomplish nothing by waiting in D.C.

Mark called Todd and Zola with the news. They agreed to meet in Zola's apartment in an hour. Ten minutes later, as Mark was sitting on his sofa in the dark, sipping a cup of coffee, his phone rang. It was Gordy's father. Mark stared at it, and, out of sympathy, reluctantly took the call. He offered condolences and was running out of things to say when Mr. Tanner said, "Say, Mark, could you do us a favor?"

Instinctively, he almost said no, but couldn't at that moment. "Well, sure."

"Could you and Todd go to the morgue and identify the body. I just can't make that drive over, not for something like this."

Mark was stunned. Three days ago the families were blaming him for Gordy's death, and now they were asking him to run the worst errand imaginable? When Mark didn't respond, Mr. Tanner said, "We're just too upset right now, Mark, and, well, you and Todd are right there. Please. I know it's an awful thing to ask, but it would help us tremendously."

Somehow, Mark forced himself to say, "Sure."

THE BODY HAD been taken to the Office of the Chief Medical Examiner which also housed the morgue. Todd parked on the street beside the modern glass building and they found the entrance. Detective Swayze met them in the lobby and thanked them for coming. He looked at Zola and said, "I really don't think you need to see this."

"I'm not going to. I'll wait."

"Good. There's a waiting room over there," he said, nodding, and Zola walked to it. Todd and Mark followed him down the stairs to a wide hallway. They stopped at a metal door beside a sign that read, "Body Storage."

Swayze said, "It's cold in there but this won't take long."

"How often do you do this?" Mark asked.

"Twice a week. The room holds two hundred. We never have a shortage of bodies here in the District."

A lady in a white lab coat met them at the door and opened it. "Tanner, right?" she asked the detective.

"That's right," Swayze said. They stepped into a large, sterile cooler filled neatly with organized metal racks holding dozens of body bags, all navy blue, all zipped tightly from above the heads to below the feet. They turned a corner, passed more racks with more bodies, and abruptly stopped. A tag attached to a body bag gave the name "G. Tanner.?? Drowning."

Mark glanced around and saw another tag. "Unknown. Gunshot."

The lady took the zipper above the head and slowly pulled it down. She stopped at the chest and opened the bag. Gordy's eyes were wide open, lifeless, as if he'd been screaming in horror as he hit the water. His skin was as white as new snow. By far the most gruesome feature was his tongue, thick and balled up and protruding grossly from his mouth. There were abrasions on his cheeks. His thick blond hair appeared to still be wet.

Mark leaned on the rack to steady himself. Todd mumbled, "Shit," and bent over as if to throw up.

"Is this Gordon Tanner?" Swayze asked casually.

Mark nodded as Todd backed away.

The lady zipped him up again and picked up a small plastic bag. She said, "There were no shoes, socks, pants, or underwear. This is what's left of his shirt. There's nothing else."

Swayze said, "That's why we couldn't do a positive ID. We figured it was him, but his wallet, keys, everything was missing. I'm sorry."

Mark closed his eyes and said, "So am I." For some reason, he touched the body bag around the ankles and gave it a pat. "So am I."

They followed the lady out of Body Storage. In the hallway, Mark asked the detective, "So what happens now?"

"The family has done the paperwork. Their funeral home will come get him. He'll be transported in a couple of hours."

"Nothing else from us?"

"No. Thanks, and again I'm very sorry."

"Thank you."

They sat with Zola in the waiting room for a long time. Things were quiet and somber until Todd said, "Let's get out of here."

Outside, Mark stopped and said, "I guess I need to call Mr. Tanner."

FOR THE REST of Tuesday and throughout Wednesday, Todd and Mark stayed close to Zola. She was unable to work and lost her job as a temp with the accounting firm. It was seasonal anyway. When Todd put in a few hours at the bar, Mark stayed with her. They took long walks around the city, hanging out in bookstores, window-shopping, and thawing out in coffee bars. When Mark puttered around Ness Skelton, Todd took her to the movies. They stayed in her apartment each night, though she assured them she was fine. She wasn't. None of them were. They were sleepwalking through a nightmare and needed each other.

As other law students drifted back to town, they wanted to talk about Gordy, conversations the three preferred to avoid. On Thursday night, one carload drove to Martinsburg for visitation at the funeral home, but Mark, Todd, and Zola decided to skip it. A party materialized later that night at a popular sports bar, and they spent an hour with friends. They left when the beer was flowing and their fellow students began offering toasts to Gordy.

Mark was relieved when Brenda did not call. He did not want to speak at the funeral, and knew it was unlikely anyway. Neither he nor Todd was asked to be a pallbearer, another relief. The service would be dreadful enough. They planned to stay away from the families and watch it from a distance, if that was possible. There was even talk of not attending, but that would have been wrong.

On Friday, Mark and Todd dressed in their nicest suits, white shirts, subdued ties, leather shoes, their best "interview uniforms," and picked up Zola, who wore a long black dress and looked like a model. They drove ninety minutes to Martinsburg and scoped out the church, a pretty redbrick building with lots of stained glass. A crowd was already milling around the front steps. A hearse was parked at the curb. At 1:30, they entered the vestibule and took programs from an usher. On the cover was a handsome photo of their friend. Mark asked the usher about a balcony and he pointed at some stairs. It was still empty when they sat down in the rear pew, tucked away in a remote corner of the sanctuary, as far away as possible from the pulpit.

Zola sat between them and wiped her cheeks with a tissue. "This is all my fault," she said and began crying. They didn't scold her and they didn't argue. Let the grieving run its course. There would be plenty of time to hash it out later. Mark and Todd felt like crying too but managed to keep their composure.

The church was beautiful, with a wood-paneled choir

loft slightly elevated behind the pulpit and a massive pipe organ to one side. Behind the loft was a painting of Christ on the cross. Stained-glass windows lined the walls and provided plenty of light. Four sections of pews formed a semicircle around a center aisle. As they waited, a crew of solemn men set up dozens of flower arrangements on both sides of the pulpit.

The pews were filling quickly and soon there were others in the balcony. The Tanners and Karveys had lived in Martinsburg for generations and an overflow crowd was expected. Mark was reminded of his little fictional scenario when the town learned that one of its favorite sons had run off with an African Muslim, jilting his childhood sweetheart. Jilting everyone who knew Gordy. It was almost humorous a few days earlier, but not so much at the moment. Fortunately, the town would never know. If things had gone as planned, in about four months Mark and Todd would have been standing down there as groomsmen watching Brenda walk down the aisle. Now they were hiding in the balcony, paying their respects while trying to avoid the family.

An organist took her position and began playing a quiet dirge that seemed perfect for the occasion. After a few minutes, the choir filed in from a side door and filled the loft. It was obvious that Gordy's farewell would get the full treatment. The mourners kept coming and were soon standing along the walls. The balcony was packed and the three squeezed together to make room for an elderly couple. At 2:00 p.m., the pastor appeared and settled in behind the pulpit. According to the program, he was the Reverend Gary Chester. He raised his arms and everyone stood. The casket was rolled down the center aisle with four pallbearers on each side. Behind it, Brenda walked alone, erect and steadfast. Mr. and Mrs. Tanner were behind her, then the rest of the family. Gordy had an older brother and a teenage sister, and she was struggling. Her brother had an arm around her shoulders, helping her. When the casket, mercifully unopened, was in place beneath the pulpit, and when the family took their seats, the Reverend Chester motioned for the crowd to sit.

Mark glanced at his watch: 2:12. How long would this last?

After a lengthy prayer by the reverend, the choir sang four stanzas of a hymn. The organist followed with a piece that could not have been more depressing. When she finished, several women were sobbing. Brenda's brother stood, walked to a lectern near the piano, and read Psalm 23. Chester returned to the pulpit and began his homily. Evidently, he had been there for a long time because he knew Gordy well. He told stories of watching the kid play football and baseball. Without using the word "suicide," he dwelled on the mysteries of death and its often confusing forms. God is always in control. He has a plan for everything. And while we are left to question death, and especially tragedies, God knows what he is doing. We may someday understand why Gordy did what he did, or we may never know, but God is the supreme architect of all life and death and our faith in him is never ending.

Chester was reassuring, a real pro. At times his voice grew weak, and he was obviously suffering. Given the impossibility of his task, he gamely offered words of comfort.

Jimmy Hasbro was Gordy's favorite childhood friend, and Mark and Todd had partied with him several times during law school. His was the first of two eulogies. As a kid, Gordy was fascinated by snakes and liked to collect them. His mother, with good reason, banned them from the house. It was a cute little hobby that came to an abrupt end when a copperhead sank its fangs into his right knee. The doctors even considered amputation. Jimmy did a fine job with the story and brought some humor to the occasion. As teenagers, their favorite cop had been an old guy named Durdin, now dead. Late one night Durdin's squad car went missing. It was found the next morning in a pond just outside town. How it got there was a great mystery that had never been solved. Until now. With a flair for drama and humor, Jimmy told the story of Gordy "borrowing" the car and driving it into the pond as Jimmy watched. The church exploded with laughter that went on for several minutes. What a perfect time to reveal what really happened after all these years.

When the laughter passed, Jimmy grew somber again. His voice cracked when he described Gordy's loyalty. He called him the epitome of a "foxhole buddy," the guy you want beside you in a fight. The guy who always had your back. Sadly, though, some of Gordy's friends had not been so loyal. When he needed them the most, when he was suffering and in need of help, some of his friends had not risen to the task.

Mark flinched and Zola grabbed his hand. Todd glanced over. All three felt sucker punched.

So this was the narrative in Martinsburg! Gordy wasn't responsible for his own actions. Brenda played no part in his crack-up. No, sir. Some friends in D.C., his law school pals, had neglected him.

His pals sat in stunned anger and disbelief.

Jimmy finally choked up and couldn't finish. Wiping

his eyes, he stepped away from the pulpit and returned to his seat in the third row. The choir sang again. A kid from the church played the flute. A friend from Washington and Lee delivered the second eulogy, one that did not include finger-pointing. After fifty-five minutes, the Reverend Chester gave the closing prayer and the processional began. With the organ roaring, the congregation stood as the pallbearers rolled the casket down the aisle. Brenda, sobbing now, dutifully followed. There was a lot of loud crying, even up in the balcony.

Mark decided that he hated funerals. What purpose did they serve? There were far better ways to console the loved ones than gathering in a packed church to talk about the deceased and have a good cry.

Todd whispered, "Let's just sit here for a moment, okay?"

Mark had the same thought. Brenda and the families were outside, wailing and hugging as they loaded Gordy into the hearse, which they would then follow to the cemetery down the road, where they would gather again for the burial, another gut-wrenching service the three had no plans to watch. And Jimmy Hasbro would be in the middle of it. If Mark made eye contact with him, he might throw a punch and ruin the day.

As the balcony emptied, they watched the same crew hurriedly gather the flowers and whisk them away, no doubt headed for the cemetery. When the flowers were gone, and the sanctuary was empty, they sat, waiting.

In a low voice, Mark said, "I can't believe this. Everybody's blaming us."

"That son of a bitch," Todd said.

"Please," Zola said. "Not in church."

They watched a custodian remove some folding chairs near the piano. He looked up, saw them sitting alone in the balcony, and seemed curious about their presence. Then he returned to his job and left the sanctuary.

Finally, Mark said, "Let's get outta here."

12

It was Friday afternoon, the end of another miserable week. They were in no hurry to return to the city, so Todd took the back roads and they crossed into Virginia. Near the town of Berryville, the boys decided they needed a drink, and Todd stopped at a convenience store. Zola, who never touched the stuff, volunteered to drive, something she often did when she was out with Gordy and the law school gang. Mark bought a six-pack and a soft drink for her.

"Where are we going?" she asked.

Todd, in the front passenger seat, pointed to a sign. "It says that's the way to Front Royal. Ever been to Front Royal?"

"No."

"Well, let's take a look." They popped tops and took off. A few miles down the road, Mark stuck his beer between his knees and checked his phone. There was an e-mail from Ness Skelton. He read it and yelled, "What! You gotta be kidding!"

"What is it?" Todd asked, startled.

"They just fired me! I've been fired!"

"Come on," Zola said.

"No, this is from Everett Boling, sorry, M. Everett Boling, a real ass who's the managing partner at Ness Skelton. Listen to this. He says, 'Dear Mr. Frazier. Today our firm announced its merger with the London-based law firm of O'Mara and Smith. This is an exciting opportunity for Ness Skelton to expand and better serve our clients. However, the merger requires a shifting of our personnel. I regret to inform you that the offer of an associate position is being rescinded. We wish you the best in your endeavors. Sincerely, M. Everett Boling.'"

"I like their timing," Todd said.

"So they're firing me before I even start the job. Can you believe this?"

"I'm so sorry, Mark," Zola said.

"Yeah, me too," Todd said. "Sorry, pal."

"And they don't even have the guts to do it in person," Mark said. "Terminated by a lousy e-mail."

"Are you really surprised, Mark?" Todd asked.

"Of course I'm surprised. Why shouldn't I be?"

"Because they're a bunch of low-end lobbyists who gave you a half-baked offer that didn't include a salary, and one contingent upon passing the bar exam. You've said yourself, and many times I might add, that you trusted no one there and never felt good about the place. They're a bunch of creeps, your term not mine."

Mark took a deep breath, put down his phone, drained his beer, crumpled the can, and tossed it on the floorboard. He ripped off another can, popped the top, and took a swig. Todd drained his and said, "Give me another." When he popped his top, he held his can up and said, "Cheers. Welcome to the world of the unemployed."

"Cheers," Mark said as the cans touched.

After another mile or so, he said, "I really didn't want to work there anyway."

"Attaboy," said Todd. Zola kept glancing at him in the mirror.

"You would've been miserable," Todd said. "They're all a bunch of turds, real pricks who hate their work. Said so yourself."

"I know, I know. But I would like to call Randall, my supervisor, just to hear him stutter and stammer."

"I guarantee you he won't take your call. Let's bet on it."

"That's a bad bet."

"Don't do it," Zola said. "Don't waste the energy."

"For some reason I'm low on energy these days," Mark said. "My worthless little brother is about to go to prison, which is a bum deal for him, but I really hate it for my mother. Then Gordy loses it. Now we're taking flak for his suicide. Zola's family gets rounded up and tossed in a prison to wait on deportation. Now this. Now we're supposed to somehow push it all aside and hustle back to law school for our last semester, which will be followed by two months in hell studying for the bar exam, so we can do something to make a little money and start repayment, which, actually, is far more impossible than it seems, and it seems awfully damned impossible at the moment. Yes, Zola dear, I'm tired. Aren't you?"

"I'm beyond exhausted," she said.

"That makes three of us," Todd added.

They slowed and passed through the small town of

Boyce. When it was behind them, Mark asked, "Are you guys really going to class on Monday? I'm not."

"That's either the second or the third time you've said that," Zola said. "If you don't go to class, then what are your plans?"

"I have no plans. My status will be day to day."

"Okay, but what are you going to do when the law school starts calling?" Todd asked.

"I won't take their calls."

"Okay, so they'll put you on inactive status and notify your loan sharks and they'll be out for blood."

"What if they can't find me? What if I change phone numbers and move to another apartment? It would be easy to get lost in a city of two million people."

"I'm listening," Todd said. "So, you start hiding. What about work and income and those little challenges?"

"I've been thinking about that," Mark said and took a long swig. "Maybe I'll get a job tending bar, for cash, of course. Maybe wait tables. Or maybe I'll become a DUI specialist like that sleazeball we met last Friday at the city jail. What was his name?"

"Darrell Cromley," Zola said.

"I'll bet Darrell nets a hundred grand a year hustling DUIs. All cash."

"But you don't have a license," Zola said.

"Did we ask Darrell to show us his license? Of course not. He said he was a lawyer. His business card said he was a lawyer, so we just assumed he had a license. He could've been a used-car salesman moonlighting at the jail."

"What about going to court?" Zola asked.

"You ever been to city court? I have, and it's a zoo. There are hundreds of Darrell Cromleys running around, hustling small-time criminals for fees, ducking in and out of courtrooms where the judges are bored and half-asleep. And the judges and clerks and everybody else in the courtrooms just assume, as we did, that the guys in the cheap suits scrambling around are really lawyers. Hell, there are a hundred thousand lawyers in this city and no one ever stops and asks, 'Hey, are you really a lawyer? Show me your license.'"

"I think that beer's gone straight to your brain," Todd said.

Mark smiled at Zola in the mirror.

13

The first day of classes for the spring semester meant money. The Department of Education wired Foggy Bottom the sum of $22,500 for each student's tuition, along with another $10,000 for living expenses. The school immediately wired the bulk of the tuition to its owners at Baytrium Group, then handed out individual expense checks to the students. The Office of Financial Aid was a busy place throughout the day as cash-starved students waited in long lines.

Mark and Todd skipped classes and arrived just before five, when the office closed. With $20,000 in their pockets, they retired to a dive they had discovered over the weekend. The Rooster Bar was tucked away on Florida Avenue in the U Street section of the District, far away from the Foggy Bottom clientele. It covered the ground floor of a four-story building that, though painted bright red, attracted little attention. Todd's boss, a bookie everyone called Maynard, owned both the bar and the building, along with the Old Red Cat and two other joints in the city. Maynard had succumbed to Todd's badgering and agreed to transfer his services. He had also agreed to hire Mark, who claimed to have vast experience mixing drinks. They would tend bar at night and on weekends, and, with new day jobs, their financial future looked much brighter. Of course, their massive debts were still on the books, though they had no intention of addressing them.

The Rooster Bar had the look and feel of an old neighborhood watering hole. Most of its regulars were government workers who lived in the area or stopped by each afternoon for a few stiff ones before heading home after the traffic thinned out. For some, the thinning out took several hours. The bar's wide, half-moon counter was polished mahogany and brass, and by five each afternoon it was packed two and three deep with important mid-level bureaucrats slugging happy hour booze and watching Fox News. Its kitchen cranked out decent bar food at decent prices.

In a corner booth, over chicken wings and draft beer, Mark and Todd spent hours plotting their next moves.

They skipped classes on Tuesday and searched the Internet for a respectable forger who could sell them new identities. They found one in Bethesda, in a garage shop where the "security consultant" printed two sets of perfect driver's licenses for each. D.C. and Delaware for Mark Upshaw and Mark Finley, formerly Mark Frazier; and D.C. and Maryland for Todd Lane and Todd McCain, formerly Todd Lucero. The cost was $200 cash for each set, and the forger offered perfect passports for another $500 each. They declined, for the moment anyway. Their current passports were valid and they had no plans to leave the country.

With new names, they purchased new cell phones and numbers. They kept their old ones to monitor who might be looking for them. They left the phone store and drove to a quick-print shop where they ordered stationery and business cards for their new venture, Upshaw, Parker & Lane, Attorneys-at-Law. Mark Upshaw and Todd Lane. New names, new phone numbers, a new future. The address was 1504 Florida Avenue, same as The Rooster Bar.

They skipped school on Wednesday, and while the Coop's other renters were in class and no one was watching they loaded up their clothes, a few books, even fewer pots and pans and dishes, and fled the building without a word to anyone. Their January rents were already past due and they expected to be sued by their slumlord, who would have an extremely difficult time finding them. They moved into a grungy three-room apartment on the top floor above The Rooster Bar, a real dump that apparently had been used for storage since the days of FDR. They had not come to terms with Maynard on the lease payments, and had floated the idea of swapping labor for rent, with, of course, everything off the books. Maynard liked it that way.

The idea of living there was not in any way pleasant, but then neither was the option of paying more or being stalked by the loan sharks. If living for a few months in a rathole kept the loan collectors at bay, then Mark and Todd could grind it out. They bought two beds, a sofa, some chairs, a cheap dinette set, and some other odds and ends from a salvage store next to a homeless shelter.

They decided to stop shaving and grow beards. As proper law students, they rarely shaved anyway. The scruffy look was expected. Now the whiskers might provide additional cover.

Wednesday afternoon they ventured for the first time into the Judiciary Square neighborhood, home to the various courthouses that handled the District's legal matters. The hub was the District Courthouse, a massive, 1970s-style concrete edifice where those accused of all manner of criminal activity were dealt with. Its jungle of courtrooms sprawled over six levels. Its hallways were crowded with lawyers ducking in and out of hearings and defendants free on bail loitering nervously with their loved ones. Court was open to the public; admission was free and easy, after the obligatory security with metal detectors and body scans. They watched jury trials in progress. They watched first appearances where inmates in jumpsuits were hauled before judges for quick paperwork, then sent back to jail. They watched motion hearings in which prosecutors and public defenders argued back and forth. They studied the dockets and collected as much paperwork as possible. They roamed the hallways, watching carefully as lawyers huddled with frightened families. Not once did they hear anyone ask a lawyer if he or she actually had a license to practice. Not once did they see anyone they recognized.

That night, they worked until ten serving drinks and food at The Rooster Bar, then retired to their grungy apartment upstairs, where they spent hours online navigating the maze of the D.C. court system. Criminal law was their future, primarily because the fees could be paid in cash and the clients would have no interest in stopping by their office for consultation. Such meetings would take place either at jail or in court, just like Darrell Cromley's.

They skipped classes again on Thursday and opened new checking accounts. There were six Swift Bank branches in the D.C. metropolitan area. Mark went to one near Union Station and deposited $500 in the name of Mark Upshaw. Todd Lane did the same at a branch on Rhode Island Avenue. Together, they visited another Swift Bank branch on Pennsylvania Avenue and opened a law firm checking account with a bogus taxpayer ID number. Thursday afternoon, they were back in court, absorbing the circus.

They skipped classes on Friday and stopped thinking about Foggy Bottom. If possible, they would never see the place again, and that in itself was exhilarating.

Gordy's DUI citation required him to appear in courtroom 117 in the District Courthouse on Friday afternoon at 1:00. At 12:45, Mark and Todd arrived outside the courtroom and tried to appear as nervous as possible. A crowd was gathering. Mark held the citation and looked as though he needed help. Both wore jeans and hiking boots and were sufficiently scruffy. Mark also wore a John Deere cap. A guy with a briefcase arrived and spotted them. He walked over and said to Mark, "You here for a DUI?"

"Yes, sir," Mark replied. "Are you a lawyer?"

"Yep. You got one?"

"No, sir."

"Can I see your citation?"

Mark handed it over and the lawyer frowned as he read it. He then pulled out a business card and gave it to Mark. Preston Kline, Attorney-at-Law. "You need a lawyer for this," Kline said. "My fee is a thousand bucks, cash."

"Really, that much?" Mark asked, shocked. Todd stepped beside him and said, "I'm his friend."

Kline said, "It's a bargain, son. I can save you a lot of money. If you're found guilty, you'll lose your license for a year but before that you'll spend some time in the slammer. I can probably get that suspended, though."

Kline wasn't nearly as smooth as Darrell Cromley, but at the moment that didn't matter. Mark said, "I got four hundred cash. I can get the rest later."

Kline said, "Okay, but it's due before your court date."

"What court date?"

"Okay, we'll walk in and see the judge, name's Cantu, a real hard-ass. I'll do the talking and you don't speak unless I say so. Cantu will go through the motions, all routine stuff, and you'll plead not guilty. He'll set the case for a hearing in a month or so and that'll give me time to do my work. I'm assuming you actually blew 0.11?"

"Yes, sir."

"You got the cash?"

Mark reached into a pocket and removed some money. He handed over four $100 bills and Kline snatched them. "Let's go inside and do the paperwork."

Todd asked, "Can I go too?"

"Sure. The zoo is open to the public."

Inside, lawyers milled about beyond the bar as a dozen or so spectators watched them. Kline directed Mark to a spot in the front row and removed some papers from his old briefcase. "This is a contract for legal services between you and me," he said, pointing. He scribbled in the sum of $1,000. "It's also a promissory note to pay the balance. Look it over, fill in your name and address, sign at the bottom."

Mark took his pen and wrote Gordon Tanner's name and his old address. He and Todd were banking heavily on the chance that no one would recognize Gordy's name from the news covering the suicide. And, they seriously doubted that anyone in the vast court system had removed Gordy's name from the DUI docket. If so, and if Mark was questioned, they planned to simply walk away. Or run.

Mark read the contract and tried to memorize as much as possible. He handed it back and asked, "You do a lot of these?"

"All the time," Kline said smugly, as if he were a high-powered litigator.

Todd said, "Say, my brother got in a fight at a Caps game and is charged with assault. Do you handle those?"

"Sure. Simple or aggravated?"

"Simple, I think. How much do you charge?"

"A thousand bucks if there's a plea. If he goes to trial then it's far more expensive."

"Can you keep him out of jail?"

"Sure, no problem. If he'll plead to a disturbance, he'll walk. Later, I can get it expunged, for another thousand. That is, if there's nothing else on his record."

"Thanks, I'll tell him."

At 1:00, Judge Cantu assumed the bench and everyone stood. The assembly line began as one DUI defendant after another walked through the gate when his or her name was called by a clerk. Only about half had lawyers. Each was asked to plead either guilty or not guilty. Those admitting guilt were handed papers by a prosecutor and asked to sit in a corner and fill in the blanks. Those pleading not guilty were assigned return dates in February.

Mark and Todd watched every move and heard every word. They'd be in the business soon enough.

When Gordon Tanner was called, Kline said, "Take off your cap." He led Mark to the bench and they looked up at the judge. "Hello, Mr. Kline," Judge Cantu said. They had watched him work for twenty minutes and the guy was Santa Claus, with a smile and kind word for everyone who appeared before him. Though traffic court was the lowest rung on the ladder, he seemed to enjoy it.

"First offense?" Judge Cantu asked.

"Yes, sir," Kline responded.

"I'm sorry," he said to Mark with a pleasant look. Mark had a knot in his stomach that felt like a bowling ball, and he half expected someone, perhaps one of the assistant prosecutors, to blurt out, "Hey, I recognize that name. Thought Tanner jumped off the bridge." But there were no surprises.

Judge Cantu said, "May I see your driver's license, Mr. Tanner?"

Mark frowned and said, "Well, Judge, I lost my wallet. Credit cards, everything."

"Well, you won't be needing your license. I'm assuming you're pleading not guilty."

Kline quickly said, "That's correct, Your Honor."

The judge scribbled here and there and said, "Okay, your court date is February 14. Should make for a nice Valentine's Day." He smiled as though he'd said something humorous.

Kline took some papers from a clerk and said, "Thanks, Judge. See you then."

They backed away from the bench, and as they started to leave the courtroom Mark whispered to his lawyer, "Say, is it okay if we hang around and watch things?"

"If you're that bored, sure."

They sat in the back row as Kline disappeared. Todd whispered, "So that's how you handle a DUI. Nothing to it." Other lawyers came and went as more defendants arrived. Ten minutes later Kline was back with another client, undoubtedly one he'd just hustled in the hallway.

They absorbed the show for the next hour and left. According to Kline's business card, his office was on E Street, not far from the District Courthouse. They walked three blocks and found the address. It was a four-story building that was evidently brimming with lawyers. A directory by the front door listed the names of a dozen small firms and several solo practitioners. Evidently, Kline practiced alone. As Mark waited outside, Todd stepped into a cramped reception area where a frazzled lady labored behind a large desk. She greeted him without a smile. "May I help you?"

"Uh, sure, I'm looking for a lawyer named Preston Kline," Todd said, glancing around. At the edge of her desk was a row of dividers with the names of a bunch of lawyers. Phone messages and letters were stacked neatly by each name.

"Are you a client?" she asked.

"Maybe. Someone referred me to him, said he was a good criminal lawyer."

"Well, he's in court. I can take your name and phone number and he'll call you back."

"And his office is here?"

"Yes, second floor. Why?"

"Well, could I see his partner or his paralegal? I need to talk to someone."

"He works alone. I'm his secretary."

Todd hesitated, looked around, and said, "Okay, I have his number and I'll give him a call. Thanks." He left before she could respond.

As they walked away, Todd said, "Just as we figured. The

guy works out of his pocket. Got a cubbyhole on the second floor with no staff. The girl at the front desk answers the phone for a whole pack of them. A real low-end operation."

"I love it," Mark said. "Now all we need is a girl."

14

Zola attended one class on Monday but found it so depressing she blew off the others. The class, Rights of the Elderly, was one of those useless electives so popular with third-year students coasting to the finish line. She and Gordy had signed up for it and planned to take turns suffering through the lectures, then compare notes at the end and get rewarded with either As or Bs. It was a small class, about twenty students, and when the seat to her right remained empty she couldn't help but think of Gordy. He should have been sitting there.

When they had started dating the previous September, they had been cautious. Gordy was a popular student with an outsized personality and commanded a lot of attention. Zola was not the first girl he'd chased, but certainly the first black one he'd fallen for. Their friends knew he had a serious sweetheart back home, one who was jealous and came to D.C. often to check on him. Zola and Gordy had been careful, but with time they had been noticed. Word had spread.

The professor had started his lecture with some sad comments about Mr. Tanner's tragedy, and Zola got a few looks. She heard little else and couldn't wait to leave the building, but not before picking up her check for $10,000. She deposited it in her bank, bundled up, and drifted through the city. When the sky turned gray, she ducked into the National Portrait Gallery and killed some time.

During law school, she had managed to find part-time jobs for a few hours here and there. She lived more frugally than the rest of her impoverished friends, and since she didn't drink, partied little, and used public transportation, she had saved money. The $20,000 the government lent her each year to live on had been more than enough, and with one semester left Zola had $16,000 in a savings account no one else knew about. Chump change in D.C., but serious money in Senegal. If her parents and brother were finally deported, the money could become crucial to their survival. Bribery was common, and though she shuddered at the thought of traveling to Senegal, and of being either detained or denied reentry, she knew that she might one day be forced to rush to the aid of her family with as much cash as possible. So she saved and tried not to think about her loans.

She had not heard from her parents. Telephone use was limited at the detention center. Her father had been confident that he would be allowed to notify her before they were finally removed and flown back to Senegal, but with deportation the rules seemed to change daily. She convinced herself they were still in the country, and that provided some comfort. Why, she wasn't sure. What was worse—living like prisoners in a federal camp or being turned loose on the streets of Dakar? Neither scenario held the slightest hope. They would never be allowed to return to their neighborhood in Newark. The menial jobs they had scrambled to get for the past twenty-six years would be taken by other undocumented workers. The cycle would continue because the work had to be done and real Americans preferred not to do it.

When she wasn't longing for Gordy and blaming herself, she was worrying about her family and their frightening predicament. And if she somehow managed to put those two tragedies aside, she was confronted with the uncertainties of her own future. As the cold, bleak days of January crept by, Zola fell into a deep and understandable funk.

After ten days of virtually living with Todd and Mark, she needed some distance. They were skipping classes and were adamant that they would not return to school. They texted her occasionally to check on things, but seemed occupied with more important matters.

Late Tuesday morning, she heard noises from across the hall and realized the Tanners were removing boxes of Gordy's belongings. She thought about saying hello and offering condolences, but let it pass. Mr. Tanner and Gordy's brother spent an hour going back and forth to a rental van parked on the street. Grim work, and she listened to their efforts through a cracked door. When they were gone, she took an extra key and walked through Gordy's apartment. The old furniture that came with the place was still there, and she sat on the sofa, in the dark, and had a good cry.

On two occasions and at very inopportune times, she had fallen asleep on that sofa, and allowed him to venture into the night. Her guilt was overwhelming.

On Wednesday, she dressed for class and was about to

leave when her father called. They were still at the detention facility without a word about their final removal. Nothing had changed since her visit. He tried to sound upbeat, a real challenge given his circumstances. Zola had been trying to locate relatives in Senegal to alert them and ask for help, but so far had not been successful. After twenty-six years of virtually no contact, a pleasant homecoming seemed unlikely. And, since her parents had no idea when they might be returned, making arrangements seemed impossible. According to her father, most of the family had fled the country years earlier. Those still there had their own problems and would not be sympathetic.

They talked for twenty minutes, and when the call ended she broke down again. Going to class seemed like such an insignificant thing to do. She was there because of a misguided dream of becoming a lawyer and fighting to protect her family and other immigrants. Now that was a hopeless cause, a broken dream.

She had collected a small library of immigration manuals and procedures, and she spent hours online reading articles and blogs and government publications. She was in contact with several rights groups and legal aid lawyers. One issue continued to frighten her. ICE, in its random eagerness to seize and deport, had made mistakes. She kept a file of cases where legitimate American citizens had been caught up in sweeps and sent back. She knew of a dozen stories in which citizens whose parents were undocumented had been mislabeled and removed. And in almost every case, the illegal seizure had occurred after the family had been detained.

Alone and vulnerable, and with her family in custody, she once again feared the knock on the door.

On Thursday, she dressed in her best for an interview at the Department of Justice. A number of starting positions were available but they were in high demand. She felt lucky just to land an interview. The salary, $48,000, was not what she had been thinking about three years earlier, but those fantasies were long gone.

The federal government had created a loan forgiveness program for young lawyers who pursued careers in public service. In the program, students who chose to work for any branch of state, local, or federal government, or for certain qualified nonprofits, could repay only 10 percent of their annual salaries, for ten years, and walk away from the rest of the debt. For many students, especially those at Foggy Bottom, it was tempting, especially in light of the soft job market in the private sector. Most preferred to work in some law-related agency, but others were signing up to teach school or join the Peace Corps.

The interview was in the basement of an office building on Wisconsin Avenue, far from the DOJ headquarters near the White House. When Zola signed in, the small waiting room was packed with third-year students, some of whom she knew from Foggy Bottom. She took a number, stood until a chair became available, and had pretty much given up when her name was called. She chatted with a harried flunky from DOJ for fifteen minutes and couldn't wait to get away.

Given the instability of her life, ten years was a long time to commit to anything.

15

Friday dinner was at The Rooster Bar, a place she had never heard of. According to Todd, he and Mark wanted to treat her to a fine meal. One look at the place, though, and she knew something was up. They were waiting in a corner booth, both dressed in new suits, both unshaven and working on beards, and both wearing odd new eyeglasses. Mark's were round tortoiseshell. Todd preferred a narrow frameless pair in the European style.

She sat across from them and said, "Okay, what's going on?"

Todd asked, "Did you go to class this week?"

"I tried. At least I made the effort. Didn't see you boys around."

Mark said, "We've dropped out, and we highly recommend it."

Todd said, "It's exhilarating, Zola. No more law school. No more worries about the bar exam."

"I'm listening," she said. "Where'd you get those suits?"

A waiter took their drink orders. Beers for the boys, a soda for her.

"It's our new look, Zola," Mark said. "We're lawyers now and we have to look the part, though in our line we can't look too sharp. DUI lawyers, as you know, rarely make the cover of *GQ*."

"I see. And who would be desperate enough to hire you?"

"We've hung out our own shingle," Todd said. "Hired ourselves. The Legal Clinic of Upshaw, Parker & Lane." He handed her a new business card with the firm's name, address, and phone number.

She looked at it, studied it, and said, "You are kidding, right?"

"Dead serious," Mark said. "And we're hiring."

She took a deep breath, slowly showed them both palms, and said, "Okay. I'm not asking any more questions. Tell me what's going on, or I'm leaving."

Todd said, "You're not going anywhere. We've moved out of our apartments, dropped out of school, changed our names, and found a way to make a few bucks. We're going to pass ourselves off as lawyers, hustle the criminal courts for fees, in cash of course, and hope like hell we don't get caught."

"We won't get caught," Mark said. "There are too many guys just like us doing the same thing."

"But they're all licensed," she said.

"How do you know? No one ever checks. And the clients have no clue. They're scared to death and overwhelmed anyway, and never think about asking. Just like we didn't ask Darrell Cromley at the jail."

"It's illegal," she said. "I haven't learned much at Foggy

Bottom but I do know that practicing law without a license is against the law."

"Only if we get caught," Mark said.

Todd added, "Sure, there's a risk, but it's not that significant. If something goes wrong, we'll just disappear again."

Mark said, "And we think we can generate some cash, tax-free, of course."

"You're crazy."

"No, we're actually pretty smart. We're hiding in plain sight, Zola. Hiding from our landlord. Hiding from the student loan services. Hiding from everyone who might want to find us. And, we'll be making decent money."

"And your debts?"

Mark sipped his beer, wiped his mouth, and leaned in closer. "Here's what will happen. The law school will one day realize that we've checked out, but it will do nothing. Most reputable law schools notify DOE and then haggle over how much of the tuition will be refunded for the semester. You can bet Foggy Bottom wants to refund nothing, so it will sit on the fact that we're gone and keep all the money. We'll check in by e-mail with our servicers and give them the impression that we're in class. Graduation is in May, and, as you know, we're supposed to agree to a repayment plan that starts six months later. When we don't pay, they'll throw us in default."

Todd added, "Did you know that last year a million students went into default?"

She shrugged. Maybe she did; maybe she didn't.

Mark continued, "So we have some time, nine or ten months before we're in default. By then, we'll be kicking ass with our little legal clinic and hoarding cash."

She said, "But default means default, a guaranteed lawsuit that you can't defend."

Todd said, "Only if they find us. My loan servicer works in a sweatshop in Philadelphia. Mark's is in New Jersey. Where is yours, I can't remember?"

"Chevy Chase."

"Okay, a bit closer, but you'll still be safe. The point is that they can't find us because we have different names, different addresses. They'll turn us over to some two-bit law firm, one no doubt owned by Hinds Rackley, and they'll file suit. Big deal. They're suing students like crazy and the lawsuits are worthless."

"But your credit is ruined."

"What credit? It's ruined anyway because we can't repay the loans. Even if we found honest work, there's no way in hell we can repay what we owe."

The waiter appeared and Mark ordered a platter of nachos. When he left, she said, "So much for a fine dinner."

"Compliments of us. It's on the firm," Todd said with a smile.

She was still holding the business card. She looked at it and asked, "Where did these names come from?"

Mark replied, "The phone book. Common, everyday names. I'm Mark Upshaw and have documents to prove it. He's Todd Lane, just another ham-and-egg lawyer hustling the streets."

"And who's Parker?"

"That's you," Todd said. "Zola Parker. We're thinking our little clinic needs some diversity so we're adding you as the middle partner. All equal, you understand. Three equal partners."

"Three equal crooks," she said. "I'm sorry, but this is crazy."

"It is. And what's even crazier is the idea of wrapping things up at Foggy Bottom, graduating in May without a job, then grinding away for the bar exam. Face it, Zola, you're not emotionally prepared for that. Neither are we, so we've already made our decision."

"But we're almost finished with law school," she said.

Mark said, "So what? So you finish with a law degree that's worthless. Just another piece of paper courtesy of Hinds Rackley and his diploma mill. We've been had, Zola, sucked into a scam of epic proportions. Gordy was right. You can't just drift along with the scam and hope for a miracle. At least we're fighting back."

"You're not fighting anything. You're just screwing the taxpayers."

Todd said, "The taxpayers are getting screwed by Congress and the Department of Education. And, of course, Rackley, who's already made his money off our backs."

"But we chose to borrow the money. No one made us."

"True, but the money was loaned to us under false pretenses," Mark said. "When you started law school, did you really believe that you would one day be sitting here with a mountain of debt and no job? Hell no. The picture they painted back then was much rosier. Take the money, get the degree, pass the bar, and go to work in a great profession that would make it easy to repay everything."

The waiter brought another round of drinks. There was a gap in the conversation as they sipped and stared at the table.

Softly, she said, "It seems awfully risky."

Mark and Todd nodded in agreement. Mark said,

"There are risks, yes, but we don't consider them to be that significant. The first risk is that we get caught practicing law without a license, but it's no big deal. A slap on the wrist, a small fine, and move on."

Todd added, "We've studied the cases and unauthorized practice is not that uncommon. It happens, and by the way the cases are fascinating, but no one goes to jail."

"That's supposed to be comforting?"

"I suppose. Look, Zola, under our plan if someone gets suspicious and reports us, and let's say the D.C. Bar Council shows up with a bunch of questions, we simply vanish again."

"And that's even more comforting?"

Mark ignored her and said, "The second risk is that we default on our loans and this somehow screws up our already screwed-up lives."

The nachos arrived and each took a bite. After the second bite, Zola touched her eyes with a paper napkin and they realized she was crying. She said, "Look, guys, I can't stay in my apartment. Every time I look at Gordy's door I almost break down. His family moved out his stuff on Tuesday and I keep going over there and sitting in the darkness. I need to get away, to somewhere."

They nodded, stopped eating, took a sip.

"And there's something else," she said. She took a deep breath, wiped her eyes again, and told the story of a college student in Texas who was yanked from her dorm room in the middle of the night by ICE agents. She was sent to El Salvador, where she was reunited with her family of undocumented workers who had been removed a month earlier. The problem was the student had been born in the

U.S. and had full citizenship. Her appeals and paperwork still languished somewhere deep in the bureaucracy.

Zola told them she had found a dozen cases of U.S. citizens being ensnared in ICE raids and removed, and each arrest had happened after the detention of family members. She was living in fear and it was debilitating.

Mark and Todd listened with sympathy. When she finished, and the tears had stopped, Mark said, "Well, we've found a great hiding place, and there's room for you."

"Where?" she asked.

"Upstairs. We're sharing a dump on the fourth floor, no elevator I might add, and there are two rooms just below us. Maynard says we can have it for very reasonable rent."

"Who's Maynard?"

"Our boss," Todd said. "He owns the place."

"It's not very nice," Mark said. "But you would have your privacy, or some of it."

"I'm not rooming with you guys."

"No, not at all. We'll be on the fourth floor and you'll be on the third."

"Does it have a kitchen?"

"Not really, but then you don't need to cook anyway."

"How about a bathroom?"

"That could be a problem," Todd said. "The only bathroom is on the fourth floor, but we can make it work. It's not ideal, Zola, but we're all scrambling here. We can tough it out for a few months and see how things go."

"It's the perfect place to hide," Mark said. "Think of Anne Frank hiding from the Nazis, only not quite that severe, you know?"

"That's supposed to make me feel better?"

"I guess I could find a better analogy."

"What about Maynard?" she asked. "How much does he know?"

Todd said, "I've worked for Maynard for three years and he's cool. He's a bit on the crooked side anyway, big-time bookie and all, and he has no idea what a legal clinic is. He thinks we're still in school but doesn't really care. We're negotiating with him, offering to swap bartending hours for rent. He'll come around."

She said, "I really can't visualize myself hustling DUI cases like that Cromley dude."

Mark said, "Of course not, Zola. So far, from what we've observed, all the hustlers are men, most of them white. You wouldn't fit in, because, well, you do tend to attract attention."

"So what's my specialty?"

"Office girl," Todd said.

"I don't like the sound of that. Where's the office?"

"Your den. It's the new home of Upshaw, Parker & Lane. UPL. Unauthorized Practice of Law."

"Clever."

"We thought so. We see your talents in the field of personal injury law, which, as we know because of our superb legal education, is still the most lucrative area of street law."

As if rehearsed, Mark took the handoff and said, "We see you working the hospital emergency rooms, trolling for injured plaintiffs. In this city, most of them are black and you can relate to them. They'll believe you and want to hire you."

"I know nothing of personal injury law," she said.

"Of course you do. You've seen a thousand ads on television, all those hucksters begging for cases. They're not the sharpest tools in the shed, so you gotta figure there can't be much to PI work."

"Thanks."

Todd added, "And it only takes a couple of really good car wrecks to make some money, Zola. I met a lawyer in the Old Red Cat who was starving until he slipped on some ice and fell. When he was laid up in the hospital, they rolled in another guy who got banged up in a motorcycle collision. A year later the lawyer settled the motorcycle accident case for almost a million and raked off one-third."

"Just like that," she said.

"Yes, and there will always be injured people and they always take 'em to the hospital. That's where you'll be waiting."

"It'll work, Zola, because we'll make it work," Mark said. "Just the three of us, all for one, one for all. Equal partners to the very end."

"And what's the end, guys? What is your endgame?"

"Survival," Todd said. "We'll survive by hiding and pretending to be other people. We'll hustle the streets because there's no turning back."

"And if we get caught?"

Mark and Todd took a sip and thought about an answer. Finally, Mark said, "If we get caught, we simply walk away again. Vanish."

"A life on the run," she said.

"We're running now," Todd said. "You might not want to admit it, but that's what we're doing. We're living a life that's not sustainable, so we have no choice but to run."

Mark cracked his knuckles and said, "Here's the deal, Zola. We're in this together, thick as thieves and loyal to the end. We have to agree, right now, up front, that if it becomes necessary, we leave together."

"And go where?"

"We'll worry about that when the time comes."

"What about your families?" she asked. "Have you told them?"

They hesitated, and the pause conveyed the answer. Mark said, "No, I have not told my mother, because she has enough problems right now. She thinks I'm in class and looking forward to graduation with a nice job all lined up. I suppose I'll wait a couple of months, then lie and tell her I'm taking a semester off. I don't know. I'll think of something."

"And you?" she asked Todd.

"Same here," he said. "Right now I don't have the balls to tell my parents. I'm not sure which version of the truth sounds worse. On the one hand, I'm $200,000 in debt and have no job. On the other hand, I've dropped out and decided to make a buck hustling DUIs for cash with a new identity. I'll wait, like Mark, and think of something later."

"And if the scheme blows up and you get into trouble?"

"It won't happen, Zola," Mark said.

"I'd like to believe you but I'm not convinced you know what you're talking about."

"We're not convinced either," Todd said. "But we've made our decision and there's no turning back. The question is whether or not you're with us."

"You're asking a lot. You expect me to walk away from three years of law school."

"Come on, Zola," Mark said. "What has law school done for you? Nothing, except ruin your life. We're offering a way out. It may not be the cleanest exit, but right now it's all we've got."

She crunched on a nacho and looked around the bar. It was packed with young men in their thirties and forties, all drinking and watching basketball and hockey on the big screens. There were a few women, but not many, and almost no students.

She asked, "And both of you guys work here?"

Todd said, "Yep. It's a lot more fun than sitting in class and studying for the bar exam."

"And what are the terms of the partnership?"

Mark said, "We're pooling our expense money for this semester. Ten thousand each. That covers the launch: new computers, new phones, some office equipment, new identities, some nicer clothes."

"Are you in?" Todd asked.

"Let me think about it, okay? I still think you're crazy."

"We won't argue that."

16

Some thirty months earlier, when Mark Frazier signed his name on the last federal loan form and jumped headlong into the quagmire of student debt, the Department of Education assigned him a loan servicer, a woman by the name of Morgana Nash. She worked for NowAssist, a private company in New Jersey hired by the DOE to service student loans, and her selection had been at random. Mark had never met her and had no reason to. As the borrower, he was allowed to establish the lines of communication and had chosen to keep the chatter to a minimum, like most students. He and Ms. Nash corresponded by e-mail only. She had once asked for his cell phone number, but since he was not required to divulge it, she didn't get it. NowAssist was one of several loan service companies, and all were supposedly monitored closely by DOE. Those with subpar performances were either given less business or terminated altogether. According to its website, DOE ranked NowAssist in the middle of the pack. Other than the suffocating debt itself, Mark had no complaints with Ms. Nash and her efforts so far. After thirty months of listening to the bitching of a bunch of law students, he knew that there were some bad service companies.

Her latest e-mail, one received on his old account, read,

> Hello, Mark Frazier: I trust your holidays went well and you've buckled down for your final semester of law school. Congrats on making it this far and best of luck in these final months. When we last communicated, in November, you were excited about your position at Ness Skelton but still uncertain as to your starting salary. An update on this issue would be appreciated. Based on your salary, I would like to begin the process of structuring a repayment plan. As you know, the law requires a repayment plan to be signed at graduation, with your first payment due exactly six months after that. I know you're busy but please check in at your convenience.
>
> Most recent installment Jan. 13, 2014 = $32,500.
> Total due, principal and interest: $266,000.
>
> Best Regards, Morgana Nash, Public Sector Representative

Mark waited two days and on Saturday morning replied,

> Dear Ms. Nash: Thank you for your note, so good to hear from you. Hope you are well. Things are sort of up in the air over at Ness Skelton these days. The firm merged with some British outfit and everything seems to be in flux. In fact, I can't find anyone there who's

willing to talk about my position. I even get the impression that the job offer might have vanished in the merger. It's very unsettling. And add the fact that my best friend jumped off the Arlington Memorial Bridge and into the Potomac (see link) last week, and, well, I haven't thought much about law school. Give me some time and I'll put myself back together. The last thing I want to talk about is repayment. Thanks for your patience. Your friend, Mark.

TODD WAS STUCK with an outfit called Scholar Support Partners, or SSP. Or simply SS, as Todd and many other students called it. It was based in Philadelphia and had a dismal record handling loans. Todd had found at least three lawsuits across the country in which SSP had been sued for abusive debt collection practices. The company had been caught tacking on unwarranted fees to its loans, and had already paid fines. Nonetheless, the DOE stuck with it.

His "counselor" was a real smart-ass named Rex Wagner, a bully Todd would love to punch if he ever had the chance, which of course he never would. He envisioned Wagner stuffed in a cubbyhole in a boiler room in some low-end basement office, probably fat and eating chips with headphones stuck to his bald head as he hounded kids on the phone and fired off pissy e-mails.

His latest read,

Dear Mr. Lucero: Down the home stretch now with graduation right around the corner, so it's time to talk about repayment, which I assume you have no desire to discuss since, based on our last correspondence a month ago, you still have not found "meaningful legal employment." I hope this has changed. Please update me on your latest efforts to get a job. I'm afraid I will not be able to accept a repayment plan predicated on your apparent desire to work only as a bartender. Let's talk, and the sooner the better.

Most recent installment: $32,500, Jan. 13, 2014; total principal and interest: $195,000.

Sincerely, Rex Wagner, Senior Loan Counselor

To which Todd eventually replied,

Dear SS Senior Loan Counselor Wagner: I can make more money tending bar than you can harassing students. I've read about your company and all its lawsuits and abusive tactics, but I'm not accusing you of any abuse, yet. I am not in default, hell I haven't even graduated, so back off. No, I don't have a real job, because there aren't any, at least not for graduates of low-end for-profit schools like FBLS, which, by the way, practically lied to us way back then when we were thinking about signing on. Boy, were we stupid.

Give me some time and I'll work out something. Todd Lucero.

Wagner replied,

Dear Mr. Lucero: I would like to keep things positive. I've worked with many students who struggled to find work, but they all eventually did so. It just takes a lot of gumption and shoe leather to get out there and knock on those doors. D.C. is full of great law firms and well-paying government jobs. I'm sure you'll find a rewarding career. I will ignore the fact that you used the words "abuse" and "harassing." All of our e-mail correspondence will become public and I suggest we choose our words carefully. I would like to discuss this with you on the phone, but of course I do not have your number.

Regards, Rex Wagner, Senior Loan Counselor

Todd replied,

Dear SS Senior Loan Counselor Wagner: My apologies if I offended you. I'm not sure you realize the pressure I am under at this point in my life. Nothing has gone as planned and the future looks awfully bleak. I curse the day I decided to go to law school, and especially the one at Foggy Bottom. Do you realize that the Wall Street dude who owns the school nets $20 million a year from it? And it's just one of eight in his portfolio? Fascinating. Looking back, I should've bought myself a law school instead of enrolling in one.

No, you can't have my phone number. According to the numerous lawsuits against SS, the worst abuse was over the phone, where it's almost never recorded. Let's stick with e-mail, where every word matters.

We're still pals. Todd Lucero.

THEY SPENT ALL of Saturday cleaning, painting, and hauling away sacks of garbage. Zola's "suite" was actually three rooms: one for the bed, one for the den/office, and a utility closet that had potential. They convinced Maynard to allow them to move a wall and add a door. One of Maynard's cousins was an unlicensed contractor who did odd jobs without bothering with the permit routine, and for a thousand bucks cash he said he could jerry-rig a small shower, commode, and vanity and convert the utility closet to a bathroom. Todd and Mark doubted that Zola would be impressed, but she really had no choice.

She had not agreed to join the partnership, but it was only a matter of time.

THE DAY WAS cool and sunny, and Zola needed fresh air. She left her apartment early Saturday morning and walked to the Mall, where she sat on the steps of the Lincoln Memorial and watched the tourists. Gazing at the Washington Monument and the Capitol in the distant background, she thought of her parents and brother locked away like prisoners in a miserable detention center, awaiting removal. Her view was majestic, with every building and monument a symbol of unbridled freedom. Their view, if they had one, was of fencing and razor wire. Because of their sacrifice, she had been given the gift of citizenship, a permanent status she had done nothing to earn. They had worked like dogs in a country they were proud of, with the dream of one day belonging. How, exactly, would their removal benefit this great nation of immigrants? It made no sense and seemed unjustly cruel.

She tried to keep Gordy out of her thoughts. His tragedy was behind her and dwelling on it served no useful purpose. They'd never had a future together and she had been foolish to think otherwise. But he was still there and she couldn't shake the guilt.

She drifted past the Reflecting Pool and tried to envision the place packed with about 250,000 people back in 1963 when Dr. King described his dream. Her father always said that the greatness of America was that anyone could pursue any dream, and through work and sacrifice the dreams could come true.

Now his dreams had become nightmares, and she was helpless.

At the Washington Monument, she fell into a long line for the ride to the top, but soon got bored and left. She loved the Smithsonian and spent a few hours lost in American history. At no time throughout the day did she waste time thinking about law school or the pursuit of "meaningful legal employment."

Late in the afternoon, Todd sent a text and suggested "another fine dinner." But she declined, saying she had plans. She read a novel, watched an old movie, and went to bed just after eleven. The apartment building was rocking with loud music and rowdy students coming and going. Saturday night in the big city. An argument in the hallway woke her around one, but she managed to drift off.

She was sleeping soundly when someone began pounding on her door. For immigrants, especially those without the paperwork, the rules of engagement were well-known. Keep clothes and shoes close by, along with the phone, do not answer the door, and hope and pray it's not ICE. If it is, they'll kick through the door anyway and there's no place to run. Though she was as legal as any ICE agent, she certainly wasn't living like it.

Zola jumped out of her skin and pulled on her jeans. The pounding continued and a loud voice yelled, "Open up! Immigration!" She eased into the den and stared at the door in horror, her heart beating like a jackhammer. She was holding her phone and was about to speed dial Mark, as if he could hustle over at two in the morning and save her. The pounding stopped. There were no more voices, only the shuffling of feet. She braced for the crash of her door, but there was nothing but silence. Then, at the far end of the hallway, laughter.

Was it really ICE, or just someone's idea of a sick joke? She waited and tried to control her breathing. As the minutes passed she stood in the darkness, afraid to move, to make a sound. It was possible that ICE might stop by for questions, but not at that hour, right? When ICE arrived they meant business. They didn't knock and walk away when no one answered.

Regardless of who was there, the damage was done. Zola slowly returned to her bedroom, pulled on a sweater, put on her shoes, and waited some more. When things were quiet, she unlocked her door, took a peek up and down the hallway, saw no one, and locked her door behind her. With Gordy's spare key, she entered his apartment, kept the lights off, and stretched out on his bare mattress.

Sleep was impossible. She could not live like this. If her two friends were crazy enough to assume new lives, she would take her chances with them.

Morgana Nash checked in:

Dear Mark: I'm so sorry about your friend. I understand why you are upset. However, let's try and nail down the situation at Ness Skelton and begin talking about a repayment schedule. My sympathies. Morgana Nash, Public Sector Representative.

Sunday morning Mark fired back:

Dear Ms. Nash: Thank you for your sympathies. It means so much. It appears as though I've been fired from Ness Skelton, fired before I even started, which is okay because it was a bad place on a good day and I despise the people who work there. So I'm unemployed again, along with the rest of my class, and I really don't have the emotional strength to start looking for another dead-end job. Please back off, okay? Love, Mark.

First thing Monday morning, she replied,

Dear Mark: I'm sorry you are upset. I'm just doing my job and my job requires me to engage you in a conversation about repayment. There are many good jobs in the D.C. area and I know you will find meaningful legal employment. Just keep me in the loop. Morgana Nash, Public Sector Representative.

Mark responded,

Dear Ms. Nash: There are no loops. There is nothing. I'm in therapy and my therapist tells me to ignore you for now. Sorry. Mark.

17

They waited until late Monday morning, when the building was empty and the neighbors were in class, and they moved Zola's boxes to her new third-floor suite above The Rooster Bar. If she was unimpressed with her new digs, she kept it to herself. In fact, she unpacked her clothes and belongings with a smile and seemed pleased with her new hiding place. It was only temporary. As a child in Newark she had lived in far tighter quarters with almost no privacy. Mark and Todd had no idea how poor her family had been in those days.

The contractor, with his crew of hardworking and undoubtedly illegal Slovakians, was busy transforming the utility closet into a bathroom, so the partners walked down the street for a late lunch. Over salads and iced tea, Todd covered some of the basic rules of engagement. They would live in a world of cash, no credit. Credit cards leave trails. They had convinced Maynard to swap labor for rent. Todd and Mark would each work twenty-five hours a week tending bar and no records would be kept. Maynard would accept this for rent and also cover the utility bills, Internet, and cable, and allow them to use the address for what little mail they anticipated. He seemed to like the idea of having three budding lawyers practically hiding in his building and appeared to miss the distinction between a legal clinic and a law firm. Maynard asked few questions.

It was ironic that their zeal to avoid credit was predicated on the fact that they collectively owed more than $600,000, but the irony was lost at the moment.

They would revisit their shady security contact and buy a fake driver's license for Zola as her only form of ID. Once she became Zola Parker, they would get her a cell phone, but they would keep their old ones to monitor the people who might be looking for them. They all would be sued by their landlords but the lawsuits would be worthless because Mark Frazier, Todd Lucero, and Zola Maal no longer existed and evidently had left town. Eventually, they would be placed in default by their student loan servicers, but that was several months down the road. You can't effectively sue someone if you can't find the person. They would try to avoid all of their old friends but continue to update their Facebook pages, though with less activity. They would have no contact with Foggy Bottom and felt sure their absence would not be noticed by anyone in administration.

At times, Zola seemed overwhelmed by the plot. It was insane and destined for a bad ending, but she felt safer, and safety was her primary concern. And, her partners were either overly confident or putting up a good front. Deep down, she knew they had no idea what they were doing, but their enthusiasm was hard to ignore. As reluctant as she was, she was comforted by their loyalty.

Mark grew serious and talked about their personal lives. It was important that they avoid new friendships and serious dating. No one else could know about their scheme. The partnership needed a wall around it that could not be penetrated.

She interrupted with "Are you kidding me? We just buried my boyfriend and you think I want to start dating again?"

"Of course not," Mark said. "Todd and I are unattached at the moment, and it's best if we all stay that way."

Todd said, "Right, and if you want sex Mark and I are always available, just to keep things in the firm, you know?"

"That's not going to happen," she said with a laugh. "Our lives are complicated enough right now."

"Sure, but just file it away," Todd said.

"Is that your best pickup line: 'Let's keep it in the firm'?"

"I don't know. I've never used it before."

"Well, don't use it again. It's not working."

"I'm kidding, Zola."

"No, you're not. What happened to that Sharon babe you were seeing last semester?"

"She's history."

Mark said, "Let's agree that all hookups will be off premises, okay?"

"Whatever," she said. "What's next on the list?"

"We don't have a list," Mark said. "You got questions?"

"More doubts than questions."

"We're listening," Todd said. "This is our big moment, our finest hour. Let's put it all on the table."

"Okay, I seriously doubt I'll be able to hustle injury cases in hospital emergency rooms. And I doubt if either of you knows how to do it either."

Todd said, "You're right, but we can learn. We have to learn. It's a matter of survival."

Mark said, "Oh, I think you'll be a natural, Zola. A beautiful young black woman in a killer dress, short skirt maybe, with stylish heels. I'd hire you in a heartbeat if my wife got banged up in a car wreck."

"My only nice dress is the one I wore to the funeral."

"We're upgrading your wardrobe, Zola," Todd said. "We're no longer law students but real professionals. New clothes for all of us. It's in the firm's budget."

"That's the only promising thing I've heard yet," she said. "And let's say we get some clients and we need to meet them at the office. What then?"

It was obvious they had thought of everything. Without hesitating, Mark said, "We tell them our offices are being renovated and we meet them downstairs in the bar."

"The Rooster Bar?"

"Sure. The drinks are on the firm as we go through the paperwork," Todd said. "They'll love it."

Mark said, "Keep in mind, Zola, most of our clients will be small-time criminals who pay in cash. We'll meet them in court or in jail, and the last place they'll want to go is a law office."

Todd said, "And we will not be having conferences with other lawyers. Nothing like that."

"Of course not."

Mark said, "If we get backed into a corner, we can always rent a room at a business center for a few hours. There's one around the corner."

"I guess you guys have thought of everything."

"No, we don't have a clue, Zola," Todd said. "But we'll figure it out, make it work, and have some fun along the way."

"What else is bugging you?" Mark said.

"Okay, I doubt I can keep this from Ronda. She's a close friend and she's worried about me."

"She also has the biggest mouth in our class," Todd said. "You have to keep her in the dark."

"That won't be easy. I doubt if I can drop out of law school without her knowing it."

"Does she know about you and Gordy?" Mark asked.

"Of course she does. He hit on her during our first year."

"What have you told her?" Todd asked.

"She wanted to talk so I met her for a sandwich last night. I said I was really struggling and skipping classes for the time being, that I might take off a semester and pull things together. She didn't pry too much, just wanted to talk about Gordy and his final days. I didn't say much. She thinks I might need to see a therapist, someone for grief counseling. I said I'd think about it. She was really sweet, and I needed that."

"You gotta cut the cord, Zola," Mark said. "Stiff-arm her, but do it gently. We have to pull away from the law school gang. If word gets out that the three of us are skipping our last semester, the school might start asking questions. That's no big deal, unless of course it decides to notify DOE."

"I thought we weren't worried about the loans."

"True, but we need to delay default as long as possible. If the loan servicers find out that we've withdrawn, they'll start barking about repayment. When they can't find us, they'll turn the files over to lawyers who'll hire investigators to sniff around. I'd rather deal with that down the road."

"I'd like to avoid it altogether,"Todd said.

"Oh, I think we will."

"But you have no idea, do you?" she asked.

Mark and Todd exchanged looks and nothing was said for a moment. Todd's cell phone vibrated and he pulled it out of a pocket. "Wrong one," he said, and pulled another phone out of another pocket. Two phones, the old and the new. One for the past, one for the present. He read a message and said, "It's Wilson, says, 'Hey, man, you skipping classes again today. What's up?'"

"This might be harder than we thought," Mark said.

18

By 8:45, they were gathering in nervous little groups in the wide hallway outside courtroom 142 in the District Courthouse. A sign by the door said it was the domain of the Honorable Fiona Dalrymple, Criminal Division 19, General Sessions Court, District of Columbia. Those summoned to the day and hour were, generally speaking, a rough-looking bunch from the tougher neighborhoods, most with black or brown skin, almost all either holding the piece of paper that had commanded them to be there or standing close to a loved one with such paperwork. No one was alone. Those accused brought with them spouses or parents or teenage children, and everyone wore some version of the same frightened, hopeless look. At the moment, there were no lawyers preying on the victims.

Zola and Todd arrived first, both dressed casually, and began watching everyone else. They leaned against a wall and waited for Lawyer Upshaw, who soon appeared with a nice suit and an old briefcase. He joined them and they clustered like the others, whispering, waiting as if someone might be chosen at random for an execution.

"I like that guy over there," Todd said, nodding in the direction of a little round Hispanic man of about forty with a piece of paper and a fidgety wife.

"I like him too," Zola added with amusement. "He could be our first client."

"There are so many to choose from," Mark said, almost under his breath.

Zola said, "Okay, Mr. Big Shot, show us how it's done."

Mark swallowed hard, offered them a fake smile, said, "Nothing to it," and walked over to the couple. As he drew close, the wife lowered her eyes in fear while the husband's eyes grew larger.

"Excuse me," Mark said in a low voice. "Are you Mr. Garcia? Looking for Freddy Garcia."

The man shook his head no, but said nothing. Mark's eyes seized upon the citation clutched in the guy's right hand and asked, "Are you going to court?"

Stupid question. Why else would the guy be missing work and waiting outside a courtroom? He nodded quickly, yes, while managing to maintain silence.

"What's the charge?" Mark asked.

Still not speaking, the man offered the citation, which Mark took and managed to scan with a frown. "Simple assault," he mumbled. "This could be bad. You been to court before, Mr. Lopez?"

Fierce shaking of the head. No. His wife broke her gaze from her shoes and looked at Mark as if she wanted to cry. Other people were moving about as the crowd grew.

"Look, you need a lawyer. Judge Dalrymple can be tough. You understand?" With his free hand, Mark whipped out a brand-new business card and forced it on the guy. "Simple assault can carry some jail time, but I can take care of that. Nothing to worry about. You want some help?"

Nodding yes, yes.

"Okay, look, my fee is a thousand bucks. Can you pay it?"

Mr. Lopez's mouth dropped open at the mention of money. From behind Mark, a sharp, crisp voice rifled his way and was no doubt meant for him. "Hey, what's going on here?"

Mark turned to see the puzzled and concerned face of a genuine street lawyer, a taller guy of forty with a worn suit and pointed nose. He assessed the situation perfectly as he joined them. "What's going on, pal?" he asked Mark in a slightly lower voice. "Are you hustling my client?"

Mark, unable to speak, took a step back just as the lawyer snatched the citation from his right hand. He looked at Mr. Lopez and said, "Juan, is this guy bothering you?"

Mr. Lopez handed the business card to the lawyer, who glanced at it and said, "Look, Upshaw, this is my client. What are you trying to do?"

Mark had to say something so he managed, "Nothing. I was looking for Freddy Garcia." Mark glanced around and noticed another guy in a suit gawking at him.

The lawyer said, "Bullshit. You're trying to hustle my client. I heard you say your fee is a thousand dollars. Right, Juan?"

Lopez, suddenly fluent and chatty, said, "Right. He say a thousand dollars, say I go to jail."

The lawyer took a step closer to Mark, their noses a foot apart. Mark thought about punching him but quickly decided that a fistfight between two lawyers in the hallway outside the courtroom would not help the situation. "Beat it, Upshaw," the lawyer hissed.

Mark tried to smile as he said, "Hey, relax, pal. I'm looking for my client, Freddy Garcia. So I got the wrong guy, okay?"

The lawyer sneered and said, "Well, if you could read, you would notice that the citation is addressed to Mr. Juan Lopez, my client here. I'll bet Freddy Garcia is not even on the docket, and I'll bet even more that you're just hustling business."

"You should know," Mark replied. "Just relax."

"I'm relaxed, now beat it."

Mark wanted to bolt, but managed to ease back a step. "You got it, asshole."

"Go bother somebody else."

Mark turned around, dreading the looks from Todd and Zola.

But they were gone.

HE FOUND THEM around the corner and they hurried to a coffee shop on the first floor. As they pulled chairs around a small table, Mark realized Todd and Zola were laughing so hard they couldn't speak. This pissed him off but after a few seconds he started laughing too. Todd finally caught his breath and said, "Nice work, Darrell."

Zola wiped her cheeks with the back of a hand. "Freddy Garcia," she managed to say. Todd erupted again.

"Okay, okay," Mark said, still laughing.

"I'm sorry," Todd said, holding his sides.

They laughed for a long time. Mark finally got it together and asked, "Who wants coffee?" He walked to the counter, bought three cups, and brought them back to the table, where the other members of his firm had regained their composure, somewhat.

Todd said, "We saw the guy coming, and when he realized what you were doing he went on the attack."

Zola said, "I thought he was going to hit you."

"So did I," Mark said. They sipped their coffees, each on the verge of more laughter.

Mark finally said, "Okay, here's the good part. It was a bad scene all right, but no one even thought about whether or not I was a lawyer. This is going to be easy."

"Easy!" Todd exploded. "You almost got in a fight over our very first client."

Zola said, "Did you see the look on Juan's face when the two of you were going at it? He must think all lawyers are crazy." She was laughing again too.

"Chalk it up to experience," Mark said, playing along. "We can't quit now."

"Darrell Cromley you're not," Todd said.

"Shut up. Let's go."

THEY DECIDED TO change strategy for their second foray into the abyss. A motley crowd was waiting outside the courtroom of the Honorable Leon Handleford, Criminal Division 10. Todd appeared first and tried to look as nervous as possible. He studied the group and focused on a young black man waiting with an older woman, probably his mother. Todd drifted over, smiled at them, and struck up a conversation. "A helluva way to spend the day, right?"

"You got that right," the young man said. His mother rolled her eyes in frustration.

"This is DUI court, right?" Todd asked.

"Traffic," the young man said.

His mother added, "Got him doing eighty-five in a forty-mile zone. Second ticket this year. Insurance is going through the roof. I swear."

"Eighty-five," Todd repeated. "That's booking it."

"So I was in a hurry."

"Cop said he's going to jail," the mother said, thoroughly frustrated.

"You got a lawyer?" Todd asked.

"Not yet," the young man said. "I can't lose my license, man. If I lose my license I lose my job."

Mark appeared with a purpose and with a phone stuck to his head. He made eye contact with Todd, hurried over, and put the phone away. Ignoring the black guy and his mother, he said to Todd, "Just talked to the prosecutor, a dude I know pretty well. I got the jail time knocked off and they'll cut the fine in half. We're still haggling over the suspension but we're making progress. You got the other half of my fee?"

"Sure," Todd said quickly as he reached into his pocket and pulled out some cash. In plain view, he peeled off five $100 bills and handed them over. As Mark grabbed the money, Todd pointed to his new friend and said, "Say, this guy got caught doing eighty-five in a forty-mile zone. What's he looking at?"

Mark had no idea, but he was Darrell Cromley now, a veteran street lawyer, and no question went unanswered. "Eighty-five," he repeated as if in awe. "You get a DUI?"

"No," he answered.

"Cold sober," his mother said. "It might make more

sense if he was drunk, but he knew exactly what he was doing."

"Come on, Mom."

Mark said, "Anything over eighty means time in the slammer."

The mother asked, "You take speeding cases?"

Mark gave her a sappy smile as if he could handle anything. "This is my beat, ma'am, traffic court. I know all the judges and all the wrinkles."

"I gotta keep my license," the young man said.

"What kind of work do you do?" Mark asked, glancing at his watch.

"Package delivery. A good job and I can't lose it."

A good job. Pay dirt! For a DUI the fee was $1,000. Mark was thinking of something less for speeding, but the notion of gainful employment raised the stakes. All business, Mark said, "Look, my fee is a thousand bucks, and for that I'll get it reduced to plain old speeding and keep you out of jail." He looked at his watch again as if important matters were pressing.

The young man looked hopefully at his mother, who shook her head to say, "This is your mess, not mine." He looked at Mark and said, "I only got three hundred on me now. Can I pay the rest later?"

"Yes, but it's due before your next court date. Let me see the citation."

He pulled it out of his pocket and handed it over. Mark scanned it quickly. Benson Taper, age twenty-three, single, address on Emerson Street in Northeast D.C.

Mark said, "Okay, Benson, let's go see the judge."

HUSTLING CLIENTS IN the hallway was nerve-racking enough, especially for a rookie pretending to be a lawyer, but walking into a courtroom and staring at the wheels of justice head-on was terrifying. Mark's knees were weak as they moved down the center aisle. The knot in his stomach grew with each step.

Brace yourself, you idiot, he said to himself. Show no fear. It's all a game. If Darrell can do it, so can you. He pointed to a spot in a middle row and, directing traffic as if it was *his* courtroom, whispered to the mother, "Take a seat here." She did, and they moved on to the front row and sat down. Benson handed over $300 and Mark produced a contract for legal services, identical to the one he'd signed on behalf of Gordy for the attorney Preston Kline. When the paperwork was finished, he and Benson sat and watched the parade.

A few feet in front of them, the bar, a knee-high railing, separated the spectators from the action. Beyond it were two long tables. The one on their right was covered with piles of paper and several young prosecutors milled about, whispering, joking, placing even more papers here and there. The table to their left was almost bare. A couple of bored defense lawyers leaned on it, chatting quietly. Clerks walked back and forth, handing papers to the lawyers and Judge Handleford. Though court was in session, the bench area buzzed with assembly-line activity and no one seemed too worried about making noise. A large sign read, "No Cell Phones. $100 Fine."

Judge Handleford was a large, bearded white man pushing sixty and thoroughly bored with his daily routine. He rarely looked up and seemed occupied signing his name on orders.

A clerk looked at the crowd and called a name. A tall woman in her fifties walked down the aisle, nervously stepped through the gate, and presented herself to His Honor. She was there for a DUI and had somehow managed to make it this far without some hungry lawyer stuck by her side. Mark made a note of her name: Valerie Blann. He would get her name from the docket and call her later. She pleaded not guilty and was given a return date for late in February. Judge Handleford barely looked up. A clerk called the next name.

Mark swallowed hard again, kicked himself for fortitude, and walked through the gate. With his best lawyerly frown, he walked to the prosecution's table, picked up a copy of the docket, and took a seat at the defense table. Two more lawyers arrived. One left. They came and went and no one noticed. A prosecutor told a joke and got a few laughs. The judge appeared to be napping now. Mark glanced at the courtroom and saw Zola seated behind Benson's mother, wide-eyed, watching every move. Todd had made his way to the front row for a closer look. Mark got up, walked over to a clerk seated beside the bench, handed her a card, and informed her that he was representing Mr. Benson Taper. She gave him a look. Who cares?

When Benson's name was called, Mark stood and motioned for his client. Side by side, they stood in front of Judge Handleford, who was barely showing a pulse. A prosecutor drifted over and Mark introduced himself. Her name was Hadley Caviness and she was extremely cute; great figure, short skirt. Mark took her card; she took his. The judge said, "Mr. Taper, it looks as though you have counsel, so I assume you're pleading not guilty."

"That's correct, Your Honor," Mark said, his first words

in court. And with them, Mark, along with his two partners, was in violation of Section 54B, D.C. Code of Criminal Procedure: unauthorized practice of law; punishable by a fine of up to $1,000, restitution, and no more than two years in jail. And it was no big deal. Because of their thorough research, they knew that in the past forty years only one impostor had served time for the unauthorized practice of law in the District. He had been sentenced to six months with four suspended, and his behavior had been particularly bad.

In the context of criminal conduct, UPL was such a minor offense. No one really got hurt. And if the three of them were diligent, their clients' interests would be served. Justice would be protected. And on and on. They could rationalize their scheme for hours.

Todd practically held his breath while his partner stood before the judge. Could it be this easy? Mark certainly fit the role, and his suit was nicer than those of the other lawyers on both sides of the courtroom. And the other lawyers? How many of them were trying to survive under a mountain of debt?

Zola was on the edge of her seat, waiting for someone to scream, "This guy's a fake!" But no one looked twice at Lawyer Upshaw. He seamlessly joined the treadmill, just another one of dozens. After watching the proceedings for half an hour, she had noticed that some of the defense lawyers knew each other and knew a prosecutor or two and seemed right at home. Others kept to themselves and spoke to no one but the judge. It didn't matter. This was traffic court, and everyone was going through the motions that never changed.

Benson's next court appearance was a month away.

Judge Handleford scribbled his name; Mark said, "Thanks, Your Honor," and led his client out of the courtroom.

The city's newest law firm had a few weeks to figure out what to do. Benson's cash paid for an early lunch at a nearby deli. Halfway through his sandwich, Todd remembered Freddy Garcia and they had another good laugh.

For the afternoon rigors, Mark changed suits—he now owned three—and Todd got dressed up. They hit the courthouse at 1:00 p.m. and trolled for clients. Evidently, there was an endless supply. At first they worked together, learning little tricks as they went along. No one noticed them and they relaxed as they blended in with the other lawyers buzzing around the sprawling courthouse.

Outside Division 6, Todd stuck his phone to his ear and had an important conversation with no one. Loud enough for all to hear, he said, "Look, I've handled a hundred DUI cases with you on the other side so don't feed me that crap. This kid blew 0.09, barely over the limit, and he has a perfect driving record. Stop beating around the bush. Reduce it to reckless driving or I'll have a chat with the judge. If you force me to, I'll take it to trial and you know what happened the last time. I embarrassed the cops and the judge tossed the charges." A pause as he listened to his dead phone, then, "That's more like it. I'll stop by in an hour to sign the deal."

When he stuck his phone in his pocket, a man walked over and asked, "Say, are you a lawyer?"

ZOLA, STILL DRESSED casually, moved from one courtroom to the other, sizing up defendants who appeared without lawyers. The judges often asked them where they worked, were they married, and so on. Most had jobs that were not that impressive. She took notes on some of the better prospects. Using the names and addresses from the dockets for reference, she made a list of names for her partners to call. After a couple of hours, she became bored with the grinding monotony of small-time criminal justice.

It might have been boring, but it was more fun than sitting in class and worrying about the bar exam.

AT FIVE, THEY entered The Rooster Bar and found a corner table. Mark fetched two beers and a soda from the bar and ordered sandwiches. He would work the six-to-midnight shift, so the drinks and food were on the house.

They were pleased with their first day on the job. Todd had snagged one DUI client and appeared before Judge Cantu. The prosecutor had mentioned that he had never seen Todd before, and he replied that he had been around for a year. Mark had hustled a simple assault in Division 9 and appeared before a judge who looked him over but said nothing. Within a few days their faces would be familiar.

Their haul was $1,600 cash, with promissory notes for another $1,400. Add the fact that their earnings were non-reportable and tax-free, and they were almost giddy with the prospects of striking gold. The beauty of their scheme was its brazenness. No one in his right mind would stand in front of a judge and pass himself off as a lawyer.

19

At midnight, Mark climbed the stairs to the fourth floor and entered his cramped apartment. Todd was waiting on the sofa with his laptop. There were two empty cans of beer on the flimsy coffee table they'd purchased for $10. Mark got a beer from the small fridge and fell into a chair across from the sofa. He was exhausted and needed sleep. "What are you working on?" he asked.

"The class action. There are now four of them filed against Swift Bank, and it looks like it's a simple matter of calling one of the lawyers and signing on. I think it's time to do it. These guys are advertising like crazy but only on the Internet. No TV ads yet, and I think the reason is that each claim is worth so little. These are not injury cases with big values. The damages are not much, just a few bucks for the bogus fees and such that Swift padded onto the monthly statements. The beauty is that there are so many of them, maybe as many as a million customers who got clipped by Swift."

"I saw where the CEO appeared before Congress today."

"Yes, and it was a bloodletting. The guy got hammered from both sides of the aisle. He was a terrible witness, I mean the guy was literally sweating, and the committee had a field day with him. Everyone is demanding his resignation. One blogger thinks Swift looks so bad it has no choice but to settle this mess quickly and move on. He thinks the bank will throw a billion or so at the class actions, then spend some real money with a new ad campaign to gloss over its sins."

"The usual. No mention of Rackley?"

"Oh no. The guy is hiding behind his wall of shell companies. I've been looking for hours and there's no mention of him or his fronts. I wonder if Gordy was right about his involvement with Swift."

"I'll bet he's right, but we need to keep digging."

They were quiet for a moment. Normally, a television would be on, but they had yet to call the cable company. They planned to piggyback on the line from the bar, but they were not ready for a lot of questions from an installer. Their two flat screens were in a corner.

Mark finally said, "Gordy, Gordy. How often do you think of him?"

"A lot," Todd said. "All the time."

"Do you ask yourself what we should've done different?"

"Truthfully, yes. We could have done this or that, but Gordy was not himself. I'm not sure we could have stopped him."

"I tell myself that. I miss him, though. I miss him a lot. I wonder what he would think if he could see us now."

"The Gordy we once knew would tell us we're crazy. But that last guy would probably want to join our firm."

"As the senior partner, no doubt." They managed a

quick laugh. Mark said, "I read a story once about a guy who killed himself. Some shrink was going on about the futility of trying to understand it. It's impossible, makes no sense at all. Once a person reaches that point, he's in another world, one that his survivors will never understand. And if you do figure it out, then you might be in trouble yourself."

"Well, I'm not in trouble, because I'll never understand it. Sure he had a lot of problems, but suicide wasn't the answer. Gordy could have cleaned up, got his meds straight, worked things out with Brenda, or not. If he had said no to the wedding, he would have been much happier in the long run. You and I have the same problems with law school, the bar exam, unemployment, loan sharks, and we're not suicidal. In fact, we're fighting back."

"And we're not bipolar, so we'll never understand."

"Let's talk about something else," Todd said.

Mark chugged his beer. "Right. What about our hit list?"

Todd closed his laptop and placed it on the floor. "Nothing. I called eight of our prospective victims and no one wanted to talk. The phone is a great equalizer, and these folks are not nearly as nervous tonight as they were in court today."

"Does it seem too easy? I mean, we signed up three thousand bucks in fees today, and we had no idea what we're doing."

"We had a good day and won't always be so lucky. What's amazing is the traffic, the sheer number of people who get chewed up by the system."

"Thank God for them."

"It's an endless supply."

"This is crazy, you know? And it's not sustainable."

"True, but we could run this racket for a long time. And it sure beats the alternative."

Mark took a sip, exhaled mightily, and closed his eyes. "There's no turning back. We're violating too many laws. Unauthorized practice. Tax evasion. And I suppose some code section on labor laws. If we join the class action against Swift, we can add that to our list."

"Are you having second thoughts?" Todd asked.

"No. You?"

"No, but I do worry about Zola. At times I feel like we've dragged her into it. She's awfully fragile right now, and frightened."

Mark opened his eyes and stretched his legs. "True, but at least she feels safe now. She has a good hiding spot and that's of the utmost importance. She's a tough girl, Todd, who's survived more than we can imagine. Right now she's where she wants to be. She needs us."

"Poor girl. She met with Ronda tonight, had a drink somewhere, and told her that she was thinking about taking a semester off, said she couldn't focus right now on law school and the bar exam. She thinks she sold the story. I talked to Wilson and told him that the two of us would eventually show up for classes. He's concerned but I assured him we're okay. Maybe these people will leave us alone."

"If we ignore them they'll forget about us. They have more pressing matters to worry about."

Todd said, "Well, so do we, our new careers. Now that we have these clients, we have to deliver our services. I mean, we're promising these people we can keep them out of jail and get their fines reduced. Any idea how we might go about that?"

"We'll figure it out tomorrow. The key is chumming it

up with the prosecutors, getting to know them and being persistent. And look, Todd, if we can't always deliver we won't be the first lawyers who promised too much. We'll get our fees and move on."

"You sound like a real street hustler."

"That's my gig. I'm going to bed."

BELOW THEM, ZOLA was awake too. She was in her flimsy bed, propped up against the pillows with a quilt covering her legs. The room was dark, the only light coming from the screen of her laptop.

Her loan counselor was a woman named Tildy Carver, and she worked for a servicing company nearby in Chevy Chase called LoanAid. Ms. Carver had been pleasant enough through law school, but her tone was changing as the semesters progressed. That afternoon, when Zola was sitting in a courtroom taking notes, she had received Ms. Carver's latest e-mail:

> Dear Ms. Maal: When we last corresponded a month ago, you were getting ready for your final semester. At that time, you were not optimistic about your employment possibilities. I'm sure you're busy with lots of interviews as graduation approaches. Could you please update me on your efforts to find a job? I look forward to hearing from you.
>
> Sincerely, Tildy Carver, Senior Loan Adviser
>
> Last installment, January 13, 2014: $32,500; total principal and interest: $191,000.

In the safety of her new hiding place, she stared at the "total" figure and shook her head. It was still difficult to believe that she had voluntarily waded into a system that allowed someone like her to borrow so much, with the thought of paying it back an absurd impossibility. Of course, now she wasn't supposed to worry about repayment, but she found that plan troublesome too. It was wrong to simply run away and blame the system.

Her parents had no idea how much she owed. They knew she was borrowing legitimate sums provided by the government, and they had innocently believed that any program provided by Congress must be thoughtful and good. Now they would never know, which was slightly comforting.

She typed,

Dear Ms. Carver: Nice to hear from you. I interviewed last week with the Department of Justice and I'm waiting for a response. I'm seriously thinking about working in the public sector or for a nonprofit to ease the strain of repayment. I'll keep you posted.

Sincerely, Zola Maal

She heard footsteps above her and knew her partners were moving about. She turned off her laptop and stretched out under the covers. She was thankful for her cozy little hiding place, thankful that there would be no sudden knock on the door. The first apartment she remembered as a child was not much larger than her new space. She and her two older brothers shared a tiny bedroom. The boys had bunk beds and next to them she slept on a cot. Her parents were close by in another cramped bedroom. She didn't realize they were poor and frightened and not supposed to be there. In spite of this, though, the home was a happy place with lots of laughter and good times. Her parents worked odd jobs at all hours, but one was usually at home. If not, there was always a neighbor down the hall checking on the kids. Their front door was usually open and folks "from home" were in and out. Someone was always cooking and the aromas hung heavy in the hallways. Food was shared, as was clothing, even money.

And they worked. The Senegalese adults put in long hours with no complaints. Zola was twelve years old before she realized there was a dark cloud hanging over her world. A man they knew was arrested, detained, and eventually sent back. This had terrified the others, and her parents moved again.

She thought of her parents and brother every hour of every day, and usually fell asleep fighting tears. Her future was uncertain, but nothing compared with theirs.

20

The king of D.C. billboards was a colorful tort lawyer named Rusty Savage. His jingle was "Trusting Rusty," and it was impossible to drive along the Beltway without being confronted with his smiling face exhorting those who'd been injured to trust him. His slick TV ads featured clients who'd suffered all manner of physical trauma but were doing swell because they had wisely picked up the phone and called 1-800-Trust-Me.

The three UPL partners had researched personal injury firms in the District and settled on Rusty. His operation had eight lawyers, several of whom were evidently able to walk into a courtroom and actually try a case. Zola made the call and explained to the lady on the other end that her husband had been badly injured in a wreck involving an 18-wheeler and she needed to see Rusty. The lady explained that he was tied up in a "major trial in federal court" but one of his associates would be happy to meet with her.

If you know nothing about personal injury law, find

someone who does. Using a name she'd selected from the phone book, Zola made the appointment.

The office suite was in a glass building near Union Station. She and Todd entered the lobby, which had the look and feel of a busy doctor's waiting room. Rows of chairs lined the walls along with racks of magazines. A dozen clients, some with crutches and canes, sat in varying degrees of discomfort. Rusty's relentless advertising blitz was apparently working well. Zola checked in with the receptionist and was given a questionnaire on a clipboard. She filled in the blanks with bogus information but gave an actual phone number, her old cell. After fifteen minutes, a paralegal fetched them and led them back to a large, open space packed with cubbyholes and workstations. Numerous underlings labored frenetically on the phones and desktops, cranking out paperwork. The lawyers had private offices to the sides with views of the city. The paralegal tapped on the door of one, and they entered the domain of Brady Hull.

From the website, they knew that Mr. Hull was about forty and had a law degree from American University. Of course, he was "passionate about fighting for the rights of his clients," and claimed an impressive series of "major settlements." The paralegal left them and introductions were made. They sat in leather chairs across from Mr. Hull, whose desk was only slightly tidier than a landfill.

Tom (Todd) explained that Claudia (Zola) Tolliver's husband was his best friend and he was there only for moral support. The husband, Donnie, had asked Tom to sit in with his wife and take notes while he, Donnie, was confined to the house with his injuries.

Mr. Hull was skeptical at first and said, "Well, I don't

normally do this. We might need to discuss things that are private and confidential."

Claudia said, "Please, it's okay. Tom is a trusted friend."

"Very well," Mr. Hull said. He had the frazzled look of a man with too much going on, too many calls to make, too many files to touch, not enough hours in the day. "So your husband got banged up?" he said, glancing at a sheet of paper. "Tell me about it."

Claudia began, "Well, it happened three months ago." She hesitated, looked at Tom, and managed to seem overwhelmed and nervous. "He was driving home from work on Connecticut Avenue, up near Cleveland Park, when he was hit by an 18-wheeler. Donnie was going north, the truck south, and for some reason it veered left, crossed the center line, and hit him. Dead on, just like that."

"So liability is clear?" Hull said.

"Yes, according to the police. The driver has said nothing, so as of now we still don't know why he crossed over."

"I need to see the accident report."

"I have it, at home."

"You didn't bring it?" Hull asked rudely.

"I'm sorry. I've never done this before. I wasn't sure what to bring."

"Well, send over a copy as soon as you can. And his medicals? Did you bring his medical records?"

"No, sir. I didn't know I needed to."

Hull rolled his eyes in frustration as his phone beeped. He glanced at it and for a second seemed poised to take the call. "How bad are his injuries?"

"Well, he almost died. Severe concussion, he was in a coma for a week. Broken jaw, broken collarbone, six broken ribs, one of which pierced a lung. A broken leg. He's had two operations and will probably need at least one more."

Hull seemed impressed and said, "Wow, he did get banged up. What's the total of his medical bills so far?"

She shrugged and looked at Tom, who shrugged back as if he had no clue. She said, "Close to $200,000, maybe. He's doing rehab now but can't get around too well. Here's the thing, Mr. Hull, I don't know what to do. The lawyers called night and day right after it happened. I finally stopped answering the phone. I've been dealing with the insurance company and I'm not sure I can trust them."

"Never trust an insurance company in a case like this," he said sternly, as if she'd already blundered. "Don't talk to them." Hull was not as distracted now and able to focus. "What kind of work does Donnie do?"

"He drives a forklift in a warehouse. Pretty good job. He makes about forty-five a year. Hasn't worked since the accident and I'm running out of money."

"We can provide bridge loans," Hull said smugly. "Do it all the time. We don't want our clients pinching pennies while we negotiate a settlement. If liability is as clear as you say, we'll get this thing settled without going to court."

"How much do you charge?" she asked. Tom had yet to say a word.

"We charge nothing," Hull said proudly. "No recovery, no fee."

Tom wanted to say, "Gee, I've seen that on about fifty billboards." But, of course he kept it to himself.

Hull went on, "We get paid when you get paid. Our fee is based on a contingency, usually 25 percent of a settlement. If we go to trial, then obviously there's a lot more work on our end, so we bump it up to one-third."

Claudia and Tom nodded. Finally, something they had learned in law school.

She said, "Well, here's the deal, Mr. Hull. The insurance company says they'll pay all the medicals, and the lost wages, and the rehab expenses, and on top of all that pay us $100,000 for a settlement."

"A hundred grand!" Hull said in disbelief. "That sounds like an insurance company. They're lowballing you because you don't have a lawyer. Look, Claudia, in my hands, this case is worth a million bucks. Tell the insurance company to screw itself and, no, wait, don't tell them anything. Don't say another word to the adjuster. Who is the company, by the way?"

"Clinch."

"Oh, of course. Sounds like Clinch. I sue those clowns all the time, know them well."

Claudia and Tom relaxed a bit. Their research had led them to Clinch, one of the leading commercial insurers in the region. Its website boasted of a long tradition of protecting freight and transportation companies.

"A million dollars?" Tom repeated.

Hull exhaled, smiled, even managed to chuckle. He clasped his hands behind his head as if the old master needed to enlighten his students. "I make no guarantees, okay? I can't properly evaluate any case until I have all the facts. Police report, medicals, lost wages, the other driver's safety record, all that jazz. And then there's the huge issue of permanent disability, which, to be brutally honest, means a lot more money. Let's hope Donnie makes a full recovery, goes back to work, and is soon clicking along as if nothing happened. If so, based on medicals in the range of what you said, I would demand something in the neighborhood of one-point-five from Clinch and haggle for a few months."

Tom gawked in disbelief.

Claudia, overwhelmed, said, "Wow. How do you arrive at that figure?"

"It's an art form, really. But not that complicated. Take the total of the medicals and use a multiple of, say, five or six. Clinch will counter with three, maybe three and a half. Clinch also knows my reputation and those folks do not want to see me in a courtroom, believe me. That will be a huge factor in this negotiation."

"So you've nailed them before?" Tom asked.

"Oh, many times. This little law firm terrifies even the biggest insurance companies."

At least that's what your TV ads claim, Tom thought to himself.

"I had no idea," Claudia said, as if in shock.

His desk phone rang again and he resisted the urge to grab it. He rocked forward, placed his elbows on the desk, and said, "Here's the drill. My paralegal will take care of the paperwork. You and Donnie sign the contract for legal services, it's all in black and white with no surprises. Once we have it, I'll contact the insurance company and ruin its day. We'll begin gathering the medical records and we're off and running. If liability is clear, we'll have it settled within six months. Any more questions?" He was obviously ready to move on to the next case.

Claudia and Tom gave each other blank looks and shook their heads. She said, "I guess not. Thanks, Mr. Hull."

Hull stood, stretched out his hand, and said, "Welcome aboard. You've just made a great decision."

"Thank you," she said as she shook it. Tom shook too

and they hustled out of the office. The paralegal handed her a folder with the words "New Client Packet: Trusting Rusty" on the cover and led them to the door.

When the elevator door closed, they started laughing. "What a nice little tutorial," Zola said.

"Personal Injury Law 101," Todd replied. "A crash course like that would take four months at Foggy Bottom."

"Yes, and taught by some clown who's never advertised on a billboard."

"Now all we need is a client or two."

As Todd drove away, Zola checked her phone and chuckled. "We're getting rich. Mark just hustled another DUI for six hundred in cash. Division 4."

CHOOSING THE RIGHT hospital proved difficult. There were so many in the city. Potomac General was a busy, sprawling, chaotic public hospital and the preferred unloading place for victims of street violence. On the high end, George Washington was where they took President Reagan when he was shot. There were at least eight more in between.

They had to start somewhere and decided it would be General. Todd dropped Zola off at the front entrance and went in search of a parking place. As a lawyer now, Ms. Parker wore a fake designer jacket and skirt that fell above the knees but wasn't too short. Her brown leather pumps were quite stylish, and with a knockoff Gucci attaché she certainly looked like a professional in some field. She followed signs and made her way to the cafeteria on the ground floor. She bought coffee, took a seat at a metal table, and waited on Todd. Not far away, a teenager in a wheelchair sat with a woman, probably his mother, and ate ice cream. One leg was in a thick cast with metal rods protruding. Judging from his mother's appearance, the family was not affluent.

Affluency was to be avoided, the UPL partners had determined. Those with money were more likely to know a real lawyer. Poor folks would not, or so they reasoned. Against a far wall, a man of about fifty had plaster on both ankles, and appeared to be in pain. He was alone and trying to eat a sandwich.

When Todd entered the cafeteria he stopped and glanced around. He made eye contact with Zola and went to buy coffee. He eventually sat at her table, where she was busy reviewing the UPL new client packet, plagiarized from Rusty's. "Any victims?" he said quietly as he picked up a sheet of paper.

She was scribbling some useless notes and said, "That kid over there with the broken leg. Dude in the far corner with matching bum ankles."

Todd slowly looked around as he sipped his coffee.

"I'm not sure I can do this," she said. "It seems so wrong, preying on unsuspecting people."

"Come on, Zola. Nobody's watching. These folks might need our services, and if we don't get them Trusty Rusty will. Besides, if they tell us to get lost we haven't lost anything."

"You go first."

"Okay, I'll take the white kid. You've got the black guy."

Todd stood and pulled out his cell phone. He walked away, deep in conversation with no one, and began pacing around the cafeteria. He circled back, and as he walked by the kid with the broken leg he said to the phone, "Look, the trial is next week. We're not taking fifty thousand because the insurance company is trying to screw you. Got that? I'll tell the judge that we're ready for trial." He stuffed the phone into his pocket, turned around, and with a big smile said to the kid, "Hey, that's a nasty-looking leg. What happened?"

"Broke it in four places," the mother said proudly. "Had surgery yesterday."

The kid smiled and seemed to enjoy the attention. Todd looked at the cast, kept smiling, and said, "Wow. Nice job. How'd you do it?"

The kid said proudly, "I was on a skateboard and hit some ice."

Skateboard = assumption of risk, self-inflicted injury. Ice = natural element. As the lawsuit dissipated, Todd asked, "Were you by yourself?"

"Yep." Personal negligence = no one else to blame.

Todd said, "Well, good luck." He yanked out his phone, took a non-call, and walked away. As he brushed beside Zola, he said, "Strike one. It's up to you." He left the cafeteria, still on the phone. He was right; no one was watching; no one cared.

Slowly, she stood and adjusted her fake reading glasses. Holding a sheet of paper in one hand and a cell phone in the other, she walked around the cafeteria. Tall, thin, well dressed, attractive. The man with the injured ankles couldn't help but notice her as she drew close, on the phone. She smiled at him as she walked by and he returned the smile. Then she was back with a pleasant "Say, are you Mr. Cranston?"

He smiled and said, "No. Name's McFall."

She was standing next to him looking at his ankles. She

said, "I'm an attorney and I'm supposed to meet a Mr. Cranston here at 2:00 p.m."

"Sorry. Wrong guy."

Evidently, McFall wasn't much of a talker. She said, "Must've been a good car wreck."

"No car wreck. I stepped on some ice and fell off the patio. Broke both ankles."

What a klutz, she thought, as another lawsuit evaporated. She said, "Well, hang in there."

"Thanks."

She returned to her table and her coffee and buried her face in paperwork. Todd returned after a few minutes and whispered, "Did you sign him up?"

"No. He fell on some ice."

"Ice, ice, ice. Where's global warming when you need it?"

"Look, Todd, I'm just not cut out for this. I feel like a vulture."

"That's exactly what we are."

21

Wilson Featherstone was another third-year student at Foggy Bottom and had been a member of the gang in the early days. During their second year, he and Todd got sideways over a girl, and they had partied with him less and less. But he was still a good friend, of Mark's anyway, and his calls had been persistent. He was not going away, and Mark finally agreed to meet for a drink. Avoiding the old neighborhood, Mark chose a dive near Capitol Hill. Late on a Thursday night, with Todd serving drinks at The Rooster Bar and Zola reluctantly trolling at GW Hospital, Mark walked in late and saw Wilson at the bar, half a beer already down.

"You're late," Wilson said with a smile and a warm handshake.

"Good to see you, man," Mark said as he slid onto the stool next to him.

"What's with the beard?"

"Can't find a razor. How you doing?"

"I'm fine. The question is, how are you doing?"

"I'm okay."

"No, you're not. You've skipped the first three weeks of classes and we're all talking about you. Same for Todd. What's going on?"

The bartender stopped by and Mark ordered a draft. He shrugged and said, "I'm taking a break, that's all. Reasonably severe motivational problems. Gordy kind of messed me up, you know?"

"You've moved out of your apartment. Todd too. No one's seen Zola. You guys cracking up or something?"

"I don't know what they're doing. We were with Gordy at the end and we're struggling, I guess."

Wilson took a drink as the bartender sat a mug in front of Mark. Wilson asked, "What happened with Gordy?"

Mark studied his beer and thought about an answer. After a few seconds, he said, "He was bipolar, off his meds, really messed up. He got a DUI; we bailed him out, took him to his apartment, and stayed with him. We didn't know what to do. We wanted to call his family, maybe his fiancée, but that freaked him out even more. He threatened me when I mentioned calling home. Somehow he got away that night and drove to the bridge. We were driving around in a panic, trying to find him, but we were too late."

Wilson absorbed this and took another drink. He said, "Wow, that's pretty awful. There's some gossip that you guys were with him at the end. Didn't know it was that bad."

"We kept an eye on him. He was locked in his bedroom. Zola was sleeping on the sofa, Todd across the hall. I had his keys in my pocket. We were trying to get him to a doctor. I don't know what else we could've done. So, yeah,

Wilson, it's safe to say that we're not doing too well these days."

"Bummer, man. I didn't see you at the funeral."

"We were there, hiding in the balcony. Todd and I met with the family after he jumped, and there was a lot of finger-pointing. At us, of course. Gotta blame somebody, right? So we wanted to avoid them at the funeral."

"It wasn't your fault."

"Well, they sure think so, and, I gotta tell you, Wilson, there's a lot of guilt right now. We should've called Brenda or his parents."

This sank in and Wilson ordered another beer. "I don't see it. You can't take the fall for his suicide."

"Thanks, but I can't let it go."

"So, what are you doing, dropping out of law school with one semester to go? That's pretty stupid, Mark. Hell, you got a job lined up for the fall, right?"

"Wrong. I got fired before I even started. The firm merged with another one, things got realigned, I got squeezed. Happens all the time in this wonderful profession."

"I'm sorry. I didn't know."

"It's okay. The firm was a dead end anyway. And you, any luck on the job front?"

"Sort of. I found a place with a nonprofit, so I'll do the public service gig and duck out on most of the loans."

"For ten years?"

"That's what they think. My plan is to grind it out for three or four years, keep the sharks at bay, and hustle on the side for a real job. Sooner or later, the market has got to get better."

"You really believe that?"

"I don't know what to believe, but I gotta go somewhere."

"After you pass the bar exam, of course."

"Here's the way I look at the bar exam, Mark. Last year, half the Foggy Bottom students passed it, half failed. I figure I'm in the top half, and if I bust my ass I can pass it. I look around the school and there are a lot of morons, but I'm not one of them. Neither are you, Mark. You're bright as hell and you don't mind the work."

"As I said, there are motivational problems."

"Then what's your plan?"

"I don't have one. I'm drifting. I suppose I'll show up at school eventually, though the idea of walking into that place makes me ill. Maybe I'll take off a semester, catch up later. I don't know."

"You can't do that, Mark. If you drop out the sharks will put you in default."

"I think I'm already in default. I look at my loan statement and see that I owe a quarter of a million dollars with no viable means of employment. To me, that sure feels like a default. And what the hell? They can sue me but they can't kill me. Last year a million students went into default, and as far as I know, they're still walking around, living and breathing."

"I know, I know. I read the blogs." Both took a drink and looked at themselves in the mirror above the rows of liquor bottles.

Wilson said, "Where are you living now?"

"You stalking me?"

"No, but I stopped by your apartment. A neighbor said you were gone. So is Todd. Have you seen him? He's not at the bar anymore."

"Not lately. I think he's back in Baltimore."

"He quit?"

"I don't know, Wilson. He mentioned taking some time off. I think he's messed up more than me. He and Gordy were especially close."

"He won't answer the phone."

"Well, you guys are not exactly best of friends."

"We got over it. Hell, Mark, I'm concerned, okay? You guys are my friends and you've just disappeared."

"Thanks, Wilson, it means a lot. But I'll be okay, eventually. Not sure about Todd."

"What about Zola?"

"What about her?"

"Well, she's missing in action too. No one has seen her. She moved out."

"I'm talking to Zola and she's a mess. She was the last one to see Gordy alive and she's taking it very hard. On top of that, her parents are about to be deported back to Senegal. She's in bad shape."

"Poor girl. Gordy was stupid to get tangled up with her."

"Maybe, I don't know. Nothing makes sense right now."

They drank for a long time without speaking. In the mirror, Mark saw a familiar face at a table across the room. A pretty face, one he'd seen in a courtroom. Hadley Caviness, an assistant prosecutor, the one handling Benson Taper's speeding case. Their eyes met briefly and she looked away.

Wilson glanced at his watch and said, "Look, this is too depressing. I gotta run. Please keep in touch, Mark, and if I can help, let me know. Okay?" He drained his beer and laid a $10 bill on the bar.

"You got it, Wilson. Thanks."

Wilson stood, patted him on the shoulder, and left. Mark looked in the mirror and noticed that Hadley was sitting with three other young ladies, all enjoying drinks and chatting away. Their eyes met again and she held his gaze for a few seconds.

HALF AN HOUR later, the girls were finished and paying their bill. As they left, Hadley circled back and walked to the bar. "Waiting for someone?" she asked.

"Yes, you. Have a seat."

She offered a hand and said, "Hadley Caviness, Division 10."

He shook it and said, "I know. Mark Upshaw. Can I buy you a drink?"

She assumed her stool and said, "Of course." Mark waved the bartender over and said, "What will it be?"

"Chardonnay."

"And I'll have another beer." The bartender left and they turned to face each other. "Haven't seen you around lately," she said.

"Well, I'm there every day, hustling the system."

"You're new in town."

"Couple of years. I was with a firm and got tired of the grind. Now I'm on my own and having some fun. You?"

"First year in the prosecutor's office so I'm stuck in traffic court. Bored. Not exactly having a ball but paying the bills. Where was law school?"

"Delaware. Came to the big city to change the world. You?" He was hoping she would not say she went to law school at Foggy Bottom.

"Kentucky, undergrad and law. I came here for a job on Capitol Hill but it didn't work out. I got lucky and found a place with the prosecutor's office. I hope it's only temporary." The drinks arrived. They touched glasses, said, "Cheers," and took a drink.

"So what's next?" Mark asked.

"Who knows in this town? I'm watching the market, looking for openings, same as thousands of others. The job situation is not that strong right now."

No kidding, Mark thought. You should hang around Foggy Bottom. "So I hear."

"What about you? Don't tell me you plan to make a career out of defending drunk drivers."

Mark laughed as if this was humorous. "Not really. I have a partner and we would like to get into personal injury."

"You'd look cute on a billboard."

"That's my dream. That and TV ads." She'd had several drinks and was sitting close, almost touching. Her legs were crossed and her skirt was high on the thighs. Lovely legs. She took a drink, sat the glass on the bar, and asked, "You got plans for later tonight?"

"None whatsoever. You?"

"I'm free. I have a roommate who works for the Census Bureau and she's gone all the time. I really hate being alone."

"You move pretty fast."

"Why waste time? I'm just like you and right now we're thinking about the same thing."

Mark paid the tab and called a car. As they drove away, she took his left hand and placed it on an exposed thigh.

He chuckled and whispered, "I love this city. Lots of aggressive women."

"Whatever you say."

The car stopped in front of a tall apartment building on Fifteenth Street. Mark paid the driver and they strolled inside, hand in hand as if they had known each other for months. They kissed in the elevator, kissed again in the tidy little den, and agreed that neither wanted to watch television. As she was undressing in the bathroom, Mark managed to fire off a quick text to Todd: *Got lucky. Won't be in tonight. Sweet dreams.*

Todd replied, *Who's the girl?*

Mark: *You'll probably meet her real soon.*

HE FOUND TODD outside Division 6 at 9:30. The hallway was swarming with the usual ragtag collection of the accused, along with several lawyers working the crowd. Todd was hustling a young woman who appeared to be in tears. When she finally shook her head no, he backed off and noticed his partner watching from a distance. Todd walked over and said, "Strike three. A slow morning. You look like hell. Up all night?"

"It was amazing. I'll tell you about it later. Where's Zola?"

"I haven't talked to her this morning. She's been sleeping in, a lot of late nights at the hospitals."

"You think she's really hustling folks or just reading a book? I mean, she hasn't hooked a client yet."

"I don't know. Let's save it for later. I'm moving down to Division 8." Todd walked away, briefcase in hand, and after a few steps whipped out his cell phone as if he had important business. Mark drifted down to Division 10 and walked inside. Judge Handleford was presiding and talking to a defendant. As always, lawyers and clerks milled about the bench, shuffling paperwork. Hadley was there, chatting with another prosecutor. When she saw Mark, she smiled and walked over. They sat at the defense table as if they had important business.

Just hours earlier, they had collapsed from exhaustion and slept wonderfully entangled and naked. Now she was fresh, clear-eyed, very professional. Mark was a bit fatigued.

In a low voice, she said, "I know what you're thinking but the answer is no. I have a date tonight."

"Hadn't crossed my mind," he said with a smile. "But you have my number."

"I have lots of numbers."

"Right. Could we discuss my client Benson Taper?"

"Sure. I don't remember him. Let me get the file." She stood and walked to a clerk's table where she riffled through a large drawer of files. She found Benson's and returned to the defense table. Scanning it, she said, "Dude was flying, wasn't he? Eight-five in a forty-mile zone. That's reckless and it could carry some jail time."

"I know. Here's the deal. Benson is a young black guy with a good job. He delivers packages, and if he gets busted for reckless, he loses his job. Can you knock it down to a lesser charge?"

"For you, anything. How about simple speeding? Pay a little fine and tell the boy to slow down."

"Just like that?" Mark asked with a smile.

She leaned closer and said, "Sure. Satisfy the prosecutor and you get good deals, at least from me."

"Does your boss have to approve this?"

"Mark, this is traffic court, okay? We're not talking about a murder charge. I'll slide this in front of old Handleford over there and he won't say a word."

"I love you, baby."

"That's what they all say." She stood with the file and extended a hand, to seal the agreement. They shook, professionally.

22

Benson was eating a sandwich in a coffee shop on Georgia Avenue in the Brightwood section of the District. He was on lunch break and looked sharp in his work uniform. He was glad to see Mark and asked about the good news. Mark pulled an order from his briefcase and said, "We've made some progress. You got the rest of the fee?"

Benson reached into a pocket and pulled out some cash. "Seven hundred," he said as he handed it over.

Mark took it and said, "Everything is reduced to simple speeding. No reckless, no jail. Fine one-fifty, payable in two weeks."

"You're kidding?"

Mark smiled and looked at the waitress who had suddenly appeared. "BLT and coffee," he said. She left without saying a word.

"How'd you do that?" Benson asked.

Slept with the prosecutor, Mark wanted to report proudly, but let it go. "I haggled with the court, told the judge what a good guy you are, good job and all, and he cut you some slack. But no more tickets, Benson, you understand?"

"Wow. You're the man, Mark. This is awesome."

"I caught the judge on a good day, Benson. Next time we won't be so lucky."

"Ain't gonna be no next time, I promise. I can't believe this. I just knew I'd get fired and lose everything."

Mark slid across a sheet of paper and gave him a pen. "This is the order. Sign there on the bottom and you don't have to go back to court."

With a big smile, Benson signed his name. "I can't wait to tell my momma. She's been on my ass ever since I got caught. You know, Mark, she likes you. She said, 'That young man knows his stuff. He's gonna be a great lawyer.'"

"Well, she's obviously very intelligent." Mark took the order and placed it in his briefcase.

Benson took a bite of his sandwich and washed it down with iced tea. He wiped his mouth with a napkin and said, "Say, Mark, do you take other kinds of cases? Big cases?"

"Sure. My firm handles a wide variety of cases. What's on your mind?"

Benson glanced around as if anyone cared. "Well, I got this cousin, he's from down in Virginia, in the Tidewater area, and he's in a mess. You got time for the story?"

"I'm waiting for my lunch," Mark said. "Fire away."

"Well, you see, my cousin and his wife had a baby, sometime back, and things got really messed up at the hospital. It was a bad delivery, everything went wrong, and the baby died two days later. It had gone smooth, the pregnancy, no signs of trouble, you know? Then, all of a sudden, a dead baby. He was their first one, a little boy, and this was after they had tried to get pregnant for a long time. The mother went off the deep end big-time, cracked up, and they started fighting. They were devastated and didn't handle it well. So they split and later divorced. A bad divorce. To this day they're still screwed up. My cousin is drinking too much and she's batshit crazy. A real tragedy, you know? They've tried to find out what happened during the delivery but the hospital won't say much. In fact, the hospital has given them the runaround at every turn. They hired a lawyer to look into it but he wasn't much. Said dead babies aren't worth a lot of money. Said it's tough to sue doctors and hospitals because they have all the records and on top of that they hire the best lawyers to keep you tied up in court forever. She, the mother, said she ain't about to go to court. My cousin still wants to find out what happened and maybe file a suit or something, but he's pretty screwed up too. Is that true, Mark, that dead babies ain't worth much?"

Mark had no idea but was intrigued with the story so far. He managed to demur like a real lawyer with "Depends on the facts of the case. I would need to see the records."

"He's got 'em, a whole stack of paperwork that the hospital gave his lawyer, or I should say his ex-lawyer. He fired the guy and now he says he wants to talk to another lawyer. You think you might want to take a look?"

"Sure."

The BLT arrived, with chips and a pickle but nothing to drink. Mark said to the waitress, "Thanks, but I also ordered a cup of coffee."

"Oh yeah," she said, irritated, and left.

Mark took a bite of the sandwich and Benson did the same. "What's the guy's name?"

Benson wiped his mouth and said, "Ramon Taper, same last name. My dad and his dad are brothers, but neither stayed around. Everybody calls him Digger."

"Digger?"

"Yeah, when he was a kid he took a little spade and dug up a bunch of flowers from a neighbor's backyard. Stole 'em, tried to replant 'em down the street. The nickname stuck."

The coffee finally arrived and Mark said thanks. "Is he trouble?" Mark asked.

Benson laughed and said, "You could say that. Digger's always been trouble. Spent some time in a juvenile facility but he's not a bad dude. No real record. He was doing okay, married a good girl, and they were holding things together all right until the baby died. After the divorce, the mother moved away, some place like Charleston. Digger drifted around and moved here a few months ago. He works part-time in a liquor store, which is the last place he needs to work. Got a thing for vodka. I'm really worried about him."

"So he's here, in the District?"

"Yep, lives around the corner, with another crazy woman."

As Mark crunched on the dill pickle something told him to just say no to Digger and his problems, but he was curious. "I'll take a look."

TWO DAYS LATER, Mark returned to the coffee shop. It was empty but for a skinny little black guy sitting at a table with a thick folder in front of him. Mark walked over and said, "You must be Digger."

They shook hands and Mark sat down. Digger said, "I prefer Ramon. Digger is not the best nickname for a black guy. Obvious reasons."

"Fair enough. I'm Mark Upshaw. Nice to meet you, Ramon."

"Same." He was wearing a driving cap pulled low in the front with the bill resting on a pair of oversized, round, black-framed reading glasses. The eyes behind them were puffy and red.

"Benson says you're a fine young lawyer," Ramon said. "Said you saved his job."

Mark smiled and tried to think of something appropriate when the same waitress appeared. "Black coffee. Ramon?"

"Nothing, just water."

She left and Mark looked at the eyes. His diction was clear enough but he had obviously been drinking. Mark said, "Benson told me a little about the case. Sounds like a real tragedy."

"You could call it that. Something bad happened in the delivery, not sure we'll ever know exactly. I wasn't there."

Mark absorbed this, and when it was apparent nothing else was coming, he said, "Can I ask why you weren't there?"

"Let's just say I wasn't there and I should've been. Asia could never get over that and, of course, I got all the blame. She's always said that if I had been there I could've made sure the hospital was doing things right."

"And Asia is your ex-wife?"

"That's right. You see, she went into labor two weeks early. It was just after midnight and the baby came quick. The hospital was real busy, there had been some shootings and a big car wreck, and, well, we've never really known what happened. But it looks like they neglected her and the baby got stuck coming out. Cut off his oxygen." He tapped the folder. "It's supposed to be in here, but we figure the hospital has covered things up."

"Who's 'we'?"

"The first lawyer, the one I fired. You see, after it all happened, Asia went crazy, kicked me out, and filed for divorce. She had a lawyer, I had a lawyer, things were bad. I got a DUI, so I had another lawyer for that. Lots of lawyers in my life, and I just didn't have the stamina for a big lawsuit." He tapped the folder again.

The coffee arrived and Mark took a sip. "Where is the first lawyer?"

"Norfolk. He wanted $5,000 to pay an expert to review the records. I didn't have $5,000 and I really didn't like the lawyer. He wouldn't return calls and seemed too busy. You gonna want $5,000 too?"

"No," Mark said, but only to prolong the conversation. He had no idea how to proceed with a malpractice case but, as usual, he assumed he could learn on the fly. His plan, if he even had one, was to sign up the case, review the records, and try to determine if there was liability. If so, he would refer the case to a real lawyer who specialized in medical negligence. If the case proceeded, he and his partners would have as little involvement as possible and, hopefully, one day take a slice of a generous fee. Yes, that was the plan.

"And Asia is out of the picture?"

"Oh yes. She's long gone. No contact."

"Will she join the lawsuit if we file one?"

"No, no way. She wants nothing to do with any of it.

She's living down in Charleston with some family and I hope they're trying to help her. She's crazy, Mr. Upshaw. Hearing voices, that kind of crazy. It's pretty sad, but she can't stand the sight of me and has said many times that she'll never go to court."

"Okay, but looking down the road, if there's a settlement, she'll be entitled to half the money."

"Why is that? Hell, it's my lawsuit. Why should she get anything from the case if she wants no part of it?"

"That's the law," Mark said, without a clue. However, something from law school was sticking and he vaguely remembered a case from first-year torts. "Let's worry about that later. Right now we need to proceed with the investigation. Any settlement is way down the road."

"Don't seem right."

"Do you want to proceed?"

"Sure, that's why I'm here. Do you want the case?"

"That's why I'm here."

"Then we got a deal. Now tell me what's going to happen."

"Well, first, you sign a contract for legal services with my firm, which will give me the authority to request all the records. I'll have them reviewed, and if there appears to be clear liability on the part of the doctors and hospital then you and I will have another conversation. We'll decide if we want to file a lawsuit."

"How long will that take?"

Clueless again, Mark said, convincingly, "Not long. A matter of weeks. We don't sit on things, Ramon. We move fast."

"And you don't want any money up front?"

"No. Some firms ask for a retainer or expense money,

but not us. Our contract calls for a contingency of one-third if there's a settlement, 40 percent if we go to trial. These are complex cases that are vigorously defended by folks with plenty of money. So, our cut is a little higher than your average injury case. And, this type of litigation is expensive. We'll front the out-of-pocket money and get repaid at settlement. You okay with that?"

Ramon took a sip of water and gazed through the window. While he pondered things, Mark removed a contract from his briefcase and filled in the blanks. Eventually, Ramon removed his bulky glasses and wiped his eyes with a paper napkin. Softly, he said, "This is so bad, Mr. Upshaw."

"Please, call me Mark."

His lips trembled and he said, "Sure, Mark. We had things going good, me and Asia. Loved that woman, I guess I always will. She wasn't strong but she was a good girl, and a beauty. She didn't deserve this. I guess no one does. We were so ready for Jackie, we had tried for so long."

"Jackie?"

"His name was Jackson Taper, and we were going to call him Jackie. After Jackie Robinson. I like baseball."

"I'm sorry."

"He lived for two days, never had a chance. They screwed him up, Mark. It should not have happened."

"We'll get to the bottom of it, Ramon. I promise."

Ramon smiled, bit his bottom lip, wiped his eyes again, and put on his glasses. He reached for a pen and signed the contract.

AS WAS THEIR habit, the partners met in the late afternoon in the same booth in the rear of The Rooster Bar to recap the daily business. Mark and Todd had beers, Zola a soft drink. After three weeks of practicing law with no authority to do so, they had learned a lot and were somewhat comfortable with their routines; Zola less so than the other two. The fear of getting caught was almost gone, though it would always nag at some level. Mark and Todd were regularly appearing in the criminal courts, same as a thousand other lawyers, and answering the same questions from bored judges. They made quick deals with prosecutors, not a single one of whom seemed the least bit curious about their credentials. They signed their bogus names on orders and other paperwork. They roamed the halls in search of clients, often bumping into other lawyers, all too busy to suspect anything. Despite their fast start, they soon learned that business was not that easy to hustle. On a good day they would rake in $1,000 or so in fees from new clients. On a bad day they would net nothing, which was not unusual.

Zola had narrowed her search to the three busiest hospitals—Catholic, General, and George Washington. She had yet to sign up a single client, but was encouraged by a few near misses. She didn't like what she was doing, preying on the injured, but for the moment she had no choice. Mark and Todd were working hard to support the business. She felt compelled to contribute something.

They debated at length about how often they should be seen hustling potential clients and standing in front of judges. On the one hand, familiarity would give them credibility as they became everyday players in the assembly line. But on the other hand, the more lawyers, prosecutors, clerks, and judges they met, the larger the pool of people who might one day ask the wrong question. And what might that question be? A bored clerk might ask, "What's your bar number again? The one I'm showing is not in the system." There were 100,000 lawyers in the D.C. Bar Council, and each one had a number that had to be added to every order and pleading. Mark and Todd were using fictitious numbers, of course. However, the sheer number of lawyers provided excellent cover, and so far the clerks had shown no interest.

Or a judge might ask, "When were you admitted to the bar, son, haven't seen you around here?" But, so far, no judge had been even remotely curious.

Or an assistant prosecutor might ask, "Delaware Law, huh? I have a friend who went there. Do you know so-and-so?" However, the assistant prosecutors were far too busy and important for such idle chatter, and Mark and Todd kept their conversations brief.

Questions were never feared from the most important folks of all: their clients.

Zola sipped her soda and said, "Okay, I have a confession. I think I've pulled a Freddy Garcia."

"Oh, we gotta hear this," Todd said with a laugh.

"So last night I was at GW, doing my act, and I noticed a young black couple at a table eating one of those dreadful pizzas. She was banged up, plaster here and there, a neck brace, cuts on the face. Had to be a car wreck, right? So I venture over, do my little dance, and they want to talk. Turns out she was hit by a taxi—*ka-ching,* lots of insurance—and their eight-year-old daughter is upstairs in ICU. The case gets better and better. Then they ask me what I'm doing hanging around a hospital cafeteria, and I deliver my lines perfectly. My mother is quite ill, on her last legs, and I'm doing the awful bedside waiting game. I give them my card and we promise to talk later. My phone rings and I scoot away to check on dear old Mom, right? I'm smiling as I leave the hospital because I've finally hooked a big one."

She paused to make them wait, and continued, "Well, this afternoon I get a phone call, not from my brand-new clients, but from their lawyer. Seems as though they've already hired one, a real nasty dude named Frank Jepperson. And, boy, did he have a lot on his mind."

Mark was laughing. Todd said, "You really did it—another Freddy Garcia."

"Yep. He accused me of trying to steal his client. I said no, we were just having a nice little chat as I took a break from sitting with Mom. Really? he asked. Then why did I give them my card? And who the hell is Upshaw, Parker & Lane? Said he'd never heard of them. And so on. I finally hung up. Look, guys, I'm just not cut out for this. You gotta find me another specialty. Some of the cafeteria workers are starting to give me dirty looks."

"You're a natural, Zola," Mark said.

Todd added, "You just need one big case, that's all. We're doing the grunt work for peanuts while you're stalking the big stuff."

"I feel like a stalker. Is there something else I can do?"

"I can't think of anything," Todd said. "You can't hustle the criminal courts like us because it's a boys' game and you'd attract too much attention."

"I'm not doing that either," she said. "You can have it."

Mark said, "I really don't see you as a divorce lawyer. For that you need a real office because divorce clients take up a lot of time and need a lot of hand-holding."

"How do you know that?" Todd asked.

"I went to Foggy Bottom."

"I made an A in Family Law," she said.

"So did I," Todd said. "And I skipped half the classes."

"Can't we rent a nice little office so I can do divorces?"

"Let's talk about it later," Mark said. "I have something that we should discuss. I think I've landed a huge case."

"Do tell," Todd said.

Mark launched into the story of Ramon's lawsuit. At the end, he whipped out a contract for legal services and pointed to the signature at the bottom. "He's all signed up," he said proudly. Todd and Zola examined the contract and thought of a dozen questions.

Zola asked, "Okay, what's next?"

"We need to spend some money," Mark said. "It'll cost us $2,000 to hire a consultant to review the records. I've been looking online and there are plenty of these guys, most are retired doctors, who do nothing but work with law firms and evaluate cases involving medical negligence. There are several here in the District. We spend some cash, get an expert opinion, and if there's liability, then we refer the case to an ace trial lawyer."

"How much do we get?" Zola asked.

"Half the fee. That's how the big tort lawyers operate, by referrals. Grunts like us go out and find the cases, then hand 'em over to the guys who know what they're doing, and then sit back and wait on the money."

Todd was skeptical. "I don't know. If we get involved in a big case, it might blow our cover. If our names are on the pleadings, a lot of people will see them. The trial lawyer, the defense lawyers, the insurance companies, the judge. I don't know. This seems too risky."

"We'll keep our names off the pleadings," Mark said.

"We'll just tell the trial lawyer to keep us out of it. That should work, right?"

"I don't know, Mark," Todd said. "We have no idea what we're getting into here. Plus, I'm not sure I want to fork over two thousand bucks."

"We could Trust Rusty, couldn't we?" Zola asked with a grin.

"Hell no. We'll hire a med mal specialist. There are several here in the District who do nothing but sue doctors and hospitals. Real trial lawyers. Come on, Todd. I don't see much of a risk. We can hide in the background, let someone else do the work, and collect a fat fee."

"How much?"

"Who knows? Say there's gross negligence on the part of the doctors and hospital. Say we settle for $600,000, just to make the math simple. Our cut will be a hundred grand and we've done nothing but hustle the case."

"You're dreaming," Todd said.

"And what's wrong with that? Zola?"

"Everything's risky in this game," she replied. "Every time we stand in front of a judge and pretend to be a lawyer we're taking a chance. I say we go for it."

"Are you in, Todd?" Mark asked.

Todd drained his mug and studied his partners. So far, at least in the brief history of UPL, he had been slightly more aggressive than the other two. Backing down now would show weakness. He said, "One step at a time. Let's see what the consultant says, then go from there."

"Deal," Mark said.

23

Frank Jepperson sat behind his oversized desk and stared at Zola's business card. As a veteran of the personal injury wars in the District, he was quite familiar with her game. In his earlier years, he too had toiled in the vineyards of the city's hospitals, stalking potential clients. He knew all the tricks. He paid kickbacks to tow truck drivers who worked accident scenes. He greased the palms of traffic cops who sent clients his way. Each morning he reviewed police reports looking for the most promising car wrecks. With success, he'd been able to hire a full-time runner, a former cop named Keefe, and it was Keefe who had hustled the family Zola approached in the cafeteria at GW. Jepperson had signed them up fair and square, and now a rookie was trying to poach.

Jepperson's turf was the mean streets of the District, where there were few rules and lots of shady players. However, when possible, he tried to protect his turf, especially when a new player looked suspicious.

Keefe sat across from him, with one ostrich-skin cowboy boot across a knee, and clipped his fingernails.

"And you found this place?" Jepperson asked.

"Yep. On the ground floor there's a joint called The Rooster Bar. The office is two floors above it and no way to get up there. I had a few drinks and chatted with a bartender, who claimed to know nothing. Really clammed up when I asked about Zola Parker."

"And the Bar Council?"

"I checked. No such lawyer on record. Lots of Parkers, but none named Zola."

"Interesting. And the firm—Upshaw, Parker & Lane?"

"Nothing, but then, as you know, law firms change so fast it's impossible to keep up with who's practicing where. The Bar Council says it has a hard time tracking firm names."

"Interesting."

"You want to file a complaint?"

"I'll think about it. Let's see if we run across these clowns again."

ON THE EIGHTH floor of the Foggy Bottom Law School, a junior administrator noticed that three professors had reported that two third-year students, Mark Frazier and Todd Lucero, had skipped all classes for the first four weeks of the spring semester. Both had received their loans for their final semester, but evidently were not bothering with classes. It was not at all unusual for graduating students to mail it in, but cutting all classes for over a month was extreme.

She sent an e-mail to Mr. Frazier. It read,

> Dear Mark: Are you okay? Your complete absence this semester has been noticed and we are concerned.

Please notify me as soon as possible. Faye Doxey,
Assistant Registrar.

She sent an identical note to Todd Lucero. After two days, neither had responded.

ON FEBRUARY 14, Zola eased into the courtroom of the Honorable Joseph Cantu and watched the proceedings. After almost an hour, a clerk called the name of Gordon Tanner. His lawyer, Preston Kline, stood before Judge Cantu and said, "Your Honor, I have not heard from my client in a month. I can only assume he's skipped out."

A clerk handed the judge a note. He read it twice, and said, "Well, Mr. Kline, it appears as though your client is dead."

"Wow, Judge. You sure about that? I had no idea."

"It's been confirmed."

"Oh, well, no one told me. I guess that explains things."

"Wait a minute," Judge Cantu said as he scanned more paperwork. "According to these entries, he died on January 4, a suicide. There's even a story from the *Post*. But he appeared with you right here in front of me on January 17. Can you explain this?"

Kline scratched his jaw as he looked at his copy of the docket. "Well, no, sir, I cannot explain. We were certainly here on the seventeenth, but, frankly, I've had no contact with him since then."

"I guess because he's dead."

"It's all very confusing, Judge. I don't know."

Cantu raised both hands in frustration and said, "Well, if the boy's dead, then I have no choice but to dismiss the case."

"Yes, sir, I guess."

"Next case."

Zola left a few minutes later and reported to her partners.

MARK ENTERED THE office building on Sixteenth Street and took the elevator to the third floor. He found the door for Potomac Litigation Consultants and stepped into the small reception room. A secretary nodded at a couple of chairs and he took a seat. Five minutes later, Dr. Willis Koonce appeared and introduced himself. Mark followed him to a small office down the hall.

Koonce was a retired obstetrician who'd practiced in the District years earlier. According to the website, he had spent the past twenty years as a litigation expert, a professional testifier. He claimed to have analyzed thousands of cases and had been called to the witness stand over a hundred times, in twenty-one states. He almost always worked on the plaintiff's side.

As soon as Mark sat down, Koonce began with "You got 'em by the balls, son. And they're covering up like crazy. Here's my report." He handed over a two-page document, single spaced. "All the technical stuff is in there. I'll save you the time by explaining it in layman's terms. The mother, Asia Taper, was left unattended, for the most part, for a crucial period of time. It's hard to tell how closely she was monitored because there are missing records, but, suffice to say, the FHR—fetal heart rate—decelerated, the uterus ruptured, and there was a significant delay in performing a cesarean section. Without the delay, the baby would have probably been fine. Instead, it sustained what is known as an ischemic insult, or profound brain injury, and as we know died two days later. Death was a good thing; otherwise the child would have lived ten years or so basically as a vegetable, unable to walk, talk, or feed itself. It all could have been prevented by proper monitoring and a quick cesarean. I would classify the negligence as gross, and as you well know, this should make the case easier to settle."

Mark did not know but nodded right along.

"However, as you also know, Virginia cut a deal with the doctors twenty years ago, in the midst of the great tort reform movement, and all damages are capped. The max you can hope to recover is two million bucks. Sad, but true. Had the child lived, the settlement would be much larger. But, it's a Virginia case."

"So we're stuck with two million?" Mark said, as if disappointed with such a paltry sum.

"Afraid so. Are you licensed in Virginia?"

"No, I'm not." Nor anywhere else for that matter.

"Have you handled a med mal case before? I mean, you look pretty young."

"No. I'll refer it. Any suggestions?"

"Sure." Koonce grabbed a sheet of paper and handed it over. "Here's a list of the top D.C. firms for cases like this. All of these guys practice in Virginia; all are good lawyers. I've worked with every one of them."

Mark looked at the names. "Anyone in particular?"

"I'd start at the top with Jeffrey Corbett. He's the best in my book. Handles only ob-gyn cases. He'll scare the hell out of the doctors and they'll settle soon enough."

Two million. A quick settlement. The cash register in Mark's brain was firing away.

Koonce was a busy man. He glanced at his watch and said, "My fee for trial work is $40,000, which covers courtroom testimony. If you and Corbett want to use me, say so as soon as possible. I have lots of cases." He was slowly getting to his feet.

"Sure thing, Dr. Koonce."

They shook hands. Mark gathered Ramon's medical records and hurried away.

LATE THAT AFTERNOON, Zola was alone in the bar, waiting for the daily UPL debriefing. She had spent the day away from the hospitals and felt much better about herself. After weeks of digging, she had finally found the right lawyer in Senegal, in Dakar, the capital. According to the website, Diallo Niang worked in a three-lawyer firm and spoke English, though on the phone he was difficult to understand. He did criminal work, as well as immigration and family matters. For a fee of $5,000, Mr. Niang would represent the interests of Zola's parents and brother when they arrived, though no one had a clue when that might happen. Wiring such a sum to a bank in Senegal made Zola uncomfortable, but under the circumstances she had no choice. Mr. Niang claimed to have plenty of contacts with important people in the government and could help the family reenter the country. Zola had read enough horror stories about the tribulations of deportees upon arriving home, unwanted.

She opened her laptop and checked her e-mails. She was not surprised to see one from the law school. Faye Doxey wrote,

> Dear Ms. Maal: Professors Abernathy and Zaran are reporting that you have not been to class this semester. We are concerned. Could you please call or write and let us know what's going on? Sincerely, Faye Doxey, Assistant Registrar.

She knew, of course, that Mark and Todd had received similar messages and had ignored them. The partners were surprised that anyone at Foggy Bottom was diligent enough to notice. She thought about the e-mail for a moment, then responded:

> Ms. Doxey: I have pneumonia and my doctors insist that I stay in bed and away from everyone. I am monitoring my classes and expect to make a full recovery. Thanks for your concern. I'll be back soon enough. Sincerely, Zola Maal.

The lying still bothered her but it was now a way of life. Virtually everything she did was a lie: the fake name and the fake firm and the fake business cards and the fake persona of a concerned lawyer preying on hapless injury victims. She couldn't continue like this. Could life be any worse if she were still in class and trying to find a real job and worrying about the bar exam and her loans?

Yes, it could. At least she felt safe and beyond the reach of immigration authorities.

The lying continued with the next e-mail. It was from Tildy Carver at LoanAid.

> Dear Ms. Maal: When we last corresponded you had just interviewed with the Department of Justice. Any

> word? You were thinking of going the public service route under the Department of Education's loan forgiveness program. I'm not sure this is best for you. It does require a ten-year commitment, which is a long time. But that decision is yours. Anyway, I would appreciate an update on your employment situation at your earliest convenience. Regards, Tildy Carver, Senior Loan Adviser.
>
> Last installment, January 13, 2014: $32,500; total principal and interest: $191,000.

As always, she stared at the figures in disbelief. The temptation was always to ignore the e-mails for a day or so, but she decided to confront this one head-on.

> Dear Ms. Carver: I didn't get the job at Justice and right now I'm unable to interview anywhere else. I'm currently bedridden with pneumonia and under a doctor's care. I hope to return to classes in a few days and I'll check in then. Sincerely, Zola Maal.

Mark arrived with a big smile and ordered a beer. Todd entered the bar, stopped long enough to get a draft, and joined them. He looked tired and haggard after a long day in the trenches and was in a foul mood. He greeted them with "I just spent eight hours hustling the losers in the courthouse and got nothing. Zero. A big, fat goose egg. And what have the two of you been doing?"

"Relax, pal," Mark said. "Some days are better than others."

Todd gulped his beer and said, "Relax my ass. We've

been doing this crap for a month and it feels like I'm carrying the load here. Let's be honest, two-thirds of the fees are from cases I've hustled."

"Well, well," Mark said, amused. "Our first fight. I suppose it happens with every law firm."

Zola closed her laptop and glared at Todd.

"I'm not fighting," he said. "Just had a bad day."

She said, "As I recall, I was advised to stay away from the criminal courts because it's a boys' game. My part of the scheme is to hang around hospitals and stalk the wounded, the theory being that one of my cases could make up for a bunch of yours. Right?"

"Yes, but you don't have any cases," Todd sneered.

"I'm trying, Todd," she said coldly. "If you have a better idea I'd love to hear it. I really don't like what I'm doing."

"Children, children," Mark said with a grin. "Let's all relax and count our money."

All three took a drink and waited. Mark finally said, "I met with our expert today, the one we paid $2,000, and he says it's a clear case of gross negligence by the doctors and hospital. I have copies of his report for you to read at your leisure. It's beautiful, worth every penny. He says, and this guy is a real professional, that in the hands of the right lawyer the case is worth the max under Virginia law—$2 million. He says the guy to hire is one Jeffrey Corbett, a med mal stud who's gotten rich off suing obstetricians. Office about four blocks from here. I checked him out online and the guy is totally legit. According to an article in a medical magazine, and one not so favorable, Mr. Corbett makes between five and ten million a year." He took another drink. "Does this help your nasty mood, Todd?"

"Yes."

"Thought so. And if you guys agree, I say I call Mr. Corbett and line up an appointment."

"It can't be this easy," Zola said.

"We're just lucky, okay? According to my research, over two thousand ob-gyns get sued every year for all manner of negligence. Lots of bad-birth cases out there, and we've managed to stumble across one."

Todd waved a waiter over and ordered another round.

24

The following Saturday, they left D.C. early in Todd's car and drove two hours to the Bardtown Federal Detention Facility near Altoona, Pennsylvania. From the outside, nothing had changed since their last visit seven weeks earlier. The razor wire glistened in the sunlight. The tall chain-link fencing looked just as foreboding. The parking lot was filled with cars and trucks of the dozens of employees protecting the homeland.

Zola wore a long, loose black dress. As Todd turned off the ignition, she pulled out a hijab and draped it over her head and shoulders. "Such a good little Muslim," Todd said.

"Shut up," she said, and got out.

For the occasion, Mark Upshaw, her attorney, wore a coat and tie. He had called ahead to arrange the meeting, hoping to avoid the drama they had created the last time. Evidently, the paperwork was in order, and they were led to the same visiting room, where they waited half an hour for her parents and brother to be brought in. Zola introduced her friends again and hugged her mother.

They controlled their emotions as Bo, her brother, explained that they had no idea when they would be shipped out. An official had told them that ICE was waiting for enough Senegalese to be processed so the chartered flight would be full. No need to waste any seats for such an expensive trip. A hundred was the number they had in mind, and they were still rounding up illegals.

Bo asked about law school, and the partners agreed that everything was going well. Abdou, her father, patted Zola's arm and said they were so proud of her for becoming a lawyer. Zola smiled and played along. She gave him a note card with the name of Diallo Niang, the lawyer in Dakar, and said that if at all possible he should call her when they were headed for the plane. Zola would immediately call Mr. Niang, who would try to facilitate their arrival. But there were many unknowns.

Zola's mother, Fanta, said little. She held Zola's hand and sat, downcast, sad, and fearful, while the men did the talking. After twenty minutes, Todd and Mark excused themselves and waited in the hall.

When the visit was over, they returned to the car and Zola removed the hijab. She wiped her eyes and said nothing for a long time. When they crossed into Maryland, Todd stopped at a convenience store and bought a six-pack. With the afternoon to kill, they decided to detour through Martinsburg and pay their respects to Gordy. In the public cemetery not far from the church, they found his new headstone, with fresh dirt around it.

ON SUNDAY, MARK borrowed Todd's car and drove home to Dover. He needed to see his mother and have a serious chat but was in no mood to deal with Louie. His situation had not changed and his case was slowly grinding through the system, with a trial date looming in September.

Louie was still asleep when Mark arrived around eleven. "He usually wakes up around noon, in time for lunch," Mrs. Frazier said as she poured fresh coffee at the kitchen table. She wore a pretty dress and heels and smiled a lot, obviously happy to see her favorite son. A pot of stew simmered on the stove and smelled delicious.

"So how's law school?" she asked.

"Well, Mom, that's what I need to discuss," Mark said, eager to get it over with. He told the sad story of Gordy's death and explained how devastating it was. Because of the trauma, he had decided to take the semester off and ponder his future.

"You're not graduating in May?" she asked, surprised.

"No. I need some time, that's all."

"What about your job?"

"It disappeared. The firm merged with a bigger one and I got squeezed in the process. It was a bad firm anyway."

"But I thought you were excited about it."

"I think I was pretending to be excited, Mom. The job market is pretty lousy these days and I grabbed the first offer that came along. Looking back, it was not going to work."

"Oh, dear. I was hoping you might be able to help Louie after you passed the bar exam."

"I'm afraid Louie is beyond help, Mom. They've got him nailed and he's looking at some hard time. Does he talk to his lawyer?"

"No, not really. He's got some public defender who's very busy. I'm so worried about him."

You should be. "Look, Mom, you need to brace yourself for the fact that Louie is going away. They caught him on video selling crack to an undercover cop. There's not a lot of wiggle room."

"I know, I know." She took a sip of coffee and held back tears. Changing the subject, she asked, "But what about your student loans?"

She had no idea how much money Mark owed and he wasn't about to tell her. "I've put them on hold for the time being. No problem."

"I see. So if you're not in school, what are you doing these days?"

"Working here and there, tending bar a lot. And what about you? Surely you don't sit around here all day with him."

"Oh no. I'm working part-time at Kroger and part-time at Target. And when I'm not working, I volunteer at a nursing home. And when I get really bored I go down to the jail and visit the lady prisoners. Jail's just full of them. All drug related, you know. I swear I think drugs will be the ruin of this country. So I keep busy and try to stay away from here."

"What does he do all day?"

"Sleeps, eats, watches television, plays video games. Gripes about his problems. I shamed him into riding my old bike down in the basement but he managed to break it. Says it can't be fixed. I buy him some beer every now and then so he'll shut up. The court order prohibits alcohol but he goes on and on until I buy beer. I figure no one will ever know."

"Have you thought about moving up his court date?"

"Can you do that?"

"I don't see why not. It'll be a plea bargain, Mom. Louie's not going to trial, because he has no defense. He'll get a better deal if he simply pleads guilty and gets it over with."

"But he says he wants to go to trial."

"That's because he's an idiot, okay? If you'll remember, I met with his lawyer when I was home for Christmas. He showed me the file and the video. Louie has convinced himself that he can smile at a jury and con them into believing that the cops entrapped him in a bogus drug deal. He thinks he can walk out of the courtroom a free man. Not going to happen."

"How does a plea bargain work?"

"It's simple. Almost every criminal case is settled with a plea bargain. He admits his guilt, avoids a trial, and the prosecution cuts him some slack on his sentence. He's looking at a max of ten years. I have no idea what a deal might look like, but he could probably get five with time served. With good behavior, crowded jails, and so on, he might be out in three years or so."

"And he wouldn't have to wait until September?"

"I doubt it. With my limited knowledge, I don't see why he couldn't do the deal much sooner than that. That would get him out of the house."

There was the slightest hint of a tiny grin at the corners of her mouth, but only for a second. "I just can't believe this," she said, her eyes drifting away. "He's such a good boy."

Maybe. Louie had flirted around the edges of the drug scene throughout high school. There were plenty of red flags but his parents had always chosen to ignore them. At every sign of trouble, they had rushed in to defend him and believe his lies. They had enabled Louie, and now the bill was due.

Mark knew exactly what was coming next. She looked at him with watery eyes and asked, "Could you talk to his lawyer, Mark? He needs some help."

"No way, Mom. Louie is going to prison and I'm not getting near his case. The reason is simple. I know Louie, and he'll blame everybody but himself. And he'll especially blame me. You know that."

"You've always been so hard on him."

"And you've always looked the other way."

A commode flushed in the back of the house. Mrs. Frazier glanced at the clock and said, "He's up early. I told him you were coming home for lunch."

Louie lumbered into the kitchen with a big smile for his brother. Mark stood, got bear-hugged, and tried to seem happy to see him. Louie resembled a grizzled bear shaken from hibernation: unshaven, matted hair, eyes puffy from too much sleep. He wore an ancient Eagles sweatshirt that was straining around the waist and baggy gym shorts that would fit a nose tackle. No shoes or socks, but the ankle monitor. It was undoubtedly the same outfit he slept in.

Mark almost made a crack about his obvious weight gain, but let it pass.

Louie poured himself some coffee and took a seat at the table. "What are you guys talking about?" he asked.

"Law school," Mark said quickly, before Mrs. Frazier could say something about Louie's case. "I was just telling Mom that I'm taking a semester off. Need some time to readjust. My job disappeared and the market is pretty soft right now, so I'm sort of catching my breath."

"That sounds fishy," Louie observed. "Why would you quit with only one semester to go?"

"I'm not quitting, Louie. I'm postponing."

Mrs. Frazier said, "His best friend committed suicide and this is really bothering him."

"Wow, sorry. But it seems weird to blow off your last semester."

Yes, Louie, but you're hardly in a position to comment on the career paths of others, Mark thought, but was determined to avoid tension. He said, "Believe me, Louie, I have things under control."

"I'm sure you do. Say, Mom, what's in that pot on the stove? Something smells good."

"Beef stew. How about an early lunch?" She was already getting to her feet. As she opened a cabinet, she threw Mark under the bus with "Mark thinks you should consider a plea bargain, Louie. Have you discussed this with your lawyer?"

Great, Mom. Now we can slug it out.

Louie smiled at Mark and snarled, "So you're practicing law now, huh?"

If you only knew. "Not at all, Louie, and I have no advice. Mom and I were just discussing things in general."

"Sure you were. Yes, Mom, I've discussed it with my lawyer, during one of our few conversations. And if I plead guilty, then off I go, with credit for time served, which includes house arrest with my little ankle bracelet. So I could spend the next six months in prison, avoiding gangs, taking cold showers with my back to the wall, eating powdered eggs and stale toast, or I can spend the next six months right here. Not much of a choice is it?"

Mark shrugged as if he had no opinion. The wrong word at this point could ignite something nastier, and he wanted no part of it. Mrs. Frazier was busy placing paper napkins and old silver on the table.

Louie went on, "I'm not pleading guilty, regardless of what the two of you think. I want my day in court. The cops entrapped me and I can prove it to the jury."

Mark said, "Great. I'm sure your lawyer knows what he's doing."

"He knows more about criminal law than you do."

"Of course he does," Mark said.

Louie slurped his coffee and said, "But, I was hoping that after you passed the bar exam this summer you might be able to help a little with my case, maybe sit with me at trial so the jury will think I have two lawyers, you know? I guess that's not going to happen."

"No, it's not going to happen. I'm taking a break."

"That's really weird."

She placed three bowls of steaming beef stew on the table. Louie attacked his as if he hadn't eaten in a week. Mark glared at his mother, then glanced at the clock. He'd been there for forty minutes and couldn't imagine staying another hour.

25

On Monday, March 3, federal agents raided the corporate headquarters of Swift Bank in downtown Philadelphia. The press was tipped off and there was plenty of footage of a small army of men with "FBI" emblazoned on their parkas hauling boxes and computers to waiting trucks. The company issued a statement saying all was well, it was cooperating and all that, while its stock price plummeted.

A business commentator on cable recapped the bank's troubles. Two congressional investigations were underway, along with the FBI's. U.S. Attorneys in three states were preening for the cameras and promising to get to the bottom of things. At least five class action suits were on the books and the lawyers were in a frenzy. More litigation was a certainty. Swift's CEO had just resigned—to spend more time with his family—and took with him about $100 million in stock options, loot that would undoubtedly make all that family time more enjoyable. The CFO was negotiating his exit package. Hundreds of former employees were surfacing, blowing whistles, and suing for wrongful terminations. Old lawsuits against Swift were reexamined and revealed that the bank's bad behavior had been ongoing for at least a decade. Customers were howling and closing accounts. Consumer watchdogs were issuing statements condemning "the most fraudulent banking practices in U.S. history."

Nine percent of Swift's stock was owned by an investment firm in L.A. As its largest stockholder, it had nothing to say. The UPL partners monitored Swift's mess on a daily basis and printed every word they could find about the bank. So far, Hinds Rackley had managed to escape attention.

They decided that with such chaos the time was right to join the fun. Mark contacted a law firm in Miami and signed on as a plaintiff in its class action. Todd called a toll-free number advertised by a law firm in New York and joined its class action. Zola stayed closer to home and joined forces with a D.C. firm well known in the mass tort business.

Within hours of becoming litigants, they were flooded with paperwork being churned out by the lawyers hounding Swift. It was an impressive collection.

According to the latest estimates, there were potentially one million Swift customers who had been subjected to the bank's corrupt practices.

RAMON CALLED EVERY day, even on weekends. He wanted updates on his case, and Mark explained over and over that the initial review, from their "first expert," was positive and they were proceeding as fast as possible. Mark had an appointment with the great Jeffrey Corbett on

Wednesday, March 19, the earliest open date on his packed schedule. Evidently, his trial calendar was something to behold and he hardly had time to consider new cases.

When Ramon called on Tuesday, he dropped the bomb that Asia, his ex, had come to life down in Charleston and was curious about the lawsuit. Mark had little doubt that Ramon, probably under the influence, had tried to impress her with big talk about hiring lawyers to pursue a malpractice case. Mark was certain she would not be a factor.

Mark was wrong. On Wednesday, he received a call from a lawyer in Charleston, a Mr. Mossberg. Since the incoming phone number was unknown, Mark, as always, debated whether to take the call. After five rings he accepted it.

Mossberg began with "I represent Asia Taper, and I understand you represent her ex-husband. That right?"

"That's correct. Ramon Taper is our client."

"Well, you can't sue without her. She was, after all, the mother of the child." Mossberg's tone was aggressive to the point of being confrontational.

Just great, Ramon. There goes a chunk of our fee. Just what we needed—another pushy trial lawyer getting in the way.

"Yes, I understand that," Mark said as he quickly searched for Mossberg online.

"My client says your client has all the medical records. That true?"

"I have the records," Mark said. Edwin Mossberg. Six-man firm specializing in personal injury, downtown Charleston. Forty-five years old. So twenty years in the trenches and far more experienced than anyone at UPL. A big guy, flabby cheeks, full head of gray hair, expensive suit and tie. Biggest victory to date an eleven-million verdict against a hospital in Atlanta. And lots of lesser, though still impressive, verdicts.

"Can you send me a copy of them?" Mossberg practically demanded.

"Sure, no problem."

"So, tell me, Mr. Upshaw, what's been done on the case?"

For the thousandth time Mark pinched the bridge of his nose and asked himself what the hell he was doing. He gritted his teeth and said, "Well, right now the medicals are being evaluated by our expert. Should have a report in a few days."

"Who's the expert?" Mossberg asked, as if he knew every expert in the field.

"We'll talk about him later," Mark said, finding his footing. One asshole to another.

"I'd like to see the report as soon as you have it. There are a lot of bad experts out there, and I happen to know the best. Guy lives at Hilton Head. I've used him several times, with great success I might add."

Oh, please add; would love to hear more about your phenomenal successes. "That's great," Mark said. "Zip me your contract and I'll be in touch."

"Sure. And, Mr. Upshaw, there's no lawsuit without my client, you understand? Asia has suffered greatly because of this, and I'm determined to get every dime of compensation she is entitled to."

Go, Superman! "So am I, Mr. Mossberg," Mark said. "Good day." He ended the call and wanted to throw his phone out the window.

TODD AND ZOLA took the news well. Mark met them for a quick lunch at a restaurant near the District Courthouse, where Todd had just pulled the firm's first double play by signing up two DUIs in one session of court. With $700 of fresh cash in his pocket, he insisted on paying for lunch and planned to take the afternoon off. Though none of the three would admit it, the idea of such a fat, easy fee from Ramon's case was intoxicating. And, it made their lives less urgent. Why bother with hustling the criminal courts and hospitals when serious money was just around the corner? All three were putting in fewer hours and spending less time together. There was no friction; they just needed some space.

The early rush at the District Courthouse provided the richest opportunities. Mark and Todd were usually there at nine going through their routines. Some days were lucky; most were not. After a few weeks at the game, both knew they couldn't last much longer. It was difficult to comprehend how Darrell Cromley and Preston Kline and the real hustlers could spend their careers roaming the hallways, ready to pounce on unsuspecting people. Perhaps they had no real choice; it was the only work for which they were suited. Perhaps it was made easier by the fact that they never feared getting caught without a license.

Zola had given up on chasing ambulances, though she had yet to inform her partners. She had changed and refined and polished her sales pitch a dozen different ways, but had yet to snare a decent client. And she was weary from the effort. It was so deceitful, and every time she zeroed in on some poor, injured soul she felt like a predator. Away from the boys, she was spending more time in federal courtrooms, watching real trials and appellate arguments. She found it fascinating, but also a bit depressing. Not too many years earlier she had started law school with the dream of becoming a real lawyer. Now she could only watch them and wonder what happened.

"Will this Mossberg guy get half the fee?" she asked over lunch.

"I don't know," Mark said. "Like most areas of our practice, this is something new. I suppose the fee split will be decided by him and Jeffrey Corbett."

"Corbett hasn't signed on yet," Todd added.

"No, he hasn't. We see him on the nineteenth."

"We?" Todd asked.

"Yes. I want you to go with me and take notes."

"So, you'll be the trial lawyer and I'll be the paralegal?"

"Junior associate."

"Gee, thanks. What if Corbett says no?"

"We have an appointment two days later with Sully Perlman, the second-best med mal lawyer in town. If Corbett doesn't work out, we go to Perlman. Otherwise, we cancel with Perlman."

"You sound like you know what you're doing," Zola said.

"Have no idea but I'm getting real good at faking things," Mark replied.

Todd asked, "Well, how are you going to fake it when someone in Corbett's firm or Mossberg's firm digs an inch or two just under the surface and realizes that we're not exactly licensed to practice law in the District, or anywhere else for that matter? That's what I don't like about this. We're fairly safe over in the criminal courts because no one seems to notice us anymore and our clients damned sure don't care if we're faking it. But this is something else.

This is big-time litigation where a lot of smart people will be paying attention."

"Agreed," Zola said. "Here's an idea. I have no clue whether it will work, because, hey, we have no clue about anything, right? We're from Foggy Bottom. But let's say that one day the case settles for two million, the max in Virginia. The lawyers get one-third off the top."

Mark held up a hand and said, "Sorry to interrupt, but it'll probably be 40 percent. I've read some cases where 40 percent was approved by the court because there were a lot of lawyers involved and the case was complicated. You can bet Corbett and Mossberg will go for 40 percent. Ramon will have no choice."

She said, "Great, let's say 40 percent. Corbett and Mossberg split evenly, so $400,000 to each firm. We get half of Corbett's, so $200,000 in our direction. Here's the crazy idea: What if we sit down with Corbett and offer to sell him our interest right now, up front, and get out of it before someone gets curious and starts digging?"

"How much?" Mark asked.

"Half. Discount it by half, and we walk off with a hundred thousand." She snapped her fingers. "Just like that. We get our money now, don't have to fool with the case, don't worry about getting caught."

"Brilliant," Todd said. "I like it. Can you sell an interest in a lawsuit?"

"I've looked pretty hard and found no ethical prohibition against it," she said.

Mark said, "Not a bad plan. We can discuss it with Corbett."

MORGANA NASH WITH NowAssist wrote,

Dear Mark Frazier: It's me again, just checking in. How are classes going this semester? Any plans for spring break? I hope you're headed to Florida or a beach somewhere. When we last chatted you were down in the dumps and less than enthused about law school. I hope things are better now. We need to discuss a repayment plan in the very near future. Please drop me a line at your convenience.

Last installment: Jan. 13, 2014 = $32,500. Total due, principal and interest: $266,000.

Sincerely, Morgana Nash, Public Sector Representative

Mark eventually wrote back:

Dear Ms. Nash: In my last e-mail I politely asked you to leave me alone because I'm in therapy and my therapist really doesn't like you. He says that because my loans are so enormous and my debt so suffocating I could be on the brink of a serious emotional breakdown. He says I'm fragile. Please, please go away or I'll have no choice but to ask my therapist to contact your lawyer.

Sincerely, Mark Frazier

Todd heard from Rex Wagner at Scholar Support Partners:

Dear Mr. Lucero: I've had the privilege of helping hundreds of students with their loans, so I've seen it all. It's not uncommon for someone like you—unemployed—to try and ignore me. Sorry, but I'm not going away, nor is your debt. We must talk about a repayment plan, if only to agree that one will be delayed until you find meaningful employment. Please contact me as soon as possible.

Last installment: $32,500, Jan. 13, 2014; total principal and interest: $195,000.

Sincerely, Rex Wagner, Senior Loan Counselor

To which Todd promptly responded,

Dear SS Senior Loan Counselor Wagner: When you feel the trapdoor closing, you think of ways to get out. Desperate ways, one of which is to quit school and go hide. Another is to face default head-on and get it over with. So I go into default? What's the big deal? As I'm sure you know, over a million students defaulted last year. They all got sued but not a single one was executed. So, you can sue me but you can't kill me, right? You can ruin my credit for the rest of my life, but here's the deal: after dealing with you and your company and the law school, I'm done with debt. Finished, forever. I will live the rest of my life debt-free.

Your friend, Todd Lucero

———

TILDY CARVER AT LoanAid sent Zola an e-mail that read,

Hello, Zola. Only two months to go and I know you must be excited about graduation. You deserve it! Your hard work and perseverance have brought you to this point and you are to be commended. Congratulations! I know your family is proud. How about an update on the employment front? We need to talk and begin the process of putting together a rough outline of your repayment plan.

I'm here for you. Sincerely, Tildy Carver, Senior Loan Adviser.

Last installment, January 13, 2014: $32,500; total due: $191,000.

Zola waited a couple of days and finally replied:

Dear Ms. Carver: I'm afraid there's nothing to report. I can't buy a job. I'll keep interviewing until I graduate, and then interview some more. If my bad luck continues, I'll probably get a job with an accounting firm. If so, I'll let you know immediately.

All best, Zola Maal

26

Jeffrey Corbett's firm occupied the top two floors of a handsome glass building near Thomas Circle. In the plush lobby, a uniformed doorman escorted Mark and Todd to "Mr. Corbett's elevator," an exclusive lift that serviced only floors seven and eight. When it opened, they walked into a stunning reception area filled with minimalist furniture and contemporary art. A comely young lady greeted them with handshakes and asked if they wanted coffee. Both watched her walk away. When she was back with the coffee, in fine china, they followed her around a corner to a conference room with a sweeping view of downtown. She left them there, and they watched her walk away for the second time.

The table was long and wide and covered with burgundy leather. Sixteen sleek leather chairs were around it. The walls held even more art. So far, the place had the seductive feel of serious success and wealth.

"Now, this is how you practice law," Todd said, admiring the decor.

"Well, we'll never know."

Mr. Corbett had his own way of doing things. At 3:00 p.m., Mark and Todd would meet with an associate named Peter and a paralegal named Aurelia. They would spend an hour or so reviewing Ramon's stack of medical records, along with the report from Dr. Koonce. The records and the report were still in Mark's briefcase. He had offered to send them over but that was not their protocol.

If the preliminary meeting went well enough, then Mr. Corbett would tear himself away from his schedule and close the deal.

Peter walked in and introduced himself. He was about thirty-five, still an associate according to the website. The firm had fifteen lawyers, about half of them partners, but it was clear, at least online, that there was only one boss. Peter was dressed casually in an expensive cashmere sweater and khaki pants. Aurelia, the paralegal, wore jeans. Everyone got themselves properly introduced.

Peter was curious about their firm, and within seconds both Mark and Todd were treading water. They gave their usual spiel—three friends who got fed up with the bigger firms and decided to make a go of it on their own. As soon as possible, Mark said, "So you guys do a lot of bad-birth cases, right?"

"That's all we do," Peter said smugly as Todd passed across copies of the report from Dr. Koonce. Aurelia had yet to speak and it was already obvious she would say as little as possible.

"May I see the medical records?" Peter asked, staring at them on the table in front of Mark.

"Certainly."

"You brought how many copies?"

"Just one."

"Okay. Mind if we run another copy real quick? Aurelia and I will skim through these and make notes. It goes faster if we both have a copy."

Mark and Todd shrugged. Whatever.

Aurelia left with the records. Peter left to tend to pressing matters in his office. Mark and Todd checked their phones and enjoyed the view of the city. Ramon had already left two voice mails.

Fifteen minutes later, Aurelia was back with two stacks of records. Peter returned and everyone took their seats. Peter said, "This might take an hour or so, for the first read-through. You're welcome to stay or you can go out for a walk."

Todd wanted to ask if he could go sit with the secretary out front, but let it pass. Mark said, "We'll stay."

Peter and Aurelia began plowing through the records and making dozens of notes. Todd stepped into the hallway to make a call. Mark sent e-mails from his phone. The minutes passed slowly. It was obvious to them that Peter and Aurelia knew a lot about medical records.

After half an hour, Peter left the conference room. He returned with Jeffrey Corbett, a slim gray-haired man of about fifty. Mark and Todd had read so much about him they felt as if they already knew him. He spoke in a rich, velvety voice, one that jurors supposedly found almost hypnotic. His smile was warm and charismatic. This was a man you could trust.

He took a seat at the head of the table and stopped smiling. He frowned at Mark and Todd and said, "You guys have really screwed up."

Mark and Todd stopped smiling too.

Corbett said, "You signed a contract with Mr. Ramon Taper on February 10. You hired Dr. Koonce two days later, and on February 19 he gave you his report, dated on that day. Six days later, February 25, the statute of limitations expired. It's a Virginia case, and Virginia has a two-year statute of limitations. Three in Maryland, five here in the District. But only two in Virginia."

Mark managed to say, "Sorry, but the delivery was last year, February 25, 2013. It's right there on the top page of the admissions log."

Looking down his nose, Peter replied, "Yes, but that date is incorrect. It's the first date you see when you look at the records, and evidently it was the only date you noticed. You and Dr. Koonce, I presume. Someone wrote '2013' instead of '2012,' and off you went. The baby was born on February 25, 2012."

For no apparent benefit, Corbett added, "Koonce is a quack, by the way, a professional testifier because he couldn't make it as a real doctor."

Well, he gave us your name, Mark almost blurted, but was too stunned to say anything. With all of the wonder and ignorance of a first-year law student, Todd looked at Corbett and asked, "So, what are you saying?"

Corbett jabbed a finger in his direction. "I'm saying, son, that you and your little law firm sat on the case while the statute of limitations ran out, and there's no way to revive this lawsuit. You committed malpractice, and you can bet your sweet ass you'll get sued by your client. You have no defense, no way out. It's a lawyer's worst nightmare and it's inexcusable. Period. Yes, your client sat on his case for almost two years, but that's not all that unusual. You had plenty of time to prepare and file a quick lawsuit to stop the clock. That didn't happen." Corbett rose to his feet and kept pointing. "Now, I want the two of you to take these medical records and get out of my office. I want no part of this. The record is clear that you contacted my office February 27, after the statute of limitations had expired. When the lawsuit lands, there can be no doubt that my firm did not see this case until it was too late."

Peter and Aurelia stood too. Mark and Todd looked up at them, then slowly got to their feet. Mark managed to mumble, "But the admissions records say it was last year, 2013."

Corbett was unsympathetic. "If you had studied the records, Mr. Upshaw, you would have realized it happened in 2012, *over* two years ago."

With a bit of drama, Peter slid the original records across the table, as if surrendering the smoking gun. Mark looked at them, bewildered, and asked, "So what do we do now?"

Corbett said, "I have no advice, never been in this spot before. But I suppose you should notify your errors-and-omissions carrier, put them on notice. What's your coverage?"

Errors and what? Coverage? Mark looked at Todd, who was already looking at him; both were thoroughly stupefied. "I'll have to check," Mark said, still mumbling.

Corbett said, "You do that. Now please leave and take your records with you."

Peter walked to the door and opened it. Mark picked up the stack of records and followed Todd out of the room. Someone slammed the door behind them. The comely secretary was not at her desk on the way out. The oak-paneled elevator seemed stuffier on the ride down. The doorman wasn't as friendly as they left the building. Not a word passed between them until they were safely locked in Todd's car, with Ramon's medical records flung across the backseat.

Todd gripped the wheel and said, "Well, that's the last case we refer to that prick."

From somewhere, Mark found humor and began laughing. To keep from crying, Todd laughed too, and they managed to keep it going until they parked behind The Rooster Bar.

ZOLA FOUND THEM in their booth, empty mugs on the table. One look into their eyes and she knew they had been there for a spell. She slid into a spot next to Mark and looked across at Todd. Neither spoke. She finally asked, "Okay, how'd it go?"

Todd asked, "You ever heard of errors-and-omissions insurance? For lawyers?"

"Don't think so. Why?"

Mark said, "Well, it appears as though every lawyer with a license carries malpractice insurance that's commonly referred to as errors-and-omissions. And this insurance comes in handy when the lawyer screws up and does something really bad like sit on a case until the statute of limitations runs out and the case evaporates, forever. The client gets pissed off and sues the lawyer, and the lawyer's insurance company comes in to defend. It's really smart insurance."

"Too bad we don't have any of it," Todd said.

"We could sure use it. We missed the statute of limitations, Zola, in Ramon's case. It ran out on February 25, two years after the baby died. Two years in Virginia. Did you learn that in law school?"

"No."

"That makes three of us. Six days after I met with Koonce and two days before I made the first call to Corbett, the statute ran out. There's no way around it, and there's no one to blame but me."

"Us," Todd said. "The firm. All for one and one for all, right?"

"Not so fast," she said.

Mark added, "Actually, a couple of his flunkies saw it when they were going through the records. They fetched him; he said get out. I thought at one point he might call security to escort us from the building."

"A real charmer, huh?"

"Can't blame him," Todd said. "He's just making sure his firm is off the hook. It's not every day that a couple of bozos walk in with a big case that's already dead and they're too stupid to know it."

She nodded and tried to absorb it all. Mark waved at a waiter and ordered another round.

Zola asked, "So how did Ramon take the news?"

Mark grunted, smiled. "I haven't called him yet. I think you should do it."

"Me!? Why?"

"Because I'm a coward. And you could pull it off. Meet him for a drink. Turn on the charm. He'll be impressed and maybe he won't sue us for $5 million."

"You are kidding," she said.

"Yes, Zola," Mark said. "I'm kidding. This one is on me. I'll eventually meet with Ramon and somehow get through it. The real problem, though, is Mossberg. He's sitting by the phone waiting to hear what our expert says. At some point, and soon, I have to tell him the truth. The lawsuit is gone for good. He'll sue us on behalf of Asia, and our cover will be blown. Simple as that."

"Why would he sue if we have no insurance and no assets?" she asked.

"Because he's a lawyer. He sues everybody."

Todd said, "Wait a minute. That's a very good question. What if we simply go to Mossberg and tell the guy the truth? He's way down in Charleston and couldn't care less about what we're doing up here. Tell him we dropped out of law school and we're trying to make a buck on the streets, without being properly admitted to the bar. Sure we screwed up his case, and we're very sorry about that. Just a bunch of idiots, right? But why sue us when we have nothing? Why waste the paper? Hell, he's got plenty of other cases."

"Okay, you drive to Charleston," Mark said. "My Bronco won't make it."

"What do you tell Ramon?" she asked.

The waiter placed two beers and a soda on the table. Mark took a long drink and wiped his mouth. "Ramon? Well, I suppose telling him the truth might be disastrous, so let's stick with the lying for now. I'll tell him our expert didn't like the facts, couldn't see any liability, and so we're looking for another expert. We need some time here, so let's stall him. Let a few months pass. Keep in mind he's been sitting on the case for two years and he runs hot and cold."

"He won't back off now," Todd said. "You've managed to get him excited."

"You got a better idea?"

"No, not at the moment. It's best to keep lying. With our practice, when in doubt—keep lying."

27

On Friday, March 21, two days after the beginning of the end of UPL, Edwin Mossberg called twice before noon. Mark ignored both calls. He was hiding in the upstairs coffee bar of an old, cramped used-book store near Farragut Square, reading the complimentary daily newspapers and killing time. Todd was supposedly stalking the halls at the District Courthouse while Zola was supposedly camping out in a hospital prayer room where families huddled with ministers. However, Mark seriously doubted either of the other two was hard at work. Their dream of a big, easy score had eased the pressure and lulled them into a false sense of security.

Now that the dream had vanished so dramatically, they were reeling. They had agreed that it was imperative to double down and rake in as much cash as possible before the sky fell, but failure killed their motivation.

Mossberg's e-mail hit like a bomb.

> Mr. Upshaw: I've called twice but no answer. Are you on top of the statute here?? My client is not sure of the

delivery date but thinks it was around this time of the year, late February or early March 2012. Again, we don't have the medical records. Virginia has a two-year statute, courtesy of tort reform, and I'm sure you're aware of this. Please call as soon as possible.

INCLUDING THE EXPENSE money so generously lent by the Department of Education, along with the fees they'd hustled in almost two months of unauthorized practice, minus outlays for a new desktop computer and printer, and new clothes, and old furniture, and food, the balance sheet of Upshaw, Parker & Lane showed net cash of almost $52,000. The three partners agreed that the firm could afford the round-trip airfare to Charleston.

Mark bought the ticket at Reagan National, flew the first leg to Atlanta and the second to Charleston. He took a cab from the airport to an old downtown warehouse that Mr. Mossberg and company had converted into a splendid office with views of the harbor. The lobby was a museum dedicated to the courtroom heroics of the firm's trial studs. Its walls were covered with framed newspaper stories detailing victories and massive settlements. In one corner a water heater was on display, one that had once blown up and killed some folks. Near a window a hunting rifle was mounted next to an X-ray of a firing pin in someone's head. A chain saw here, a lawn mower there. After ten minutes amid the carnage, Mark was convinced that no product was safe.

As with Corbett's operation, Mossberg's reeked of easy millions and phenomenal success. How had some lawyers managed to strike it so rich? Where did Mark's legal career take a left turn and fall off the rails?

An assistant fetched him and led him up the stairs to a massive office where Edwin Mossberg was standing in front of a tall window, looking at the harbor and listening on the phone. He frowned at Mark and motioned for him to sit on a thick leather sofa. The office was larger than the entire fourth floor where Mark and Todd were currently hiding.

Mossberg finally stuck his phone in his pocket, thrust forward a hand, and without a smile said, "Nice to meet you. Where are the medical records?"

Mark had arrived with nothing, not even a briefcase.

"Didn't bring them," he said. "We need to talk."

"You missed the statute, right?"

"Right."

Mossberg sat on the other side of a coffee table and glared at him. "Figured as much. What did your expert say?"

"Said we had 'em by the balls. Gross negligence, the works. He missed the date too, Corbett said he was a quack, and the statute ran out six days later, two days before I made the first call to Corbett's office."

"Jeffrey Corbett?"

"Yes. Know him?"

"Oh yes. He's a fine trial lawyer. So you just left two million on the table."

"I suppose."

"What are the limits of your liability?"

"I have no insurance."

"You're practicing law with no errors-and-omissions coverage?"

"That's correct. I'm also practicing law without a license."

Mossberg took a deep breath and exhaled loudly in a rasping, almost growling sound. He flopped his hands and said, "Just tell me the story."

In ten minutes Mark covered it all. Three good friends in a bad law school. Heavy debts, soft job market, Gordy and the bridge; the horror of the bar exam; the insanity of repayment; the crazy idea to hustle the criminal courts; a fine romp with a cute assistant prosecutor that led to a great deal for Benson that led to the referral to Ramon. And here we are.

"And you thought you wouldn't get caught?" Mossberg asked.

"We haven't been caught. Only you know, and why should you care? You have enough cases to keep you busy. You have more money than you can spend. You're a long way from D.C. and we're not exactly taking fees out of your pocket."

"Except for this little med mal case."

"True. We screwed it up. But let's not forget the fact that your client and my client sat on the case until the very end."

"What will you tell your client?"

"That there's no liability, and there's not. Maybe he'll go away; maybe he'll cause trouble. We'll wait and see. Looks like you have the same problem."

"Not really. I don't have a signed contract with Asia. In med mal, son, you never sign a contract for representation until you've reviewed the medical records. Chalk that up to something else you haven't learned."

"Thanks. What will you tell her?"

"I don't know. I haven't thought about it. She's not the most stable person in town."

"You could tell the truth and sue me on her behalf, but why bother? I don't have a dime and I'll just bankrupt any judgment. Honestly, you couldn't even find me in D.C. if you wanted to. Others are looking."

"Is Mark Upshaw your real name?"

"No."

"And Parker and Lane?"

"Bogus."

"No surprise. We couldn't find any record of you and your firm in the D.C. bar directory. You're leaving a pretty wide trail, son."

"Did you call anyone there?"

"I don't think so. One of my paralegals dug a little."

"I'd appreciate it if you wouldn't dig anymore. I've told you the truth."

"So, allow me to summarize. You dropped out of law school, assumed another name, and you're practicing law without a license, which is a crime, and taking your fees in cash, without proper reporting, I assume, which is also a crime, and now you've ruined a beautiful med mal case that cost your client and my client more money than they'll ever see. Not to mention defaulting on your student loans. Have I missed anything?"

"Maybe a couple of items."

"Of course. And so what am I supposed to do?"

"Nothing. Let it slide. Ignore me. What do you have to gain by reporting me to the D.C. Bar?"

"Well, for one, it would be a nice step in the direction of cleaning up our profession. We have enough problems without deadbeats like you scamming the system."

"I could argue that we provide valuable services to our clients."

"Ramon Taper?"

"No, not him. The other guys. Ramon was our first venture into the minefield of personal injury law, and, frankly, I think we've had enough. We'll stick to DUIs and leave the car wrecks to the guys on the billboards."

"That's good to hear."

"I'm begging for a favor, Mr. Mossberg. Just leave us alone. Things are tough enough anyway."

"Get out of my office," Mossberg said, standing.

Mark rolled his eyes as his shoulders sagged. Under his breath he mumbled, "I think I've heard that before."

Mossberg walked to the door and yanked it open. "Out!"

Mark strolled through the opening, avoided eye contact, and found the stairs.

HIS RETURN FLIGHT was delayed in Atlanta, and it was almost midnight when Mark arrived at his apartment. The delay possibly kept him from getting shot, or something close to it.

Around nine that night, Ramon found The Rooster Bar and parked himself at the long counter. Todd was behind the bar mixing drinks. The after-work crowd had cleared and half a dozen regulars were watching college basketball.

Ramon ordered a vodka tonic and Todd placed it before him with a small bowl of peanuts. "You know this dude?" Ramon asked, showing Todd the business card of one Mark Upshaw of the firm of Upshaw, Parker & Lane. Address right there, right where he was sitting: 1504 Florida Avenue.

Todd looked at it and shook his head. He and Mark had convinced the other bartenders and waiters to play completely dumb if anyone showed up asking questions about them, their firm, or their offices. So far, the little conspiracy was holding.

Ramon said, "Dude's my lawyer, and his card says his office is right here, but this is a bar, right?" His tongue was a bit thick, some of his words not so clear.

Todd was suddenly captivated by his customer and wanted to know more. "He might be upstairs. Don't know what all's up there, but you won't find a lawyer working at this time of night."

"Dude's running from me, you know what I mean? Been calling him for three days now and he won't answer."

"He must be busy. What kinda case you got?"

"Big one." He closed his eyes and nodded, and Todd realized he was drunker than he'd thought.

Todd said, "Well, if I bump into him, what do I say? Who's looking for him?"

"Name's Ramon," he said, barely lifting his head. He had yet to touch his drink.

Todd took a deep breath and eased away. He stepped into the kitchen and sent a text to Mark. *Our client Ramon is here, drunk. Stay away. Where r u?*

Atlanta airport, delayed.

Call him and feed him a line. Something.

Will do.

Todd returned to the bar and stood a few feet from Ramon, who made no effort to pull out his phone. If Mark was calling, Ramon wasn't responding. Still holding the business card, he waved Todd over and said, "This say Florida Avenue, right? So where's the law office?"

"Don't know, sir."

"I think you're lying," Ramon said, louder.

"No, sir. You're right, this is Florida Avenue, but I don't know of any law office."

Even louder, Ramon said, "Well, I got a gun in my car, you know that? And if I can't get justice one way, I might just get it another. Know what I mean?"

Todd nodded at another bartender as he stepped closer to Ramon. "Look, sir, if you're going to threaten folks we'll have no choice but to call the police."

"I gotta find this dude, okay? Mr. Upshaw, Attorney-at-Law. He's got my case and I think he's running from me. And don't go calling no police, okay?"

"Why don't you finish your drink and I'll call you a cab?"

"Don't need a cab. Got a car out there with a gun under the seat."

"That's the second time you've mentioned a gun. That makes us very nervous around here."

"Just don't call no police."

"They've already been called, sir."

Ramon's back stiffened and his eyes popped wide open. "What? Why'd you do that? I ain't hurt nobody."

"Sir, we take gun talk seriously in this city."

"How much is the drink?"

"It's on the house if you want to hustle on out of here."

Ramon slid off the stool and said as he headed for the door, "Don't know why you had to call the police." Todd followed him outside and watched him disappear around the corner. If he had a car, Todd didn't see it.

28

Late on a Saturday morning, Todd woke up in the bed of Hadley Caviness, for the second night in a row, and realized she was missing. He rubbed his eyes, tried to remember how much he'd drunk, and decided it wasn't much at all. He felt great and enjoyed the extra hour of sleep. She returned, in nothing but a large T-shirt, with two cups of coffee. They propped up pillows and sat in the darkness.

There was movement in the next room, a rattling sound as if a bed was shaking. Then the muted groans of pleasure.

"Who's that?" he whispered.

"My roommate. She came in late last night."

"Who's her buddy?"

"Don't know. Probably just some random guy."

"So she's into the random stuff as well?"

"Oh yes. We're sort of having a contest. A numbers game."

"I like it. Do you count me once or twice?"

Hadley took a sip of coffee, and they listened as things intensified. "I get one point for you, one for your partner."

"Oh, so Mark's been here?"

"Nice try. I saw you guys talking in court the other day while you looked me over. I could almost read your lips. Sure enough, you walked in the next day all smiles."

"I confess. Mark said you're great in bed."

"Is that all?"

"Great body, very aggressive. Now I know why. You and your roomie are keeping score."

"We're both twenty-six years old, single with no desire to try the monogamy thing, and we're free and loose in a city with about a million young professional men. It's become a sport." The male partner reached the summit as the floor shook, then the bed stopped rattling.

"That was too fast," Hadley said. Todd cracked up and said, "So you compare notes?"

"Absolutely. We have a ball debriefing, especially after she's been out of town all week and sleeping with all kinds of men."

"I don't want to know my scouting report."

"I have an idea. There's a bagel shop just around the corner. Let's get out of here and find something to eat. I have far better taste in men than she does and I really don't want to meet her latest stranger."

"Thanks, I guess."

"Let's go."

They dressed quickly and eased out of her apartment without confronting the other pair. The bagel shop was packed with the weekend crowd. They found a table by the door and wedged themselves into the chairs. As they crunched on toasted bagels, Todd said, "You know, you're too cute to be sleeping with half the town."

She looked around. "Not so loud, okay?"

"I'm practically whispering."

"What, you want to settle down and get married or something?"

"Not quite ready for that. It just seems odd that a knockout like you is so into the random game."

"That's chauvinistic. It's okay for you to hook up every night, but if a cute girl does it then she's nothing but a slut."

"I didn't call you a slut."

A guy at the next table glanced over. Hadley took a sip of coffee and said, "Let's talk about something else. I'm intrigued by your little law firm. I've met you and Mark Upshaw. Who is Zola Parker?"

"A friend."

"Okay. Does she hustle the criminal courts like you and Mark?"

"Oh no. She does personal injury." Todd kept his answers short and wanted to change the topic.

"Does she have a license to practice law?"

Todd chewed on his bagel and studied her beautiful eyes. "Of course."

"Well, I got curious and checked with the Bar Council. Seems they haven't heard of you, Mark, or Ms. Parker. You guys need to sign up. And the bar numbers you're using are not in their data bank."

"Their records are notoriously sloppy."

"Oh really. Never heard that."

"Why are you so curious?"

"My nature. You say you went to law school at Cincinnati. Mark studied at Delaware. I checked with both schools and they've never heard of you. Zola claims to have a law degree from Rutgers but somehow she slipped through the cracks of their alumni association." Hadley was talking with a nasty, know-it-all smile.

Todd managed to eat with an unconcerned air. "You are quite the stalker, aren't you?"

"Not really. It's none of my business. Just seems odd."

Todd smiled while at the same time wanting to slap the smile off her face. "Well, we're hiring if you ever get tired of the prosecutor's routine."

"I'm not sure we'd get much work done around the office. You do have an office, don't you? I know you have an address, but anybody can claim a street number."

"What are you getting at?"

"Nothing. Just curious."

"Have you shared your curiosity with anyone else?"

"No. I doubt if anyone else has noticed. You've picked the perfect place to practice, with or without a license. It's a zoo and no one cares. However, just a bit of advice, I'd stay away from old Witherspoon in Division 7. He's nosier than most judges."

"Thanks. Anyone else to avoid?"

"Not really. Just don't avoid me. Now that I'm onto your little scam, I'll help when I can."

"You're a doll."

"That's what they all say."

MARK WAS SERVING drinks at The Rooster Bar when Todd rolled in at noon. Todd punched the clock, put on his official red apron, and filled a few mugs. At the first opportunity, he pulled his partner aside and said, "Houston, we have a problem."

"Only one?"

"I was with Miss Hadley again last night."

"You dog. I was out looking for her."

"I found her first. Had a little chat this morning over breakfast. She's onto our scam, knows we're not licensed, checked with the Bar Council. She knows where we didn't go to law school."

"Damn it."

"My first reaction too. However, she might be cool, says she hasn't told anyone and likes to keep secrets. Even offered to help when possible."

"What does she want?"

"More of the same, I think. She and her roommate are really into the random hookup game. It's all about numbers."

Mark managed a laugh, but it wasn't because of anything humorous. "Wonder if they're busy tonight."

"I'll bet they are, with someone else."

Mark said, "Shit!" and walked away to take an order. Todd was drying beer mugs when he brushed by and said, "This feels like the beginning of the end."

LATE SUNDAY NIGHT, Ramon Taper was arrested for driving under the influence. He was taken to Central Jail, where he spent the night in the drunk tank. Monday morning, his girlfriend arrived to check on him. As she waited, she met one Darrell Cromley, a friendly lawyer who seemed right at home in the waiting room at Central. In short order, Cromley arranged for Ramon to be released on a recognition bond. Outside the jail, as Darrell was going through his standard routine of explaining what was next, Ramon said, "Say, man, I got a lawyer but he's trying to dodge me."

"A lawyer for what?" Darrell said, pouncing.

"I got a big case down in Virginia, medical malpractice. My little baby died at the hospital a couple of years back and I hired this crook named Mark Upshaw. Ever hear of him?"

"No, but there's a lot of lawyers around here you can't trust."

"He ain't much, I tell you. I need to fire him but I can't find him. You do medical malpractice?"

"It's one of my specialties. Tell me about the case."

29

Two days later, Mark was sitting in the courtroom of the Honorable Fiona Dalrymple, waiting for a client who would plead guilty to shoplifting. As usual, he pretended to review an important document while watching the lawyers come and go as their cases were called. It was a zoo all right, with the monkeys firmly in control. Some of the faces were familiar, others he'd never seen before, and once again he marveled at the number of lawyers it took to keep the wheels of justice churning along. A blast from the past appeared in a hideous suit and scanned the courtroom, the way all lawyers did when they wanted to be seen. He walked through the bar, chatted with an assistant prosecutor who looked around, saw Mark, and nodded.

Darrell Cromley walked over and sat down next to Mark. He thrust over a business card and said softly, "I'm Darrell Cromley, and you're Mark Upshaw, right?"

We've met before, Mark thought, and this cannot be good. "That's right."

"I've been hired by Ramon Taper. Let's step outside and talk."

Mark glanced at his business card. Darrell Cromley, Personal Injury. He specifically remembered that his other card was for Darrell Cromley, DUI Specialist. Darrell must be a man of many talents.

In the hallway, Darrell was all business as he delivered the dreaded news. "My firm has been hired by Mr. Taper, who had the misfortune of getting picked up while driving under the influence."

So that's the connection. Cromley froze and looked at Mark closely. "Have we met before? You sure look familiar."

"Haven't had the pleasure. There are a lot of lawyers around here."

"I guess so," Darrell said, still not convinced. He whipped out some paperwork from his battered briefcase and handed it to Mark. "Here's a copy of our contract with Mr. Taper, along with a letter from him terminating your representation. We've spent the last two days investigating his med mal case down in Virginia, and it seems as though the statute of limitations has expired. You're aware of that, right?"

"Sure. We looked at the case and had it reviewed by a doctor. He said there's no negligence. It's a dead end." Mark felt a slight weakness in his knees as his heart pounded away.

"Well, it's certainly dead now that the statute has run. Did you guys file a quickie lawsuit to toll the statute?"

"Of course not. There's no liability. A lawsuit is a waste of time."

Darrell shook his head, frustrated, as if he were dealing with an idiot. Mark wanted to hit him but thought better of it. A veteran street hustler like Cromley was probably a pretty fair brawler himself.

"We'll see about that," Cromley said like a real tough guy. "First, I want the medical records. I'll have them reviewed by a real expert, and if there's even a hint of liability, then your goose is cooked, pal."

"It's a dead end, Darrell."

"If I were you, I'd put my errors-and-omissions carrier on notice."

"So you'd sue another lawyer?"

"Damned right, if the facts are there. I've done it before and I'll do it again."

"I'm sure you would."

"Send the records over, okay?"

At that moment, a frightened young woman approached them and asked, "Say, are you guys lawyers?"

Mark was too paralyzed to speak. Darrell, though, was quick on the draw. With his frown, he said, "Sure, what's the problem?"

Mark backed away and left them to their business.

AT THE ROOSTER BAR, the partners huddled in a booth, as far away as possible from the late afternoon crowd. Mark had just finished his Cromley story and they were deflated. Zola asked, "So what happens next?"

Mark said, "Let's assume the worst. The likeliest scenario is that Cromley looks at the medical records, which I can delay for a few days but he's not going away, and then he has them reviewed by another expert. If liability is as clear as Koonce says it is, Cromley will know before long that Ramon and his ex-wife had a damned good case.

Since he can't sue the doctors and the hospital, he'll have no one to come after but us. So he'll file a $10 million lawsuit against our little firm and then the fix is in. At some point, and we can't predict exactly when, we'll be exposed. He'll check with the Bar Council and learn the truth. The Bar Council will then notify the courts and start an investigation. Our names are on dozens of court orders, so it won't take long to piece things together."

"And this will be a criminal investigation?" Zola said.

"Yes, we knew when we started that unauthorized practice is a crime. Not a serious one, but a crime nonetheless."

"But a felony, as opposed to a misdemeanor."

"A felony."

Todd said, "There's something else, Zola. We were going to tell you but just didn't get the chance."

She said, "Can't wait. Let's hear it."

Mark and Todd exchanged looks, and Todd began, "Well, there's this cute little prosecutor in Division 10, name of Hadley Caviness. Mark met her in a bar a few weeks back and they hooked up. Evidently, she hooks up a lot and likes variety. I met her in court one day, one thing led to another, and we had some fun. Twice. Over a bagel the morning after she lets me know that she's onto our little fake firm. She says she's cool, thinks it's funny, likes to keep secrets, and so on, but in this business you can't trust anyone."

"Especially fake lawyers," Zola said. "I thought we agreed to limit our contact with others."

"I tried," Mark said.

"She's very cute," Todd added.

"Why haven't you told me before now?"

"It just happened last weekend," Mark said. "We think she's harmless."

"Harmless?" Zola said, rolling her eyes. "So, we have cute little Hadley to think about and Darrell Cromley to actually worry about."

"And don't forget Mossberg down in Charleston," Mark said. "He's an ass and he'd love nothing more than to burn us."

"Brilliant," she said. "After three months in business, Upshaw, Parker & Lane is going under." She took a sip of her soft drink and looked around the bar. Nothing was said for a long time as the three licked their wounds and pondered their next moves. Finally, she said, "Signing up the med mal case was a bad move, wasn't it? We had no idea what to do with it, and we really screwed it up. A disaster for us, but think about Ramon and his ex-wife. They get nothing because of us."

"They sat on the case for two years, Zola," Mark said.

Todd said, "We can rehash this forever and get nowhere. We need to focus on tomorrow."

Another long gap in the conversation. Todd walked to the bar, got two more beers, and returned with them to the table. He said, "Think about this. When Cromley sues us for legal malpractice, the named defendants will be Todd Lane, Mark Upshaw, and Zola Parker. Three people who do not exist. How can he discover our true identities?"

Zola said, "And we're assuming cute little Hadley does not know our real names either, right?"

"Of course not," Mark said.

"And Mossberg?"

"He has no clue."

"So, we have to either hide or run," she said.

"We're already hiding," Todd said. "But they'll find us. Hell, if Ramon can get this close, I'm sure professional investigators can track us down. Our address is on at least a million of those business cards we've been throwing at people."

"Nothing will happen fast," Mark said. "It'll take Cromley a month or so to file a lawsuit. We'll know when he does because we'll be watching the dockets. Then he'll realize he's sued some people who don't exist, and that'll screw him up for even longer. The Bar Council will chase its tail looking for three phantom lawyers."

Todd said, "I guess we need to stay away from the criminal courts."

"Oh, yes. Those days are over. No more hustling the poor and oppressed."

"What about our pending cases? We can't just drop these people."

Mark said, "That's exactly what we'll do. We can't close these cases because we can't risk going back to court. Again, those days are over. Starting now, don't take any phone calls from a client or anyone else for that matter. Let's use prepaid cell phones to keep in touch and ignore all other calls."

Zola said, "I'm already carrying two phones. Now a third?"

"Yes, and we have to monitor all of them to see who's looking for us," Mark said.

"And my days as a hospital vulture are over?" she asked and managed a smile.

"Afraid so."

"You weren't very good at it," Todd said.

"Thanks. I hated every minute of it."

A manager walked over and said, "Hey, Todd, you're on tonight. We're shorthanded and need you now."

"Be there in a sec," Todd said and waved the guy off. When he was gone, Todd asked, "So, gang, what's next?"

"We go after Swift Bank," Mark said.

"And dig a deeper hole," Zola replied, but it was not a question.

MORGANA NASH AT NowAssist sent Mark an e-mail that read,

> Dear Mark: I have just been informed by the administration at Foggy Bottom Law School that you have been placed on withdrawal status. I called the law school and was informed that you have not been to class this semester. This is very troubling. Please contact me immediately.
>
> Last installment Jan. 13, 2014: $32,500; total principal/interest: $266,000.
>
> Sincerely, Morgana Nash, Public Sector Representative

Late that night, and after several more beers, Mark responded,

> Dear Ms. Nash: Last week my therapist had me admitted to a private psychiatric hospital in rural Maryland. I'm not supposed to use the Internet but these clowns around here are not too sharp. Would you please stop hounding me? According to one shrink here

I'm borderline suicidal. A bit more abuse from you and I could go over the edge. Please, please, leave me alone!!

Love, Mark Frazier

Rex Wagner of Scholar Support Partners e-mailed Todd:

Dear Mr. Lucero: I have been informed by your law school that you are now officially considered "Withdrawn." I called the law school and was told that you have not attended a single class this semester, your last before graduation. Why would any sane student drop out of law school during his last semester? If you are not in school I can only assume you are working somewhere, probably in a bar. Employment of any nature while not enrolled in school triggers either the need for a repayment plan or, in the absence of one, default. Default, as I'm sure you know, means a lawsuit filed against you by the Department of Education. Please contact me immediately.

Last installment: $32,500, Jan. 13, 2014; total due: $195,000

Sincerely, Rex Wagner, Senior Loan Counselor

While Mark was typing his response to Morgana Nash, Todd fired off one to his loan counselor.

Dear SS Counselor Wagner: You hit the nail on the head with that sanity question. Nothing is sane about my world these days, most especially my insurmountable debts. Okay, the fix is in. Jig's up. I dropped out because I hate the law school, hate the law, etc. I'm currently earning about $200 a week, cash, tending bar. So let's say that's $800 a month, tax-free because I haven't filled out those forms yet. To maintain my impoverished lifestyle, I need about $500 a month for food, rent, things like that. And you should see where I'm living and what I'm eating. Analyzing these figures, I suppose I could agree to a repayment plan of something like $200 a month, beginning in six months. I know you'll hit the "Interest" button as soon as possible and kick in the 5 percent per annum. Five percent of $195,000 is about $9,750 a year. Let's just round it to $10,000 in interest. Under my proposed repayment scheme, I can swing about a fourth of that each year. You loan sharks will then add the interest in arrears to the ballooning principal, and hit that with another 5 percent per year. The math gets a bit bewildering, but my spreadsheet says that in ten years I will owe almost $400,000. And this does not include all the little secret fees and add-ons and other illegalities that SSP has been caught padding onto the student loans it handles. (I've read the lawsuits and, boy, would I love to file one myself. You and your company should be ashamed—piling hidden fees onto the backs of students already drowning in debt.)

So, are you willing to accept my offer of $200 a month? Beginning in six months, of course.

Your pal, Todd Lucero

Evidently, Mr. Wagner was working late, or, as Todd imagined, was sitting in his recliner, in nothing but his boxers, watching porn and monitoring his e-mails. Within minutes he replied,

Dear Todd: The answer is no. Your offer is ridiculous. I find it hard to believe that a person as clever as you will spend the next ten years mixing drinks. There are plenty of good jobs out there, law related and otherwise, and if you'll get off your butt you can find one. Then we can have a serious conversation about repayment.

Sincerely, Rex Wagner, Senior Loan Counselor

To which Todd immediately replied,

Dear SS: Great. I withdraw my offer. T.L.

Zola's correspondence was slightly more professional. Tildy Carver at LoanAid wrote,

Dear Zola Maal: I have been informed that you have withdrawn from law school. Such a dramatic action presents several issues and we must discuss them at once. Please call or e-mail me as soon as possible.

Tildy Carver, Senior Loan Adviser

Last installment, January 13, 2014: $32,500; total principal and interest: $191,000

Zola was almost asleep. She responded,

Dear Ms. Carver: After the suicide of my friend in January, I found it impossible to continue with my studies. So I decided to take a gap semester instead, with the possible plan of resuming law school in a year or so. I will contact you later.

Sincerely, Zola Maal

30

On a warm spring day in late April, with the cherry trees in full bloom and the air clear after a good rain, the partners gathered in the firm's headquarters to launch their last Hail Mary at the practice of law. The firm's headquarters also doubled as Zola's den, and over the past three months she had managed to add some life and color to her hiding place. She had painted both rooms a soft beige and hung some contemporary art. In one corner there was a small refrigerator, the only sign of a kitchen. On an old metal table, there was a new desktop computer with a thirty-inch screen, and next to it was a high-speed laser printer. Sagging bookshelves were mounted on two walls and were filled with piles of paperwork, the fruits of their diligent tracking of all matters related to Swift Bank.

Each of the three had joined, as an aggrieved plaintiff, a separate class action against the bank. There were now six spread across the country, all led by lawyers who specialized in such massive lawsuits.

In the meantime, Swift Bank was on the ropes, cut and

bloodied, and barely able to survive its daily thrashing. New allegations of wrongdoing poured forth. Whistle-blowers were singing at full volume. Upper managers were pointing fingers. Indictments were being promised. Stock-holders were embarrassed, but they were also furious because the stock had fallen from $60 to $13 in less than four months. Rumors roared through the Internet and cable news. The most prominent was a recurring one that Swift would have no choice but to throw billions at its problems.

That prospect only incited the class action industry.

Comparing the responses from the three firms they had hired, it was clear that a Miami outfit called Cohen-Cutler was a few steps quicker than the other two, one in New York and one in D.C. Cohen-Cutler had a nice reputation in the rough-and-tumble world of mass torts. It was huge, with a hundred lawyers and plenty of muscle. Its paper-work was more efficient.

Thus, the fading law firm of Upshaw, Parker & Lane made the decision to join hands with the mighty Cohen-Cutler.

Zola sat at the table with a cup of tea and studied the desktop. Todd sat in the only chair with his laptop. Mark sprawled on the floor. Gone were their beards and fake eyeglasses, as well as their suits. The courtroom days were over; no need to hide behind disguises. They would spend the next few weeks hiding above The Rooster Bar. Beyond that, they had no plan.

Mark said, "There's a Swift branch on Wisconsin Avenue in Bethesda. Let's start there. Check out the white pages for Bethesda. We're looking for generic names that can easily be misspelled."

"Got one," Todd said. "Mr. Joseph Hall, 662 Manning

Drive, Bethesda. Change the last *l* to an *e* and he's now Joe Hale. Our first fake client."

Zola opened a document copied from the Cohen-Cutler materials. It was known internally as a PIS, Plaintiff Information Sheet. "Date of birth?" she asked.

Mark said, "Make him forty years old. Born March 3, 1974. Married, three kids. Swift Bank customer since 2001. Checking account and savings account. Debit card."

She typed away, filling in the blanks. "Okay, account numbers?"

"Let's leave them out for now. We'll fabricate them later if we have to."

"Next?"

Todd said, "Ethel Berry at 1210 Rugby Avenue. Change the *e* in Berry to an *a* and you still have the same Ethel Barry."

Mark said, "That's our girl. Ethel's kind of an old-fashioned name so let's give the gal some years. Born on December 5, 1941, two days before Pearl Harbor. Unmarried widow. No kids at home. Checking, savings, too old for a debit card. Doesn't like credit."

Zola filled in the blanks, and Ethel Barry became a class action plaintiff. "Next?"

Todd said, "Ted Radford, 798 Drummond Avenue, Apartment 4F. Change the *a* to an *e* and he's now Ted Redford, like Robert, the actor."

Mark said, "And when was Robert Redford born? Hang on." He pecked and scrolled and said, "August 18, 1936. So give Ted the same birthday."

Todd asked, "Is Robert Redford really seventy-seven years old?"

"Still looks good to me," Zola said, typing.

Mark said, "*The Sting* and *Butch Cassidy* are two of my favorite movies. We can't have a Redford without a Newman."

Todd hunted and pecked. "Got one. Mike Newman at 418 Arlington Road, Bethesda. Change the *w* to a *u* and he's now Mike Neuman."

Zola typed and mumbled, "Aren't we having fun?"

After rampaging through Bethesda, and collecting fifty plaintiffs, the firm turned its sights to the suburbs of Northern Virginia. There was a Swift branch on Broad Street in Falls Church. The area around it proved fertile as dozens of new fake clients were added to their lawsuit.

By noon, they were bored and decided to have lunch and move outdoors. They took a cab to Georgetown, to the Waterfront, where they found a table with a view of the Potomac. No one mentioned Gordy, but each remembered their last visit to the area. They were standing nearby on that awful night when they saw flashing lights on the Arlington Memorial Bridge in the distance.

They ordered sandwiches and iced tea, and all three opened laptops. The search continued for aggrieved Swift customers.

LONG AFTER THEY had eaten, the waiter politely asked them to leave; said he needed the table. They closed shop, walked around the corner to a coffee bar, found another table outside, and commenced operations. When they added their one hundredth new client, Mark placed the call to Miami. He asked to speak to a senior litigator with Cohen-Cutler, but of course the great man was away on business. Mark kept pushing and was finally routed to a lawyer named Martinez, who, according to the website, was fighting Swift on the front lines. After introducing himself and mentioning his little firm, Mark said, "So, we have about a hundred Swift customers and we'd like to join your class action."

"A hundred?" Martinez repeated. "You're kidding, right?"

"No, I'm dead serious."

"Look, Mr. Upshaw, as of today our firm has almost 200,000 Swift plaintiffs. We're not taking referrals for anything under 1,000. Find a thousand cases and we'll talk business."

"A thousand?" Mark repeated and looked wild-eyed at his partners. "Okay, we'll get to work. Say, just curious, what's the big picture look like?"

Martinez coughed and said, "Can't say much. Swift is under enormous pressure to settle but I'm not sure their lawyers understand this. There are a lot of mixed messages. We think it will settle, though."

"How soon?"

"We're guessing early summer. The bank wants this mess behind it and has the cash to make it go away. The federal judge sitting on the case in New York is really pushing the litigation. You're watching the headlines."

"You bet. Thanks. We'll be in touch."

Mark placed his phone next to his laptop and said, "We've only just begun."

31

The District Bar Council had almost 100,000 members, about half of whom worked in the city. The other half were scattered through all fifty states. Since membership, as well as the payment of dues, was mandatory, the administration of the bar's activities was a challenge. A staff of forty worked diligently in its headquarters on Wisconsin Avenue, keeping up with the names and addresses of its members, planning educational courses and seminars, promulgating standards of professional responsibility, publishing a monthly magazine, and dealing with disciplinary matters. Complaints against judges and lawyers were directed to the Office of Disciplinary Counsel, where one Margaret Sanchez managed a staff of five lawyers, three investigators, and half a dozen secretaries and assistants. To receive a proper review, a complaint had to first be filed in writing. Often, though, the first hint of trouble came by phone, and usually from another lawyer who did not want to get too involved.

After several efforts, Edwin Mossberg from down in

Charleston managed to get Ms. Sanchez on the line. He told her of his encounter with one Mark Upshaw, a young man claiming to be a lawyer but apparently using an alias. Mossberg had checked and found no record of such a person in the bar's directory. Or in the phone book, or online, or anywhere else for that matter. He described in general Upshaw's negligence in allowing an important statute of limitations to expire, and his subsequent trip to Charleston to beg Mossberg to keep quiet.

Ms. Sanchez was captivated by the story. Complaints of unauthorized practice were rare and almost all involved paralegals who either deliberately or inadvertently stepped out of bounds and did things that only their bosses were supposed to do. A quick reprimand usually got them back in line without substantial damage to the clients.

Mossberg was reluctant to file an official complaint, said he didn't have time to fool with it, but just wanted to tip off the bar and let it know there was a problem. He e-mailed a copy of Upshaw's business card with the name of his firm, its address on Florida Avenue, and a phone number. Ms. Sanchez thanked him for his time.

The story was made even more interesting by the fact that it was the second phone call dealing with the law firm of Upshaw, Parker & Lane. The previous week, a local ambulance chaser named Frank Jepperson had unofficially tipped her off that one Zola Parker had tried to hustle one of his clients in a hospital cafeteria. Ms. Sanchez knew Jepperson from two prior complaints about his own unethical behavior. Jepperson had sent her a copy of Zola Parker's business card.

Sitting at her desk, Ms. Sanchez compared the copies of the two cards. Same firm, same address, different phone numbers. A quick review of the bar's directory verified that neither Mark Upshaw nor Zola Parker was a member. She summoned a member of her staff, Chap Gronski, whose official title was assistant disciplinary counsel, and gave him the two copies of the firm's business cards. An hour later, Gronski was back with some research.

He said, "I've checked the criminal dockets and found fourteen cases in which Mark Upshaw is the attorney of record. Nothing on Zola Parker. There's a guy named Todd Lane who's been active for the past three months, found his name on seventeen entries. There's probably more. The odd thing is that there is nothing prior to January of this year."

"Sounds like a start-up, a brand-new firm in town," she said. "Just what we need."

"Shall I open a file?" Gronski asked.

"Not yet. There's no official complaint. When are they due in court again?"

Gronski flipped through some printouts. "Looks like Upshaw has a sentencing hearing for a DUI client in Division 16 at ten in the morning."

"Ease over and take a look. Have a chat with Upshaw and let's see what he has to say for himself."

AT TEN THE next morning, Chap Gronski was sitting in Judge Cantu's courtroom watching the parade. After the third guilty plea and sentencing, the clerk called the name of Jeremy Plankmore. A young man in the back row stood nervously, looked around for help, and stutter-stepped down the aisle. As he approached the bench, alone, Judge Cantu asked, "Are you Mr. Plankmore?"

"Yes, sir."

"Says here your lawyer is Mark Upshaw. I don't see him in the courtroom."

"No, sir, me neither. I've been calling him for three days and he won't answer his phone."

Judge Cantu looked down at a clerk, who shrugged as if she knew nothing. He looked at the assistant prosecutor, who gave the same shrug. "Very well, step aside, Mr. Plankmore, and I'll deal with it later. Let's see if we can get Mr. Upshaw on the phone. He must've got his schedule mixed up."

Plankmore sat in the front row, frightened and confused. Another lawyer moved in for the kill.

Gronski reported back to Ms. Sanchez. They decided to wait two days until Mr. Lane's next scheduled court appearance.

JEREMY PLANKMORE DECIDED to dig a bit deeper. With a friend as extra muscle, he waited until later that afternoon and visited the address on his lawyer's business card. Upshaw had charged him a thousand bucks, $800 of which he'd paid in cash. The balance was in his pocket, but he had no plans to hand it over. Indeed, his plans were to confront Mr. Upshaw and demand a refund. At the address on Florida Avenue, he couldn't find the law firm. At The Rooster Bar, he and his friend bought beers and chatted with the bartender, a heavily tattooed young lady named Pammie. Pammie had little to say, especially when Jeremy started poking around with questions about Mark Upshaw and a law firm in the building. She claimed to know nothing and seemed irritated by the questions. Jeremy got the impression she was stonewalling, and he wrote his name and phone number on the back of a paper napkin. He handed it to Pammie and said, "If you bump into Mark Upshaw, tell him to call me. Or else I'll report him to the Bar Council."

"Like I said, I don't know the guy," Pammie replied.

"Yeah, yeah, but if you happen to meet him." Jeremy and his friend left the bar.

SNIFFING A JACKPOT, Darrell Cromley moved with extraordinary speed. He paid $3,500 to a retired doctor for an "expedited review" of Ramon's medical records. In conclusion, the expert wrote, in language blunter than Dr. Koonce's, that "the actions taken by the hospital staff and attending doctors fell far below acceptable standards of care and constituted gross negligence."

Darrell grabbed the two-page summary, attached it to his two-page lawsuit, and filed it on behalf of his client, Ramon R. Taper, against Attorney Mark Upshaw and his firm in the Circuit Court of the District of Columbia. The gist of the lawsuit was obvious: Attorney Upshaw had sat on a clear case of medical negligence and allowed the statute of limitations to expire, thus extinguishing any chance of recovery from the hospital and its doctors. Ramon was seeking actual and punitive damages that totaled $25 million.

Darrell mailed a copy of the lawsuit to the address at The Rooster Bar, and paid a process server $100 to personally deliver it to Mr. Upshaw, as required. At the bar, though, the process server had trouble finding the firm. He assumed it was housed somewhere above the bar—he counted three levels up there—but the only visible door, one to the side, was locked. Inside the bar, he asked around, and was told by the manager that there was no such law firm. No one seemed to know anything about Mark Upshaw. The process server tried to leave the lawsuit with the manager, but he adamantly refused to accept it.

For the next three days, the process server tried to find either the law firm or Mark Upshaw, but had no luck.

At no time did Darrell Cromley consider checking with the District Bar Council to determine if Mark Upshaw was a member.

THE LAW FIRM had adopted the strategy of mobility. It left the building each morning and drifted around the city, from coffee shops to libraries to bookstores to outdoor cafés, anywhere the partners could camp out with their laptops and comb the white pages for more clients. An observer might have been curious as to what all three were working on with such diligence, mumbling softly to each other, offering names and addresses while their assortment of cell phones vibrated in a muted chorus of neglected calls. The three were certainly in demand, yet they rarely took a call. Such an observer, and there were none, would not have a clue.

TODD WAS BEHIND the bar late one night tidying things up as the last of the customers paid their tabs and left. Maynard, who rarely came to The Rooster Bar, appeared from the kitchen and asked, "Where's Mark?"

Todd replied, "Upstairs."

"Get him down here. We need to talk."

Todd knew it was trouble. He called Mark, who was two floors above him in the firm's office laboring through the white pages with Zola and adding names to their class action. Within minutes, Mark entered the bar. They followed Maynard to an empty booth. Their boss was scowling, in a foul mood, and wanted answers.

Maynard tossed a business card on the table and asked, "Ever hear of a guy named Chapman Gronski? Goes by Chap?"

Mark picked up the card and felt sick. "Who is he?" Todd asked.

Maynard said, "An investigator for the District Bar Council. He's been around twice looking for the two of you. Mr. Mark Upshaw, Mr. Todd Lane. Don't know these guys. I do know Mark Frazier and Todd Lucero. So what the hell's going on?"

Neither knew what to say, so Maynard continued. He tossed a napkin on the table and said, "A guy named Jeremy Plankmore left this yesterday, said he was a client, said he was looking for his lawyer, a Mr. Mark Upshaw." He tossed another card on the table and said, "And this guy has been by three times, a little guy named Jerry Coleman. He's a process server for some lawyer who wants to sue you and your law firm." He tossed another card on the table and said, "And this is from a father who said his son hired you, Todd, to handle a simple assault case. Said you didn't show up for court."

Maynard stared at them and waited. Mark finally said, "Well, it's a long story, but we're in a bit of a jam."

Todd said, "We can't work here any longer, Maynard. We need to disappear."

"You got that right and I'm going to help you. You're fired. I can't have these people harassing the other bartenders. They're tired of covering for you guys anyway. Next thing I know the cops will be stopping by with all sorts of questions, and I don't have to tell you that cops make me real nervous. I don't know what you're doing but the party's over. Get out."

"I understand," Todd said.

"Can we keep the upstairs for a month?" Mark asked. "We need some time to wrap up some things."

"Wrap up what? You guys have been running a fake law firm and now half the city's looking for you. What are you doing?"

Todd said, "Don't worry about the cops. They're not involved. Let's just say we have some disgruntled clients."

"Clients? But you're not lawyers, right? Last I heard you guys were in law school getting ready to graduate."

"We dropped out," Todd said. "And we've been hustling clients in the criminal courts, all fees in cash."

"That's pretty stupid if you ask me."

No one asked you, Mark thought, but let it go. And, yes, at the moment it seemed pretty stupid. He said, "We'll pay you a thousand bucks in cash for another thirty days and you'll never see us."

Maynard took a sip of ice water and glared at them.

Todd, stung, said, "Look, Maynard, I've worked for you for, what, the last three years. You can't just fire me like this."

"You're fired, Todd. Got that? Both of you. I can't have this place crawling with investigators and pissed-off clients. You've been lucky that someone hasn't walked in and recognized you."

"Just thirty days," Mark said. "And you'll never know we're here."

"I doubt that." He took another sip and kept glaring. Finally, he asked, "Why do you want to stay here when everybody seems to know your address?"

Mark said, "We need a place to sleep and finish our work. And, they can't get to us. The door to the upstairs is always locked."

"I know. That's why they hang around the bar hassling the other bartenders."

Todd said, "Please, Maynard. We'll be out by the first of June."

"Two thousand dollars cash," Maynard said.

"Okay, and you'll keep our cover?" Mark asked.

"I'll try, but I really don't like all this attention."

32

At the Bardtown Federal Detention Facility, Zola's parents and brother were awakened at midnight and told to gather their things. Each was given two canvas bags to fill with their possessions and thirty minutes to prepare for the trip. Along with about fifty other Africans, some of whom they'd met in detention and knew to be primarily Senegalese, they were loaded onto a white unmarked bus that was designed to transport federal inmates. They were handcuffed and remained so on the bus. Four heavily armed ICE agents, two wielding shotguns, escorted them to their seats and instructed them to sit quietly and ask no questions. Two of the agents assumed positions in the front of the bus, two in the rear. The glass windows were locked and covered with thick metal screens.

Zola's mother, Fanta, counted five other women in the group. The rest were men, almost all under the age of forty. She was stoic and determined to keep her composure. Emotions were raw, but they had long since accepted the reality of removal.

After four months in captivity, they were relieved to be out of detention. Of course they preferred to remain in the country, but if life in the U.S. meant living in a cage, things could not be much worse in Senegal.

They rode in quiet darkness for almost two hours. The agents occasionally talked and laughed, but the passengers made no sounds. Highway signs told them they were entering Pittsburgh and the bus headed to the airport. It was cleared through security gates and parked inside a large hangar. An unmarked passenger jet waited nearby. On the other side of the airport, far away, the bright lights of the terminal were visible. The passengers left the bus and were herded into a corner where more ICE agents were waiting. One by one, the detainees were questioned and their paperwork reviewed. Once they were cleared, their handcuffs were removed and they were allowed to retrieve their two bags, the contents of which were examined again. The processing moved slowly; no one was in a hurry, especially those headed home.

Another bus arrived. Two dozen Africans got off, all looking as dazed and defeated as those on the first bus. Someone's paperwork wasn't in order so the others waited. And waited. It was almost 5:00 a.m. when an official led the first group of passengers to the airplane. A line formed behind them. Slowly, they climbed aboard with their bags and were directed to their seats. Boarding took another hour. The passengers were relieved to know they would not be handcuffed for the flight. Another official read the rules regarding movement while in flight, use of the restrooms, and so on. Yes, they were allowed to talk, but quietly. At the slightest hint of trouble, all passengers would be handcuffed. Any disturbance would lead to an automatic arrest upon arrival. Half a dozen armed agents would accompany them. The flight would take eleven hours, nonstop, and food would be provided.

It was almost seven when the jet's engines began making noises. The doors were shut and locked and an official instructed them to fasten their seat belts. He then went through the safety and emergency procedures. Brown bags were given to all passengers. A cheese sandwich, an apple, and a small container of juice. At 7:20, the airplane shuddered and began moving toward a taxiway.

Twenty-six years after arriving in Miami as stowaways on a Liberian freighter, Abdou and Fanta Maal were leaving their adopted land as criminals, and headed for an uncertain future. Their son Bo, who was seated behind them, was leaving the only country he'd ever really known. As the plane lifted off, they held hands and fought tears.

AN HOUR LATER, a caseworker at Bardtown called Zola with the news that her family was en route to Dakar, Senegal. It was a routine call made to the contact person listed by each detainee. Though Zola knew it was coming, she nonetheless took it hard. She walked upstairs and informed Mark and Todd, and they spent an hour trying to console her. They decided to take a long walk and find some breakfast.

It was a somber meal. Zola was too worried and preoccupied to touch her waffle. Todd and Mark were genuinely concerned about her family, but they had stayed up most of the night fretting over their own predicament. Darrell Cromley had filed suit much faster than they had expected. The Bar Council was on their trail, no doubt tipped off by either Cromley or that prick Mossberg down in Charleston. Not that it really mattered; their little charade was over. They felt lousy about a lot of things, but the clients they were stiffing really bothered them. Those people had trusted them, had paid them, were now getting cheated, and would get chewed up again by the system.

As they ate and watched Zola, she picked up her phone and called Diallo Niang for the second time. Dakar, Senegal, was four time zones ahead and the workday was in full swing. Again, Diallo Niang did not answer his cell, nor did anyone answer his office line. In return for the $5,000 retainer Zola had paid weeks earlier, Niang had agreed to meet her family at the airport, arrange temporary housing, and, most important, keep the authorities happy. He'd claimed to be an expert on immigration matters and knew exactly what to do. When she couldn't get him on the phone, she became frantic.

With so many people looking for them, returning to their address was not a good idea. They walked a few blocks, found a Starbucks, bought coffee, opened their laptops, logged in, and returned to the white pages. The search for more fake clients gave them something to do, something else to think about.

AS THE MONOTONY of the flight wore on, the passengers became less subdued and more talkative. Almost all claimed to have a friend or relative waiting on the ground, though the uncertainty was palpable. No one even pretended to be optimistic. They had been away for years and had no valid paperwork or identification, at least not of the Senegalese variety. Those who'd had fake U.S. driver's licenses had been forced to surrender them. The Dakar police were notoriously rough on returnees. Their attitude was simple—if you don't want to be here, who needs you? The U.S. is kicking you out, so no one really wants you. They were often treated like outcasts. Housing and employment were difficult to find. Though many of their countrymen dreamed of immigrating to the U.S. and Europe, they were scornful of those who'd tried and failed.

Abdou and Fanta had relatives scattered throughout the country, but they were not to be trusted. Over the years, they had been contacted by various siblings and cousins who wanted help entering the U.S. illegally. Abdou and Fanta had been unable, or unwilling, to get involved. It was dangerous enough living without documentation. Why risk detection by assisting others?

Now that they needed help, there was no one they could trust. Zola had assured them that Diallo Niang was on retainer and would take care of them. They were praying fervently for his intervention and assistance.

They flew into the sunlight and back into the night. After eleven hours, and two more rounds of brown bag food, the plane began its descent into Dakar, and once again the mood on board became somber. Their return trip ended after midnight, a twenty-four-hour adventure none of them had bargained for. The plane taxied to the main terminal and stopped at the last gate of a long concourse. The engines died but the doors remained closed. An ICE official explained that once inside they would be handed over to Senegalese officials, outside U.S. jurisdiction. Good luck.

When the doors finally opened, they grabbed their bags, shuffled off the plane and down the ramp. Inside they were led to a large open area separated from the concourse by a row of uniformed policemen. Cops were everywhere, none of them even remotely friendly. An official in a suit began barking instructions in French, the official language of Senegal.

When they were arrested four months earlier, and removal looked likely, Abdou and Fanta resumed speaking in their native French. After twenty-six years of trying to avoid the language and working hard to learn English, they struggled at first. But it eventually came back, and perhaps the only positive aspect of their detention was the rediscovery of a language they loved. Bo, on the other hand, had never heard French around the house and was not encouraged to learn it at school. He couldn't speak a word, at first, but became highly motivated while at Bardtown. After four months of nonstop French with his parents, he was somewhat proficient.

But the official spoke rapidly and with a full vocabulary. Most of the refugees were somewhat rusty and found it hard to follow. The processing began as the police reviewed the paperwork from the U.S. An officer waved the Maals over and asked questions. What part of Senegal were they from? When did they leave? Why did they leave? Where did Abdou work before he left Senegal? How long were they in the U.S.? Did they leave family behind? Did they have family in Dakar, or another city, or the countryside? Where did they plan to live? The questions were pointed, the responses scoffed at. Several times the officer warned Abdou that he'd better be truthful. Abdou assured him he was.

Bo noticed that other returnees were being escorted away from the area to a place down the concourse where people were waiting. Evidently, the lucky ones were being released to their friends and relatives.

The officer asked if they had a contact in Dakar. When Abdou gave the name of Diallo Niang, their attorney, the officer asked why they needed a lawyer. Abdou tried to explain that one had been arranged by his daughter in the U.S. because there was no family to rely on. The officer studied a sheet of paper and said Mr. Niang had not contacted the police. He was not waiting for the family. The officer pointed to a row of chairs, told them to wait there, and walked over to a man in a suit.

An hour passed as the police escorted more of their fellow passengers away from the area. When a dozen or so remained, the man in the suit approached the Maals and said, "Mr. Niang is not here. How much money do you have?"

Abdou stood and said, "About five hundred U.S."

"Good. You can afford a hotel room. Follow that officer. He will take you."

The same policeman nodded and they picked up their bags. He led them along the concourse, out of the terminal, and into a parking lot where a police van was waiting. He sat with them in the rear, said nothing for the twenty minutes they weaved through empty streets, and told them to get out in front of a grungy five-story hotel. At its front door, he said, "You will stay here because the jail is full. Do not leave under any circumstances. We will be back in a few hours to get you. Any questions?"

His tone left little doubt that questions would not be appreciated. At that moment, they were grateful to be where they were and not in jail.

The cop stared at them as if something more needed to

be said. He lit a cigarette, blew smoke, and said, "And I would like to be paid for my services."

Bo looked away and bit his tongue. Abdou set down his bags and said, "Of course. How much?"

"One hundred U.S."

Abdou reached into his pocket.

THE CLERK AT the front desk was napping in a chair and seemed irritated at being bothered at such an hour. At first he said there were no vacancies; the hotel was full. Abdou assumed the hotel and the police were in business together and the no-vacancy routine was part of the act. He explained that his wife was ill and they had to sleep somewhere. The clerk studied his computer screen and managed to find a small room, at a premium rate, of course. Abdou seemed unfazed and chatted away like a real charmer. He said he had only U.S. cash, which, of course, was unacceptable. Only West African francs. Fanta managed to act as though she might faint at any moment. Bo was having trouble following the exchange in French, but he wanted to leap across the desk and strangle the guy. Abdou refused to take no for an answer and practically begged for a room. The clerk relented somewhat, and said there was a bank down the street. They could check into the room, but first thing in the morning he wanted his money in the local currency. Abdou promised and thanked him profusely, and the clerk reluctantly handed over a key.

Abdou asked if they could use the phone for a call to the U.S. Absolutely not. When the room was paid for, a phone call would be allowed, but only if its charges were prepaid. It was almost 3:00 a.m. local time—11:00 p.m. in the U.S.—when they entered the small, stuffy room on the fourth floor. A single, narrow bed hugged the far wall. The men insisted that Fanta take it. They slept on the floor.

ZOLA WAS AWAKE at 3:00 a.m. because sleep was impossible. She had worked through the night calling, texting, and e-mailing Diallo Niang, but without any response. When her phone beeped with an unknown caller she grabbed it. It was Bo, and for a few seconds the sound of his voice was a relief. He gave her a quick version of what had happened, said there was no sign of the lawyer, and that the police had just left the hotel with Abdou.

"Are you and Mother safe?"

"Well, we're not in jail, yet. They've said twice that we can stay at this hotel because the jail is full. Guess they found a spot for Dad. We can't leave the hotel."

"I've called the lawyer a hundred times," she said. "Have you tried to call him from there?"

"No. I'm using the phone at the front desk and the clerk is staring at me and listening to every word. He doesn't like folks using his phone, but I begged him for this one call."

"Give me the number and I'll think of something."

Bo handed the phone back to the clerk, then found a café near the lobby. He bought two croissants and coffee, and took them to the room, where he sat with Fanta in the semidarkness. Fanta was relieved that he had spoken with Zola.

They ate and sipped coffee, and waited once again for the knock on the door.

33

By 10:00 a.m., Zola had made the decision to go to Senegal.

They were sitting in the café at Kramer Books in Dupont Circle, laptops open, papers spread over the table as if they worked there every day, but they were not working, not as fake lawyers anyway.

They debated scenarios throughout the morning. Mark and Todd fully understood her need to go, but the obvious fear was that she would be detained and not allowed to return. Her father was already in jail. Fanta and Bo might soon join him. If Zola showed up and caused trouble, anything might happen. She argued that she was a U.S. citizen with a valid passport, and since a visa was no longer required for stays of fewer than ninety days, she could leave immediately. Zola said she would notify the Senegalese embassy in Washington of her plans, and if anyone in Dakar tried to block her return home, she would contact the U.S. embassy there. She saw little risk of being detained and, under the circumstances, was willing to accept it.

Mark suggested she wait a day or two and try to find another lawyer in Dakar. They found plenty online, many in what appeared to be old, reputable firms. Indeed, some of the firms looked so promising that Todd quipped about setting up a shop there once they were forced to flee the U.S. "Are there any white people in Senegal?" he asked.

"Sure," she said. "Two or three."

"I like it," Mark said in an effort at a little humor. "A foreign branch of Upshaw, Parker & Lane."

"I'm done with that firm," she said and managed a smile. But she didn't like the idea of again wiring money to someone she didn't know. Money was not a problem, they assured her. There was $50,000 in their firm account, and all of it was available. She was touched by their generosity and eagerness to help, and for the first time revealed the little nest egg she'd been hoarding for just such a situation. They were impressed that she had managed to save over $16,000 during law school. It was unheard of.

They really couldn't blame her for wanting to leave town. They were currently being sued by their landlords for skipping out in January. Darrell Cromley had just hit them with a $25 million lawsuit for gross malpractice. The federal government would soon pile on to the tune of something over $600,000, combined. Dozens of angry clients were looking for them. Clerks from the courts were calling. Maynard fired them, so they were genuinely unemployed. And their most urgent problem was the investigation by the District Bar Council. It was just a matter of time before their real identities were revealed and they would be leaving town too.

They drove to The Rooster Bar, where the boys watched the door while Zola ran upstairs and packed a bag. They stopped by her bank, where she withdrew $10,000 from her savings account. The bank could not convert any of it to West African francs, so they tracked down a currency exchange shop near Union Station. At a phone store, they paid $390 for four GSM unlocked international cell phones, complete with SIM cards, cameras, Bluetooth, full keyboard, and fully optimized for social networking. They would keep three and leave the other with Bo, if possible. At 4:30 they drove to Dulles and walked to the Brussels Airlines counter. Using an old credit card, Zola paid $1,500 for a round-trip ticket to Dakar, with a four-hour layover in Brussels. Barring delays, she would arrive in Dakar around four the following afternoon, after an eighteen-hour journey.

At departure security, they had a good hug and cry. They watched her until she disappeared into a mass of fellow travelers.

They returned to the city, and, on a whim, went to a Nationals game.

AT NINE THE following morning, as Zola was somewhere between Belgium and Senegal, Mark and Todd strolled into the student union on the campus of American University and found a table in a half-empty cafeteria. With jeans and backpacks they looked like everyone else. They bought coffee and made themselves at home, as if settling in for some serious studying. Mark pulled out one of his phones and walked to a wall of windows overlooking the campus. He called the Miami firm of Cohen-Cutler and asked to speak to a lawyer named Rudy Stassen. According to the firm's website, Stassen was one of several

Cohen-Cutler partners spearheading the Swift Bank litigation. A secretary said Mr. Stassen was in a meeting. Mark said it was important and he would hold. Ten minutes later, Stassen said hello.

Mark introduced himself as a lawyer in D.C. and claimed to have eleven hundred Swift customers all signed up and ready to join one of the six class actions.

"Well, you've come to the right place," Stassen said with a laugh. "We're suing like crazy. Two hundred thousand at last count. Where are your clients?"

"All in the D.C. area," Mark said as he placed his phone on the table and sat across from Todd. He punched the speaker button and lowered the volume. "I'm sort of shopping around, looking for the best deal. What are your fees?"

"Not sure. We think the attorneys' fees will be negotiated separately. As of now, we have 25 percent contracts with our clients, and we'll take an extra 8 percent off the gross settlement. All subject to court approval, of course. What's your name again, Upshaw? I'm not finding a website."

"Don't have one," Mark said. "I've solicited with direct mail."

"Okay, that's odd."

"It works. What can you say about the negotiations?"

"Stalled, as of now. Swift is claiming, in the press of course, that it wants to settle and move on, but its lawyers are dragging their feet. They're padding the file like crazy, billing millions, the usual routine. But we still think the bank will cave in and settle. You want in? You said you're shopping around."

"Eight percent sounds good. I'm in. Send me the paperwork."

"Good move. I'll turn it over to an associate named Jenny Valdez and she'll walk you through it."

"Got a question for you," Mark said.

"Sure."

"How does your law firm handle 200,000 clients?"

Stassen laughed and said, "With a lot of muscle. Right now we have ten associates who are supervising thirty paralegals and legal assistants. It's a bitch, all right, the biggest class we've ever put together, but we can handle it. Your first class action?"

"Yeah. Looks like crazy work."

"'Crazy' is a good word, but, believe me, it's worth it. We do all right, Mr. Upshaw."

"Just call me Mark."

"Thanks for the business, Mark. We'll get you included and you can tell your clients they'll be signed up within twenty-four hours. After that, it's just a waiting game. Here's the number for Jenny Valdez. Got a pen?"

"Yep." Mark wrote down the number and ended the call. He pecked away on his laptop while Todd left to fetch something to eat. Little was said as they chewed on muffins and sipped coffee. They were thinking about Zola, who had sent them a text with the message that she was on the ground, her flight uneventful.

Finally, Mark took a deep breath and called Jenny Valdez. He chatted with her for fifteen minutes, scribbled notes, and assured her their paperwork was in order. He was ready to zip along the PIS statements for all eleven hundred of their Swift clients. When he put his phone down, he looked at Todd and said, "When I push this Send button, we will be committing eleven hundred new felonies. Are we ready for this?"

"I thought we'd made that decision."

"No second thoughts?"

"Everything's a second thought. And third and fourth. But, it's our only chance of escape. Let's do it."

Mark gently pushed the Send key.

ZOLA'S CAB INCHED along in traffic far more chaotic than she had ever seen. Her driver said the air-conditioning was broken, but she doubted it had worked in years. All the windows were down and the air was thick and rancid. She wiped sweat from her forehead and realized her blouse was soaked and sticking to her skin. Outside, small cars, trucks, and vans were bumper to bumper with horns honking and drivers yelling at each other. Scooters and motorcycles, most with two passengers and even some with three, cut and weaved through the gridlock, missing each other by inches. Pedestrians darted from cab to cab selling bottles of water while others begged for coins.

Two hours after leaving the airport, the taxi stopped at the hotel and Zola paid in West African francs, the equivalent of $65. She walked into the lobby and was relieved to find cooler air. The clerk spoke bad English but managed to understand her request. He called the room and within minutes Bo bounced off the elevator and hugged his sister. They had not heard a word from Abdou, nor had they seen the police all day. They were still under orders to remain in the hotel and afraid to leave. As Bo had realized, the hotel was used by the police to keep track of other newly returned detainees.

Of course, there was no sign of Diallo Niang. Zola had called his number while sitting in traffic, but got nothing.

With Bo translating, Zola paid cash for two larger rooms that connected, and went upstairs to see her mother. After they changed rooms, Zola began calling lawyers. During her flight, she had spent hours online searching for the right one. She wasn't sure she had located her, but she had a plan.

34

Over at the Bar Council, Margaret Sanchez had become obsessed with the case of Upshaw, Parker & Lane. As Chap Gronski slowly pieced together its scheme and scam, and the extent of its brazenness became clear, Ms. Sanchez was determined to nail the three. But first she had to find them. With a nod from her boss, she contacted the District police and, with some difficulty, convinced a detective to take a look. In the scope of the District's criminal activity, the police department had little interest in some law students who were gaming the system and not physically harming anyone.

Detective Stu Hobart got the nod and reviewed the case with Ms. Sanchez. Chap had tracked down the owner of The Rooster Bar, and he and Hobart made the visit together. They found Maynard in his office, one floor above the Old Red Cat in Foggy Bottom.

Maynard was fed up with Mark and Todd and their shenanigans, and he had no patience with anything that might provoke the cops to come sniffing around. Since he knew little of what was actually going on upstairs at 1504 Florida Avenue, he didn't say much about it. He did, however, possess the critical information.

He said, "Their real names are Todd Lucero and Mark Frazier. Don't know about the black girl. Lucero worked for me here for about three years, great bartender, everybody's favorite. Last January, he and Frazier moved to the other building and set up shop. They worked off the rent by tending bar."

"For cash, of course," Hobart said.

"Cash is still legal," Maynard said. He was dealing with a city cop, not the IRS, and he knew Hobart really didn't care how he paid his employees.

"Are they still living there?" Hobart asked.

"As far as I know. They're on the fourth floor, the girl is on the third, at least that's what I've been told. I fired Mark and Todd last week, but they're renting the place through June 1."

"Why'd you fire them?"

"That, sir, is none of your business. But I fired them because they were attracting too much attention. I can hire and fire at will, as you know."

"Of course. We checked the door to the upstairs and it appears to stay locked. I guess we could get a warrant and kick it in."

"I suppose you could," Maynard said. He opened a drawer, pulled out a ring of keys, found the one he wanted, unhooked it, and tossed it across the table. "That'll do it, but please don't involve the bar. It's one of my better ones."

Hobart picked up the key and said, "You got it. Thanks."

"Don't mention it."

AFTER DARK, ZOLA'S cab left the hotel and weaved through the thinning traffic of central Dakar. Twenty minutes later, it stopped at a busy intersection and she got out. She walked to a tall modern building where two security guards blocked the front door. They spoke no English but were impressed with her looks. She handed them a scrap of paper with the name of Idina Sanga, *Avocat,* and they quickly opened the door and led her through the lobby to an elevator.

According to her profile, Madame Sanga was a partner in a firm of ten lawyers, half of them women, and she spoke not only French and English but Arabic as well. She specialized in immigration matters, and, at least on the phone, seemed confident that she could handle the situation. She met Zola at the elevator on the fifth floor and they walked to a small conference room with no windows. Zola thanked her for staying after hours.

Judging from her photo on the firm's website, Madame Sanga was about forty years old, but in person she seemed much younger. She had been educated in Lyon and Manchester and spoke perfect English with a lovely British accent. She smiled a lot, was easy to talk to, and Zola spilled her guts.

For a modest retainer, Madame Sanga would take charge. The case was not unusual. No laws had been broken, and the initial harassment was typical. She had the right contacts with the police and immigration, and she was confident that in short order Abdou Maal would be released. Fanta and Bo would not be arrested. The family would be free to move about, and Madame Sanga would go about the task of obtaining proper documentation.

MARK AND TODD were sleeping soundly on their cheap twin beds on the fourth floor of 1504 Florida Avenue when someone knocked on the door. Mark stepped into their cramped den, flipped on a light, and said, "Who is it?"

"The police. Open up."

"You got a warrant?"

"Got two of them. For Frazier and Lucero."

"Shit!"

Detective Stu Hobart entered with two uniformed officers. He handed a sheet of paper to Mark and said, "You're under arrest." Todd stumbled out of the bedroom, wearing nothing but a pair of red boxers. Hobart handed him a warrant of his own.

"What the hell for?" Mark asked.

"Unauthorized practice of law," Hobart said proudly, and Mark laughed in his face. "Are you kidding me? Don't you have better things to do?"

"Shut up," Hobart said. "Get dressed and let's go."

"Go where?" Todd asked, rubbing his eyes.

"To jail, ass face. Let's go."

"What a crock," Todd said. They retreated to the bedroom, threw on some clothes, and returned to the den. A cop whipped out a pair of handcuffs and said, "Turn around."

"You gotta be kidding," Mark said. "We don't need handcuffs."

"Shut up and turn around," the cop snarled, eager for a confrontation. Mark turned around and the cop yanked his hands in place and slapped on the handcuffs. The other cop secured Todd, and the two were shoved out the door. Another uniformed cop was waiting at the curb, smoking a cigarette and guarding two D.C. patrol cars, engines running. Mark was pushed into the rear seat of one, Todd the other. Hobart assumed the passenger's seat, and as they drove away Mark said, "Right now in this city you've got gang wars, drug deals, rapes, and murders, and you guys are busy arresting two law students who wouldn't harm anyone."

"Just shut up, okay?" Hobart snarled over his shoulder.

"I don't have to shut up. There's not a law on the books that says I have to shut up, especially when I'm being arrested for some lousy misdemeanor like this."

"It's not a misdemeanor. If you knew anything about the law you'd know it's a felony."

"Well, it should be a misdemeanor, and you should be sued for wrongful arrest."

"That's terrifying, coming from you. Now shut up."

In the rear seat of the car behind them, Todd casually asked, "Does this give you guys a real thrill, knocking on doors in the middle of the night and slapping on handcuffs?"

"Just shut up, okay?" snarled the cop behind the wheel.

"Sorry, pal, but I don't have to shut up. I can talk all I want. The District has the highest murder rate in the country and you're wasting your time harassing us."

"Just doing our job," the driver said.

"Your job sucks, you know that? I guess we're lucky you didn't send in a SWAT team to kick in the door and spray bullets everywhere. That's your biggest thrill, right? Get all dressed up like Navy SEALs and pounce on people."

"I'm going to stop this car and kick your ass," the driver said.

"You do that and I'll sue your own fat ass at nine o'clock Monday morning. Big lawsuit, federal court."

"You gonna do it yourself or hire a real lawyer?" the driver said, and the other cop howled with laughter.

Ahead, Mark was saying, "How'd you find us, Hobart? Somebody at the Bar Council picked up our trail and called the cops? Figures. You must be real low on the pole to get stuck with a petty crime like this."

"I wouldn't call two years in jail petty," Hobart said.

"Jail? I'm not going to jail, Hobart. I'll just hire me another street lawyer, probably one without a license, and he'll be ten steps ahead of you. There's no way we're going to jail. We'll pay a small fine, get the old slap on the wrist, promise to never do it again, and walk out of court. Hell, we'll be back in business while you're still chasing jaywalkers."

"Just shut up."

"Not going to happen, Hobart."

At Central Jail, Mark and Todd were pulled out of the rear seats and jostled roughly into a basement entry. Once they were inside, the handcuffs were removed and they were separated. Over the next hour, each filled out two intake forms, got fingerprinted, and then was set in front of a camera for the standard mug shot. They were reunited in a holding cell where they waited for another hour, certain that they were about to be thrown in a cell with some real criminals. At 5:30, though, they were released on their own recognizance and informed that they could not leave the District of Columbia. Their citations directed them to appear in Division 6 in a week for their first appearances. They knew the place well.

Throughout the morning, they monitored the *Post* online and saw nothing about their arrests. Certainly, they could not be that newsworthy. They decided to wait before telling Zola that there was an arrest warrant with her name on it. She had enough on her mind anyway, and she was safely out of reach.

In their apartment, they spent two hours writing checks from the firm account. Refunds, to current clients who'd paid them in cash and were now getting stiffed because their lawyers were out of business. As bad as they needed the money, they simply could not walk away from their clients. The total was almost $11,000 and it was painful to part with, but they felt better when they mailed the envelopes. Mark managed to sell his Bronco for $600 at a used-car lot. He took the money in cash, signed over the title, and resisted the urge to look over his shoulder at the old wreck he'd driven for the past nine years. After dark, they loaded the firm's new desktop computer, color printer, and three boxes of files into the back of Todd's car. They threw some of their clothes into the rear seat, had one last beer at The Rooster Bar, and drove to Baltimore.

While Mark killed time in a hotel sports bar, Todd finally told his parents that he would not be graduating in a week. He admitted he had not been truthful, had in fact not gone to class at all that spring, did not have a job of any sort, was $200,000 in debt, and was now drifting and trying to figure out life. His mother cried while his father yelled, and the episode was even uglier than he had anticipated. On his way out, he said he was taking a long trip and needed to leave his car in the garage. His father yelled no, but he left it anyway and walked half a mile to the hotel.

The following morning, Mark and Todd caught a train to New York City. As it was leaving Penn Station, Todd handed over the *Washington Post*. At the bottom of the front page of the Metro section, a small headline read, "Two Arrested for Unauthorized Practice of Law." They were described as law school dropouts, former students at Foggy Bottom, where no one in administration had anything to say. Nor did Margaret Sanchez with the D.C. Bar Council. The two had apparently been roaming the city's courtrooms soliciting clients under assumed names and routinely appearing before judges. An unnamed source described them as "pretty good lawyers." A former client said Mr. Upshaw worked very hard on her case. A current client said he just wanted his money back. There was no mention of Zola Maal, though the story said "a third suspect is involved." If found guilty, they could face up to two years in prison and a fine of $1,000.

Their phones were crazy with calls from old friends at Foggy Bottom.

Todd said, "My dad will love this. Me, a felon."

Mark said, "My poor mother. Both of her sons headed to the slammer."

35

Zola was horrified at the news that her partners had been arrested. Even worse, the cops were looking for her as well, though she wasn't too worried about being tracked down in Senegal. Mark and Todd were in Brooklyn and claimed to have things under control, but she had serious doubts about that. They had been wrong about almost everything since January, and she found it difficult to accept their abundant confidence at this point. She found the story online and monitored it. Her name had not been mentioned and she found nothing about herself in the court dockets. Her Facebook page was flooded with comments and questions from friends, but she had stopped responding weeks earlier.

Idina Sanga had not been allowed to visit Abdou in jail, and after two days of waiting Zola was even more concerned. The police had been to the hotel twice to check on her mother and brother, but offered nothing in the way of news. Being with her family was comforting, and her presence and reassurances gave them hope. Bo and Fanta asked repeatedly about her studies, and graduation from law school, and the bar exam, and so on, but she managed to deflect their questions and keep the conversations away from the mess she had created back home. If they only knew. But, of course, they would not. They would never again set foot on U.S. soil, and Zola wasn't sure she wanted to either.

On the flight over, Zola had read a dozen articles about the crowded and dangerous conditions in Dakar's jails and prisons. She hoped that Bo and her mother had not been so curious. The places were deplorable.

Eventually, Zola ventured out of the hotel and went for walks around Dakar. The city sprawled across the Cap Vert peninsula and was a jumble of villages and former French colonial towns. The streets were hot and dusty and badly maintained, but brought to life each morning with heavy traffic and swarms of people. Many of the women wore long, sweeping dresses made of bright fabrics. Many of the men wore fine suits and seemed just as busy as those in D.C., with cell phones and briefcases. Horses pulling carts laden with fruits and produce battled with sleek new SUVs in the clogged intersections. As frantic as it looked at first, the city had a laid-back feel to it. Everyone seemed to know everyone else and few seemed to be in a hurry. Chatter and laughter filled the air. Music was everywhere, roaring from car stereos and shop doors and thumping from street bands giving impromptu concerts.

During her second full day in the city, Zola found the U.S. embassy and registered as a tourist. An hour later, as she was nearing the hotel, two policemen stopped her and asked for identification. She knew the police had broad powers to question and even detain. For almost any reason, anyone could be jailed for forty-eight hours.

One of the cops spoke a little English. She said she was an American and spoke no French. They were surprised to see her U.S. passport and her (real) New Jersey driver's license. She had wisely left the fake stuff at the hotel.

After a very long fifteen minutes, they handed her documents back and let her go. The incident was frightening enough, and she decided to save the tourist stuff for another day.

HER PARTNERS WERE set up in a small suite at a budget hotel on Schermerhorn Street in downtown Brooklyn. One bedroom, a fold-out sofa, small kitchenette, $300 a night. From an office supply store they paid $90 to rent for one month a printer/copier/scanner/fax machine.

Wearing coats and ties, they walked into a Citibank branch on Fulton Street and asked to see an account manager. Using their real names, driver's licenses, and Social Security numbers, they opened a checking account for the Legal Clinic of Lucero & Frazier. Using an old story, they said they were friends from law school and had grown weary of the grind in the big Manhattan firms. Their little clinic would help real people with real problems. They borrowed an address from an office building six blocks away, though an address was needed only to print on their new checks, which they would never see anyway. Mark wrote a personal check for $1,000 to open the account, and as soon as they were back in their suite they faxed a wiring authorization to their bank in D.C. The balance, just under $39,000, was wired to their new account, and the old one was closed. They e-mailed Ms. Jenny Valdez at Cohen-Cutler in Miami with the news that their firm of Upshaw, Parker & Lane had merged with a firm in Brooklyn, Lucero & Frazier. She e-mailed a pile of forms making the necessary changes, and they spent an hour on the paperwork. She asked them again about the Social Security numbers and bank account numbers for the eleven hundred clients they had referred to the class action, and they demurred again, saying simply that they were in the process of gathering that information.

Getting Hinds Rackley on the phone would be impossible, so they decided to begin with one of his law firms. The website for Ratliff & Cosgrove was useful enough and did a passable job of glossing over the fact that it was little more than a four-hundred-member firm that handled mortgage foreclosures, repossessions, delinquent accounts, bankruptcies, debt collections, and student loan defaults. Gordy had described it as "the gutter end" of financial services. It had about a hundred lawyers in its home office in Brooklyn, and its managing partner was Marvin Jockety, a sixtyish guy with a fleshy face and less than sterling résumé.

Mark sent him an e-mail:

> Dear Mr. Jockety, My name is Mark Finley, and I'm a freelance investigative journalist. I'm working on a story about Mr. Hinds Rackley, who I believe is a business associate of yours. After weeks of digging, I have discovered that Mr. Rackley, through his Shiloh Square Financial, and Varanda Capital, and Baytrium Group, and Lacker Street Trust, owns a total of eight for-profit law schools scattered around the country. Judging

from the bar exam results, it appears as though these eight law schools cater to a segment of the population that has no business studying law or sitting for the exam. However, it appears as though the schools are quite profitable.

I would like to arrange a meeting with Mr. Rackley as soon as possible. I have mentioned this story, without too many details, to the *New York Times* and the *Wall Street Journal,* and both are interested. Time is of the essence.

My phone number is 838-774-9090. I am in the city and eager to speak with Mr. Rackley or his representative.

Thanks, Mark Finley

It was Monday, May 12, at 1:30 p.m. They noted the time and wondered how long it would take Mr. Jockety to respond. As they waited and killed time in the suite, they launched an assault upon the unsuspecting folks in the suburbs of Wilmington, Delaware. Using online directories, they returned to their mischief and began adding additional names to their class action. Once you've committed eleven hundred felonies, what's another two hundred or so?

At 3:00, Mark re-sent the e-mail to Jockety, and did so again at 4:00. At 6:00, they took the subway to Yankee Stadium, where the Mets were playing in an overhyped crosstown grudge match that was not a sellout. They bought two tickets to the cheap seats in center field and paid $10 for twelve ounces of light beer. They moved to the top row to get far away from the other fans scattered through the bleachers.

They were due in court on Friday and had decided it would be wise not to miss the date. With their vast experience, they knew that bench warrants would be issued for their arrests. Todd called Hadley Caviness, who answered after the second ring.

"Well, well," she said. "Looks like you boys found trouble after all."

"Yes, dear, we are in trouble. Are you alone? Fair question."

"Yes, I'm going out later."

"Happy hunting. Look, yes, we need a favor. We're supposed to be arraigned this Friday but we've skipped town with no plans to return anytime soon."

"I don't blame you. You've caused quite a stir around the courthouse. Everybody has a story."

"Let 'em talk. Back to the favor."

"Have I ever denied you anything?"

"No, you have not, and I love you for it."

"That's what they all say."

"So, here's the favor. Do you think it's possible to ease over to Division 6 and ask the clerk to bump us down the road for a couple of weeks? It should be a simple matter of shuffling some paperwork, which you're a pro at."

"I don't know. There might be some people watching. If asked, what's the reason?"

"Tell them we're trying to hire a lawyer but we have no money. It's just a couple of weeks."

"I'll give it a look, see what I can do."

"You're a doll."

"Yeah, yeah."

In the bottom of the third, Mark's phone buzzed with an unknown number. He said, "This could be good."

It was Marvin Jockety and he began with "Mr. Rackley has no desire to meet with you, and he'll sue like hell if you get anything wrong."

Mark smiled, winked at Todd, touched the speaker button, and replied, "And good evening to you, sir. Why would Mr. Rackley be so eager to threaten a lawsuit? Does he have something to hide?"

"He does not. He is quite serious about his privacy and keeps some pretty nasty lawyers on retainer."

"I'll say. He has his finger in at least four law firms, including yours. Tell him to sue away. I don't have a dime."

"That won't stop him. He'll sue and he'll ruin your reputation as a journalist. And who do you work for, by the way?"

"No one but myself. I'm a freelance kind of guy. Come to think of it, Mr. Jockety, a lawsuit could be just the ticket I need because I'll countersue and go for some real money. I can collect a fortune in sanctions for a frivolous lawsuit."

"You're out of your league, buddy."

"We'll see. Tell Mr. Rackley that when he sues me he'll also be suing the *New York Times* because I'm meeting with them tomorrow afternoon. They want to run the story Sunday, front page."

Jockety laughed and said, "Mr. Rackley has more contacts with the *Times* and the *Journal* than you can possibly imagine. They won't touch a story like this."

"Well, I guess that's a chance he'll have to take. I know the truth and it'll make a helluva splash on the front page."

"You will regret it, sir," Jockety said and ended the call.

Mark stared at his phone, then put it in the pocket of his jeans. He took a deep breath and said, "Tough guy. This will not be easy."

"They're all tough. You think he'll call back?"

"Who knows? You gotta figure he talked to Rackley and they're spooked. The last thing Rackley wants is publicity. There's nothing illegal about his law school scam, but it stinks just the same."

"They'll call. And why not? If you were Rackley, wouldn't you be curious about how much we know?"

"Maybe."

"They'll call."

36

Mark was sleeping on the fold-out sofa when his phone erupted at 6:50 Tuesday morning. Jockety said, "Mr. Rackley can meet with you at ten this morning in our offices. We're in downtown Brooklyn, on Dean Street."

Mark said, "I know where you are." He didn't but the firm would be easy to find.

"I'll meet you downstairs in the lobby at 9:50. Please be prompt. Mr. Rackley is a very busy man."

"So am I. And I'll have a friend with me, another journalist, name of Todd McCain."

"Okay. Anybody else?"

"Nope, just the two of us."

Over coffee, they speculated that Rackley did not want them near his domain on Water Street in Manhattan's financial district. It was undoubtedly the gilded lair befitting a man of his stature, something a couple of reporters would have a field day describing. Better to meet them on turf crawling with his own lawyers. Litigation had already been threatened. They were stepping into his world, a rough place where his privacy would be protected at all costs and intimidation was always a useful tool.

They didn't shave and dressed in jeans and old jackets, the shaggy look of journalists unimpressed with anyone's surroundings. Mark packed a well-used nylon attaché case they'd found in a secondhand store in Brooklyn, and when they left the hotel on foot they certainly looked like a couple of guys not worth suing.

The building was tall and modern, one of many packed in the center of downtown Brooklyn. They killed time in a coffee shop around a corner and entered the atrium at 9:45. Marvin Jockety, looking at least ten years older than his website photo, was standing near the security counter, chatting with a clerk. Mark and Todd recognized him and introduced themselves, with Jockety reluctantly shaking hands. He nodded at the clerk and said, "This guy needs to see some identification." Mark and Todd reached for their wallets and handed over their fake D.C. driver's licenses. The clerk scanned them, glanced at both to compare faces with photos, and handed them back.

They followed Jockety to a row of elevators where they waited without conversation. When they stepped onto the empty elevator, he turned his back, faced the door, and said nothing.

Friendly bastard, Mark thought. What a jerk, Todd mumbled to himself.

The elevator stopped at the seventeenth floor and they stepped into the rather pedestrian lobby of Ratliff & Cosgrove. In their brief careers as lawyers they had visited several nice offices. Jeffrey Corbett's splendid digs in D.C. were by far the most impressive, though Mark still favored Edwin Mossberg's unique trophy museum down in

Charleston. Trusty Rusty's was by far the worst, with its medical office feel and wounded clients. This place was only slightly better. What the hell. They weren't there to analyze the decor.

Jockety ignored the receptionist, who ignored them in return. They rounded a corner, walked through a door without knocking, and entered a long, wide conference room. Two men in dark, expensive suits were standing at a sideboard sipping coffee from porcelain cups. Neither stepped forward. Jockety said, "Mr. Finley and Mr. McCain."

Mark and Todd had three images of Hinds Rackley, all from magazine articles. One was from Gordy's research, the enlarged head shot he had tacked to his unforgettable wall. The other two they had found online. Rackley was forty-three years old, with dark, thinning hair severely slicked back and narrow eyes behind semi-rimless frames. He nodded at Jockety, who left without a word and closed the door.

"I'm Hinds Rackley and this is my chief counsel, Barry Strayhan." Strayhan scowled and nodded and made no effort to take the introduction any further. Like his client, he held the cup in one hand and the saucer in the other; thus, they were unable to offer anything to shake properly. Mark and Todd kept their distance, which was at least ten feet away. A few awkward seconds passed, long enough for the two trespassers to get the message that notions of politeness had already gone out the window. Finally, Rackley said, "Have a seat," and nodded at the row of chairs on their side of the table. They sat down. Rackley and Strayhan sat opposite them.

Todd placed his cell phone on the table and asked, "Mind if I record this?"

"Why?" Strayhan asked like a real ass. He was at least ten years older than his client and gave the impression that everything in his life was contentious.

Todd said, "Just an old habit that most reporters have."

"Do you plan to transcribe the recording?" Strayhan asked.

"Probably," Todd said.

"Then we'll want a copy."

"No problem."

"And I'll record it too," Strayhan said as he laid his cell phone on the table. Dueling cell phones.

Throughout the exchange Rackley glared at Mark with a smug, confident look, as if to say, "I have billions and you don't. I'm superior in all respects so accept it."

One benefit of practicing street law without a license was that it had chipped away all traces of reticence. As Mark and Todd had brazenly gone about their business in the D.C. courts, they had grown accustomed to pretending to be people they were not. If they could stand before judges and use fake names and assume the roles of lawyers, they could certainly sit across from Hinds Rackley and act like journalists.

Mark returned the stare without blinking. Rackley finally said, "You wanted to see me."

Mark said, "Yes, well, we're working on a story and we thought you might want to comment on it."

"What's the story?"

"Well, the headline will be 'The Great Law School Scam,' for starters. You either own or control or somehow have your finger in several companies that own eight for-profit law schools. Really profitable law schools."

Strayhan said, "Have you found a statute somewhere prohibiting anyone from owning a for-profit law school?"

"I didn't say it was against the law, did I?" He looked to his right, at Todd, and asked, "Did I say that?"

"I didn't hear it," Todd said.

Mark said, "It's not against the law and we're not alleging anything criminal. It's just that these law schools are nothing more than diploma mills that entice lots of students to apply, regardless of their LSAT scores, and then to borrow heavily to cover the high tuitions charged by your schools. The tuitions are, of course, passed along to you, and the students graduate with tons of debt. About half of them are able to pass a bar exam. Most of them can't find jobs."

"That's their problem," Rackley said.

"Of course it is. And no one forces them to borrow the money."

Todd asked, "Do you admit that you own or control eight law schools?"

"I don't admit or deny anything, especially to you," Rackley snapped. "Who the hell do you think you are?"

Now that's a good question, Todd thought. As his many aliases blurred together, he often caught himself trying to remember his current name.

Strayhan laughed sarcastically and asked, "Do you happen to have any proof?"

Mark reached into his cheap attaché and removed a sheet of thick paper, twelve inches square. He unfolded it, then unfolded it again, and slid it across the table. It was a condensed version of Gordy's wall, the grand conspiracy, with Hinds Rackley's name all alone in the top box and the maze of his empire flowing below him.

For a second or two, Rackley looked at it with little curiosity, then picked it up and began a casual perusal. Strayhan leaned over for a closer look. Their initial reaction would be revealing. If Gordy was right, and they were convinced that he was, Rackley might realize that they were on his trail and had the proof. He might nitpick here or there, or concede the truth that he owned or controlled the swarm of entities. He might also deny everything and threaten to sue.

He slowly placed the chart back on the table and said, "Interesting, but not accurate."

Mark said, "Okay, care to discuss the inaccuracies?"

"I don't have to. If you publish a story based on this little flowchart, you'll be in serious trouble."

Strayhan added, "We'll sue for defamation and hound you for the next ten years."

Mark shot back, "Look, you've already tried the litigation scare tactics, okay, and obviously that's not working. We're not afraid of all your big talk about suing us. We own nothing. Fire away."

Todd said, "True, but we'd certainly like to avoid getting sued. What, exactly, do you find wrong with our research?"

"I'm not answering your questions," Rackley said. "But any half-assed reporter should know that it's illegal for me or anyone else to own a law firm that I'm not a member of. A lawyer cannot be a partner in more than one firm."

Mark replied, "We're not alleging ownership in the four law firms, only control. This firm, for example, Ratliff & Cosgrove, is run by your friend Marvin Jockety, who happens to be a limited partner in Varanda Capital. The other three firms have similar relationships. That's the connection, the control. And you use the four firms to hire graduates from your law schools at attractive salaries. Your law schools then advertise these wonderful jobs to entice even more unsuspecting kids to enroll and pay your jacked-up tuitions. That's the scam, Mr. Rackley, and it's brilliant. It's not illegal; it's just wrong."

"You guys are all wet," Strayhan said with another laugh, but one with a slight trace of nervousness.

Rackley's cell phone beeped and he removed it from a pocket. He listened and said, "Okay, step in please."

The door opened immediately and a man entered. He closed the door and stood at the end of the table holding some papers. Rackley said, "This is Doug Broome, my chief of security."

Mark and Todd looked at Broome, who did not acknowledge them. Broome adjusted his reading glasses and said, "Can't find anything on Mark Finley and Todd McCain. We searched all night and all morning, nothing. Not a single article, or blog, or book, or report anywhere online. There's a Mark Finley who writes about gardening for a newspaper in Houston, but he's fifty years old. There's another one who blogs about the Civil War, but he's sixty years old. There's another one who once wrote for a campus newspaper in California, but he graduated and became a dentist. Beyond that, nothing. For Todd McCain, all we found was a guy in Florida who writes for a local magazine. So, if these two claim to be journalists, then their careers must be off to a slow start. As far as the names, there are 431 Mark Finleys and 142 Todd McCains in this country. We've checked every one and nothing matches. And most interesting of all, the two driver's licenses presented at the security desk downstairs are from the District of Columbia. Surprise, surprise, they're both fake."

Rackley said, "Thanks, Doug. That's all." Doug left the room and closed the door.

Rackley and Strayhan were both grinning. Mark and Todd kept their cool. At this point, there was no turning back. Mark managed to control his nerves by maintaining the attack. "Very impressive! That's some outstanding work."

"Really impressive," Todd chimed in, but both were thinking of bolting for the door.

Rackley said, "Okay, boys, with all credibility shot to hell, why don't you tell us who you are and what's your game?"

Mark said, "If you're not answering our questions, then we're not answering yours. Who we are is really not that important. What's important here is that our little chart is close enough to the truth to expose your scam and embarrass the hell out of you."

Strayhan demanded, "You want money? Is this extortion?"

"No, not at all. Our plans haven't changed. We'll sit down with the right reporter and hand it over. There's a lot more in the file. For example, we have testimony from former associates of your law firms who feel as though they were used as propaganda. We have statements from former law professors. We have all the data regarding the rotten bar exam pass rates of your graduates. We have the data that clearly shows that you greatly expanded your enrollments at the same time the Feds opened the Treasury to thousands of unqualified students. We have dozens of testimonials from these students who graduated with tons of debt but couldn't find jobs. The file's pretty thick, and it will make a helluva splash on the front page."

"Where is this file?" Strayhan asked.

Todd reached into a shirt pocket, removed a thumb drive, and casually bounced it across the table. "It's all right there. Read it and weep."

Rackley ignored it and said, "I have contacts with the *Times* and the *Journal*. They assure me they know nothing about this."

With great relish, Mark smiled at Rackley and said, "Bullshit. Arrogant, preposterous bullshit. You expect us to believe that you know everyone at these newspapers, and not only do you know them but they trust you enough to pass along inside information? What a joke! And this from a man who is notorious for dodging reporters. Come on, Mr. Rackley."

Strayhan said, "Well, I certainly know the attorneys for the *Times* and the *Journal,* and you can bet your sweet ass they want no part of a defamation suit."

"Are you kidding?" Todd said, laughing. "They'll love it because they can crank up the firm at a thousand bucks an hour. They want their clients to get sued every day."

"You're clueless, son," Strayhan said, but it meant nothing. The chart had clearly rattled them, along with the fact that Mark and Todd were not who they claimed to be. Rackley shoved his chair back, stood, and took his cup to the coffeepot. Nothing in the way of beverages had been offered to the impostors. He slowly poured from a silver pot, added two cubes of sugar, stirred slowly, deep in thought, then returned to the table. He sat down, took a sip, and calmly said, "You're right. It's a nice front-page splash, but it's a twenty-four-hour story because everything is proper and legal. I don't cross the line, and right now I'm really not sure why I'm wasting my time explaining this to you."

Mark replied, "Oh, it's more than a twenty-four-hour story. By the time they flesh out the law school math and print the numbers that show you net about twenty million bucks a year from each of your eight schools, the story will have serious legs. Tie the money back to the federal treasury, and you'll have a public relations nightmare that won't end."

Rackley shrugged and said, "Maybe, maybe not."

Todd said, "Let's talk about Swift Bank."

Rackley said, "No, we're tired of talking, especially to a couple of guys who use fake names and fake IDs."

Todd ignored him and said, "According to your SEC filings, Shiloh Square Financial owns 4 percent of Swift, making it the second-largest stockholder. We think you own a lot more than that."

Rackley blinked and recoiled slightly. Strayhan frowned, as if confused. Mark reached into his attaché case and removed another sheet of paper. He unfolded it once but did not slide it over.

From the grave, Gordy landed a final blow.

Todd continued, "We have a list of Swift Bank's largest shareholders, about forty in all. Most are investment funds that own 1 or 2 percent of the company. Some of these funds are foreign and appear to be legitimate investments. Some, though, are offshore shells, fronts for other fronts that own pieces of Swift. Shady-looking names of companies domiciled in places like Panama, Grand Cayman, the Bahamas. They are almost impossible to penetrate, especially for a couple of non-journalists like us. We can't issue subpoenas and warrants; we can't tap phones and make arrests. But the FBI certainly can."

Mark slid the second sheet of paper across the table. Rackley took it calmly and studied the chart. It was a continuation of the first one, with all the activity flowing under Swift Bank. After a few seconds, Rackley shrugged again, even smiled, and said, "I don't recognize any of these companies."

Strayhan managed to mumble, "Just garbage."

Mark said, "And we're not alleging you're involved with them, you understand? We have no way of digging inside offshore companies."

"I got it the first time," Rackley said. "What do you want?"

"Are you after money?" Strayhan demanded.

"No, and you've already asked that once," Todd said. "What we want is the truth. We want you and your great law school scam exposed on page 1. We're victims of it. We signed on at one of your diploma mills, racked up a fortune in federal debt, none of which we can repay because we can't find jobs, and now we're a couple of dropouts staring at a pretty dark future. And we're not alone. There are thousands of us, Mr. Rackley, all victimized by you."

Mark said, "The guy who drew those charts was our best friend. He cracked up and killed himself in January. There were several reasons, and plenty of blame all around. And some of it lies with you. He owed a quarter of a million dollars in student loans, money passed along to you. All of us got caught up in the law school scam. I guess he was a little more fragile than we realized."

Nothing that registered on the faces of Rackley and Strayhan could even remotely be described as remorse.

Calmly, Rackley said, "I'll ask you again. What do you want?"

Mark said, "A quick settlement of all six Swift Bank class actions, beginning with the one filed by Cohen-Cutler in Miami."

Rackley raised both hands, held them in the air as if flabbergasted, and finally said to Strayhan, "I thought we were settling those cases."

"We are," Strayhan said, frowning.

Mark added helpfully, "Well, according to reports that the bank keeps leaking to the press, it is in the process of negotiating settlements, but that's been the story for the past ninety days. The truth is that your lawyers are dragging their feet. There are one million customers out there who've been screwed by Swift and they deserve to be compensated."

"We know that!" Rackley snapped, finally losing his cool. "Believe me, we know all that, and we're trying to settle, or at least I thought we were." He turned, glared at Strayhan, and said, "Find out what's going on." Then to Mark he said, "What is your interest in the litigation?"

"It's confidential," Mark said smugly.

"Really can't talk about it," Todd added. "Right now it's almost 10:30 on Tuesday. How long would it take before the bank could announce a settlement for all class actions?"

"Not so fast," Rackley said. "What happens to your story about the great law school scam? The front-page sensation?"

"Here's the deal," Todd said. "Tomorrow at 4:00 we meet with a reporter for the *Times*."

"A real reporter?" Rackley asked.

"Damned right. One who can peel skin. And we'll give

him the story. If he runs it, and we have no reason to think he will not, then you're the villain of the month. Worse, the story attracts the attention of the FBI, which, as I'm sure you know, is already hot on Swift's trail anyway. The bit about the offshore ownership will be like throwing gasoline on a fire."

"I get all that," Rackley said. "Cut to the chase."

"If Swift announces a full settlement within twenty-four hours, we won't meet with the reporter."

"And you walk away?"

"We walk away. You ramp up the settlement. Make sure the Miami class gets its money first, and when that cash hits home, we walk away. Not a word. The law school scam story is left for someone else to pursue."

Rackley stared at them for a long time. Strayhan knew better than to speak. A minute passed, though it seemed like half an hour. Finally, Rackley stood and said, "The bank has no choice but to settle anyway. It will make the announcement this afternoon. Beyond that, I suppose I'll have to trust your word."

Mark and Todd stood, more than ready to leave. Mark said, "You have our word, for what it's worth."

"You can go now," Rackley said.

37

Idina Sanga made no progress over the weekend. The police refused her access to Abdou, though they claimed he was safe and being properly treated. She called Zola around noon on Monday with the update that little had changed. Idina was leaning on her contacts at various levels of the state bureaucracy, and said repeatedly that these matters take time.

After four days of waiting around the hotel, Zola was climbing the walls. She sat with Fanta in their suite and talked for hours, something the two had not done in years. She and Bo lounged in the small hotel café and drank tea several times a day. She called her partners for the latest developments in their misadventures.

The two rooms were costing her the equivalent of about $100 a day. Add in their meals in the café, and Zola was beginning to worry about her finances. She had arrived with roughly $10,000 U.S., and she paid about $3,000 as a retainer to Madame Sanga's firm for representation and clout. Assuming Abdou would soon be released, the family would need housing, clothing, food, and so on, and her balance would soon be gone. She had $6,000 in her account in D.C., and she knew her partners would help in a pinch, but she was suddenly fretting over money. When they had been seized by ICE, Abdou had $800 in cash. Bo had $200. The family's savings had been wiped out when they hired an immigration lawyer who did nothing. Whatever future they had in Senegal was dependent upon Zola's meager savings.

And the likelihood of bribery had yet to be addressed.

Late Monday afternoon, their shaky financial condition worsened. Two police cars parked at the curb in front of the hotel and four uniformed officers jumped out. Zola and Bo were drinking tea in the lobby and recognized two of the officers. They were told to stay where they were as the desk clerk handed over keys to their rooms on the fourth floor. One cop stayed with them as the other three took an elevator. Minutes later, Fanta was escorted off the elevator and parked in the lobby with Zola and Bo.

"They're searching our rooms," Fanta whispered to Zola. As terrifying as it was, Zola was relieved to know that her cash and valuables were in the hotel safe behind the front desk.

They waited for an hour, certain that their rooms were being trashed. When the three cops returned to the lobby, the leader, a sergeant, handed a sheet of paper to the desk clerk, who quickly complied. The sergeant said in English, "We have a search warrant for the hotel safe."

"Wait a minute," Zola demanded as she stepped toward the desk. "You can't search my stuff." A cop stopped her.

Fanta rattled away in French and Bo tried to help her but got shoved in the process. The desk clerk disappeared and returned with a small metal box, identical to the one Zola had rented. She had watched the clerk slide it into the master safe with a dozen others. It was not equipped with a lock.

The sergeant looked at Zola and said, "Over here." She stepped to the counter and watched as he opened the box. He opened an envelope and pulled out some U.S. cash. Slowly, he counted twenty $100 bills. He removed a thick stack of West African francs, and counted. At an exchange rate of 600 francs to one U.S. dollar, the counting took some time. Zola watched it carefully, seething at this violation but thoroughly powerless. The combined cash totaled almost $6,000 U.S. Satisfied with the haul so far, the sergeant emptied the metal box. Rubber banded together were three cards—her fake D.C. driver's license, her Foggy Bottom student ID card, and an expired credit card. Her collection of cell phones was hidden in a bag stuffed under her mattress.

In her purse, clutched tightly to her side, she had her passport, New Jersey driver's license, about $500 cash, and two credit cards. If they reached for it, she would not let go without a fight. Her knees buckled when the sergeant said, "Passport?"

She unzipped her purse, fished around, and produced it. He examined it carefully, stared long and hard at her purse, then handed it back. While this unfolded, another cop was listing the contents of the metal box. Evidently, the contents would be taken away.

With her purse secure, Zola asked, "Are you taking my stuff?"

"We have a warrant," the sergeant said.

"But for what? I haven't committed a crime."

"We have a warrant," he said. "Sign here." He pointed to the crude inventory list.

"I'm not signing anything," she said, but she knew she had no choice. At that moment, though, she knew the reality. She took a deep breath and acknowledged the futility of resisting.

The sergeant placed her cash and cards into a large hotel envelope and handed it to another cop. He looked at Bo and said, in French, "You are coming with us."

Bo didn't understand until the nearest officer whipped out a pair of handcuffs and grabbed his wrist. He instinctively jerked away and this caused another officer to grab his arm.

"What are you doing?" Zola demanded in English while Fanta protested in French. Bo took a deep breath and relaxed as his hands were cuffed behind him. "It's okay," he said to Fanta.

"What are you doing?" Zola demanded again. The sergeant unclipped his set of handcuffs and dangled them in her face. "Quiet! You want these?"

"You can't take him away," she said.

"Quiet!" the sergeant snarled. "Or we take your mother too."

Bo said, "It's okay, Zola. It's okay. I'll check on Dad."

Two of the officers shoved Bo toward the front door, and they left, the sergeant holding the envelope. Zola and Fanta watched in disbelief as Bo was manhandled to the cars and thrown into a rear seat.

As they drove away, Zola called Idina Sanga.

AT 4:00 ON Tuesday afternoon, May 13, lawyers for Swift Bank announced the proposed settlement of the six class action lawsuits scattered around the country. Given the rumors and speculation during the past three months, the news was almost anticlimactic. Predictions of a massive settlement by Swift had gone stale.

Under the terms, Swift would pay into a settlement fund the initial sum of $4.2 billion to cover the anticipated claims of about 1.1 million potential customers. The six class actions included 800,000, leaving 300,000 out there as fair game for the mass tort bar. With 220,000 plaintiffs, the Cohen-Cutler class was the largest, the first to be filed, and the best organized, and it would be at the front of the line to collect its money.

The settlement covered three levels of plaintiffs. The first were the most aggrieved, those homeowners who had been forced into foreclosure by Swift's bad behavior. This was by far the smallest group, with an anticipated number of about five thousand. Level two was composed of about eighty thousand Swift customers whose credit had been ruined or severely damaged by the bank's actions. Level three was everybody else—those Swift customers who had been cheated by hidden fees and reduced interest rates. Each would receive $3,800 for their troubles.

The attorneys' fees were negotiated separately and would be paid into another fund. For each individual case, the fee was $800, regardless of actual damages. Cohen-Cutler, as well as the other lead class action firms, would get an additional 8 percent of the gross.

The business commentators were immediately buzzing with the news, and the general belief was that Swift was doing exactly what it was expected to do. Throw a pile of money at its problem, make it go away, and move on. With windfalls all around, the settlement was expected to be approved by the courts within days.

By 5:00 p.m., not a single class action lawyer was on record opposing the settlement. They were too busy hustling the unsigned Swift plaintiffs.

HADLEY CALLED TODD late Tuesday afternoon with some dreadful news. She had been unable to work her magic and bump their case down the road a week or two. Instead, the prosecutor handling their charges was adamant that they show up in court Friday for their initial appearances. Hadley said the case was getting some attention. Everyone was so bored with druggies and DUIs it was rather refreshing to have such an unusual case on the docket. Sorry, boys.

"We have to hire a lawyer," Todd said. They were sitting on a park bench at Coney Island, smoking long black cigars and sipping bottled water.

"Let's argue," Mark said. "I say we don't hire a lawyer."

"Okay. We don't show up in court Friday. What happens then? The judge will probably issue bench warrants and our names go into the system."

"So? Big deal. It's not like we're narco-traffickers or al-Qaeda. We're not peddling drugs or plotting terror. Do you really believe that anyone will be serious about tracking us down?"

"No, but we'll be wanted, dead or alive."

"What's the big deal if no one is looking for us?"

"What if we find ourselves in a bind and need to leave the country? We pull out our passports at the airport and a bell goes off somewhere. Outstanding warrants in D.C. The customs guy couldn't care less what crime we're charged with. We try to explain that it's nothing but a couple of clowns pretending to be lawyers, but he's not impressed. All he sees is a red flag, and suddenly we see the handcuffs again. Gotta tell you, I'd love to avoid any more handcuffs."

"And what's a lawyer going to do?"

"Delay, delay, delay. Buy us some time, keep the warrants at bay. Negotiate a deal with the prosecutor, keep us out of jail."

"I'm not doing jail, Todd. I don't care what happens."

"We've had this discussion. What we need is time, and the lawyer can stall this thing for months."

Mark pulled on his cigar; got a mouthful; blew a thick cloud. "Got anybody in mind?"

"Darrell Cromley."

"What an ass. I hope he's still trying to find us."

"I'm thinking about Phil Sarrano. He was a third year at Foggy Bottom when we started. Good guy, works with a small criminal firm near Capitol Hill."

"I remember him. What's he gonna charge?"

"We won't know until we ask. Five to ten grand, don't you think?"

"Let's haggle, okay? We're still on a tight budget."

"I'll call him."

Phil Sarrano wanted a $10,000 retainer. Todd gasped, choked, stuttered, appeared to be stunned, and explained that he and his co-defendant were just a couple of law school dropouts with no jobs and about half a million in debts between them. Todd assured him the case would not go to trial and would not consume much of his time.

Slowly, he chiseled away at the number, and they finally agreed on $6,000, money Todd said he would be forced to borrow from his grandmother.

An hour later Sarrano called back with the bad news that the judge assigned to the case, the Honorable Abe Abbott, wanted the two defendants to appear in person at 10:00 a.m. Friday, Division 6, in the District Courthouse. Evidently, Judge Abbott was intrigued by the case and rather eager to get to the bottom of things. Thus, no postponement of the initial appearances.

"And he wants to know where Zola Maal is these days," Sarrano said.

"We're not in charge of Zola Maal," Todd said. "Try Africa. Her family just got deported and maybe she went with them."

"Africa? Okay, I'll pass that along."

Todd broke the news to Mark that they would be headed back to D.C. a lot sooner than they had expected. Todd had appeared before Judge Abbott on one occasion; same for Mark. The upcoming reunion was not a welcome thought.

38

The Frazier home was on York Street in Dover, Delaware. The Lucero family still lived on Orange Street in south Baltimore. Thus, York & Orange Traders came to life via the astonishingly efficient incorporation laws of Mark's home state. For $500, paid by credit card, the charter was granted online, and the fledgling company used as its business address one of the many corporate services available in Delaware. Once up and running in the U.S., York & Orange Traders immediately began to expand. It looked southward and chose the Caribbean nation of Barbados as its first branch. For a fee of $650, the company got itself registered in the Lesser Antilles.

Opening a bank account there, though, would not be as easy as registering a business.

After weeks of online research, Mark and Todd knew better than to try their luck with Swiss banks. Any whiff of ill-gotten gains, and the Swiss would refuse to do business. As a whole, their banks were wary of the U.S. regulators, and many flatly refused new business from the States.

Things appeared to be a bit more laid-back in the Caribbean.

WALL STREET LIKED the news of the proposed settlement. Swift Bank opened sharply higher and continued to rise on heavy trading throughout the morning. By noon Wednesday, it had doubled and was nudging $27 a share.

Swift's lawyers were scrambling to get approvals from the six federal judges handling the class actions. Not surprisingly, at least not to Mark and Todd, who were monitoring minute by minute with several court watch apps, the judge in Miami crossed the finish line first and signed off on the deal before 2:00 p.m., less than twenty-four hours after Swift announced its plans.

Not long thereafter, Marvin Jockety called Mark and, with strained politeness, said, "Please call Barry Strayhan."

"Sure. The number?"

Jockety gave him the number and went away. Mark immediately called Strayhan, who said, "We've upheld our end of the bargain. What about you?"

"We've canceled our meeting with the *Times*. We'll sit on things until the money comes through, then we'll go away. Just as we promised."

"What's your angle with the settlement?"

"Harvard Law School, right, Mr. Strayhan? Class of 1984?"

"Correct."

"Didn't they teach you at Harvard to avoid questions that will not be answered?"

The line was dead.

ON WEDNESDAY MORNING, Idina Sanga presented herself at the jail and announced to the clerks that she was not leaving until she had consulted with her clients. And, she had the name and phone number of a ranking judicial minister at the ready. She made as much noise as possible for an hour and was finally led to a wing filled with tiny rooms, most of which she had seen before. There were no windows, no fans, no draft of any sort, and for another hour she waited in the thick and sweltering heat until Bo was brought in, handcuffed. His left eye was swollen and there was a small cut over it. His guards left but the handcuffs remained in place.

"I'm fine," he said. "Please don't mention this to Zola or my mother."

"What happened?" she asked.

"The guards, just having some fun, you know."

"I'm sorry. Should I complain?"

"No, please. It will only make matters worse, if that's possible. I'm in a cell with five other men, all sent back from the U.S. Conditions are not good but we're surviving. Complaints complicate things."

"And no sign of Abdou?"

"No. I have not seen my father and I'm worried about him."

"Have you been interrogated?" Idina asked.

"Yes, this morning, by a ranking officer. Just the two of us, no one else was in the room. They think my sister is a wealthy American lawyer, and, of course, they want money. I tried to explain that she is only a poor law student with no job, but he doesn't believe it. He called me a liar. They have the proof. They found the cash in Zola's box at the hotel. He called that a down payment, said he wants more."

"How much more?"

"Ten thousand U.S. for my father, eight thousand for my mother, another eight for me."

"That's outrageous," Idina said, stunned. "Bribery is not uncommon, but not in those sums."

"Again, he thinks Zola is wealthy. If she came here with a lot of cash, then there must certainly be more back home."

"What about the six thousand they've already taken?"

"He said that's the price for Zola. I argued that she's an American citizen who's already signed in at the U.S. embassy down the street. He was not impressed. He said they plan to arrest her and my mother if the money is not paid."

"This is preposterous. I have important friends in the government and I plan to call them at once."

Bo shook his head and grimaced. "Don't do that, please. Two men died here last week, so I'm told. Things can get a lot worse. We hear screaming occasionally. Again, if we complain, who knows what will happen." With his wrists stuck together, Bo awkwardly wiped his mouth with the back of his hand. "I have friends in the U.S., but they're all working people like us, with little money. My brother, Sory, lives in California now, but he never saves his money and is always broke. I can't think of anyone to call. My boss, or my ex-boss, is a good man but he will not get involved. No one wants to get involved when illegals are rounded up and sent back. We were in the detention center for four months and lost contact with almost everyone on the outside. Once your friends know you're getting removed, they are no longer your friends. It's every man for himself." He closed his eyes and frowned as if in pain. "I don't know of anyone to call. You'll have to ask Zola."

THE METS WON the first two games at Yankee Stadium. The next two would be at Citi Field. Once again, Mark and Todd bought the cheapest seats possible and found themselves high in left field, far above the action. Hyped as it was, the third game was far from a sellout.

They sipped beer, watched the game, cheered for neither team because Todd was an Orioles fan while Mark pulled for the Phillies, and quietly planned the next few days. In the morning, they would take the train to D.C., and meet with Phil Sarrano, who would talk to the prosecutor and get a feel for his mood.

Todd was buying a bag of peanuts when Mark's phone buzzed. It was Zola, still holed up in a grungy hotel where nothing was certain. Either Mark or Todd had spoken with her every day, though the chats were brief. They used e-mails for updates, but were careful not to put everything in writing. On the topic of bribery, it was best to correspond by phone.

"Serious trouble," Mark said as he put away his phone. He summarized what she'd told him, and finished with "She needs $26,000. She has six in her bank in D.C. That's twenty from the firm account."

Todd thought for a second and said, "The old firm account is taking a beating these days. Plenty of outflow with nothing coming in."

"Balance is $31,000, right?"

"Just over. How good do you feel about wiring twenty thousand to anyone in Senegal?"

"She wants it sent to her lawyer's trust account. From there, who knows, but I'm sure Zola can figure it out."

"What if they bust her for bribery?"

"I'm not sure anyone gets busted for bribery over there. It's a chance we'll have to take."

"So, we're doing it? Just like that? Saying good-bye to twenty thousand bucks earned the hard way, hustling drunks in city courts?"

"Well, most of it came from the taxpayers, if you'll recall. We pooled our loans meant for living expenses. We're in it together, Todd, nothing has changed. Zola needs it. We have it. End of conversation."

Todd cracked a shell and tossed some peanuts into his mouth. "Okay. But they can't arrest her, can they? She's registered with our embassy."

"You're asking me what the police can and cannot do in Dakar, Senegal?"

"No, as a matter of fact, I'm not asking you that."

"Good. She's an American kid, Todd, just like us, and we're sitting here enjoying a baseball game while she's sweating it out back in Africa, a place she's never seen before. We're worrying about facing an unfriendly judge on Friday while she's worrying about being thrown in jail, where anything might happen. Can you imagine the guards when they get a look at her?"

"Are you lecturing me again?"

"I don't know what I'm doing, really, except drinking beer. We owe her big-time, Todd. Five months ago her life was pretty good. She and Gordy were having fun. She was about to finish law school and do whatever the hell she thought she was going to do. Then we came along. Now she's in Senegal, terrified, broke, unemployed, freshly sued, soon to be indicted, and on and on. Poor girl. She probably curses the day she met us."

"No, she loves us."

"She'll love us a lot more when we wire over the twenty grand."

"She's probably more fragile than we realize."

"I think you're right. Good thing you and I are not fragile. Crazy maybe, but not fragile."

"I'll go with crazy. A couple of lunatics."

"Do you ever ask yourself why we did it?"

"No. You spend too much time looking back, Mark, and maybe I don't spend enough. But what's done is done. We can't go back and change anything, so stop thinking about it and trying to make sense of it. It happened. We did it. We can't unwind it. Hell, we have enough to think about in the near future."

"No regrets?"

"I don't do regrets, you know that."

"I wish I could just turn it off like that." Mark took a sip of beer and watched the game. After a moment, he said, "I regret the day I showed up at law school. I regret borrowing all that money. I regret what happened to Gordy. And I'll really regret things if they give us six months in the slammer and label us as convicted felons."

"Great. Now you have regrets. What's the benefit of whining about them now?"

"I'm not whining."

"Sounds like it to me."

"Okay, I'm whining. And if you end up in jail, you still won't have any regrets?"

"Mark, you and I both know that we are not going to jail. Period. Some judge might one day sign an order sentencing us to jail, but we will not be in the courtroom when that happens. We will not be in the city, probably not the country. Agreed?"

"Agreed."

39

At nine Thursday morning, Mark and Todd entered their new bank on Fulton Street as it opened. They had an appointment with an account manager and soon fed her a convoluted tale of their urgent need to wire $20,000 to a law firm in Senegal. Zola had e-mailed the precise wiring instructions. The manager had not yet performed such a task in her brief career. She made a few phone calls and learned, as did Todd and Mark, that the exchange rate between U.S. dollars and West African francs was important. The dollars were first converted to francs, then the wire was authorized by Mr. Lucero, senior partner. The wire was initiated and the money would arrive in Senegal in about twenty-four hours, if all went well. The transaction took an hour, plenty of time for Mark and Todd to charm the account manager with their clever remarks and winning personalities.

With the money on the way, Mark and Todd took the train into Manhattan and eventually arrived at Penn Station. Killing time and in no hurry whatsoever to return to D.C., they boarded at noon and napped all the way home.

Home? Though they had been gone for only five days, D.C. seemed like a different world. For years it had been their chosen ground, the place where they would begin and build their careers in the midst of endless opportunity, a city brimming with lawyers and firms and young professionals, all moving up. Now it was the place where they had failed miserably, with the damage meter still clicking away. They would soon leave D.C. in a hurry, and in disgrace, and with people looking for them, and so they found it difficult to gaze at the city from the backseat of a cab and feel any twinge of nostalgia.

Phil Sarrano's office was on Massachusetts Avenue near Scott Circle. He was one of four associates in a ten-member firm that specialized in white-collar criminal defense, work that usually meant nice fees from well-heeled politicians, lobbyists, or government contractors. Somehow the firm found time for two dropouts who'd made a rather brazen raid into the city's proud legal profession and were too broke to hire a more experienced lawyer.

Phil was only one year older than Todd and Mark. He had finished law school at Foggy Bottom in 2011, the year they had started. Looking around his office, though, they could see no diploma from the diploma mill. On the Ego Wall behind his desk was a handsome, framed certificate from the University of Michigan conferring upon him a degree in liberal arts, but nothing from Foggy Bottom. It was a nice office in a nice little firm that gave every impression of being prosperous and engaging. Phil certainly seemed to enjoy his work.

Where had they gone so wrong? Why had their careers fallen off the tracks?

"Who's prosecuting?" Todd asked.

"Mills Reedy. Know her?"

"Nope. Never slept with her. Did you?" he asked Mark.

"Not that one."

"I beg your pardon?" Phil said.

"Sorry, inside joke," Todd said.

"Better keep it inside."

"Is she tough?" Mark asked.

"Yes, a real ballbuster," Phil said, reaching for a file. "She sent over the file and I've gone through it. They have copies of all of your court appearances, with those other names of course, so I gotta ask the question that I don't usually ask: Do you guys have any defense to these charges?"

"Nope," Mark said.

"None whatsoever," Todd said. "We're guilty as hell."

"Then why'd you do it?" Phil asked.

"Isn't that another question you're never supposed to ask a client?" Todd asked.

"I suppose. Just curious, that's all."

Mark said, "We'll talk about that later, maybe over a drink. My question has to do with the prosecution. Are they really serious about this crap? It's such a minor little crime. In fact, in half the states unauthorized practice is not even a felony. It's a low-grade misdemeanor."

"This ain't half the states," Phil said. "This is D.C. and, as you would probably know if you actually had licenses, the Bar Council takes its work very seriously. And it does a good job. I've had one conversation with Ms. Reedy and she was all business. Reminded me that the max is two years in jail and a $1,000 fine."

"That's ridiculous,"Todd said.

"We're not serving time, Phil," Mark said. "And we gave our last $6,000 to you, so we're even broker."

"Had to borrow it from my grandmother,"Todd said.

"You want it back?" Phil asked, bristling.

"No, no, you keep it," Mark said. "We just want you to know that we're broke and we're not going to jail, so write that down somewhere."

Todd said, "And we can't post a bond either."

Phil was shaking his head. "I doubt that'll happen. So, if you have no defense and you won't accept any of the penalties, what exactly do you want me to do?"

"Stall," Mark said.

"Delay,"Todd said. "Drag it out, let it blow over. If you asked for a trial date what would you get?"

"At least six months, maybe a year," Phil said.

"Beautiful," Mark said. "Tell Ms. Reedy we're going to trial and we'll have plenty of time to work a deal."

"You guys sound like a couple of real lawyers," Phil said.

"We were educated at Foggy Bottom,"Todd said.

AFTER DARK THEY sneaked into their apartment above The Rooster Bar, to check on things and perhaps settle in for the night. But it was even gloomier than they remembered, and after an hour they called a car and went to a budget motel. Each had $5,000 cash in a pocket, which meant that the Lucero & Frazier firm checking account was down to its last $989.31. They found a pricey steak house and splurged on filets and two bottles of fine California cabernet.

After the table was cleared and the wine was almost gone, Todd asked, "Remember the movie *Body Heat*? Kathleen Turner and William Hurt?"

"Sure, a great movie about an incompetent lawyer."

"Among other things. Mickey Rourke plays a guy in jail, and he has this famous line, something like, 'When you commit a murder you make ten mistakes. If you can think of eight of them, then you're a genius.' Remember that?"

"Maybe. Have you killed someone?"

"No, but we've made mistakes. In fact, we've probably made so many mistakes we can't even think of half of them."

"Number one?"

"We blew it when we told Rackley about our friend committing suicide. That was really stupid. His security guy, what's his name?"

"Doug Broome, I think."

"That's it. Broome scared the shit out of us when he walked in and told us they had checked every Mark Finley and every Todd McCain in the country, right?"

"Yes."

"So, it's obvious Rackley is a fanatic about security and intelligence. It wouldn't take much of an effort to research recent suicides by students at his law schools. Gordy's name would pop up. Broome and his boys could snoop around Foggy Bottom and someone could drop our names, which were in the *Post* last week, by the way. Without too much effort, Broome could track down our real names, which, of course, would lead to our new law firm up in Brooklyn."

"Wait, I'm not following. Even if he knows our real names and where we're from, how can he find Lucero & Frazier in Brooklyn? We're not exactly registered up there.

We're not in the phone book, not on a website. I don't get it."

"Mistake number two. We overplayed the Miami class action. Rackley and Strayhan must have asked themselves why we are so interested in the Cohen-Cutler lawsuit. That's our angle, so we must have some skin in that game. What if, and I'm not sure about this, but what if Broome can find out that the firm of Lucero & Frazier has referred thirteen hundred cases to Cohen-Cutler?"

"Stop right there. We are not the attorneys of record and our firm name is off the books, same as dozens of other lawyers who've referred their cases. Cohen-Cutler has the information, but it's confidential. There's no way Rackley could penetrate Cohen-Cutler. Besides, why would he want to?"

"Maybe he doesn't have to. Maybe he just informs the FBI that there is potential fraud in the Swift Bank settlement."

"But he wants the settlement to be done, and as soon as possible."

"Maybe, but I have a hunch Rackley would react badly if he suspected we were stealing from him."

"I doubt he'll venture anywhere near the FBI when it comes to Swift."

"True, but he can find a way to blow the whistle."

Mark twirled his wine around his glass and admired it. He took a sip and smacked his lips. Todd was staring into the distance.

Mark said, "I thought you don't do regrets."

"These are mistakes, not regrets. Regrets are over and done with and a waste of time to rehash. Mistakes, though, are bad moves in the past that might affect the future. If we're lucky, the mistakes can possibly be contained or even corrected."

"You're really worried."

"Yes, same as you. We're dealing with some very rich people with unlimited resources, and we're also breaking laws right and left."

"Thirteen hundred to be exact."

"At least."

Their waiter stopped by and asked about dessert. They ordered brandy instead. Todd said, "I called Jenny Valdez at Cohen-Cutler four times today, never got her. I can only imagine the chaos down there as they try to process 220,000 claims. I'll keep trying tomorrow. We need to make sure our firm name is kept buried, and if somebody calls sniffing around, then we need to know it."

"Good. You think Broome might show up in court tomorrow?"

"Not in person, but he might have someone take a look."

"You're making me paranoid."

"We're on the run, Mark. Paranoia is a good thing."

40

To avoid the halls of justice they once haunted, the defendants used a service elevator connected to a rear entrance that few lawyers knew about. But Phil did, and he led his boys through a maze of short hallways lined with offices for judges, secretaries, and law clerks. Mark and Todd wore coats and ties, certain that they would get themselves photographed for a newspaper or two, and they spoke to no one and tried to avoid eye contact with the few familiar faces.

At 9:50, they emerged from the back and entered the courtroom of the Honorable Abraham Abbott, Division 6, General Sessions Court. Eager to see who the curious were, both defendants quickly scanned the audience. There were about thirty spectators, a bit more than normal for a first appearance calendar. They took their seats at the defense table with their backs to the crowd as their lawyer stepped over to chat with the prosecutor. Judge Abbott was on the bench, going through some paperwork. From nowhere cute Hadley Caviness popped over and leaned down between them.

"Just here for a little immoral support, boys," she whispered.

"Thanks," Mark said.

"We thought about calling you last night," Todd said.

"I was busy," she said.

"What about tonight?"

"Sorry, already got a date."

"What's the rap on Ms. Reedy?" Mark asked, nodding at the other table.

"Totally incompetent," Hadley said with a smile. "And too stupid to know it. A real bitch, though."

"Any newspapers here?" Todd asked.

"The *Post* is left side, fourth row, guy in a tan jacket. Don't know about anybody else. Gotta run. Don't lose my phone number and call me when you get out." She disappeared as quickly as she had materialized.

"Get out? As in jail?" Mark whispered.

"I love that little slut," Todd mumbled.

A door opened on the far right side and three inmates in orange jumpsuits were led in chained together. Three young black men, fresh from the mean streets of D.C., and likely headed to prison for years. If not already gang members, they would join one soon enough and band together for protection. During their brief careers as criminal defense lawyers, Mark and Todd had heard enough stories about the horrors of prison.

A clerk called the names of Frazier and Lucero. They stood, walked to the bench with Phil, and looked up and into the unsmiling face of Judge Abbott. His first words were "Can't say that I recognize either of you, though I'm told you've been here before."

Indeed they had been, but they gave no thought to uttering a word.

He continued, "Mr. Mark Frazier, you are charged with violating Section 54B of the D.C. criminal code, the unauthorized practice of law. How do you wish to plead?"

"Not guilty, Your Honor."

"And, Mr. Lucero, for the same charges?"

"Not guilty, Your Honor."

"And there is a third defendant, a Ms. Zola Maal, also known as Zola Parker, which I assume is her professional name. Where is Ms. Maal?" He was staring at Mark, who shrugged as if he had no clue. Sarrano said, "Well, Your Honor, it seems as though she has left the country. Her family has been deported back to Africa; I'm told she might have gone there to assist them. I don't represent her."

Judge Abbott said, "Very well, a strange case gets even stranger. Your cases will be referred to the grand jury for consideration. If indicted, you will be notified of the date for your arraignment. But I'm sure you know the drill. Any questions, Mr. Sarrano?"

"No, Your Honor."

Mills Reedy had wedged herself into the picture. She said, "Your Honor, I would request that bail be set for these two defendants."

Phil grunted in frustration, and Judge Abbott looked surprised. "Why?" he asked.

She said, "Well, evidently these defendants use different identities, and that could mean they are a flight risk. Posting a bond will ensure their return to court when directed."

Abbott said, "Mr. Sarrano?"

"Not necessary, Your Honor. My clients were arrested

last Friday and told to show up this morning at 10:00. They hired me and we arrived fifteen minutes early. Tell them when to be here and I'll have them here."

Like hell you will, Todd thought. Take a good look, Abe buddy, because you'll never see me again.

A flight risk, Mark thought. How about a phantomlike disappearance from the face of the earth? If you think I'll voluntarily subject myself to a life in prison, then you're crazy.

Ms. Reedy said, "Their co-defendant has already skipped the country, Your Honor. They have assumed false identities."

The judge said, "I really see no need for bail at this point. Mr. Sarrano, can your clients agree to remain in the District until their cases are presented to the grand jury?"

Phil looked at Mark, who shrugged and said, "Sure, but I need to go see my mother in Dover. I guess she can wait, though."

Todd added, "And my grandmother is quite ill up in Baltimore, but I guess she can wait. Whatever the court wants." The lying was so easy.

Sarrano said, "These guys are not going anywhere, Your Honor. Bail for them is a needless expense."

Old Abe looked frustrated and said, "Agreed. I don't see the need for it."

Ms. Reedy pressed on: "Well, Your Honor, could we at least make them surrender their passports?"

Mark laughed and said, "We don't have passports, Your Honor. We're just a couple of broke former law students." His real passport was in a hip pocket, just itching to be used. In an hour, he would purchase a fake passport just in case.

His Honor raised a hand to silence him. "No bail. I'll see you two in a month or so."

"Thanks, Judge," Sarrano said.

As they backed away from the bench, Darrell Cromley walked through the bar holding some paperwork. Loudly, he said, "Sorry to interrupt things, Judge, but I need to serve process on these two. This is a copy of the lawsuit I've filed on behalf of my client Ramon Taper."

Sarrano said, "What the hell are you doing?"

"I'm suing your clients," Cromley said, enjoying the attention. Mark and Todd took copies of the summons and lawsuit as they retreated to the defense table. Judge Abbott seemed to be amused. From the front row, another gentleman stood and announced, "Say, Judge, I need to serve papers on them too. I represent Kerrbow Properties and these two skipped out on their leases back in January." He was waving more paperwork. Sarrano stepped over and accepted it. Four rows behind the guy from Kerrbow, a man stood and said, "And, say, Judge, I hired that guy, Mark Upshaw, to handle a DUI for my son, paid him a thousand bucks in cash, and he skipped out. There's a warrant out for my son and I want my money back."

Mark looked at the guy, who was suddenly familiar. In the center aisle, Ramon Taper staggered forth and said, at full volume, "These guys took my case and screwed it up, Judge. I think they should go to jail."

A uniformed bailiff stepped to the bar to block Ramon. Judge Abbott rapped his gavel and said, "Order, order."

Phil Sarrano looked at his clients and said, "Let's get out of here." They scooted around the bench and disappeared through a side door.

FOUR MONTHS AFTER buying fake driver's licenses and launching their ill-fated adventure into the practice of street law, Mark and Todd returned to the Bethesda workshop of their favorite forger to obtain fake passports. Another crime, no doubt, but the guy actually advertised fake passports online, along with dozens of others in the "documents trade." He verbally guaranteed that his passports could fool any customs and immigration officer in the world. Todd almost asked him how he would make good on this promise. Were they expected to believe he would dash off to the airport and haggle with the guards? No. Mark and Todd knew that if they got caught, the guy would not answer the phone.

After posing for photographs, and signing the names Mark Upshaw and Todd Lane on the signature pages, they watched for an hour as he meticulously cut and pieced together the data and endorsement pages, then stamped them with an amazing collection of entries, clear proof that they had traveled extensively. He selected two well-used covers for regular passports, and even added security stickers to the backs of both. They paid him $1,000 in cash, and as they left he said, "Safe travels, boys."

THE GRADUATION PARTY was an impromptu celebration that materialized in a sports bar in Georgetown. Wilson Featherstone sent a text message invitation to Mark, and because he and Todd had nothing better to do on Friday night, they arrived late and joined half a dozen old law school pals for some serious drinking. Tomorrow, Foggy Bottom would go through the formality of a proper commencement service, though, as always, it would be sparsely attended. Only two of the gang planned to actually attend and receive their near-worthless degrees, and they were doing so only because their mothers insisted.

So they drank. They were fascinated by the adventures of Mark and Todd over the past four months, and the two regaled them with the escapades of Upshaw, Parker & Lane. The table roared with laughter as Mark and Todd tag teamed through stories involving Freddy Garcia, and Ramon Taper and his beautiful lawsuit that went sour on their watch, and their visits to the offices of Trusty Rusty, Jeffrey Corbett, and Edwin Mossberg, and poor Zola hanging around hospital cafeterias, and ducking process servers at The Rooster Bar, and being hounded by their loan counselors. There were no secrets any longer. They had become legends at Foggy Bottom, and the fact that they were now facing jail time, and laughing about it, only enriched their stories.

When quizzed about their plans, Mark and Todd said they were considering opening a branch of UPL in Baltimore and hustling the criminal courts there. Who needs a real license to practice? At no time, though, did they reveal their grand scheme.

Of the eight, six would sit for the bar exam in two months. Three had jobs, though two involved nonprofit work. Only one would be employed by a law firm, and that was contingent upon passing the bar. Every one of them had a mountain of debt, thanks to the great law school scam orchestrated by Hinds Rackley.

Though his presence was felt, Gordy was never mentioned.

41

Todd won the coin flip and took a cab to Dulles late Saturday morning. He paid $740 for a round-trip ticket to Barbados on Delta. His fake passport worked with ease at both the Delta desk and the security checkpoints. He flew two hours to Miami, snoring most of the way. He knocked out his cobwebs in an airport lounge during the three-hour layover, and almost missed his flight south. He arrived in Bridgetown, the capital, at dark, and took a cab to a small hotel on a beach. He heard music, kicked off his shoes, rolled up his pants, and walked through the warm sand to a party at a resort next door. Within an hour, he was flirting with an attractive fiftyish woman from Houston whose husband had passed out in a nearby hammock. So far, Barbados was agreeable.

Mark boarded the train at Union Station, and left D.C. behind, forever. He arrived in New York at 5:00 p.m., took the subway to Brooklyn, and found their suite just as they had left it on Thursday.

Zola's Saturday was more eventful. Mid-morning, an

important cop in a coat and tie arrived at the hotel with two uniformed officers at his side. He left them in the lobby and rode with her to her room on the fourth floor. With Fanta translating, Zola handed over a thick envelope filled with West African francs, the equivalent of $26,000 U.S. He counted the money slowly and seemed pleased with the transaction. From one coat pocket he withdrew her cards. From another he pulled out a thinner envelope and said, "Here is your money."

"What money?" she asked, obviously surprised.

"The money from the hotel safe. About $6,000 U.S. The hotel has a record of it."

Honor among thieves, she thought, but couldn't find any words. She took his envelope as he took hers and crammed it in a pocket. "I'll be back in an hour," he said and left the room.

Exactly one hour later, a police van stopped in front of the hotel. Abdou and Bo crawled out of the back, free from handcuffs, and strolled into the lobby like a couple of tourists. They wept when they saw Zola and Fanta, and the whole family had a good cry. They retired to the café and feasted on eggs and muffins.

Idina Sanga found them there and snapped everyone into action. They hurriedly packed their bags and prepared to leave. Zola settled her account with the front desk as Idina called two taxis. They hustled out of the hotel, without once looking back, and drove away. Forty-five minutes later, they stopped in front of a cluster of modern high-rise buildings. Idina was working her phone and a clerk of some variety met them in the lobby of the tallest building. Their temporary apartment was on the seventh floor. It was sparsely furnished, but who cared? After four months in a detention center and a week in a Dakar jail, Abdou viewed the place as a castle. His family was together, free, and safe.

Idina rattled off instructions. The apartment was leased for ninety days. On Monday, she would begin the task of securing documentation. Their Senegalese citizenship would be restored in short order—after all they had been born there—and Zola would be naturalized as well. Based on the reports from her two law partners, she was in no hurry to return to the U.S.

FOR THE SECOND morning in a row, Todd woke up with an aching head and parched mouth. He rallied somewhat with strong coffee by the pool, and by noon was ready to go shopping. He took a taxi to a new development on the northern edge of Bridgetown, a sprawling mess of prefab condos that was far more appealing on the website than on the ground. Websites. For no reason he could discern, he still glanced at the Foggy Bottom website when he was in a foul mood and cursed the smiling faces of the attractive and diverse students who were happily pursuing the challenge of law school. Who can trust a website?

At any rate, he met an agent who walked him through two apartments available for sale or lease at ruinous prices. He chose the smaller of the two, and, after haggling over the earnest money, signed a contract to purchase it, and handed over a Lucero & Frazier check for five grand, a check that would bounce all the way back to Brooklyn. With the contract in hand, he returned to his hotel, checked in with his partners, put on some shorts, and went to the pool, where he bought a frozen daiquiri at a tiki bar and began roasting in the sun.

LATE SUNDAY AFTERNOON, Barry Strayhan was summoned to the Fifth Avenue mansion of Hinds Rackley. They opened a bottle of wine and sat in the sun on a terrace with Central Park below them. Doug Broome and his team had indeed tracked down Mark and Todd and were still busy putting together the pieces. The news reports of Gordy's suicide led them to the Foggy Bottom Law School, where an investigator sat through the dismal commencement service the day before. With a list of graduates from the program, some easy phone work produced the names of Frazier and Lucero, a couple of third-year students who had been close to the deceased and who dropped out back in January. A fellow student even volunteered that they had been arrested for practicing law without a license. A brief story in yesterday's *Post* detailed their eventful appearance in court on Friday. Rackley wasn't the only person looking for them; seems they were leaving a trail of disgruntled clients and people who wanted to sue them. Their Facebook pages had been closed two months earlier, but a hacker hired by Broome managed to retrieve some photos. There was no doubt that Frazier and Lucero were the two boys posing as journalists in the meeting with Rackley and Strayhan five days earlier in Brooklyn.

Rackley looked at a series of photos and compared them with the mug shots from their fake D.C. driver's licenses. He tossed them on a table and asked, "So what's their game?"

Strayhan said, "Two and a half months ago Mark Frazier joined the class action in Miami as an aggrieved customer of Swift Bank. He opened an account with a branch in D.C. back in January."

"Big deal. So he gets a few bucks in the settlement. There has to be more to the story."

"Todd Lucero joined the class action in New York and their pal Zola Maal joined the one in D.C. Not sure what they were doing but maybe they just wanted to see how the racket worked."

"There's more to it. They wouldn't go to so much trouble for such small settlements. What do we know about the Cohen-Cutler class?"

"The largest of the six. Two hundred and twenty thousand clients referred by dozens of smaller law firms. Most of the plaintiffs can be found online using one of the litigation tracking services, but not all. As you might guess, with that many, and with the settlement happening so fast, things are somewhat chaotic. Cohen-Cutler is not required to list the names of the referring firms. But Broome is still digging."

"How can we get inside Cohen-Cutler?"

"We can't. It's confidential. But the FBI can certainly ask questions."

"I don't want the FBI snooping around."

"Understood. But there are ways to tip them off."

"Figure out a way and do it fast. When does the money change hands?"

"Soon. This week, by agreement and court order."

"I'm in a box here, Barry, and I don't like it. I want the settlement done, and quickly, so the bank can put this nightmare to bed. At the same time, I can't stand the idea of getting ripped off. You and I know that nobody can trust these class action lawyers, and with a million possible plaintiffs out there, it's nothing but a frenzy. There's gonna be fraud, and a lot of it."

MONDAY MORNING, TODD dressed in his best and took a cab to the Second Royal Bank of the Lesser Antilles on Center Street in the business district of Bridgetown. His 10:00 a.m. appointment was with a Mr. Rudolph Richard, a dapper old fellow whose specialty was welcoming foreign clients. Todd's spiel was that he and his partners back home had knocked a home run in the litigation wars, and, at the ripe age of twenty-seven, he was cashing in his chips and moving to the Caribbean. He was shutting down his law firm and would spend the next few years running his new hedge fund, York & Orange Traders, from the side of a pool with a view of the ocean. He presented his fake passport, his contract for the condo, a place he would never see again, and a rather gushing letter of recommendation from the Citibank account manager in Brooklyn. Mr. Richard wanted $10,000 to properly open a bank account, but Todd would have none of it. The big money was a week or two away, he explained in legalese that Mr. Richard had a difficult time following, and the best he could do was $2,000 in U.S. cash. If that wasn't enough, he would simply walk down the street, where there were at least a hundred other banks looking for business. After an hour of Todd's smiling, lying, and cajoling, the account was opened.

He left the bank and found an empty sidewalk café where he texted his partners with the delightful news that they were now in business in Barbados.

Back home, Mark was hammering away at Jenny Valdez and Cohen-Cutler. The Swift settlement had been approved at all levels, so where was the damned money? She wasn't sure, these things take time, she explained, but they were waiting on the wire transfer. It did not arrive on Monday. Mark roamed the streets of downtown Brooklyn, where the skies were overcast and gloomy, and tried not to think of his partner lying in the sun and pickling his liver. To make matters worse, every hour or so Todd zipped along another photo of another hot babe in a string bikini.

LATE TUESDAY AFTERNOON, two FBI agents entered the offices of Cohen-Cutler in downtown Miami and were quickly led to the office of Ian Mayweather, the firm's managing partner. Special Agent Wynne did most of the talking, and the meeting was tense from the opening bell. The Feds wanted information that was confidential and not to be shared.

"How many law firms referred clients to your class?" Wynne asked.

"Several dozen and that's all I'm saying," Mayweather replied, somewhat abruptly.

"We are requesting a list of these firms."

"Great. Show me a court order and we'll comply. You're asking for confidential information, gentlemen, and absent an order from a court we cannot hand it over."

"Well, we suspect there may be some fraud involved with your class."

"That wouldn't surprise me. Fraud is not that unusual in these massive settlements, as you know. We've seen it before and we do our best to prevent it. But we're dealing with over 200,000 individual plaintiffs and dozens of law firms. We cannot check everything."

"When will you pay out the money?"

"Our disbursement staff is working around the clock right now. The first tranche arrived from Swift this afternoon. We will start disbursing first thing in the morning. As you might guess, with so much money involved our phones are quite busy. We are instructed by the court to disburse as quickly as possible."

"Can you delay this for a day or two?" Wynne asked.

"No," Mayweather answered angrily. "We are under a court order to disburse as soon as possible. From what I gather, gentlemen, the FBI is in the early stage of an investigation, so you are, basically, just fishing right now. You show me a court order and this firm will do as instructed."

Never stand between a mass tort lawyer and his money from a class action settlement. The FBI knew that Cohen-Cutler's estimated haul from the Swift litigation was expected to be something close to $80 million.

Wynne stood and said, "Okay, we'll be back with a court order." He and his partner left the office without another word.

42

At 9:40 Wednesday morning, Mark received an e-mail from Cohen-Cutler informing him that well over $4 million was being wired from its disbursement office to the Citibank account of Lucero & Frazier, Attorneys-at-Law. The sum represented damages of $3,800 for each of the firm's 1,311 clients, less the 8 percent cut Cohen-Cutler took off the top to manage the class, so $4,583,256.00 to be exact.

Mark sprinted to Citibank and waited in the offices of his favorite account manager. For one agonizing hour, fifty-six minutes to be exact, he paced around the office, unable to sit still and thoroughly unable to act as though it was just another routine settlement. The account manager was nervous about the situation, but she had spent so much time with Mark she liked him and was excited for the young lawyer. As the minutes dragged by, Mark asked her to prepare six certified checks, three to the loan servicers for the outstanding balances of Todd Lucero, Zola Maal, and Mark Frazier. The total was $652,000. The fourth check was payable to Mr. Joseph Tanner, Gordy's father, and it was for $276,000. A fifth check in the amount of $100,000 was payable to Mark's mother, and a sixth, in the same amount, was to Todd's parents. The checks were prepared but not issued.

The wire landed at 11:01, and Mark immediately signed an authorization to wire $3.4 million of the money to the account of York & Orange Traders at the Second Royal Bank of the Lesser Antilles in Barbados. He left a few bucks in the law firm's account, took the six certified checks, thanked the account manager profusely, and stepped into the bright Brooklyn sunshine far wealthier than he had ever dreamed. Walking briskly, he called Todd and Zola with the thrilling news.

Mark entered a FedEx office on Atlantic Avenue and asked for six overnight envelopes and four domestic air bills. On a sheet of yellow legal paper he penned a note to Gordy's father. It read,

> Dear Mr. Tanner: Enclosed please find a certified Citibank check in the amount of $276,000. This should cover the balances of Gordy's student loans. Sincerely, Mark Frazier.

The transaction was far from clean and final. There were tax issues, gift and perhaps income, but those problems now belonged to Mr. Tanner. Mark would not give them another thought. He folded the note, placed the check inside, and put them in an envelope. He addressed air bills to Mr. Tanner in Martinsburg, and to the three loan counselors: Morgana Nash at NowAssist in New Jersey, Rex Wagner at Scholar Support Partners in Philadelphia, and Tildy Carver at LoanAid in Chevy Chase. The paperwork took half an hour, during which Mark managed to calm his nerves and stop looking over his shoulder. He reminded himself that he'd been living on the run for several months now, and the worst thing he could do was to appear nervous. Still, the arrival of the money made him jittery.

He handed the six express envelopes to the clerk, paid for their shipment in cash, and left the office. Outside, he texted Todd and Zola with the news that their student debts had been paid in full. In his hotel suite, he called Jenny Valdez at Cohen-Cutler and inquired about the disbursement for the attorneys' fees. Lucero & Frazier was due another $1,048,800, or $800 for each client. Ms. Valdez said that money should "go out tomorrow."

He sent an e-mail to his loan counselor:

Dear Morgana Nash: I'm sure you are aware of my current legal problems here in the District. No worries. A rich uncle died recently and left me a bundle. I have just sent by overnight letter a certified check in the amount of $266,000 to NowAssist as payment in full. It's been a real pleasure. Mark Frazier.

From Barbados, Todd wrote,

Dear SS Counselor Rex Wagner: Well, I finally took your advice and found a job. And it's a helluva job, I gotta tell you. I'm making so much money these days I can't spend it all. I can buy anything, but the one thing I really want is to get you off my back. Tomorrow by FedEx you'll receive a certified check in the amount of

$195,000, as payment in full. Go pester someone else. Your pal, Todd Lucero.

From Dakar, Zola wrote,

Dear Tildy Carver: I just won the lottery so I'm sending you a check for $191,000. It should arrive tomorrow. Best wishes, Zola Maal.

TODD SPENT the afternoon hanging around the office of Mr. Rudolph Richard at the Second Royal Bank of the Lesser Antilles. When the wire finally arrived at 4:15, he thanked Mr. Richard and left to call his partners.

Ten minutes later, a team of FBI agents entered the offices of Cohen-Cutler in Miami and met Ian Mayweather and his team of lawyers in the firm's largest conference room. Special Agent Wynne handed over a search warrant, which Mayweather scrutinized. He then gave it to the firm's chief criminal lawyer, who read every word. Satisfied that they had no choice, Mayweather nodded at another partner who produced a list of the fifty-two law firms that had referred 220,000 clients to the class. Wynne scanned the list, saw what he was looking for, and asked, "This law firm in New York, Lucero & Frazier, what do you know about it?"

Mayweather looked at his copy of the list and said, "They sent us thirteen hundred cases."

"Have you dealt with them before?"

"No, but then that's true for almost all of these firms. There are six class actions against Swift, and these firms shop around. I guess this one chose us."

"And you don't check to make sure the law firms are legitimate?"

"We're not required to, no. We assume the firms are legit, along with their clients. You know something about this firm?"

Wynne deflected the question and said, "We'd like to see the names of the thirteen hundred clients from Lucero & Frazier."

"They're posted online in the case file," Mayweather replied.

"Yes, along with a million others, and they are not grouped by referring attorneys. Makes it rather difficult to investigate each individual. We need to see the Lucero & Frazier clients."

"Sure, but your court order doesn't go that far."

On one side of the room the FBI agents glared at the lawyers, who held their ground and stared right back. This was their turf, not the government's, and as very rich lawyers they resented the intrusion. The Feds were meddling in their jackpot. But the Feds didn't care; their job was to investigate and all turf belonged to them. And so both gangs watched each other, waiting to see who would blink.

An agent handed Wynne a file. He removed some paperwork and said, "Here's another search warrant. The judge says we can examine any suspicious activity involving Mark Frazier and Todd Lucero, a couple of guys who are not really lawyers to begin with."

"You're kidding," Mayweather said, blinking.

"Do we appear to be kidding?" Wynne asked. "We have cause to believe that these two bogus lawyers have filed a bunch of bogus claims with your class action. We need to verify it."

Mayweather read the court order, then tossed it on the table. He shrugged in defeat and said, "Very well."

MARK WAS TRYING to eat a sandwich in a Brooklyn deli, though he had no appetite. His emotions were in near-violent conflict. On the one hand, he wanted to gloat over the money. But on the other, he knew it was time to run. He reveled in the knowledge that they had pulled off a beautiful reverse scam against the Great Satan, as Gordy called Rackley, and stolen money from a crook. But he was also terrified at the thought of getting caught.

Todd was sitting on a beach, cold drink in hand, and watching another perfect Caribbean sunset. Safe, at least for the moment, he smiled at the future and tried to imagine what he would do with his share of the fortune. But the thrill was dampened by thoughts of his parents and their embarrassment when he never returned to D.C. Return? Would that ever be possible? Was it worth it? He tried to shake off these thoughts by telling himself that they had committed the perfect crime.

Zola was enjoying life with her family in Dakar. They were dining in an outdoor café not far from the ocean, on a lovely spring night, with their biggest troubles far behind them.

None of the three had the slightest hint that, at that moment, a dozen FBI agents were working the phones and discovering that their Swift clients did not exist.

LONG AFTER THE SUN set, Todd called Mark for the fourth time that day. The first two calls had been exhilarating as they celebrated the apparent success of their heist. With the third, though, reality was setting in and they began to worry.

Todd said bluntly, "I think you should leave. Now."

"Why?"

"We have enough money, Mark. And we've made mistakes that we don't even know about. Get out of the country. The attorneys' fees will be wired tomorrow, icing on the cake, and the bank knows where to send the money. I'd feel better if you were on a plane."

"Maybe so. And your new passport worked fine?"

"As I've said, there were no problems. It actually looks more authentic than my real one, which hasn't been used that much. These things cost us a thousand bucks, if you'll remember."

"Oh yes. How could I forget?"

"Get on a plane, Mark, and get out of the country."

"I'm thinking about it. I'll keep you posted."

Mark placed his laptop and some files into a larger briefcase, the one from his street lawyer days, and packed a small carry-on bag with some clothing and a toothbrush. The room was a wreck and he was sick of it. After spending nine nights there he saw no need to check out at the front desk. The room charges were covered for two more days. So he walked away, leaving behind dirty clothing that belonged to both him and Todd, stacks of paperwork, none of which was incriminating, some magazines, discarded toiletries, and the rented printer, from which he had removed the memory chip. He walked a few blocks, hailed a cab, and rode to JFK, where he paid $650 cash for a round-trip ticket to Bridgetown, Barbados. The guard at passport control was half-asleep and hardly looked at his documents. He killed an hour in a lounge, took off at 10:10, and landed in Miami on time at 1:05 a.m. He found a bench in an empty gate and tried to sleep, but it was a long night.

THREE MILES AWAY, Special Agent Wynne and two colleagues once again entered the offices of Cohen-Cutler. Ian Mayweather and a partner were waiting. Now that the firm was cooperating, albeit by the coercion of court orders, some of the pressure was off and the air was almost cordial. A secretary brought in coffee and they sat around a small table.

Wynne began with "Well, it was a long night. We went through the list you gave us, made a bunch of phone calls, and compared names with our records from Swift Bank. It appears as though all thirteen hundred are bogus clients. We have a court order freezing all disbursements for forty-eight hours."

Mayweather was not surprised. His team of grunts had worked through the night as well and reached the same conclusion. They also had the file on Frazier and Lucero and the charges they were facing in D.C. Mayweather said, "We're cooperating. Whatever you say. But you're not going to check all 220,000 of our clients, are you?"

"No. It appears as though the other firms are legit. Give us some time and we'll back off when we're satisfied the fraud is contained to this small group."

"Very well. What's up with Frazier and Lucero?"

"Don't know where they are, but we'll find them. The money you wired to them yesterday was immediately wired to a bank offshore, so they barely managed to get it out of the country. We suspect they're on the run, but they've proven to be, let's say, unsophisticated."

"If the money's offshore you can't touch it, right?"

"Right, but we can certainly touch them. Once we have them in custody and locked up, they'll be eager to cut a deal. We'll get the money back."

"Great. My problem is the settlement. There's still a lot of money in play and I've got a bunch of lawyers screaming at me. Please hurry."

"We're on it."

AT NINE, MARK finished another double espresso and headed for his gate. At a U.S. Postal Service drop box, he placed a small padded envelope into the slot, and kept walking. It was addressed to a reporter at the *Washington Post,* a tough investigative journalist he had been following for weeks. Inside the envelope was one of Gordy's thumb drives.

As he waited in line at his gate, he called his mother and fed her a story about a long trip he and Todd were taking together. They would be gone for months and not available by phone, but he would check in whenever possible. The mess in D.C. was under control and nothing to worry about. Heads up for a FedEx package today. There's some money in it, to be used at your discretion, but please don't waste it on a lawyer for Louie. Love you, Mom.

He boarded without incident and took his seat by a window. He opened his laptop, logged in, and saw an e-mail from Jenny Valdez at Cohen-Cutler. The disbursements for attorneys' fees were being delayed until further notice due to an "unspecified problem." He read it again and closed his computer. Surely, with such a massive settlement, problems were bound to occur, so it had nothing to do with them. Right? He closed his eyes and was breathing deeply when a flight attendant announced over the speaker that there would be a slight delay due to a problem with "documentation." The flight was packed with vacationers headed for the islands, some of whom appeared to have spent time in a bar before boarding. There were groans, but also laughter and shouting.

The clock ticked slowly as Mark's blood pressure rose and his heart pounded. The flight attendants brought out the drink carts and the booze was on the house. Mark asked for a double rum punch and drained it in two gulps. He was about to ask for another when something jolted the aircraft, and it started moving back. As it taxied away from the terminal, he texted Todd and said he was about to take off. Minutes later, he watched from his window as Miami disappeared through the clouds.

43

Pursuant to Todd's instruction, Zola went to the Senegal Post Bank early Thursday, and took her lawyer with her. Idina Sanga agreed, for a fee of course, to help facilitate the opening of an account. They had an appointment with a vice president, a pleasant lady who spoke no English. Idina explained in French that her client was an American who was moving to Dakar to be with her family. Zola produced her passport, New Jersey driver's license, and a copy of the apartment lease. Her story was that her American boyfriend, who was quite wealthy, wished to send her some money for support and also to buy a home. He traveled the world with his ventures and planned to spend time in Senegal. There was even the likelihood that he would open an office there. The story flowed well and convinced the vice president. The fact that Zola was represented by a lawyer with a good reputation helped immensely. Idina stressed the need for extreme privacy and explained that a lot of money would soon arrive by wire. An initial deposit that equaled about $1,000 U.S. was agreed upon, and the paperwork was reviewed by Idina. Bank cards would soon be in the mail. The transaction took less than an hour. Back in the apartment, Zola e-mailed the bank account information to Todd.

When Mark landed in Bridgetown at 1:20, Todd met him at the gate. "Nice tan," Mark observed.

"Thanks, but I'm ready to get out of here."

"Talk to me."

They ducked into a bar and ordered beers. In a corner, they sat at a small table and took long drinks. Mark wiped his mouth and said, "You seem rather jumpy."

"I am. Look, I know you're thinking about a few days on the beach, but we're on the run now. I mean, really on the run. The FBI can trace the wire to our bank."

"As we've discussed about a dozen times."

"Yes, and that's as far as they can go, at least with the money. But when they can't find us there they might want to look here. There's nothing to gain by hanging around the island. Zola opened the account this morning in Dakar with no problems. The hang-up with the last disbursement may or may not be related to us, but why take the chance? For all we know, the Feds could be one step behind us. Let's move on while they're still scrambling."

Mark took another drink and shrugged. "Whatever. I guess I can get some sun in Dakar."

"There are some fabulous beaches there, with resorts that rival anything here. And it looks like we'll have plenty of time to play by the pool."

They drained their beers, walked outside into a blinding sun, and caught a cab to the Second Royal Bank, where they waited an hour to see Mr. Rudolph Richard. Todd introduced Mark as his partner in York & Orange, and explained that they wished to wire $3 million of their account to a bank in Dakar. Mr. Richard was curious but did not pry. Whatever his clients wished was fine with him. They withdrew $20,000 in cash and left the bank. At the airport, they studied routes and saw that almost all went through Miami or JFK, places they preferred to avoid. They paid $5,200 in cash for two one-way packages, and left Barbados at 5:10 p.m. bound for London Gatwick, forty-two hundred miles and eleven hours away. En route, Mark checked his e-mails, and the one from the account manager at Citibank in Brooklyn informed him that the second wire had not arrived. "We can forget that million for attorneys' fees," he mumbled to Todd.

"Well, we really didn't earn it," Todd quipped.

They drank beers for two hours at Gatwick before boarding a flight for Algeria, a thousand miles away. The layover there was eight hours, an interminable time in a hot and crowded airport. However, as the miles passed and the cultures changed, they became convinced that they were leaving the bad guys farther and farther behind. Two thousand miles and five hours later, they landed in Dakar at 11:30 at night. Though it was late, the airport was bustling with loud music and aggressive vendors offering jewelry, leather goods, and fresh fruits. Outside the main entrance, the beggars flocked to those arrivals with lighter skin—whites and Asians. Mark and Todd were jostled but managed to find a cab. Twenty minutes later they arrived in front of the Radisson Blu Hotel at the Sea Plaza.

Zola had reserved two poolside rooms in her name and paid for a week's stay. Evidently, she had schmoozed well because Mark and Todd were greeted like dignitaries. No one asked to see their passports.

It was their first visit to Africa and neither ventured a guess as to how long it would last. Their pasts were a mess. Their futures were uncertain. So, somewhere along the way they decided to live in the present with no regrets. Life could be worse. They could be studying for the bar exam.

AROUND NOON SATURDAY, as the midday sun baked the ceramic tile walkways around the pool and along the terraces, Mark staggered out of his room, squinted into the blinding light, rubbed his eyes, walked to the edge of the water, and fell in. Salt water, pleasant and warm. He dog-paddled back and forth for a few laps, then gave up. He sat in the shallow end with the water touching his chin and tried to remember where he was a week ago. Washington. The morning after a drinking session with his law school pals. The day after their appearance in court with Phil Sarrano, and all those angry people after them. The day he was supposed to graduate from Foggy Bottom, then go forth and conquer the world.

It wasn't conquered but it was certainly different. Some weeks drag by and nothing happens. Others, like this one, are so tumultuous you can't keep up with the days. A week ago they were dreaming of the money. Now it was tucked away in a Senegalese bank where no one could find it.

Because their bodies were tuned to the same clock, Todd soon emerged and made a splash. He gave no thought to swimming laps, but instead waved over a cabana boy and ordered drinks. After two rounds, they took showers and dressed in the clothes they'd been wearing. Shopping was high on their list.

Their partner, however, wore something they'd never seen before. Zola arrived at the hotel restaurant in a bright red and yellow dress that flowed to the floor. With a necklace of large colorful beads and balls, and a flower in her hair, she looked very African. They hugged and carried on, but were careful not to attract too much attention. The restaurant was half-full of guests, almost all of whom were European.

As they sat down, Todd said, "You look beautiful."

Mark said, "Zola, let's get married."

Todd said, "Hey, I was going to ask."

Zola said, "Sorry, no more white boys. Far too much trouble. I'm going to find a nice African dude I can boss around."

"You've been bossing us around for three years," Mark said.

"Yeah, but you talk back and you lie a lot. I want a guy who never speaks unless spoken to and always tells the truth."

"Good luck," Todd said.

A waitress stopped by and they ordered drinks. Beers for the boys, tea for Zola. They asked about her family. They were safe and happy. After the initial jail scare, things settled down. They had not seen the police nor had they heard from other authorities. She and Bo were thinking about renting a small apartment near their parents; they needed some space. Abdou was back home in Senegal, in Muslim territory, and was reasserting his dominance. But he and Fanta were already bored because they were not working. After four months of idleness in detention, they needed to get busy. All in all, their lives were good, if a bit unsettled. Their lawyer was working to revive their citizenship and secure documentation.

Zola wanted the details of the last two weeks, beginning with their arrests, their escape to Brooklyn, then on to Barbados. Mark and Todd alternated stories and everything was funny. The waitress returned with the drinks, and Zola insisted they order chicken *yassa,* a traditional Senegalese dish of roasted chicken and onion sauce. When the waitress left, Todd and Mark resumed their storytelling. The scene in Judge Abbott's courtroom—when half the spectators seemed ready to rush the bar and grab them—required both of their efforts because all three were laughing so hard.

They got some looks from the other tables and tried to keep a lid on things. They enjoyed the chicken *yassa* and passed on dessert. Over strong coffee, their voices got lower as the conversation became serious. Mark said, "Our problem is obvious. We are here on vacation for a few days and we're traveling with fake passports. If we got busted, they'd haul us off to the same jail where they took your father and Bo. Two little white boys in a really bad jail."

Zola was shaking her head. "No, you're fine here. You can stay as long as you want and no one will say anything. Just stay where the white folks are and don't venture away from the beaches. Don't do anything to attract attention."

Todd asked, "How do these folks feel about homosexuals?"

She frowned and said, "Well, I haven't really asked. You guys gay now? I leave you for two weeks and—"

"No, but we got some looks when we checked in last night. We're a pair. Folks make assumptions."

Mark said, "I've read that the gay life is frowned upon in most African countries, especially the Muslim areas."

"It's not as accepted as in the U.S., but no one is going to harass you. There are dozens of Western-style hotels along the beach here and lots of pale-skinned tourists, mostly from Europe. You'll fit in."

"I read something about the cops being pretty tough," Todd said.

"Not around the beaches. Tourism is too important. But keep in mind that here they can stop you for any reason and ask to see some ID. A couple of white guys in the wrong part of town could attract their attention."

"Sounds like racial profiling," Mark said.

"Oh, yes, but the shoe is on the other foot."

They had been talking for almost two hours. After a lull in the conversation, Zola leaned in a bit closer and asked, "So, how much trouble are we really in?"

Mark and Todd looked at each other. Todd spoke first: "Depends on the settlement. If it's completed and no one gets suspicious, then perhaps we've pulled off the perfect crime. We'll hang around here for a couple of weeks, maybe wire over the rest of the money from Barbados, make sure it's all safely tucked away."

Mark added, "Then we'll ease back home, stay away from D.C. and New York, and spend a lot of time watching and listening. If the Swift story eventually goes away, then we're free and clear."

Todd said, "On the other hand, if somebody gets suspicious, we might be forced to go to plan B."

"Which is?"

"Still working on it."

"And the mess in D.C.?" she asked. "I gotta tell you

boys, I don't like the fact that I've been indicted, even if it is for something as trivial as unauthorized practice."

Mark said, "We haven't been indicted yet. And keep in mind we paid a lawyer a fat retainer to delay the case and work a deal. I'm not worried about D.C."

"Then what are you worried about?"

Mark mulled it over for a moment and said, "Cohen-Cutler. They've delayed the disbursement for the attorneys' fees. That could be a red flag."

AFTER LUNCH ZOLA left and they napped and swam and drank by the pool. As the afternoon went on, the pool scene improved dramatically with the arrival of some young couples from Belgium. The music picked up, the crowd continued to grow, and Mark and Todd were on the fringes, enjoying the show.

At seven, Zola was back with two large bags filled with goodies—new laptops and new prepaid cell phones. Each of the three set up several e-mail accounts. They walked through different scenarios involving security, and talked about the money, but made no serious decisions. Jet lag hit hard and Mark and Todd needed to sleep. Zola left them just after nine and returned to her apartment.

44

The call came in on Todd's third phone, the first of his prepaid variety, the one he'd purchased in D.C. the day Zola left for Senegal. Now that he had a fourth phone, he and his two partners were wondering how they might consolidate devices and live with only one. That did not appear likely.

The third phone number was the one he'd given to Mr. Rudolph Richard, and the call was devastating. Mr. Richard said he was using the phone because he did not want to leave an e-mail trail. The FBI had just contacted him with questions about the wire transfer sent from the Lucero & Frazier account with Citibank in Brooklyn. He, of course, answered none of their questions and did not confirm the existence of the York & Orange account with his bank. He gave them nothing, as usual, and under the laws of Barbados the FBI could not obtain information about the account. However, he, Mr. Richard, felt duty bound to inform his client that the FBI was on the way.

Todd thanked him, then ruined Mark's day. Mark's first

thought was to contact Jenny Valdez and fish for information, but that was quickly dismissed as a rather stupid idea. If the FBI was using a full-court press, then any phone call to Cohen-Cutler would be recorded and traced.

It took Zola an hour to get to the hotel. They sat under an umbrella on a terrace and admired the ocean, though pleasant thoughts were impossible. Their worst nightmare was unfolding, and though they had often considered what might happen if things went off track, they were stunned by the reality. The FBI was on their trail. Which meant, of course, that their class action scam had been discovered, and that would lead to indictments, arrest warrants, travel alerts. Given the importance of fighting terrorism and narco-traffickers, it was impossible to know how seriously the FBI would pursue a little class action mischief, but they were assuming the worst.

Zola was particularly terrified, and with good reason. She had used her valid American passport to travel to Senegal, thus leaving a trail that any blind investigator could follow. The FBI could easily track her movements. And, to make bad matters worse, she had registered with the U.S. embassy in Dakar upon her arrival two weeks earlier.

Decisions were necessary. Since they had no idea what the FBI was up to, or how deep they were digging, or how close they might actually be in pursuit, the three decided to make plans. Todd would contact Mr. Richard in Barbados and transfer the remaining balance to the bank in Senegal. Zola would confide in Bo and tell him everything, but not her parents; maybe later, but not now. She would see Idina Sanga first thing the next morning and push along the process of becoming naturalized. If she were a proper Senegalese, extradition to the U.S. would be almost impossible. And she would gently explore the possibility of obtaining new documentation for a couple of friends.

Throughout Tuesday and Wednesday, the three were glued to their laptops as they searched the Internet for anything relevant to the Swift settlement. Nothing. Their chunk of the attorneys' fees did not arrive at Citibank in Brooklyn, a rather clear indication that something was wrong. Finally, on Thursday morning, a financial site reported a slight snag in the Swift matter. A federal judge in Miami had halted further disbursements pending an investigation into allegations of fraud. A federal judge in Houston did the same. Nationwide, Swift had already paid almost $3 billion of the $4.2 billion settlement, but problems were popping up.

Although the fraud was not described, the three partners knew precisely what the investigators were finding.

MARK'S IDEA WAS to leave the country, and to do so without bothering with customs and passport control at the airport. They had the money to do anything, so his plan was to hire a car and a driver and hit the road. They could meander south through West Africa, take their time and enjoy the trip, and eventually make it to South Africa. He'd read that Cape Town was the most beautiful city in the world, plus they spoke English there. Todd was lukewarm to the idea. He wasn't keen on spending a month bouncing along the outback and holding his breath every time some border guard with an assault rifle and an itchy finger studied his passport. He didn't say no, because such an escape might one day become necessary, but he didn't approve of it either.

Zola, however, said no. She was not leaving her family after what they had been through.

The investigation continued, though there was virtually no news about it. And so they waited. Zola felt far safer in Dakar, but once again she was living with the fear that someone might knock on the door.

THE RESORT CITY of Saint-Louis sits on the Atlantic, two hundred miles north of Dakar. With 175,000 residents, it is much smaller and quieter, but still large enough to get lost in. It had once been the capital of the country, and the French had built fine homes that had been well preserved. The city was known for its colonial architecture, laid-back lifestyle, pretty beaches, and the most important jazz festival in Africa.

Zola organized the trip. She paid a driver with an air-conditioned SUV, and she and Bo and her two partners left for a few days in Saint-Louis. Her parents were not invited. She and Bo were feeling suffocated by Abdou and needed a break. What they really needed was another place to live, with some distance between themselves and their parents. She had a hunch Saint-Louis might be just the spot.

Leaving Dakar, they realized their driver spoke little English, and as the time passed they talked more openly about the past six months. Bo had questions, some rather pointed at times. He couldn't believe they had actually done the things they'd done, and Mark and Todd struggled to justify them. Bo was irritated that they had dragged his little sister into their schemes and scams. Mark and Todd were quick to take responsibility, but Zola stood her ground. She had a mind of her own and was capable of making her own decisions. Sure, they had made mistakes, but she was a part of every one of them. She blamed no one but herself.

Bo knew there was money in the bank, but had no idea how much. He was struggling to accept a future away from the U.S., the only home he'd ever known. He left a girlfriend behind and was heartbroken. He left a lot of friends there, kids from school, guys from the neighborhoods. He left a good job.

As the hours passed he lost his edge. He knew he would still be in jail if not for the money Mark and Todd had entrusted to Zola. He could not ignore the adoration those two had for his sister.

After six hours on the road, they crossed the Senegal River on the Faidherbe Bridge, designed by Gustave Eiffel, he of the tower fame. The old town was on N'Dar Island, a narrow strip of land with the ocean on both sides. They passed through blocks of beautiful old buildings and finally stopped at the Hôtel Mermoz near the beach. After a long dinner on the terrace, with the ocean below them, they went to bed early.

Real estate listings for the area were not as detailed as any place in the States, or in Dakar for that matter, but with a little effort Zola found what she was looking for. The house was built in 1890 by a French merchant and had changed hands many times. It was a three-story villa that looked nicer from the street than from behind its doors and windows, but it was charming and spacious. The wooden floors sagged here and there. The furniture was ancient, covered with dust, and mismatched. The shelves were filled with pots and urns and old books in French. Some of the plumbing worked; some did not. The round refrigerator was from the 1950s. The courtyard and balcony were shaded by thick bougainvillea and designed for the tropics. There was a small television in the living room. The listing promised Internet service, but the agent said it was slow.

They separated and drifted through the house, which would take hours to fully inspect. On a second-floor balcony, just off a bedroom suite that Todd was already claiming, he bumped into Mark. "They'll never find us here," Todd said.

"Maybe, but can you believe we're actually here?"

"No. This is surreal."

Regardless of their feelings, Zola loved the house and signed a six-month lease that equaled about $1,000 U.S. per month. Two days later, they moved in, with Todd and Mark taking the top floor—three bedrooms, two baths, and not a single working shower—while Zola took the master suite on the ground floor. Bo was stuck somewhere in between with more square footage than anyone. They stayed two more days and nights, buying supplies, changing lightbulbs and fuses, and trying to learn as much as possible about the house. It came with a gardener, Pierre something, who didn't speak a word of English but was proficient at pointing and grunting.

The island was like Venice, a self-contained city surrounded by water, except it had beautiful beaches. The sand brought the tourists, and there were dozens of quaint, pretty hotels near the water. When they were not in the house doing chores for Zola, Mark and Todd were at the beach, drinking rum cocktails and looking for girls.

When Zola and Bo left in the SUV, Mark and Todd hugged them good-bye and said hurry back. They planned to be gone about a week, enough time to pack a few things and get disentangled from their parents.

That night, in the semi-lit living room of an old mansion built by Europeans in another century, another time, the two worked on a bottle of scotch and tried to put their lives in perspective. It was an impossible chore.

ON SUNDAY, JUNE 22, the *Washington Post* ran a front-page story under the headline "For-Profit Law School Scam Linked to New York Fund Manager." Beneath the fold there was a large photo of Hinds Rackley. The story was basically a better-written version of what Gordy had plastered to his den wall, with dozens of companies and fronts and shells and law schools. Swift Bank, though, received little attention. It was obvious, at least to Mark and Todd, that the journalist had been unable to penetrate Rackley's offshore companies that allegedly owned stock.

But the story was vindication, at some level. Gordy's work had been validated. The Great Satan would now endure a PR nightmare, and though the story did not imply it, there was a good chance Rackley was now on the FBI's radar.

They reveled in the story for a couple of days, then abruptly forgot about it.

Two days later, on June 24, Mark Frazier, Todd Lucero, and Zola Maal were indicted on federal racketeering charges by a grand jury in Miami. The charges were part of an ongoing investigation into numerous allegations of class action fraud in the Swift Bank settlement. More indictments were likely, according to the first report on Bloomberg. As Mark and Todd watched, the story spread throughout the web, but never achieved headline status. In the world of major business news, it wasn't much of an event.

Perhaps not to the nation, but to the three defendants it was a rather big deal. Though they had been expecting it, the news was still frightening. However, they were prepared. They had a suitable hiding place and the FBI didn't have a clue.

Zola was another matter. Mark and Todd doubted the FBI would go to the trouble of tracking her all the way to Dakar, and expect the police there to cooperate with an arrest, and then expect the Senegalese courts to extradite her, all for a crime that had nothing to do with terrorism, murder, or drug trafficking. They believed this, but they kept it to themselves. They were fully aware that by now Zola had little confidence in anything they said or believed, and with good reason.

Zola was making her own plans. She summoned them back to Dakar for an important meeting, one she had been putting together for some time. With the help of an intermediary referred by Idina Sanga, Zola had slowly worked her contacts until she found the right person. The deal was as simple as it was complicated. For $200,000 each, the government would issue new identities, new ID cards, new passports, and new proofs of citizenship to the three former UPL partners. The facilitator was a career state department official with clout. Zola met with him three times before they fully trusted one another. It was never clear how much the facilitator would earn, but Zola expected the loot would be diminished as it moved upward.

The deal was simple because it was cash for citizenship,

a transaction hardly unique to Senegal. It was complicated because it required the rejection of who they were and where they were from. It was possible to maintain dual citizenship, but not in their real names. If they wished to become Senegalese and thus protected by the government and ostensibly hidden from the U.S. authorities, they could no longer be Mark, Todd, and Zola. Dual citizenship meant dual identities, something no government sanctioned.

They took the deal with no hesitation, except for some minor bitching over its cost. Their stash was now down to about $2.5 million, a nice cushion but the future was so uncertain.

They returned to Saint-Louis, and to their decaying villa, with new ID cards, new credit cards, and rather handsome new passports with their smiling faces. Mr. Frazier was now Christophe Vidal, or simply Chris. His sidekick was Tomas Didier, or Tommy around the house. Just two young men of French descent, though neither spoke a lick of their native tongue. The Caucasian population of Senegal was less than 1 percent, and the addition of two more gringos hardly moved the needle.

Zola was now Alima Pene, a proper African name. They began calling her Alice.

Bo, who wasn't facing a string of felonies in the U.S., remained who he was. His paperwork would be far less expensive but take longer.

THE LAZY LIFE of sleeping, reading, watching the Internet, strolling the beaches, drinking, and having oceanside dinners at midnight soon gave way to boredom. After a month or so of being full-blooded Senegalese, Chris and

Tommy were looking for work, preferably something legitimate this time.

Their favorite bar was a thatched-roof hut nestled between two small resorts on the main beach, a five-minute walk from their villa. They spent hours there, playing dominoes, throwing darts, chatting with tourists, soaking up the sun, having lunch, and drinking Gazelles, a lager that seemed to be the Senegalese national beer. The bar was owned by a cranky old German woman whose husband had recently died. She waddled in occasionally to drink a few and snarl at the staff, all of whom rolled their eyes behind her back. Tomas began flirting with her and before long introduced his friend Christophe. They charmed her over a long lunch. The next day she was back for more, and during the fourth lunch Tomas asked if she had ever thought about selling the place. They were looking for something to do, and so on. She admitted to being old and tired.

They bought the bar and closed it for renovations. With Alice on board, they pumped in $80,000 for a fancier kitchen, bar equipment, and big televisions, and they doubled the seating capacity. Their business plan was to make it more of an American-style sports bar while keeping the local music, food, drinks, and decor. When it reopened, Alice was in charge of the dining room. Chris and Tomas worked the bar. Bo supervised a small staff in the kitchen. The place was packed from the opening bell, and life was good.

For the sake of memory, and a tip of the hat to another lifetime, they called it The Rooster Bar.

AUTHOR'S NOTE

As usual, I played fast and loose with reality, especially the legal stuff. Laws, courthouses, procedures, statutes, firms, judges and their courtrooms, lawyers and their habits, all have been fictionalized at will to suit the story.

Mark Twain said he moved entire states and cities to fit his narrative. Such is the license given to novelists, or simply assumed by them.

Alan Swanson guided me through the streets of D.C. Bobby Moak, a tort specialist with an encyclopedic knowledge of the law, once again reviewed the manuscript. Jennifer Hulvey at the University of Virgina School of Law walked me through the complex world of student lending. Thanks to all. They are not to be blamed for my mistakes.

The question all writers hate is: "Where do you get your ideas?" With this story the answer is simple. I read an article in the September 2014 edition of *The Atlantic* titled "The Law School Scam." It's a fine investigative piece by Paul Campos. By the end of it, I was inspired and knew I had my next novel.

Thank you, Mr. Campos.

Read on for a sneak peek at

CAMINO ISLAND

We hope you have enjoyed *The Rooster Bar.*
We're pleased to present you with a sneak peek of
John Grisham's novel, *Camino Island*,
available now. Enjoy!

CHAPTER ONE

THE HEIST

1.

The imposter borrowed the name of Neville Manchin, an actual professor of American literature at Portland State and soon-to-be doctoral student at Stanford. In his letter, on perfectly forged college stationery, "Professor Manchin" claimed to be a budding scholar of F. Scott Fitzgerald and was keen to see the great writer's "manuscripts and papers" during a forthcoming trip to the East Coast. The letter was addressed to Dr. Jeffrey Brown, Director of Manuscripts Division, Department of Rare Books and Special Collections, Firestone Library, Princeton University. It arrived with a few others, was duly sorted and passed along, and eventually landed on the desk of Ed Folk, a career junior librarian whose task, among several other monotonous ones, was to verify the credentials of the person who wrote the letter.

Ed received several of these letters each week, all in many ways the same, all from self-proclaimed Fitzgerald buffs and experts, and even from the occasional true scholar. In the previous calendar year, Ed had cleared and logged in 190 of these people through the library. They came from all over the world and arrived wide-eyed and humbled, like pilgrims before a shrine. In his thirty-four years at the same desk, Ed had processed all of them. And, they were not going away. F. Scott Fitzgerald continued to fascinate. The traffic was as heavy now as it had been three decades earlier. These days, though, Ed was wondering what could possibly be left of the great writer's life that had not been pored over, studied at great length, and written about. Not long ago, a true scholar told Ed that there were now at least a hundred books and over ten thousand published academic articles on Fitzgerald the man, the writer, his works, and his crazy wife.

And he drank himself to death at forty-four! What if he'd lived into old age and kept writing? Ed would need an assistant, maybe two, perhaps even an entire staff. But then Ed knew that an early death was often the key to later acclaim (not to mention greater royalties).

After a few days, Ed finally got around to dealing with Professor Manchin. A quick review of the library's register revealed that this was a new person, a new request. Some of the veterans had been to Princeton so many times they simply called his number and said, "Hey, Ed, I'll be there next Tuesday." Which was fine with Ed. Not so with Manchin. Ed went through the Portland State website and found his man. Undergraduate degree in American lit from the University of Oregon; master's from UCLA; adjunct gig now for three years. His photo revealed a rather plain-looking young man of perhaps thirty-five, the makings of a beard that was probably temporary, and narrow frameless eyeglasses.

In his letter, Professor Manchin asked whoever responded to do so by e-mail, and gave a private Gmail address. He said he rarely checked his university address. Ed thought, "That's because you're just a lowly adjunct professor and probably don't even have a real office." He often had these thoughts, but, of course, was too professional to utter them to anyone else. Out of caution, the next day he sent a response through the Portland State server. He thanked Professor Manchin for his letter and invited him to the Princeton campus. He asked for a general idea of when he might arrive and laid out a few of the basic rules regarding the Fitzgerald collection. There were many, and he suggested that Professor Manchin study them on the library's website.

The reply was automatic and informed Ed that Manchin was out of pocket for a few days. One of Manchin's partners had hacked into the Portland State directory just deep enough to tamper with the English department's e-mail server; easy work for a sophisticated hacker. He and the imposter knew immediately that Ed had responded.

Ho hum, thought Ed. The next day he sent the same message to Professor Manchin's private Gmail address. Within an hour, Manchin replied with an enthusiastic thank-you, said he couldn't wait to get there, and so on. He gushed on about how he had studied the library's website, had spent hours with the Fitzgerald digital archives, had owned for years the multivolume series containing facsimile editions of the great author's handwritten first drafts, and had a particular interest in the critical reviews of the first novel, *This Side of Paradise.*

Great, said Ed. He'd seen it all before. The guy was trying to impress him before he even got there, which was not at all unusual.

2.

F. Scott Fitzgerald enrolled in Princeton in the fall of 1913. At the age of sixteen, he was dreaming of writing the great American novel, and had indeed begun working on an early version of *This Side of Paradise.* He dropped out four years later to join the Army and go to war, but it ended before he was deployed. His classic, *The Great Gatsby,* was published in 1925 but did not become popular until after his death. He struggled financially throughout his career, and by 1940 was working in Hollywood, cranking out bad screenplays, failing physically and creatively. On December 21, he died of a heart attack, brought on by years of severe alcoholism.

In 1950, Scottie, his daughter and only child, gave his original manuscripts, notes, and letters—his "papers"—to the Firestone Library at Princeton. His five novels were handwritten on inexpensive paper that did not age well. The library quickly realized that it would be unwise to allow researchers to physically handle them. High-quality copies were made, and the originals were locked away in a secured basement vault where the air, light, and temperature were carefully controlled. Over the years, they had been removed only a handful of times.

3.

The man posing as Professor Neville Manchin arrived at Princeton on a beautiful fall day in early October. He was directed to Rare Books and Special Collections, where he met Ed Folk, who then passed him along to another assistant librarian who examined and copied his Oregon driver's license. It was, of course, a forgery, but a perfect one. The forger, who was also the hacker, had been trained by the CIA and had a long history in the murky world of private espionage. Breaching a bit of campus security was hardly a challenge.

Professor Manchin was then photographed and given a security badge that had to be displayed at all times. He followed the assistant librarian to the second floor, to a large room with two long tables and walls lined with retractable steel drawers, each of which was locked. Manchin noticed at least four surveillance cameras high in the corners, cameras that were supposed to be seen. He suspected others were well hidden. He attempted to chat up the assistant librarian but got little in return. He jokingly asked if he could see the original manuscript for *This Side of Paradise*. The assistant librarian offered a smug grin and said that would not be possible.

"Have you ever seen the originals?" Manchin asked.

"Only once."

A pause as Manchin waited for more, then he asked, "And what was the occasion?"

"Well, a certain famous scholar wished to see them. We accompanied him down to the vault and gave him a look. He didn't touch the papers, though. Only our head librarian is allowed to do so, and only with special gloves."

"Of course. Oh well, let's get to work."

The assistant opened two of the large drawers, both labeled "This Side of Paradise," and withdrew thick, oversized notebooks. He said, "These contain the reviews of the book when it was first published. We have many other samples of later reviews."

"Perfect," Manchin said with a grin. He opened his briefcase, took out a notepad, and seemed ready to pounce on everything laid on the table. Half an hour later, with Manchin deep in his work, the assistant librarian excused himself and disappeared. For the benefit of the cameras, Manchin never looked up. Eventually, he needed to find the men's room and wandered away. He took a wrong turn here and another one there, got himself lost, and eased through Collections avoiding contact with anyone. There were surveillance cameras everywhere. He doubted that anyone at that moment was watching the footage, but it could certainly be retrieved if needed. He found an elevator, avoided it, and took the nearby stairs. The first level below was similar to the ground floor. Below it, the stairs stopped at B2 (Basement 2), where a large thick door waited with "Emergencies Only" painted in bold letters. A keypad was next to the door, and another sign warned that an alarm would sound the instant the door was opened without "proper authorization." Two security cameras watched the door and the area around it.

Manchin backed away and retraced his steps. When he returned to his workroom, the assistant was waiting. "Is everything okay, Professor Manchin?" he asked.

"Oh yes. Just a bit of a stomach bug, I'm afraid. Hope it's not contagious." The assistant librarian left immediately, and Manchin hung around all day, digging through materials from the steel drawers and reading old reviews he cared nothing about. Several times he wandered off, poking around, looking, measuring, and memorizing.

4.

Manchin returned three weeks later and he was no longer pretending to be a professor. He was clean shaven, his hair was colored a sandy blond, he wore fake eyeglasses with red frames, and he carried a bogus student card with a photo. If someone asked, which he certainly didn't expect, his story was that he was a grad student from Iowa. In real life his name was Mark and his occupation, if one could call it that, was professional thievery. High-dollar, world-class, elaborately planned smash-and-grab jobs that specialized in art and rare artifacts that could be sold back to the desperate victims for ransom. His was a gang of five, led by Denny, a former Army

Ranger who had turned to crime after being kicked out of the military. So far, Denny had not been caught and had no record; nor did Mark. However, two of the others did. Trey had two convictions and two escapes, his last the year before from a federal prison in Ohio. It was there he'd met Jerry, a petty art thief now on parole. Another art thief, a onetime cellmate serving a long sentence, had first mentioned the Fitzgerald manuscripts to Jerry.

The setup was perfect. There were only five manuscripts, all handwritten, all in one place. And to Princeton they were priceless.

The fifth member of the team preferred to work at home. Ahmed was the hacker, the forger, the creator of all illusions, but he didn't have the nerve to carry guns and such. He worked from his basement in Buffalo and had never been caught or arrested. He left no trails. His 5 percent would come off the top. The other four would take the rest in equal shares.

By nine o'clock on a Tuesday night, Denny, Mark, and Jerry were inside the Firestone Library posing as grad students and watching the clock. Their fake student IDs had worked perfectly; not a single eyebrow had been raised. Denny found his hiding place in a third-floor women's restroom. He lifted a panel in the ceiling above the toilet, tossed up his student backpack, and settled in for a few hours of hot and cramped waiting. Mark picked the lock of the main mechanical room on the first level of the basement and waited for alarms. He heard none, nor did Ahmed, who had easily hacked into the university's security systems. Mark proceeded to dismantle the fuel injectors of the library's backup electrical generator. Jerry found a spot in a study carrel hidden among rows of stacked tiers holding books that had not been touched in decades.

Trey was drifting around the campus, dressed like a student, lugging his backpack, scoping out places for his bombs.

The library closed at midnight. The four team members, as well as Ahmed in his basement in Buffalo, were in radio contact. Denny, the leader, announced at 12:15 that all was proceeding as planned. At 12:20, Trey, dressed like a student and hauling a bulky backpack, entered the McCarren Residential College in the heart of the campus. He saw the same surveillance cameras he had seen the previous week. He took the unwatched stairs to the second floor, ducked into a coed restroom, and locked himself in a stall. At 12:40, he reached into his backpack and removed a tin can about the size of a twenty-ounce bottle of soda. He set a delayed starter and hid it behind the toilet. He left the restroom, went to the third floor, and set another bomb in an empty shower stall. At 12:45, he found a semi-dark hallway on the second floor of a dormitory and nonchalantly tossed a string of ten jumbo Black Cat firecrackers down the hall. As he scrambled down the stairwell, the explosions boomed through the air. Seconds later, both smoke bombs erupted, sending thick clouds of rancid fog into the hallways. As Trey left the building he heard the first wave of panicked voices. He stepped behind some shrubs near the dorm, pulled a disposable phone out of his pocket, called Princeton's 911 service, and delivered the horrifying news: "There's a guy with a gun on the second floor of McCarren. He's firing shots."

Smoke was drifting from a second-floor window. Jerry, sitting in the dark study carrel in the library, made a similar call from his prepaid cell phone. Soon, calls were pouring in as panic gripped the campus.

Every American college has elaborate plans to handle a situation involving an "active gunman," but no one wants to implement them. It took a few dumbstruck seconds for the officer in charge to push the right buttons, but when she did, sirens began wailing. Every Princeton student, professor, administrator, and employee received a text and e-mail alert. All doors were to be closed and locked. All buildings were to be secured.

Jerry made another call to 911 and reported that two students had been shot. Smoke boiled out of McCarren Hall. Trey dropped three more smoke bombs into trash cans. A few students ran through the smoke as they went from building to building, not sure where exactly the safe places were. Campus security and the City of Princeton police raced onto the scene, followed closely by half a dozen fire trucks. Then ambulances. The first of many patrol cars from the New Jersey State Police arrived.

Trey left his backpack at the door of an office building, then called 911 to report how suspicious it looked. The timer on the last smoke bomb inside the backpack was set to go off in ten minutes, just as the demolition experts would be staring at it from a distance.

At 1:05, Trey radioed the gang: "A perfect panic out here. Smoke everywhere. Tons of cops. Go for it."

Denny replied, "Cut the lights."

Ahmed, sipping strong tea in Buffalo and sitting on go, quickly routed through the school's security panel, entered the electrical grid, and cut the electricity not only to the Firestone Library but to half a dozen nearby buildings as well. For good measure, Mark, now wearing night vision goggles, pulled the main cutoff switch in the mechanical room. He waited and held his breath, then breathed easier when the backup generator did not engage.

The power outage triggered alarms at the central monitoring station inside the campus security complex, but no one was paying attention. There was an active gunman on the loose. There was no time to worry about other alarms.

Jerry had spent two nights inside the Firestone Library in the past week and was confident there were no guards stationed within the building while it was closed. During the night, a uniformed officer walked around the building once or twice, shined his flashlight at the doors, and kept walking. A marked patrol car made its rounds too, but it was primarily concerned with drunk students. Generally, the campus was like any other—dead between the hours of 1:00 and 8:00 a.m.

On this night, however, Princeton was in the midst of a frantic emergency as America's finest were being shot. Trey reported to his gang that the scene was total chaos with cops scrambling about, SWAT boys throwing on their gear, sirens screaming, radios squawking, and a million red and blue emergency lights flashing. Smoke hung by the trees like a fog. A helicopter could be heard hovering somewhere close. Total chaos.

Denny, Jerry, and Mark hustled through the dark and took the stairs down to the basement under Special Collections. Each wore night vision goggles and a miner's lamp strapped to his forehead. Each carried a heavy backpack, and Jerry hauled a small Army duffel he'd hidden in the library two nights earlier. At the third and final level down, they stopped at a thick metal door, blacked out the surveillance cameras, and waited for Ahmed and his magic. Calmly, he worked his way through the library's alarm system and deactivated the door's four sensors. There was a loud clicking noise. Denny pressed down on the handle and pulled the door open. Inside they found a narrow square of space with two more metal doors. Using a flashlight, Mark scanned the ceiling and spotted a surveillance camera. "There," he said. "Only one." Jerry, the tallest at six feet three inches, took a small can of black paint and sprayed the lens of the camera.

Denny looked at the two doors and said, "Wanna flip a coin?"

"What do you see?" Ahmed asked from Buffalo.

"Two metal doors, identical," Denny replied.

"I got nothing here, fellas," Ahmed replied. "There's nothing in the system beyond the first door. Start cutting."

From his duffel Jerry removed two eighteen-inch canisters, one filled with oxygen, the other with acetylene. Denny situated himself before the door on the left, lit a cutting torch with a sparker, and began heating a spot six inches above the keyhole and latch. Within seconds, sparks were flying.

Meanwhile, Trey had drifted away from the chaos around McCarren and was hiding in the blackness across the street from the library. Sirens were screaming as more emergency vehicles responded. Helicopters were thumping the air loudly above the campus, though Trey could not see them. Around him, even the streetlights were out. There was not another soul near the library. All hands were needed elsewhere.

"All's quiet outside the library," he reported. "Any progress?"

"We're cutting now," came the terse reply from Mark. All five members knew that chatter should be limited. Denny slowly and skillfully cut through the metal with the torch tip that emitted eight hundred degrees of oxygenated heat. Minutes passed as molten metal dripped to the floor and red and yellow sparks flew from the door. At one point Denny said,

"It's an inch thick." He finished the top edge of the square and began cutting straightdown. The work was slow, the minutes dragged on, and the tension mounted but they kept their cool. Jerry and Mark crouched behind Denny, watching his every move. When the bottom cut line was finished, Denny rattled the latch and it came loose, though something hung. "It's a bolt," he said. "I'll cut it."

Five minutes later, the door swung open. Ahmed, staring at his laptop, noticed nothing unusual from the library's security system. "Nothing here," he said. Denny, Mark, and Jerry entered the room and immediately filled it. A narrow table, two feet wide at most, ran the length, about ten feet. Four large wooden drawers covered one side; four on the other. Mark, the lock picker, flipped up his goggles, adjusted his headlight, and inspected one of the locks. He shook his head and said, "No surprise. Combination locks, probably with computerized codes that change every day. There's no way to pick it. We gotta drill."

"Go for it," Denny said. "Start drilling and I'll cut the other door."

Jerry produced a three-quarter drive battery-powered drill with bracing bars on both sides. He zeroed in on the lock and he and Mark applied as much pressure as possible. The drill whined and slid off the brass, which at first seemed impenetrable. But a shaving spun off, then another, and as the men shoved the bracing bars the drill bit ground deeper into the lock. When it gave way the drawer still would not open. Mark managed to slide a thin pry bar into the gap above the lock and yanked down violently. The wood frame split and the drawer opened. Inside was an archival storage box with black metal edges, seventeen inches by twenty-two and three inches deep.

"Careful," Jerry said as Mark opened the box and gently lifted a thin, hardback volume. Mark read slowly, "The collected poems of Dolph McKenzie. Just what I always wanted."

"Who the hell?"

"Don't know but we ain't here for poetry."

Denny entered behind them and said, "Okay, get on with it. Seven more drawers in here. I'm almost inside the other room."

They returned to their labors as Trey casually smoked a cigarette on a park bench across the street and glanced repeatedly at his watch. The frenzy across the campus showed no signs of dying down, but it wouldn't last forever.

The second and third drawers in the first room revealed more rare books by authors unknown to the gang. When Denny finished cutting his way into the second room, he told Jerry and Mark to bring the drill. It, too, had eight large drawers, seemingly identical to the first room. At 2:15, Trey checked in with a report that the campus was still in lockdown, but curious students were beginning to gather on the lawn in front of McCarren to watch the show. Police with bullhorns had ordered them back to their rooms, but there were too many to handle. At least two news helicopters were hovering and complicating things. He was watching CNN on his smart phone and the Princeton story was *the* story at the moment. A frantic reporter "on the scene" continually referred to "unconfirmed casualties," and managed to convey the impression that numerous students had been shot "by at least one gunman."

"At least one gunman?" Trey mumbled. Doesn't every shooting require at least one gunman?

Denny, Mark, and Jerry discussed the idea of cutting into the drawers with the blowtorch, but decided against it, for the moment anyway. The risk of fire would be high, and what good would the manuscripts be if they were damaged. Instead, Denny pulled out a smaller one-quarter drive drill and began drilling. Mark and Jerry bored away with the larger one. The first drawer in the second room produced stacks of delicate papers handwritten by another long-forgotten poet, one they'd never heard of but hated nonetheless.

At 2:30, CNN confirmed that two students were dead and at least two more were injured. The word "carnage" was introduced.

5.

When the second floor of McCarren was secured, the police noticed the remnants of what appeared to be firecrackers. The empty smoke bomb canisters were found in the restroom and the shower. Trey's abandoned backpack was opened by a demolition crew and the spent smoke bomb was removed. At 3:10, the commander first mentioned the word "prank," but the adrenaline was still pumping so fast no one thought of the word "diversion."

The rest of McCarren was quickly secured and all students were accounted for. The campus was still locked down and would remain so for hours as the nearby buildings were searched.

6.

At 3:30, Trey reported, "Things seem to be settling down out here. Three hours in, fellas, how's the drilling?"

"Slow," came the one-word response from Denny.

Inside the vault, the work was indeed slow, but determined. The first four opened drawers revealed more old manuscripts, some handwritten, some typed, all by important writers who didn't matter at the moment. They finally struck gold in the fifth drawer when Denny removed an archival storage box identical to the others. He carefully opened it. A reference page inserted by the library read, "Original Handwritten Manuscript of The Beautiful and Damned—F. Scott Fitzgerald."

"Bingo," Denny said calmly. He removed two identical boxes from the fifth drawer, delicately placed them on the narrow table, and opened them. Inside were original manuscripts of *Tender Is the Night* and *The Last Tycoon.*

Ahmed, still glued to his laptop and now drinking a highly caffeinated energy drink, heard the beautiful words: "Okay, boys, we have three out of five. *Gatsby*'s here somewhere, along with *Paradise.*"

Trey asked, "How much longer?"

"Twenty minutes," Denny said. "Get the van."

Trey casually strode across the campus, mixed in with a crowd of the curious, and watched for a moment as the small army of policemen milled about. They were no longer ducking, covering, running, and dashing behind cars with loaded weapons. The danger had clearly passed, though the area was still ablaze with flashing lights. Trey eased away, walked half a mile, left the campus, and stopped at John Street, where he got into a white cargo van with the words "Princeton University Printing" stenciled on both front doors. It was number 12, whatever that meant, and it was very similar to a van Trey had photographed a week earlier. He drove it back onto campus, avoided the commotion around McCarren, and parked it by a loading ramp at the rear of the library. "Van in place," he reported.

"We're just opening the sixth drawer," Denny replied.

As Jerry and Mark flipped up their goggles and moved their lights closer to the table, Denny gently opened the archival storage box. Its reference sheet read, "Original Handwritten Manuscript of The Great Gatsby—F. Scott Fitzgerald."

"Bingo," he said calmly. "We got Gatsby, that old son of a bitch."

"Whoopee," Mark said, though their excitement was thoroughly contained. Jerry lifted out the only other box in the drawer. It was the manuscript for *This Side of Paradise,* Fitzgerald's first novel, published in 1920.

"We have all five," Denny said calmly. "Let's get outta here."

Jerry repacked the drills, the cutting torch, the canisters of oxygen and acetylene, and the pry bars. As he bent to lift the duffel, a piece of the splintered wood from the third drawer nicked him above his left wrist. In the excitement, he barely noticed and just rubbed it for a split second as he removed his backpack. Denny and Mark carefully placed the five priceless manuscripts into their three student backpacks. The thieves hustled from the vault, laden with their loot and tools, and scampered up the stairs to the main floor. They left the library through a service entrance near a delivery ramp, one hidden from view by a thick, long hedge. They jumped through the rear doors of the van and Trey pulled away from the ramp. As he did so, he passed two campus security guards in a patrol car. He flicked a casual wave; they did not respond.

Trey noted the time: 3:42 a.m. He reported, "All clear, leaving the campus now with Mr. Gatsby and friends."